Finding My Way

DEDICATION

As always this is for Heather

ALSO WRITTEN BY Mavis Applewater AND
AVAILABLE FROM Wednesday Afternoon Press:

- ❖ The Brass Ring
- ❖ Checkmate
- ❖ My Sister's Keeper
- ❖ Tempus Fugit
- ❖ Whispering Pines
- ❖ Home For The Holidays
- ❖ Everlasting

www.wedapress.com

Finding My Way

By

Mavis Applewater

This is a work of fiction. All characters, locales and events are either products of the author's imagination or are used fictitiously.

Finding My Way

Cover design by Sandy Castle
Cover Photo: Marie-Louise
Edited by Tara Young

A Wednesday Afternoon Press Book
Wednesday Afternoon Press
Boston, MA. USA

www.wedapress.com

ISBN: 13 978-0692452691
      10 069245699

First Edition, June, 2015

Printed in the United States of America and in the United Kingdom

ACKNOWLEDGEMENTS

This book very special, it was the first one I dared shared and posted. It was the one that started it all. It is also the first one I've released since losing my Mom. I would like to thank Tara Young for doing an amazing job on editing. You really do make me look good. There are hundreds of people who have pushed for this book and I thank all of you. The most important person to thank is my loving wife Heather, who for some reason married this insane writer. Thank you for always having my back.

Prologue

I had always thought I knew myself so much that at one time, I had mapped out my entire future. Now I laugh at my assumptions, knowing that life is a constant cycle of change. Funny that it was that reality that took me off course, leading me to veer in a direction I never allowed myself to see. My story is simple. My life—or should I say my living—began one summer morning. I was standing at the back of a classroom listening to a woman speak. I was completely unaware that my life was about to change. If you like, I can tell you my story. It all began late in the summer almost ten years   ago.

Chapter One

I had just been hired to teach at the prestigious Prower University in the quaint town of Prowers Landing, Massachusetts, which was about ninety miles north of Boston. Despite its stellar reputation, I wasn't hoping for Prower. I was hoping that Brown, where I had been teaching while another professor was on sabbatical, would offer me a position.

I was told by the department head that they wanted me to come on board. Alas, as is often the case in the academic world, there wasn't a spot for me. Prower wanted me, and Brown did not. Life is just that simple. Prower was still Ivy League, but it wasn't Harvard or my alma mater Yale.

There's something you need to understand—I love history. When I had the chance to start college early, I didn't even consider studying anything else. My dear grandmother, who was raising me, was pissed that I would waste my opportunity by studying things that had already happened. She wanted me to study something more lucrative. She wanted me to become a doctor specializing in nip and tuck. For Grandma, that meant money, and money equaled success.

I had arrived on campus a bit early. I couldn't help myself, I was never on time. I was always early. Mostly because I have a fear of being late. Which in itself should tell you how tightly wound I am. Dr. Camden, the head of the department, was busy when I arrived. She suggested that I sit in on a class taught by a professor I hadn't met during the interview process.

The classroom was packed, it was amazing, especially in the middle of summer, and her classroom was standing room only. Hiding in the back, I found myself mesmerized as I watched her speak. The woman was electrifying, the kind of teacher I had always dreamed of becoming. I couldn't understand how she managed to captivate a room full of students. And still despite my fascination, I was apprehensive.

The problem was that I had met this woman before. Her name was Alexandra Kendell, and the first time we met was far from a pleasure. Her cruelty at the time left me cold, and to be honest, a little fearful. Hence my hesitation to buy the act I was watching. Still on that warm summer day, standing there while she held court, I failed to see any resemblance to the arrogant lawyer who had dismissed me without a second glance.

I was on time, just barely, which bothered me. Then it happened. I presented myself to her assistant and was turned away. I pleaded, begged, and basically made an ass out of myself, demanding to see the great Alexandra Adams Bowman Kendell. I know, who does that to a kid?

I was so certain that there had been some kind of misunderstanding that I refused to leave, until there was the threat of calling security. Embarrassed, I left before I was escorted from the building.

I stood on the busy sidewalk trying to figure out what had gone wrong. I was at a complete loss over what to do. There I was being jostled by the hurried pedestrians, on my birthday no less, after just having my dreams crushed.

I understand that in the grander scheme of things, who really cared that some rich guy paid a kid off to take his place. I wanted to know, hell, I needed to know. That was the kind of dorky bookworm I was. The only thing I knew for certain at that moment was that I needed to get in touch with Nicole. I felt that she would straighten out the whole mess.

I held up my arm and flagged down a taxi. Suddenly, I felt as if my luck was about to change. Wrong again. Someone reached for the door of the taxi. Appalled by her rudeness, I reached out and grabbed the woman. She spun around, and there stood Alexandra Kendell. She looked so much like her sister, there was no mistaking her.

She was tall and gorgeous and wearing a suit that probably cost more than my grandmother earned during her entire life. She was nothing short of breathtaking. Well, once you got past the cigarette dangling from her lips and the snarl holding it in place.

"Alexandra Kendell?" I coldly asked.

"Yes," she replied in an annoyed tone.

"I'm Stephanie Grant," I shot out boldly as I blocked her from entering the taxi.

"So?" She snarled, clearly irked by my audacity.

"You were supposed to meet with me today." I was infuriated by this woman's arrogance.

"Right, the student, and…?"

I was so appalled by her lack of manners that I stood there slack-jawed.

"I don't have time for this, kid," she chastised me when I failed to respond. She shifted in an attempt to enter the taxi. I did the only thing I could think of and blocked her path when she tried to push past me.

"Your sister said you have the diaries," I blurted out, not entirely confident that she would understand what I was talking about. Much to my dismay, she just stared down at me. "Your sister, Nicole, I spoke with her," I prompted hopefully, insanely thinking that she might give a damn.

"And?" she repeated as she pushed to get past me.

"Come on, ladies, I don't have all day!" the cab driver bellowed. There was nothing like the sound of a pissed off New York cabbie to brighten an already horrible experience.

"Hold your water!" I shouted back, raising my voice for perhaps the first time in my life. "Look, Ms. Kendell, I came a long way to see you because your sister promised me that you would be willing to show me the diaries."

"After how many martinis?"

"Excuse me?" I gulped, knowing that my world was about to crumble.

"You don't remember, do you?" She groaned, running her fingers through her hair. "Bombay Sapphire, extra dry with three olives. She rarely drinks less than a dozen and more than likely stuck you with the bill."

There was no rebuttal. Lunch with Nicole had in fact consisted of liquids, and she did stick me with the tab. I felt like a complete idiot. I should have been suspicious when Nicole excused herself to call Alex to arrange things. On the surface, it sounded plausible, except that she had returned to the table with a fresh drink. I had arrived on her doorstep expecting to turn over her ancestors' secrets based on a drunken promise.

"My sister is an alcoholic Ms…?"

"Grant! Stephanie Grant!" I snapped, my anger returning in full force.

"Ms. Grant," she repeated in quiet yet firm tone. "As I was saying, my sister will say anything you want to hear so long as you're the one buying the drinks. I'm sorry that you wasted your time. Good luck with your paper."

"It's my dissertation, and this is my cab," I bitterly spat out. I remembered her laughter when I jumped into the cab. I'd never felt so foolish in my entire life, and with my childhood, there had been plenty to feel foolish about. I still couldn't get past the fact that I had failed because I had allowed myself to be duped by a drunken debutant and verbally bitch-slapped by someone who seemed to enjoy it.

And that was my first introduction to the great Alexandra Kendell. I scrapped my thesis and started over. Only to find myself a decade later in the back of a classroom hiding from her. I wondered just why Dr. Camden had asked to meet me there. I flipped through the catalogue that listed the courses for the fall semester. The description of Ms. Kendell's classes looked like an easy ride consisting of nothing more than fluff.

I jerked my head up when the sound of a television filled the room. "What in the name of—?" I muttered.

Alexandra wove her spell over her audience as she sat there on her desk, her blue jean-clad legs crossed. I thought she looked more like a student than the professor. I felt overdressed in my best Donna Karan suit. Like most things in my life, I had chosen my attire carefully. I brushed an imaginary wrinkle from my skirt when the classroom erupted in laughter. There was something about her commanding performance that made me feel inadequate.

"The episode was called Plato's Stepchildren," she explained to her eager listeners. "Come on, none of you knows why this episode is a big deal?"

"Did we miss something?" a young woman in the front row

asked.

"No, thankfully, none of you saw anything wrong with Captain Kirk kissing Lt. Uhura," she brightly continued. "Just before this episode aired in November 1968, the network was sick with worry. This episode of *Star Trek* is often credited with being the first interracial kiss aired on television."

"First?" Someone gasped.

"Not really, but it's remembered as the first," she explained. "I know. What's the big deal? Here in the late twentieth century, we see this and so much more displayed in our living rooms."

And with that introduction, she managed to engage her students in a lively discussion on what was happening in the United States in 1968. I was shocked that she truly educated them by playing a video clip from *Star Trek,* of all things. I just couldn't understand how she made that happen.

It wasn't hard to feel inferior around someone like her. After all, she was a Kendell. Not just any Kendell, she was Alexandra Kendell, the heir apparent of the Kendell fortune. The one who walked away from a top Wall Street law firm to become a history professor. In the world I grew up in, people didn't throw away a lucrative career to be a teacher.

Not knowing her, I just couldn't understand why anyone would leave all that money and prestige. Seeing her had come as a surprise. When I accepted the position at Prower University, I had no idea I would be working with her.

How in the name of all that is sacred did this happen? After all my planning and hard work, the crap still managed to hit the fan. I was about to face an uncertain future while sitting side by side with the woman who had prevented me from writing my first book. To be fair, she technically hadn't prevented the writing of the book. I was forced to scrap my thesis and start over again, all because of Alexandra Kendell.

While I pondered the possibility she would not only remember but feel a need to torment me, someone tapped my shoulder. I turned to see Dr. Camden motion for me to follow her. Maureen Camden had pursued me to apply my talents at the university. In the beginning, I hadn't been interested. That was until I discovered that

Prower was my only option. At a university like Prower, I would advance more quickly, then after my résumé was better padded, I could make the jump over to Harvard or Yale. Dr. Camden was thrilled when I finally accepted her offer. I didn't have the heart to tell her that I was simply using Prower as a steppingstone to a higher position at a more prestigious university. No one had to know about that; it was part of my life plan.

"Did you enjoy the lecture?" Dr. Camden asked.

"It was something else," I stammered, uncertain what I should say. I had no idea if she had sent me there to show me what not to do or if there was something else going on. "Why did you send me over there?"

"I wanted you to see Alex in action," she casually threw out. "Since the two of you will be sharing an office."

"Oh?" I shuddered while thinking, 'Well, whoopee for me.' "Tell me, Dr. Camden—" I started to say.

"Maureen," she interrupted.

"Maureen," I responded with a smile. "What's your opinion of Professor Kendell's classes?"

"What do you mean?"

"Pop Culture, the History of Television and courses on the evolution of TV commercials?" I asked in confusion. Quite frankly, none of these subjects struck me as important or appropriate. "I heard that she teaches a course on soap operas. How does any of this relate to American history?"

The older woman, who stood slightly taller than I, chuckled. "To fully understand, you would need to see her in action," Maureen tried to explain. "Alex is unconventional, to say the least, but she really gets through to these kids. And for the record, she doesn't teach a course in soap operas, she shows examples of them and their effects on society in one of her more advanced popular culture courses."

"I guess it just seems like fluff and not real hard-core academics."

"On the surface, maybe, but she brings history alive and shows how this country tries to redefine its history through media interpretation."

Based on her reaction, I knew that I needed to tread carefully.

Just by the way she shortened Ms. Kendell's first name made it was obvious that the two women were friends.

"I'll make a point on sitting in for much longer next time," I lied, not wanting to start off on the wrong foot with the head of the department. In all honesty, I had no intention of attending any more lectures given by Alexandra Kendell.

Maureen showed me around campus. It was beautiful, with ivy-covered stone buildings possessing that old New England charm. I had to admit, this was going to be a very nice place to live and work. Well, until a better offer rolled along. Still it was a comfortable place to spend the next two or three years, and maybe once Peter could relocate, we could start thinking about moving our relationship along. This move gave us the opportunity to try living together for the first time. Everything was falling into place, just as I had planned.

After we completed the grand tour, Maureen showed me my new office. Although the space was small, it possessed an arched window that spanned from floor to near ceiling. My space was barren with the exception of a desk, chair, and an empty mahogany bookcase. The other half was filled with clutter. Books, magazines, food wrappers, and what looked like stray clothing covered the desk and computer, and I could detect the outline of what I assumed was a sofa. It was buried so deeply beneath clutter that I couldn't say for certain that there was an actual piece of furniture beneath.

"My God, she's a slob," I whispered, thankfully low enough to be heard only by Dr. Camden.

Suddenly, the massive pile near a file cabinet began to move. I was ready to sprint out of there when a large figure appeared. My heart leapt as Alexandra Kendell emerged from behind sporting an odd smile.

"Alex!" Maureen scolded the woman, who displayed a look similar to a deer caught in someone's headlights. "Are you smoking again?"

"No," Alex said innocently as a puff of smoke escaped from her lips.

"Alex, you know the rules. Smoking is not allowed on campus," Maureen chastised her.

"Sorry," she grumbled before she extinguished her cigarette into an ashtray that magically appeared. "I really needed it," she added sheepishly.

"I cannot believe that you started again." Maureen wagged her finger at Alex, whose only defense was to roll her eyes. "When are you going to clean up this mess? I swear, you're worse than my kids."

"I try," Alex teased with a devilish smirk.

"Behave," Maureen cautioned.

"Or?"

"Stop, you have company." Maureen groaned with exasperation. "Professor Alexandra Kendell, this is Dr. Stephanie Grant. Dr. Grant is your new cell mate."

"Stan's gone?"

"Yes, you finally drove him out. He asked about switching office space the moment Carl announced his retirement."

"You know what this means, you owe me dinner at the Top of the Hub." Alex triumphantly smirked.

"Yes, but you've started smoking again."

"So Dutch treat at Church Street?" Alexandra conceded. She finally turned and acknowledged my presence.

To say that I was stunned by their casual banter would be an understatement. In previous appointments, it was all business. It was professor this or doctor that. I rarely heard anyone address the department head by her first name. Something niggled at me; perhaps it was the first hint that my life was about to change.

"So, roomie, tell me about yourself," Alexandra said in a friendly manner.

"I gave you her résumé since you weren't around for her interview," Maureen scolded.

"You did?" she asked in a puzzled tone as she looked around the mess that constituted her half of the office.

"I need to get back to work." Maureen excused herself. "Play nice." She directed her stern warning toward Alex as she made her departure.

"I'm always nice," Alex barked with a hint of laughter.

I stood there feeling completely out of sorts uncertain how I should behave. Alexandra Kendell was in some ways larger than life. She approached me, and my pulse quickened. I swallowed deeply as she reached out her hand.

"Alex," she said with a bright smile.

"Stephanie," I answered before I took her hand and shook it firmly.

"Welcome aboard." She added released my hand from her grip. My body felt a strange sense of loss as her fingers left my own. "Sorry about the mess," she apologized. "I did it mostly to annoy Stan." Then she mumbled something I couldn't quite catch. The only word I was certain of was "bastard." The woman who stood before me was not the same person I met in New York. I couldn't help but wonder what had brought on such a miraculous change.

"So you're taking over the early American history classes?"

"Yes, and you teach postmodern American?"

"Thanks for not calling it pop culture. I always thought that sounded too seventies. Like you'd take it along with yoga and macramé or hugging 101."

I felt a twinge of guilt at the reference that I had tossed out so casually just before meeting her. She looked so endearing, nothing like the demon woman I remembered. The last thing any new staff member needed was an enemy. The tight-knit world of academia was a shark-infested cesspool. The only way to ensure a long career was to make friends, and of course, never forget— publish or perish. Publishing hadn't been a problem for me, which made me marketable. Making friends and contacts sadly never came easy for me.

"We need to get you started, and the first thing you need to know is Louisa is God around here," Alex's lilting voice advised me.

"Louisa? Oh, Dr. Camden's assistant."

"Louisa is all knowing and has the keys to everything," Alex stressed. "The other thing to know is where the coffee maker is. Lucky for us, it's just outside our office. Makes it a little noisy at times, but we don't have far to travel when we need a fix."

"Thank God," I blew out with appreciation. "Do you know a good Realtor? I was slow to accept the offer to come here and had to move quickly."

"No one comes to mind." She grimaced. It was strange she seemed genuinely concerned. "I kind of lucked into my place."

I doubted that anyone with the last name of Kendell had trouble finding a nice place to live. Unaware of my misgivings, she suggested that we grab some coffee before searching for Louisa. She took the time to brew a fresh pot, chatting away while she prepared coffee for us. She then prepared a cup for Louisa and snagged a pastry.

"A little bribe never hurts," she added playfully.

Bribes secured, we easily found Louisa. The petite woman with salt and pepper hair was holding court, easily deflecting questions from frazzled students and faculty. After a quick introduction and a little bribery, Louisa and I were on our way to becoming fast friends.

After ingratiating myself to the department head's right hand, Alex guided me around and introduced me to my new colleagues. I had met most of the staff during the interview process. Of course, that was months ago, and at the time, I was trying to impress, not make friends.

I had worked at several different universities over the years, but this was the first time I felt myself fitting in. I knew I had Alex to thank. She had a way about her that seemed to put almost everyone at ease. There were a couple of exceptions. The most notable was Stan Bibilliti. He was pleasant enough when he spoke. However, by the way he bristled each time Alex spoke, it was painfully clear that the pair barely tolerated each other. It wasn't surprising that they weren't close. Alex was vibrant and electric, and Stan was the definition of drab. Honestly, next to this guy, I was a firecracker.

I was curious if the kinship displayed by the faculty was genuine. Prower University seemed to lack the cutthroat backstabbing kill-or-be-killed attitude that existed in the arena of academia. During my interview, Maureen had stressed that she did not tolerate such things. It was one thing to say that, quite another to see it work. At the time, I was convinced that the happy, all-for-one attitude wouldn't last. I understood all too well that a new hire meant someone was leaving, budgets simply didn't allow for extra staff members. Alumni donations only go so far. Perhaps that was why I was reluctant to contact a Realtor.

"Over there is Samuel Ezra Prower's house," Alex explained as she gave me the grand tour. "Our founding father's last dwelling. It houses the theater department now. They say it's haunted."

"Oh course it is." I laughed at the notion. "I wonder what old Sam Prower would think about his family home being used by a bunch of actors."

"He was big on education." Alex shrugged it off. "That's probably why he built the college and willed most of his fortune to keep it going. I don't know how he felt about the arts."

I don't know why I went on another tour. Maureen had just shown me everything, yet for some reason, I followed along when she offered to show me around. She pointed out every nook and cranny, from housing to where the recycling was stored. I couldn't be sure, but the confident woman seemed to be babbling slightly.

During the tour, I became painfully aware that I couldn't stop looking at Alex. I tried to be discreet as I studied her. I don't know why. Perhaps I was waiting for her to morph into a three-headed demon. I was tempted to ask if she had an evil twin. There was something else, I just couldn't put my finger on it. Each time she ran her fingers through her long brown hair, I shivered. It happened so many times, she finally asked me if I was feeling all right.

"The sea air," I quickly lied. "I'm just not used to it."

"I love it," she practically purred, and I shivered once again.

"I need to go," I blurted out, wondering if I was indeed coming down with something.

"Wait," she softly requested, picking up the telephone that was on my desk. "Sorry, it would take forever to find mine. Louisa, would you know a good Realtor?" She looked around for a pen and paper. I quickly dug into my bag and retrieved a pen and a Dunkin' Donuts napkin. Alex scribbled furiously after I handed her the items.

"Here you go," she beamed, handing me the napkin with the name and phone number. "I told you Louisa knows all."

"I'll need to pick up some muffins on my way in tomorrow," I blew out, feeling slightly relieved. I dialed the number and made an appointment with Dan Brewster. "I guess I need to get going, he can show me some places today. Thank you so much, you've made my first day painless."

"I do what I can." She chuckled. "Well, I guess I'll get cracking on clearing out some of this mess. Maybe I'll find your résumé."

I wished her luck and made my departure. As I walked across the campus to my rental car, I was filled with the strangest sensation. I couldn't put my finger on it. I drove off dismissing my feelings as nothing more than nervous jitters.

***

Dan was a nice enough fellow, sadly none of his rentals was. My needs were simple—clean and affordable, with room for me and Peter. My misfortune was that I had waited and found myself moving into town right at the same time the students and others were returning. The first place he showed me looked as if the former owner was a hoarder. Not just an average hoarder, a world-class collector of disgusting things that smell and attract vermin. To his credit, Dan did look embarrassed when we opened the door and the smell hit us.

The second place was probably the best place in town to find a party. Loud music assaulted us before we stepped onto the sidewalk. Once again, Dan had the good manners to look embarrassed.

"This place is popular with a younger crowd," he feebly explained.

"No kidding." I shook my head, knowing there was no way I could endure living in party central. "So, next?"

"I'm sorry. At this time of year, there really isn't much left on the market," he said. "There are a couple that are nicer, but the landlords don't like to rent to unmarried couples."

"It's the twenty-first century. Never mind." I pushed down my anger. "Just show me what else is available."

I spent the better part of three hours looking at the worst apartments on the face of the planet. I agreed to look at more places the following day. It was clear to me that Dan did know what he was doing, he just didn't have anything to offer me. Alas, I was in dire need and fearful that I would need to lower my standards significantly.

I stopped at the university bookstore to ensure the reading list for my classes were in stock. I headed back to my modest motel room. I grabbed a burger from the nearest Mickey D's. I had intended to call Peter, but the excitement of the day caught up with me. I ended up falling asleep while watching the local news.

Chapter Two

After surviving my first day on campus, I discovered that life in Prowers Landing was going to be much easier than I thought it would be. During the first week, Alex made herself available for any and all questions I threw at her. I was really hitting it off with her. She quickly proved that she wasn't the cold-hearted lawyer I remembered. She taught me the ins and outs of the university's red tape, including the best times to hit the copy center. She even expedited the arrival of my computer.

Things were moving along smoothly. With the one notable exception of finding a place to live. Dan was telling the truth when he said there was very little on the market. The only places available were either rat holes or filled with students. If I had learned anything by spending most of my life in college, it was that students liked to party. I, on the other hand, liked to study and work. Something that could be difficult to accomplish when there was a keg party in the next room every other weekend.

I went to my new office in an effort to get organized. When I stepped inside and spied Alex trying to clean up the mess, I felt slightly light-headed. For a brief moment, I thought I might be coming down with something. Just as quickly, the odd feeling passed.

"How is the apartment hunting going, roomie?" she asked.

"Not so good." I made my way over to my desk. I blew out an exasperated sigh as I tried to organize my things. "I wish I had started looking sooner. How is your day going?"

"I need more coffee," she jested. "But then again, when don't I? I have my morning class, I should get going."

"May I join you?"

I heard the words come out of my mouth and couldn't believe

what I had just requested. I almost didn't hear her response. I was too busy being befuddled by my words.

"If you want." She seemed surprised. "I hope you won't get bored," she shyly added.

I wasn't certain what shocked me more—her shyness or that I had asked to sit in on her class. I had no valid reason to do it. In fact, I had work to do, lessons to plan, not to mention calling Peter. Unable to verbalize a response, I blindly followed after her.

I sat in the back during the lecture, and I was once again mesmerized by her. Based on the way her students responded, I wasn't alone.

"What about the explosion of reality shows?" she asked. "I'm sure more than a few of you are eagerly awaiting the next season of the *Real Housewives* of wherever. My question is, how real is real when a camera is following you around?"

The answers came in rapid-fire succession. My mouth hung open as I listened to the students voicing their opinions. Hearing their excitement, I almost jumped into the conversation.

"Hold on." Alex held up her hand and smiled. "It's that time again. We need to table this conversation. "Our time is up. We'll pick this up next time."

The room was filled with groans and disappointed mutterings. The only time I heard grousing of that nature was when I announced that there was going to be a test. The students dragged their feet when it came to leaving.

"Wow, that was something," I said once we were alone. "They totally got into it."

"You know how it is." She shrugged. "When you love what you do, it shows. I believe that we must learn from history or we're destined to repeat it."

"I feel the same way," I reluctantly admitted, wondering why I couldn't get through to my students the way she did.

"You're not going to believe this," she started with a chuckle. "I used to be a lawyer. How freaky is that?"

"I...." I hesitated, not wanting to reveal how I already knew what she had just told me. "I heard that," I finally sputtered.

"Sometimes I forget how quickly bad news travels in a small town."

"Bad news?" I was curious about the statement.

"Not important."

I glanced at my watch and grimaced. "I have another appointment," I grumbled, not wanting to end the conversation. "I hope this place will be livable."

"Good luck."

***

My meeting with Dan wasn't what I had hoped it would be. Once again, the places he showed me were nothing short of rat traps. At one place, I wasn't certain, but I could have sworn I really did see a rat scurry when we entered the dilapidated dwelling. There was one suitable place that was nothing short of magnificent. Sadly, the price reflected its grandeur. The only way I could afford to rent the three-bedroom condo would be if I gave up eating and sold a kidney.

***

The following morning, Alex and I were in our office furiously trying to organize our lesson plans for the semester.

"Busy tonight?" Alex asked. "The movie theater in town is playing *African Queen*."

"*African Queen*?"

"If you want to see new movies, you need to cross the town line." Alex snickered. "The Paramount is an old vaudeville-house-turned-movie-theater when talkies caught on. It only shows classics or hosts movie festivals. The building is amazing. So what do you say?"

"I've never seen it," I confessed, recalling how my grandmother would watch the oldies on the small black and white television nestled in the kitchen. It was the only TV we owned. Whenever she was watching her shows, I'd sneak out to help Jenny practice softball. "What time? I have an appointment to see an apartment at six."

"The movie starts at eight," she quickly said. "Interested?"

I agreed, eager to see the movie not only for the first time, but on a big screen.

***

I met with my new best friend Dan that night, only to be disappointed. I stopped by my motel, and for some unknown reason,

I changed my outfit five times. I found the theater easily and felt a sense of excitement when I spotted Alex standing out front.

"Wow, this place is amazing." I gaped at the ornate ceiling after we had purchased our tickets and snacks. "I love Art Deco."

"They refurbished the building back in the nineties," Alex explained as we handed our tickets to the usher. "Somehow, they managed to save the artwork, staircases, and those fabulous ceilings."

"I have to admit that I don't go to the movies very often."

"I kind of suspected," she said brightly just as the lights were dimming.

During the movie, which was phenomenal, I experienced the oddest sensations that were a mix of nervous energy and happiness. I reached into the tub of popcorn that Alex had settled between the two of us, and my stomach fluttered upon feeling her fingers brush against my own. It happened several times; each time, I trembled. I don't know if I was relieved or upset when we finished the popcorn halfway through the movie and Alex moved the box to the floor.

Once the barrier between us was gone, each time something exciting happened or Kate gave it to Bogie really good, Alex's hand landed on my knee. Her touch was brief, but there was something about it that made me feel alive. Curious that I could still feel her caress long after I had returned to the motel.

***

Time passed all too quickly, with all the work preparing for the upcoming semester and discovering things about the town I was about to call home. Over the passing weeks, Alex did everything she could to show me around. We did brunch almost every Sunday, had dinner together at least twice a week, and managed to see a couple more movies at the Paramount.

What I hadn't accomplished was finding a place to live. Discouraged, my interest in finding an apartment waned. I found myself sitting in on Alex's classes more and more. Time somehow had gotten away from me. Before I realized it, the new semester was about to begin. I had less than a week, and I still hadn't found anything that suited my needs or budget. I was against the fence knowing that after the semester began, there wouldn't even be a rat hole available. It was the downside of living in a college town. I had run out of options. The only choice left was to expand my search to a neighboring town. Which meant I would have to buy a car. Something that I hadn't planned on doing. I could afford it with the new job still it was one more thing to add to the list.

Normally, I would have been on top of things. Taken the bull by the horn, so to speak. This time, I chose to let the time slip away and found myself in trouble. I couldn't even apply for university housing. The grand old homes that lined the quaint campus were only available to those who had garnered tenure. I heard that even with tenure, there was a waiting list.

There I was living in a dinky motel on the edge of town spending a fortune on taxis every day. I wished I had kept the rental car longer. The worst part was playing phone tag with Peter. If he managed to transfer, it meant that I needed to find a place where both of us could live comfortably.

It was strange not to have him around to talk to every day. My arrival in Prowers Landing marked the first time since we had become a couple that we had spent this much time apart. He was looking for work in the area and hopefully would be joining me soon. That was one of the reasons I needed to select the perfect apartment. Everything seemed to be falling into place. One of the reasons I knew that Peter and I would be a good match was the work he did. Working with computers, he could not only maintain stability, but he could find work anywhere. If I received an offer that I wanted to accept, we could just pick up and go. The other reason that Peter was perfect was before we had started dating, we had been truly good friends.

A suitable partner was an important aspect of my life plan. Over the years, I had been teased about my plan. I knew I was right. I never thought it odd that I had planned out my life. A map to the future as it were. I watched as my girlfriends from high school and college suffered one heartache after another. I was never one to get all giggly and insecure over some boy. Peter and I had become friends during my years at Yale. He was a computer geek. He failed to understand that at a certain level history classes consisted of more than regurgitating dates. My time in graduate school was good for me. It wasn't long after I earned my PhD that Peter and I started dating. It wasn't all hearts and flowers. In my humble opinion, romance was overrated.

My attitude more than likely stemmed from losing my parents at such a young age. From what I had seen in their marriage, I knew I had to be sensible about the men in my life. My mother had made the wrong choice in marrying my father. It caused her nothing but heartache. At a young age, I vowed that was not going to happen to me. I know it sounds harsh talking about my father being a mistake. The truth was, I barely knew him. He wasn't around much. I would later learn the reason. He spent most of his time drinking, gambling, and chasing other women. Dear old Dad would only come home now and then, usually to announce that we were moving. Our constant moves were related to some kind of trouble he had gotten himself into. His death, although it was never proven, was payback from a jealous husband.

During her marriage, my mother doted on my father, when he could be bothered to come home. She was devastated after his death. I wish I could say I missed him. But how can you grieve for a stranger who ignored you? Dad did have a pet name for me—the brat. It didn't take a rocket scientist to figure out I was the reason he married my mother. I often wondered why he bothered. Maybe if he had bolted from the get-go, Mom might have had a shot at a decent life. Since everything was about my father, the void he left drained what little energy she possessed. She was gone within a year. I was sent to live with my grandmother. I finally was able to stop packing up my meager belongings every couple of months. I was happy living with my grandmother. The little affection she bestowed upon me was far more than I had ever received from either of my parents. It helped that she strictly reinforced my practical nature.

I didn't date in high school; then again, I wasn't in high school for very long. I was very young went I was skipped ahead of Junior High. It hadn't taken the faculty long to determine that even in the advanced classes, I was smarter than my teachers. With the aid of a special program, I was sent off to UConn before I got my braces off.

There you have it. I grew up overly bright, yet in solitude. Hence my need for a life plan. I was determined not to become a fractured adult carrying baggage. I wanted to be happy. For me, happiness meant working in a field I loved and finding the man who

I knew would be there. Heck, wasn't that what most of us wanted out of life? The difference for me was I actually wrote it down, complete with charts and graphs.

My life was different, to say the least. I had been spared from the sorrows of adolescence and at the same time denied the joy. Among my true peers, other gifted children, there was so much competition. Close friendships never formed. I didn't even begin to make friends until I was at Yale. I ended up losing my virginity just to get it over with. That, and I was curious as to what the fuss was all about. I was still curious.

It was all really quite simple when you sat down and thought about these things logically. There were only a few distractions in my past, but they were silly, really. I was young, and each time, I had been drinking. Besides, it was never more than kissing, and they had been women. I knew that would never happen again. It was curiosity, nothing more. Again, my logic at times was positively— well, to quote Mr. Spock—illogical. Yet it worked for me, or so I thought.

***

There I sat in the back of Alex's classroom. I was blowing off apartment hunting so we could hang out. It was out of character for me to take such a laid-back attitude. I reasoned that Alex and I were becoming friends, I could put off managing the details of my life for one more day. I found it hard to believe that we were getting so close. Only a few short weeks ago, I was terrified that I was going to be forced to sit side by side with a narcissistic bully. Instead, I ended up with a friend. I felt a small pang of guilt that I hadn't secured a place to live. My misery was short-lived when Alex's class erupted in laughter.

"Okay," Alex said, bringing order back to her class. "For next time. *The Brady Bunch* and *Gilligan's Island*. I want you to tell me your favorite Brady, then have five of your friends name theirs. Also explain to me why the professor could build a nuclear reactor from two coconuts but couldn't fix the hole in the boat. Kidding on that one. I want you to think of an episode that reflected the events that happened while the show was on the air. Now it's a beautiful day outside, so get out of here so I can enjoy it."

I watched the students reluctantly leave their seats. Again I was amazed. I usually needed to wake my students after one of my lectures. Alex finally forced the last of her students out the door.

"*Gilligan's Island?*"

"You should have been around for my lecture on *Hogan's Heroes.*"

"I bet that was a kick in the pants."

"It's a trick." She chuckled. "How many African-Americans do you recall seeing on that show? How is it that it aired during the Vietnam War and the war was never mentioned? The media's use of escapism. They think they're going to have an easy lecture comparing Ginger to MaryAnn, but what they're really going to be doing is talking about what was happening in this country. The pilot for the show was delayed because of JFK's assassination. That alone should get the ball rolling. This is the MTV generation. If they don't see it on Nick at Nite, then it didn't happen."

"And *The Brady Bunch?*" I pushed, suddenly intrigued by her theories.

"Don't knock the Bradys," she teased. "They managed to slip in a few social issues, not many, but one or two. Besides, your favorite Brady can reveal a great deal about your personality."

"Really?"

"It's true."

"I don't believe you."

"Your favorite Brady was Jan," she said in a cocky manner.

"Yes!" I was stunned. "How did you know?"

"It's simple really." Alex's overconfidence could really be annoying and somehow downright adorable. "Jan was the middle child, often overlooked, an outsider. She didn't bother with attracting boys the way Marcia did. She simply tried to fit in. The only person in the family she was close to was Alice, an older woman who felt the same way."

"I still don't understand how you knew that. I—" I felt an uneasiness. It wasn't as if I broadcast the fact that I spent the majority of my life playing the role of a misfit. "You will have to explain this theory of yours over lunch," I tossed out in an effort to shrug off her shrewd observation.

"Some other time."

"Are you canceling?" I was more than a little disappointed.

"No, you are."

"I am?"

"Have you found an apartment yet?"

"No."

"Stephanie, classes start soon," she began. "You can't work out of that crappy motel you're staying in. Taking a taxi every day must be adding up. A small apartment has just opened up in my building. Oh, and when I say small, I really mean it. This isn't like the time I told you Stan wouldn't mind if you used his stapler."

"Yes, thank you again for that. That man is much too uptight."

"No kidding. Like I was saying, it's a small place, but it should get you through a semester or two."

I was overwhelmed by her friendship. Without thinking, I jumped up and hugged her. She gently pushed me away. Somehow, her reaction left me feeling cold and confused. I couldn't look at her. I ran my hand through my short blond hair and stared at my shoes. Displays of affection weren't my forte. Apparently, I had gotten it wrong. I often wished that my social skills matched my academic capabilities.

"I'm guessing that you would like to see the apartment?" she said softly. I looked up and was captured by those baby blue eyes and bright smile. "Stephanie?" Her deep voice called me back from my wanderings.

"Sorry." I released a soft gasp when I realized that I had been staring. I wasn't just staring, I was gawking at the poor woman. I felt flushed. Not for the first time in my life, I stood there, mute. My mind tried to process what was going on. The only reasonable conclusion I could conjure up was a sudden onset of illness. Which would explain the heat coursing through my body, but not my blush.

"Are you all right?"

"I'm fine," I lied. Mentally, I was still trying to diagnose the mysterious illness that was forcing me to act like a blathering idiot and cause my heart to palpitate.

"You do want to see this apartment, don't you?"

"Yes." I said it a couple of times, thinking that by speaking, I could restore order to what was quickly becoming an awkward situation.

Chapter Three

We walked away from the sprawling campus. I noticed that Alex was strangely quiet. Her silence disturbed me. I assumed that my earlier odd behavior had upset her. My normal reaction to a silent companion was to let it slide. I never really got the hang of idle chitchat. Silent pauses for me were a relief. For some unknown reason, Alex's sudden silence worried me.

"Why don't you and Stan get along?" I asked in an effort to engage her. In the back of mind, I wondered why her silence bothered me.

"He didn't like my T-shirt."

"Stan is very old-fashioned," I said, knowing there had to be more to the ongoing feud than Alex's choice in clothing. "Jeans and T-shirts aren't his style. After all, he is Mr. Bow Tie."

"It was what it said," Alex said without explaining it further.

I couldn't help wondering just what was printed on Alex's T-shirt that ruffled Stan's feathers. Then again, the guy was wrapped tighter than my grandmother's girdle, which meant her shirt could have been emblazoned with nothing more than the Beatles. Knowing Alex, it might have been racy.

My curiosity was piqued. Many things about Alex caught my attention. She was direct. She had this way of drawing attention to herself. I for one found her laugh infectious. I could see that for introverts like myself and Stan, someone with Alex's charisma could be intimidating.

I followed after Alex, becoming increasingly annoyed with myself for not being able to keep a conversation going. This happened to me a lot. I'd start off okay, then nothing. I could present a paper, defend a theory, explain the reasoning behind complex historical battles, yet I couldn't share a simple conservation. So caught up in my thoughts, I failed to realize that Alex had stopped walking. I plowed right into her firm body. She managed to grasp my shoulders before I toppled over.

"Hey, are you okay?" The concern in her voice warmed me. Or perhaps it was the way she was caressing my shoulders. Or the way my body was tingling for some unknown reason.

"Sorry."

"Hey, no worries," she said. "You looked like you were a million miles away."

"I just, um…"

"Are you all right?" she asked while I scrambled for something to say. My natural awkwardness was in full force.

"There's something I need to tell you." She stared at me with a startled look that could only be described as fear. For the life of me, I couldn't understand why I felt a need to bring the subject up. In hindsight, I think I was just looking for something to say.

"Whoa." I gasped, wondering what I done to cause this strange reaction from my new friend. "What's with the look? You would think that I was about to tell you that your favorite pet died."

"Cheep-Cheep?" She gasped in mock terror.

I playfully swatted her on the arm and received the trademark Alex Kendell icy stare. I laughed at her attempt to intimidate me with a glare. Granted, ten years ago, that look scared the bejesus out of me. At that moment in time, it put me at ease.

"Alex?" I shot back with a glare of my own.

"Nice try." She smirked. "It needs work. So what did you want to tell me?"

"We've met before."

"You mean—" She looked at me strangely as she spoke. "Like in a past life? Are you from LA?" She began to laugh.

"No, I'm from Connecticut, thank you very much." I laughed along with her, giving her a playful swat on the arm. "You're such a jerk."

"Sorry, so when did we meet?"

"It was quite some time ago," I began slowly. "You were a lawyer then."

"I didn't sue you, did I?" she asked in a serious tone. "Or cheat your grandmother?"

I was taken aback when I realized that this time she wasn't joking. "No, it was nothing like that," I said quickly, hoping to erase the guilty expression from her face.

"I was a real bitch, wasn't I?" she said quietly.

I noticed that it was an admission and not a question. "I thought so at the time."

"I probably was," she muttered as she stared at her feet unable to look at me. "Whatever it was, I'm sorry for what I did. I'm equally sorry for not remembering you."

"It's not important," I lied. "I just wanted to say something just in case you did remember."

"Boy, I must have been in rare form to forget you."

"It was a long time ago," I offered, gently resting my hand on her arm. She looked up at me, the guilt still visible. "I was a kid. I looked totally different, my hair was longer and something my dear grandmother would have thought was slutty. Look, what happened back then—like my slutty hairdo—is best forgotten."

"I'm so sorry, Stephanie," she apologized again. "I wasn't a nice person back then. I'll tell you about it sometime."

"Later," I said in an effort to reassure her. "For now, I want to see this apartment, and on the way, you can tell me all about Cheep-Cheep."

She released a hearty laugh that warmed me. Alex had such an infectious laugh. There were times I still found it hard to believe that she was the same woman I had met all those years ago. Looking back on the events that happened back then, I could see her side of things. There I was, a snot-nosed, wet-behind-the-ears kid demanding her time. Which, from what I later learned about the legal profession, came at a high price. Alex seemed a bit more at ease. She guided me along the tree-lined streets of Prowers Landing.

"Come on, tell me about little Cheep-Cheep," I encouraged while I enjoyed our stroll and the late summer weather.

"I don't know," she teased. "It's really a tragic story. Are you sure you want to hear it?"

"Definitely."

We walked along until we reached the end of upper Essex Street. During our journey, Alex spun the tragic tale of her poor duckling. Cheep-Cheep, as it turned out, was her younger brother's first pet. The duckling suffered from epilepsy caused by inbreeding.

According to Alex, it would waddle for a few steps, have a seizure, and keel over. Her parents were forced to have the duckling put down. Like most parents, they did not have the heart to tell their young son. So they did what all parents do—they told David that the duckling went to live on a farm. It wasn't until David was in high school that he learned the truth. Alex explained in great detail that David failed to take the news very well.

"Poor little Cheep-Cheep." I was filled with a sense of relief that we were talking again. Over the years, my female friends for one reason or another had drifted out of my life. I couldn't deny that I felt very comfortable with Alex and resolved that I would not let that happen to us.

"Poor David." Alex sighed as a darkness overcame her. I reached out to her, wanting to ease whatever it was that was causing her such pain. "We're here," she said quickly as she broke away before my hand could reach her. I looked up and gasped when I saw Alex's building. It was a large Victorian house with a huge front porch.

"It's perfect."

"Don't let Mrs. Giovanni hear you, or she'll double the rent," Alex cautioned. Just as the words escaped her lips, we were greeted by a tiny redhead woman who shuffled across the street. "She lives in the big yellow house, and she's very particular as to whom she rents to."

"I heard that." Mrs. Giovanni snorted with a thick accent. To her credit, she did seem to try to speed up her shuffle.

"Of course you did." Alex smiled and went to assist the elderly woman. Mrs. Giovanni slapped Alex away. "You don't miss a trick, do you?" Alex teased her. I found it hard to believe that this dark-haired beauty who was helping an elderly woman cross the street was the same woman I had at one time been convinced was the incarnation of evil.

"Smart mouth," Mrs. Giovanni chastised Alex. "This one is fresh." She wagged her finger at Alex. "It comes from living in New York."

"She knows everything, too," Alex cautioned me.

"That's right," Mrs. Giovanni said proudly. "I know that Chris was no good for you."

"My ex," Alex explained shyly. "I told you she knows everything. Enough sharing, Mrs. G. I don't think Stephanie needs to hear about that. Lord knows I'm not in a hurry to hear it again."

"No need to interrupt the lady," I told Alex because I did want to know. I just didn't understand why. Normally, I couldn't have cared less about the details of someone else's life. I never liked gossip. It was hurtful, and most times when you discovered the truth, it was a horrible letdown. I mean, was it really gossiping with Alex standing right there?

"Deep down, Alexandra is a good girl. Sometimes, it's hidden very deep down," Mrs. G teased. "If you're a friend of hers, you can stay." Mrs. Giovanni patted Alex's face gently.

I know I must have looked like an idiot. I just stood there with my mouth hanging open. Surely, this nice woman hadn't just offered me an apartment in a very nice house that was walking distance from my job.

"So we look at the apartment," she announced, confirming that she was indeed renting me an apartment just because I showed up with Alex. "And then we'll go across the street and have tea and you can tell me all about yourself."

"Be careful," Alex said. "She'll pry every last detail of your life out of you before you know what hit you. Worst of all, she'll have you thinking it was your idea to spill your guts."

"I heard that." Mrs. Giovanni snorted.

I blindly followed after the tiny woman. She seemed harmless enough, and she did offer to make me tea. We stepped into the foyer, which was beautiful and surprisingly immaculate.

"Your apartment is the only one on the first floor," Mrs. Giovanni explained, extracting a large ring of keys from the pocket of her muumuu. It was clear that she had already decided that I was going to rent the apartment. Suddenly, I feared the consequences if for some reason I declined the offer.

When she opened the door and I stepped inside, I knew there was no way on God's green earth I was going to refuse. The apartment was indeed small, but it oozed charm. The only hiccup was that it wasn't an apartment, it was a studio. The bedroom and living room were one and the same. The kitchen was nestled toward the back of the room. It consisted of a small countertop and a tiny stove and a sink. Above the stove and sink was a beautiful bay window that overlooked a garden. The front of the studio was adorned with glass French doors. The front door opened into a large foyer with a gorgeous mahogany staircase that led to the second floor. The moment I entered the studio, a warm sensation encompassed me. It was one of the few times in my life I realized that sometimes things are just as they seem.

Sadly, there was one problem. Although there was ample room for a small bed or futon and I could manage to create a nice work space in the corner by the bay window, any sort of roommate was out of the question. Even if Peter and I could survive in such cramped surroundings, I sensed that Mrs. Giovanni was not the type of lady who would allow an unmarried couple to rent from her.

"What I am I going to do? I love this place."

Alex excused herself, allowing me privacy to think. I wished that she had stayed. I needed someone I could talk to. Alex was very good at listening. I stood there, happily envisioning myself living in the cozy nook. Then I remembered the source of my initial angst. On the pro side, the list seemed to be endless—the nearness to work and a friend already living in the charming building. There was only one check in the con column—Peter.

Then again, Peter hadn't found a job in the area yet. It could take a while for him to secure something. I was already past due on settling into proper accommodations. I needed to say yes. More importantly, I wanted to say yes.

The possible obstacle would be if the rent involved selling a kidney. I had already said no to that once. In affluent college towns, broom closets could be listed for over a grand a month. The studio I was looking at would fetch more. I slipped my briefcase/messenger bag onto my shoulder and went searching for Mrs. Giovanni. If the rent was too high or she wanted me to sign a long-term lease, I would have to say no and head back to the motel.

Mrs. Giovanni was all smiles when I found her waiting for me on the large wraparound porch. I followed her across the street to her equally charming home. She put the teakettle on and offered me some fresh-baked cookies. I sat at her kitchen table while she served tea and chatted about the weather. Again, my suspicious nature took over. I feared the kindly elderly lady was setting me up in an effort to garner an exorbitant rent. I felt bad thinking that this sweet woman might be a shark clad in a disarming muumuu.

Finally, the subject of the studio came up. She offered to rent it to me for a whopping four hundred dollars a month. I had been prepared to haggle, I just hadn't been prepared to haggle for her to raise the rent. Before I could voice my objections or question her sanity, she had the lease laid out in front of me. How could I refuse? The rent should have been at least a thousand dollars more.

When I left, I had the keys to my new home and a sudden realization. During the brief chat, Mrs. Giovanni had managed to learn almost everything about my childhood. I couldn't help wondering if perhaps before becoming a charming landlady Mrs. Giovanni had worked for the CIA.

"Well?" Alex asked when I found her sitting on the front porch swing sipping a cup of coffee.

"Howdy, neighbor."

"That's great. I was worried about you finding a place," Alex said in a soft warm tone that sent a strange chill down my spine. "This time of year, anything decent gets snatched up by the kids who couldn't get into the dorm."

"There's one slight problem."

"I know, no bathtub," Alex said with a grimace. "Hate to say it, but a man must have designed that bathroom. They just don't understand that sometimes a gal needs to chill with a nice bubble bath. Fear not, milady. For a small fee, I will let you use mine when you need to escape."

"Thank you," I said, not understanding why I was blushing. "But that's not the problem. I was supposed to be looking for a place for two."

"Oh?" A look of disappointment clouded her smile. Her gaze drifted as she took a sip from the coffee mug she had been holding.

"I suppose Peter will have to understand."

"Peter?" Alex choked on her coffee.

"Are you all right?" I asked as she continued to choke. She pulled away when I patted her on the back.

"I'm fine, sorry."

"Why?"

"Nothing," she choked out with a small chuckle. "My mistake. I may have to rethink my Jan Brady theory."

"What?"

"Nothing." She shook her head, apparently amused by something I had said. I was completely at a loss as to what she found so funny. She quickly shifted gears and smiled back at me as if nothing had occurred. "I have some time before my dinner with Maureen. Why don't we get your stuff from the motel?"

"I can't thank you enough." I was practically doing a happy dance. Just knowing that I wouldn't be spending another night in a tacky motel thrilled me to no end. I did notice that she had changed out of her work attire into even more casual clothing.

My first thought was, "Perfect she's already prepared to do some heavy lifting," then I took a closer look. She had changed into a pair of faded blue jeans, a white T-shirt with bold purple lettering, and a denim jacket. It was the T-shirt that made me gasp. Not so much the T-shirt but what was written across the front of it. *Pretty, Witty & Gay.*

"Oh?" I managed to sputter out.

"Stephanie?"

I heard her voice and realized that I had been standing there gaping at her. In my muddled mind, I was trying to find a way to apologize for my overt touching. I was filled with a sudden fear that there was a girlfriend out there who wouldn't like the fact that I had been hugging Alex.

"Yo, Stephanie," she said once again. "You okay?"

"Sorry." I shook the jumbled thoughts from my head. "Would this be the T-shirt that Stan did not approve of?" I asked in an effort to regain my footing.

"Yes," Alex said, her tone more than a little defensive. "My guess is he's not a *West Side Story* fan."

"That must be it."

"You didn't know?"

"Not a clue."

"Wow." She snickered. "Been a long time since that's happened."

"Just so we're clear, I don't care."

"Good." She smiled back at me. "I hate all of that uncomfortable crap."

"Speaking of crap, let's go get my stuff," I pulled her off the swing. "I can't believe you were worried. What'd you think—I would ask you not to make a pass?"

"It wouldn't have been a new experience."

"I can think of worse things." Alex looked at me with a curious expression. "Come on." I gave her a playful shove. "Let's put those muscles of yours to good use."

"Oh, so now I'm slave labor," she teased in return as we climbed into her black Subaru Outback.

Once we returned to my new home, I realized how little I actually owned. I had traveled light, not knowing what I could expect to find in the small college town. Still the meager belongings I was looking at really was the sum of things.

"You need furniture," Alex stated the obvious.

"My last place was a sublet."

She glanced at her watch. "It's too late to pick up a futon. Everything but the bars close early around here."

I had already checked out of the motel, and the thought of sleeping on the floor was less than appealing. I was contemplating buying an air mattress at the local hardware store. Until I realized that would be closed, as well. The first downside to Prowers Landing was that the sidewalks rolled up fairly early.

I supposed that I could spend one night roughing it. Suddenly, I wished I hadn't been kicked out of the Girl Scouts. I might have learned a few outdoorsy skills. I still maintained that it was Jenny Brucker's idea to play doctor and not mine. Ah, Jenny, my downstairs neighbor who I used to sneak out to watch playing softball. I had wanted to play, as well, but my grandmother thought it was undignified for a girl to play sports. Something about wanting to be men and other such nonsense.

"You can crash on my couch tonight." Alex's offer tore me from my unexpected trip down memory lane.

"Thank God."

"Look, I'm having dinner with Maureen," Alex said. "You can join us or unpack. Well, you could unpack if you had something to put your clothes in."

"Dinner sounds great."

"It's settled then. Tonight we eat, and tomorrow we shop," Alex graciously offered. "With my car, we can probably get everything in one trip."

"Thank you."

"Thank Chris." She waved off my gratitude. "If it wasn't for her, I'd still be driving my sporty little BMW."

"Ouch."

"Hey, I love my Outback," she asserted. "Meet me upstairs when you're ready. I'll leave the door unlocked."

"Is that safe?"

"In Prowers Landing?" She sounded amused. "I should be fine. But if some thug tries to kidnap me, I'm counting on you to come save me."

"Good luck with that."

Chapter Four

I showered, carefully I might add, since I had yet to purchase a shower curtain. I knew I was taking far too long in the shower. I felt grungy from the move. Although I wouldn't have admitted it at the time, I wanted to look good for my first big night out. I told myself that I wanted to make a good impression. Even though I would only spend two years at Prower, the bonds you formed in the political cesspool of academia were very important.

After I emerged from my shower, I planned to get dressed as quickly as possible. I failed to accomplish the simple act. For the first time in my life, I was in a quandary as to what to wear. Normally, I would go with one of my three standards—my expensive business suit for an interview or meeting, my everyday suits for the classroom, I owned four, or a faded pair of Levis for my downtime. The Levis were purchased as a form of rebellion against my grandmother, who insisted that girls never under any circumstances wear pants.

I knew we were going to a place called Church Street, but I knew nothing about the restaurant. Then I remembered the pair of black jeans I had purchased on a whim. I threw them on along with an emerald green blouse. I didn't know why, but I wanted to look good.

"It will have to do," I mumbled, still adjusting the blouse and my hair. Realizing that I had taken far too long, I grabbed my wallet and rushed upstairs. Despite her telling me that the door would be unlocked, I knocked lightly, only to receive no answer. I knocked a little louder, my heart racing with anticipation. Thankfully, I heard Alex calling for me to come in.

Upon entering her home, I was stunned. Her apartment was virtually a palace compared to the studio directly below it. For starters, there was a staircase off to the right that led to a second level. Her living room, complete with a marble fireplace, was bigger than my entire studio. She also had French doors. Mine opened into the garden, hers opened onto a small balcony.

"I'll be out in a moment," she called from what I assumed was the bathroom.

I took the opportunity to expand my viewing of her place. Despite the size, there was a feeling of warmth. The mantel above the fireplace was covered with pictures of her family. Above the pictures hung a carefully framed shadow box containing a saber. I gasped, reaching up to touch it. My heart was racing from being so close to something that had belonged to a man I had spent almost two years of my life researching.

"It belonged to one of my ancestors," Alex said from behind me.

I turned to explain to her that I already knew this tidbit of information, and my lungs seized. There she stood wearing nothing but a fluffy terrycloth robe and a smile. I felt a blush creep up on me when I realized that I was staring.

"I...um..." I began to babble. I took what I hoped would be a calming breathe before I tried the art of speaking. "Master Sergeant Stephan James Ballister," I managed to sputter out.

"That was a hell of a guess."

"American history," I offered, wondering just how dorky I sounded. "I mean, I'm familiar with the Knights."

"I'm guessing very familiar if you knew he was an ancestor of mine." It sounded like a compliment, yet I still felt uncertain. "Ready for a good old-fashioned girls' night? Probably our last chance before the semester starts."

"Can't wait."

"There should be some wine in the fridge. I think," she added with a shrug. "Make yourself comfortable while I finish getting ready."

Comfortable? I tried to tell myself that I could do comfortable, casual, maybe even relaxed. Of course, while telling myself all this, I was standing there feeling like a total loser. I shook out my hands in an effort to calm myself. I pondered taking a seat on the sofa when she emerged from the other room.

Alex smartly dressed in black slacks and a matching blazer. I felt my pulse quicken for the hundredth time that day. This time, my heart was racing when I noticed the pearl silk camisole underneath her blazer. For some odd reason, I was miffed that Alex couldn't wear a blouse like a normal person. I wasn't angry with the outfit per se. I was angry that I was so flustered. I wanted to look good that evening, and there she stood having casually thrown together an outfit and looked stunning.

She didn't notice, far too busy smoking while reading a piece of paper. I blew out a terse breath and watched her reading. She stood there amused by what she was reading, a cigarette dangling between her slender fingers.

"What are you reading?"

"Your résumé, I just found it."

"Here?"

"I lack organizational skills." She snarled playfully while taking another drag from her cigarette. "Top five percent of your class at Yale, very impressive. Couldn't get into Harvard?" she teased before taking a long drag on her cigarette. I walked over and took the cigarette away from her and took a healthy drag. I laughed when she gazed at me with a shocked expression.

"Now and then," I said in answer to her unspoken question. "Probably not even an entire pack in my life."

"I hate people like that," she shot out, grabbing the cigarette from me.

"I could have sworn just yesterday you told me that you had quit."

"I'm working on it."

"Just where did you go to school, Miss Kendell?"

"I did my undergrad at Wellesley, then Harvard Law. I went back to Harvard when I decided to chuck the law."

"You know that makes us sworn enemies," I taunted her as I removed her cigarette from her mouth. I looked around and discovered an ashtray on the coffee table and extinguished the cigarette. "Last one," I admonished her.

"I'll try," she offered a lighthearted promise. "I just found it, I must have hidden it for an emergency." She blushed at her lack of self-control. Quickly, she turned her attention back to my résumé.

"You got your PhD at twenty-one. That's disgusting!"

"It's the truth. I completed my dissertation the same week I bought my first legal drink. I almost did it at twenty, but I had to scrap my original thesis," I quietly explained, curious if I should tell her the whole truth.

"That sucks." She grimaced, still perusing my résumé. "So how old were you when you started college?"

"Twelve," I shyly admitted. "That's when I started at UConn. I finished when I was sixteen. Because I was so young, I couldn't live on campus. The university arranged for me to be shuttled back and forth. The driver was the nicest older woman who just loved to talk. Good thing my grandmother had a somewhat narrow view of the world."

"Sounds like my Dad's mother." She grunted. "Thankfully, my grandmother on Mom's side, Gamma was terrific. She was a bit of a Bohemian. Which is funny because Gampa was an investment banker. They made quite a pair. Here it is!" she exclaimed before I could make a comment regarding her lineage. I trembled when she draped one arm over my shoulders.

For a brief moment, I was struck mute. Something about the way she was touching me felt right. "What did you find?" I finally asked.

"This," she said, holding up my résumé. "I knew I've heard of your work. Your first book was about the executions of Corcoran and O'Brien. The first executions in the Confederate Army. They were in the Louisiana Knights, my great-great-grandfather's company."

"I know." Unconsciously, I leaned closer to her as if my body had a will of its own.

"Well, you would," she stated the obvious. "Is that how we met before?"

"Yes."

"Which would explain how you knew about my famous ancestor." Her words were quiet. "You were doing research on Company D. Sorry I don't remember."

"I wouldn't expect you to." I tried to sound causal about the whole thing. In hindsight, what had happened really wasn't that big of a deal. At the time, for me, it was catastrophic. "I had heard about the diaries. Thought I might get a peek. That was about it."

"Oh?" She pursed her lips. "I must have said no since my family doesn't share them with anyone. Was I bitchy about it?"

"Um…"

"That would be a yes."

"I originally wanted to write about Stephan Ballister," I confided, confused as to why I leaned even closer to her. "You declined to show me the diaries, and that was the end of that."

She closed her eyes and pressed her body closer to mine. I felt her heart beating. I reveled in her warmth. Thoughts escaped me. My breathing ceased. Nothing mattered, only the feel of this woman against me. Just as suddenly, the intimate moment was over. Alex stepped away, and I felt a sense of loss.

"You should call Peter and let him know about the apartment."

My head snapped at the harshness of her voice. I stepped away from her rapidly, suddenly feeling ashamed. I was embarrassed that my body was tingling, and Peter had completely vanished from my thoughts.

"I tried earlier," I meekly offered. It was a lie. The truth was, it hadn't occurred to me to call him. "We've been playing phone tag for weeks. I'll catch up with him tomorrow. I wonder how long it'll take to get a phone hooked up."

"You don't have a cellphone?"

"No." I rolled my eyes. It was a familiar argument. "I've never had any interest or desire to own one. Who would I need to call at a moment's notice?"

"Um…your boyfriend," she said.

I had no idea what had just happened. On the surface, we were just two academics chatting about her famous ancestor. Just how I ended up practically snuggling with her was a complete mystery.

Add to the mix, I was filled with an overwhelming sense of guilt. I hadn't thought much about Peter that day. He was nothing more than a passing thought when I realized the studio I had rented wouldn't be big enough for two. Granted, I was never all gooey when it came to my boyfriend. Still, I found it odd that since my arrival in Prowers Landing, Peter was rarely in my thoughts.

We just stood there not saying anything. "Do you know a good place to buy a shower curtain?" I blurted because the situation was getting too funky for words.

"Shower curtain?"

"I don't have one," I sputtered like an idiot. "I made a mess when I took my shower. I don't even have towels to clean it up. Well, I had one towel that I used to dry off, but it didn't do a whole lot when it came to cleaning the floor. I'm going to need to make a list. I had one, but now I'm not so sure about what I'll need," I rambled like a lunatic.

"Checkers."

"Checkers?"

"It's the local everything shop," she explained, turning away from me. "Prices are good, but sometimes, the selection is a bit limited."

"Oh."

"You could always take the train into Boston."

"Might be best."

"Yup."

It was the shortest, strangest conversation I had ever been involved with. Naturally, it led to a prolonged silence. I was on edge by the time Maureen arrived. Alex appeared calm when she told our boss that I would be joining them. Her soothing voice would have eased my fears if we hadn't just spent twenty minutes sitting around without speaking.

"Great. Now we can get her drunk and learn all her deep dark secrets," Maureen gloated. Her joyful tone worried me that she wasn't joking.

"Too late, Mrs. Giovanni already beat you to it," I quickly countered. "She promised not to tell where I've hidden the bodies."

"Clever girl," Maureen said with a laugh. "So how did Mrs. G get a hold of you so soon?"

"Stephanie is renting the studio downstairs," Alex explained in full big sister mode. "Now on to a more interesting subject. Who's driving?"

The driver was decided by flipping a coin; Maureen lost. "Damn, how is it that you win every time? I just wasted a good babysitter," she grumbled while we gathered our coats.

"What are you bitching about?" Alex teased her. "We're the

ones who have to be seen in a minivan."

As Maureen drove down Route 128, I felt something I hadn't experienced in a long time—fear. I was relieved once we left the highway. My reprieve was short-lived. The roads in the city were a mess. Every few feet, there seemed to be a detour. I was more than happy no one had asked me to drive.

"What is this?" I exclaimed as we sat in bumper-to-bumper traffic.

"Bureaucracy in action." Maureen snarled.

"Suddenly, I feel like Connecticut is another country. I mean, we have our share of traffic problems but nothing like this," I wryly commented when we finally entered Cambridge.

"We Bostonians are not known for our ability to play well with others while commuting," Alex said. "Driving is considered a contact sport. Use of directional signals is a sign of weakness. Trust me, driving in Massachusetts is not for the faint of heart."

"Moron!" Maureen screamed as she blared the horn.

Unable to watch, I tried looking out the window, only to see a group of college-aged people wandering into traffic, apparently having no regard for the crosswalk or traffic lights.

"What the hell is wrong with them?"

"This is MIT." Alex pointed to the domed building. "Where they can split an atom, but they can't cross the street like a normal person."

"Oh, Lord, help me!" I shouted as Maureen sped through traffic, hitting the accelerator harder when we approached the rotary. "I need a drink," I added as we flew around the circle of traffic.

"Well, you're in luck," Alex said lightly as we entered Harvard Square. For the life of me, I couldn't understand how she remained so calm. Maureen maneuvered around the twist and turns past the famous university. "Church Street is the best TexMex in the area. But watch out for the margaritas."

"Are they bad?" I held on to my seat for dear life, thankful that Alex had called shotgun and I could hide in the back. "How can you be so calm? I've already rattled off twelve Hail Marys in the last thirty seconds, and I'm not even Catholic."

"I used to live right over there." She pointed to a building that quickly turned into a blur. "As for the margaritas, they're very good. In fact, they're too good. After a couple of those babies, you lose all control."

"Space!" Maureen squealed like a small child on Christmas morning.

"Hold on!" Alex cautioned me as Maureen threw the minivan into reverse on a busy street. Her children's toys bombarded me as I held on for dear life while the sounds of honking horns from irate drivers cursing echoed in my ears.

"Yes!" Maureen congratulated herself once she had successfully parked. At least I had hoped that we had stopped, but since I had closed my eyes somewhere along the line, I couldn't be certain.

"Still alive back there, Stephanie?" I opened my eyes to find Alex's warm gaze staring back at me. "Stephanie?"

"I think I'm going to be sick." I gasped, pulling various squeaky toys off my lap.

"I have that effect on women," Alex taunted me. "Welcome to Massachusetts."

"Does everyone drive like that?"

"Only if you want to get anywhere."

***

The restaurant was very noisy and crowded and possessed an eclectic décor. Since there was a line of people that stretched out onto the street, we decided to wait at the bar for our table. Maureen took the pager that would alert us when it was our turn to be seated. We pushed our way through the crowd and managed to grab two seats. I offered to stand and pay for the first round. The skinny blond bartender raced over the moment Alex took her seat.

"Hey, girl. How are you?"

"Same old, same old," Alex responded flatly.

"So grand gold New Orleans-style, rocks, no salt?" the bartender cooed and leaned slightly over the bar. I couldn't help but notice that movement allowed her a better view of Alex's cleavage.

"You know it," Alex said politely as she turned to me. "Stephanie, what would you like?"

"The same."

"Make that two, Sara," Alex told her.

"I'm sorry, I didn't see you," little Miss Perky lied. "Maureen, what can I get for you?"

"Pepsi."

"Lost the coin toss again?"

"Yes, damn it."

Sara returned with the drinks, along with a basket of freshly made corn chips, chili con queso, and homemade salsa. She explained that the snacks were on her. I was more than a little miffed when I went to pay and was forced to shove the money at Sara, who had not taken her eyes off of Alex. Fortunately, another customer clamored for the amorous bartender's attention. I couldn't help thinking that customer just may have saved Sara's life.

"I was really hoping it was her night off," Alex groused, clearly just as annoyed as I was.

"Why?" Maureen asked. "All you have to do is bat those baby blues, and we get our drinks right away, plus free snacks. I didn't get this much attention when I was pregnant. So she's tried to slip you her number a couple of times. Fine, more than a couple of times. You've made it clear that you're not interested. Hey, if she wants to woo you with free chips and tequila, then I say let her."

"People offered you margaritas when you were pregnant?" I teased, not agreeing with her even just a little.

"Funny." Maureen smirked. "Come on, it's free stuff."

"Granted, the chips and margaritas are excellent." I tried to stay calm. "I'm certain that it's making Alex uncomfortable. If a man did that to you—"

"I'd tell him off," Maureen grumbled. "Alex has made that point more than once."

"See, I'm not the only one who thinks Sara is out of line," Alex piped in before taking a sip of her drink.

"How is everything?" Sara interrupted in an over-chipper tone.

"Fine," Alex curtly responded.

I couldn't help noticing that Sara was only interested in Alex's response. Without looking at or addressing me or Maureen, she moved to the next customer. It was safe to assume that I did not like Sara or her perky attitude. Less and less when she repeated the action several times. Each time she stopped, she made an extremely lame attempt to flirt with Alex.

It wasn't simply her lame attempts to flirt with Alex, it was the way she tried to nudge me away from her. Based on Maureen's posture, I could only assume that she had seen this show before. Every time Alex and I began to engage in a conversation, there was Sara. No matter how many times Alex brushed her off, she was relentless. The final straw came when she delivered another round of drinks for Alex and Maureen, once again pretending to have forgotten that I was there. The first time had annoyed me. The second time irked me. The third time, I was ready to lunge over the bar.

Alex's voice stopped me from reaching over and choking the life out of Sara's perky little body. "Sara? If it's not too much trouble, do you think you could bring my friend another drink?"

"Oh? I'm so sorry," Sara lied once again. I might have had a little more tolerance for the situation if the girl wasn't so bad at hiding her disgust with me. "What is that you're drinking?" Her words might have held some credence if she hadn't feigned ignorance. This girl knew her job and knew what everyone was drinking. I was the lone exception. Which in itself was hard to swallow since I was sitting next to her favorite guest drinking the exact same thing.

"Stephanie will have what I'm having. It shouldn't be too difficult for you to remember that!" Alex's harsh timbre cut through the crowded bar, silencing the restaurant. The icy glare that accompanied Alex's cold tone forced the skinny bimbo to shrink back in horror.

"Right away." Sara gulped before darting away.

"Excuse me," Alex politely said with a gentle touch to my arm.

I munched on some chips, watching Alex make her way through the crowd. We watched as Alex cornered Sara at the opposite end of the bar. To this day, I have no idea what was discussed. Based on the menacing look in Alex's eyes and Sara's look of sheer terror, I could only guess that Sara's shameless flirting ended then and there. I shouldn't have been happy about it, but I was.

"Well, there goes all the freebies." Maureen sighed.

"I don't think Sara likes me very much."

"She does seem to have it in for you," Maureen agreed. "Maybe she thinks you're a threat."

"A what?" I sputtered. I couldn't understand why the girl would view me as a threat, A part of me was flattered; another was pissed that Sara couldn't or wouldn't open her eyes to the fact that Alex wasn't interested in her.

Maureen's look of pure bewilderment confused me even further. Before Maureen had a chance to explain her observations, I felt a warm caress on my shoulder. I turned to find Alex smiling down at me, explaining that our table was ready.

"But the beeper didn't go off," Maureen said.

"Our table is ready," Alex repeated.

Before she could explain the how or why, a stocky dark smartly dressed man approached us. "Ms. Kendell, I would be happy to show you and your party to your table."

"Okay, not a waiter." Maureen snickered and handed the man our beeper.

No one said a word as we followed him to the downstairs dining area. We bypassed the other diners and were led to a private dining area. Located away from the maddening crowd in a quiet comfortable area.

I couldn't help noticing that our host was dressed far too well to be a server or even a manager. He seemed nervous as he pulled out our chairs. He apologized for any inconvenience and informed us that this evening everything was on the house, and if it met with our approval, the chef was preparing his signature dish along with all the house specials. He apologized one last time when a waiter appeared with a fresh round of margaritas. I was stunned by the sudden turn of events.

The table was silent. I sat back and watched mountains of food being delivered to our table. The wait staff seemed nervous to be around us. Alex passed a margarita to Maureen.

"Looks like we're going to be here for a while. One should be all right," she said with a mischievous grin. Maureen raised her glass and saluted Alex. "To lawyer Barbie," Alex said before taking a healthy sip of her drink. Maureen joined in on the merriment. I sat back uncertain what was real or if I had consumed more tequila than I thought I had.

"I don't wish to appear ungrateful," I said finally. "But the few times in my life when I have worked up the courage to complain about the service, the most I ever received was 'we're sorry' and a coupon for a free appetizer. How is it that we scored all of this because of one frisky bartender?"

"I'm a Kendell," Alex said in a dry voice.

"I see," I said, suddenly thinking that Alex had lost some of her charm. I sat there wondering if my first impression of Alex had been the real deal. I jumped when Maureen and Alex erupted into a riotous laughter. "Did I miss something?" I asked, feeling left out on the joke.

"Alex's family," Maureen choked out as she tried to stifle her laughter. "Great old family name. One of the country's founding families. Ah, to be a Kendell, the prestige, the history. One slight problem, though."

"No money." Alex shrugged.

"Excuse me?" I gasped. "That's like saying the Rockefellers live on food stamps."

"It's true," Alex mournfully confessed. "Well, I don't know about the Rockefellers' state of affairs. I do know that my family's fortune was blown decades ago. It's an old story. One generation slaves away to amass a fortune that should last forever. Except the next two generations go through everything without a second thought for the future. Basically because they have no intention of ever working for a living. Too busy drinking and getting laid. By the time my Dad graduated from Harvard, all that was left was a great name and a huge debt."

"It must be infuriating to have people assume that everything was handed to you."

"At times." She shrugged again as if it was no big deal. "I'm sure people would be shocked to know that I had a paper route when I was a kid. Being a Kendell made it difficult to find a job. I quickly learned to use the family connections. There were still times when I was turned away because people assumed I was rich and didn't need the money. I give my dad a lot of credit. Unlike the way he was raised, we were never led to believe that we were rich. Of course, I'm not entirely certain that my grandmother knows the money is long gone."

"I'm guessing this isn't Gamma you're talking about."

"Correct, I'm referring to my father's mother. She just keeps spending and sticks poor Dad with the bills," she continued. "Thank God he makes a good living. But between the bills my grandfather left and his mother's spending habits, it's never enough. Everything my parents and I have, we earned. All the money I made working on Wall Street went to helping my dad pay off Gramps's debt. That and my kid sister, Nicole's, love affair with gin and sleazy men, and of course, there was all the money I spent trying to get my little brother out of that cult. I did manage to help save the family estate, and thanks to God and AA, Nicole finally got her life together. Unfortunately, David is hanging around Logan Airport handing out flowers."

"You left out how Chris wiped you out," Maureen hissed with a sneer.

"She didn't get everything," Alex protested. "I kept my cottage in Ptown. Fortunately, I bought that before we were together."

"What about Wellesley and Harvard?" I asked quickly, not wanting to hear any of the gory details regarding the infamous Chris.

"Working my butt off and academic scholarships."

"Speaking of Chris," Maureen cut in.

"Let's not." Alex groaned.

"Is she still trying to use your cottage?" Maureen pried.

"Yes," Alex said reluctantly. "I said no. I told her that she brought plenty of women there while we were together, she can rent a room at the Boat Slip like everyone else."

"I can't believe her." Maureen moaned in disgust.

"Chris is Chris."

"She's—"

"What do you expect? She's a lawyer. New subject. Let's eat!" Alex insisted when the waiter arrived with a fresh round of margaritas. While Maureen passed on more alcohol, Alex and I indulged. The food was fantastic. I enjoyed the conversation. The tequila began to have an effect on me. More than once, I caught myself touching Alex's hand or knee. She seemed to ignore my contact until I rested my hand on her thigh.

"Stephanie, tell us about Peter," Alex said briskly as she brushed my hand from her thigh.

"Who?" Maureen asked, seemingly unaware of my transgression.

"Stephanie's beau," Alex said directly.

The hint of harshness in her voice was my cue. I pushed my drink away and tried to clear my head by switching to water. I caught a look of surprise clearly written on Maureen's face. For a brief moment, I thought she had been aware of what my hands had been doing. I stared at my hands for a moment, trying to understand why they had suddenly developed free will. It wasn't in my nature to be a touchy person. Caressing someone's thigh during a meal was completely out of character for me. My boyfriend had never experienced me being so rambunctious. Which led to the question, why had I suddenly become Miss Frisky Buttons?

"Peter?" Maureen stammered, breaking me out of my thoughts.

It was then I realized that Maureen's surprise came from not knowing I was in a relationship. I also realized that Alex had skillfully moved away from my grasp. Her message was clear. I had crossed a line.

"Sorry," I softly directed toward Alex. To her credit, she simply nodded, accepting my apology. "Peter and I have been together about five years now." I began to prattle on, filling them in on my boyfriend. It was the standard conversation, how we met, what he did for a living, and so on. The conversation moved to Maureen's husband and children.

When Maureen started talking about her children, Alex finally rejoined the discussion. Alex's face lit up during the conversation. It was clear that she adored Maureen's children, especially Mary who was the youngest and Alex's goddaughter. After Maureen gave Alex a halfhearted lecture about spoiling the children, we agreed that it was time to go.

Chapter Five

We stood outside in the cool autumn air waiting for Maureen to bring the car around. Alex was quiet. I knew I should say something. I had no idea what to say. I hadn't molested her, but rubbing her leg was way out of line. If a male colleague had done that, he'd be facing harassment charges. I needed to clean up the mess I had created. In many ways, my behavior was no better than Sara's. I silently vowed to try to understand why I had suddenly turned into grabby little idiot later. First things first.

"Alex," I began, taking a moment to clear my throat, still at a loss as to what to say. "I...um...I'm sorry," I stammered, feeling like an idiot. "I'm not sure what that was all about."

"It's okay."

"But," I tried to argue. "That's not me."

"Tequila has a way of making people horny and stupid."

"Horny? No, I don't—"

"Stephanie, you're a little tipsy," she tried to reason with me. "No harm, no foul."

"No." I shook my head. The movement made me feel light-headed. "I'm not a touchy person, that's all. As for having a case of the hornies—"

"A case of the hornies?" She laughed at my behavior. "Yeah, you're as sober as a judge."

"Oh, come on," I tried to argue, unaware that I was speaking very loudly. "Sex is tedious."

"Tedious?" She laughed even louder. "Sorry, can't agree with you on that one. You don't do a lot of girl talk, do you?"

"Me?" I snorted, feeling amused by her comment. Then I furrowed my brow, confused by what I had been saying. "No, I don't do girl talk. I also don't drink very often. I guess you've already figured that part out. Look, I just wanted to say that I'm sorry for, you know. Friends?" I asked hesitantly. To my relief, she nodded. I leaned over and gave her a quick hug. The gesture failed to be the quick friendly gesture I had intended. Instead, we melted into each other.

"You feel good," I whispered against her chest.

"So do you," she sweetly murmured. "Whoa!" she sputtered, stepping away from me. "Speaking of being tipsy."

I had no idea what had happened. The night had become more and more confusing. One moment, I was apologizing for behaving like a pig; the next, I was hugging her. It was at that moment I swore off tequila for the rest of my natural life. We stood in silence lost in our thoughts until Maureen drove up. I climbed into the back of the minivan and listened to the chatter in the front seat. The traffic was much lighter at this hour, and the return trip was far more relaxing. I might have nodded off once or twice during the ride home.

When we arrived back home, I quickly exited the vehicle. I was eager to make a hasty retreat. Unfortunately, the effect of the tequila reared its ugly head and redefined gravity. Just as I was certain that my face was about to be introduced to the sidewalk, I felt strong arms wrap around me.

"Easy there, sailor," Alex comforted me. "I guess you don't have your sea legs yet."

"Yeah." I groaned. "It's a good thing you warned me about the margaritas, or I could have made a complete ass out of myself."

"No worries." Alex laughed. "Let's get you inside."

"Good night, Maureen," I shouted for some unknown reason.

I stumbled along the walkway. Thankfully, Alex held me tightly. When we entered the foyer, I was convinced that the wallpaper was spinning. Alex tightened her hold on me as I teetered up the staircase.

"I could have sworn that I was beginning to sober up." I groaned. "Hey, how come you aren't drunk?"

"Who says I'm not? Trust me, if I let go of you, I'd be ass over teakettle."

"Uh-huh."

I parked myself against the wall while Alex fumbled for her keys. She placed a reassuring hand on my chest to keep me from sliding to the floor. My only game plan at that moment was to pass out on her sofa and forget as much of the evening as possible. I stumbled when she finally managed to open the door. Again, I found myself wrapped in a warm embrace. Without a word, Alex swiftly guided me through her apartment. I shivered when we entered the bedroom. She gently lay me on the bed. I was about to protest when

I felt her removing my shoes.

"You'll be more comfortable here. I'll take the sofa," she said.

"No, not going to happen."

My eyes strained against the darkness. In the back of my mind, I knew that my protest must have sounded childish. I reached out, needing to find her. My hand clasped what I hoped was her shoulder and pulled her toward me. I could hear her groaning as she stumbled. The air escaped my lungs when her body landed on top of my own. Her body pressed against mine, and my mind went blank. The only clear thought I could comprehend was how warm her body felt.

In the darkness, I could finally see her looking down at me. She moved slightly closer, and I shivered. Our lips were so close to touching I could feel her breath on my skin. I hated when these feelings would overtake my sense of reality. Yet I was helpless to resist.

"It's the alcohol," I reasoned. "Just like the other times."

"What?"

What about Gigi? You weren't drunk then! my inner voice questioned. "We were kids. It was nothing," I slurred out loud.

"Come again?" I heard Alex ask, reminding me that she was lying on top of me. "I should—" she began, her fingers brushing against my cheek.

"Come here," I whispered, unconsciously pulling her closer.

Although my mind was screaming to stop, my body had other ideas. I raised my head and brushed her lips gently with my own. The heat from the caress overwhelmed me. Parting my lips, I invited her in. Alex accepted my invitation eagerly. The kiss deepened as our bodies pressed against each other. Without realizing it, I parted my legs, allowing her thigh to nestle between them. Soon our hips began to move in rhythm. It felt so right. For the first time in my life, I was on fire.

Alex gasped for air as she broke away. I looked into her eyes, and I knew I wanted her. I reached up and unbuttoned her jacket before I gently slid it off her shoulders. I could see the passion in her eyes as she gazed down at me.

She lowered herself and unbuttoned my blouse. In response, I reached up and fulfilled a fantasy that had been running through my head all evening. My fingers caressed the silk camisole. Soon, the touch of silk wasn't enough. I wanted to feel her. I ran my hand down the silk garment until I could feel the tight muscles of her stomach. I tugged the camisole out her pants and ran my hand up her tight body.

While I was preoccupied with my own explorations, Alex had managed to not only open my blouse, but had unclasped my bra, as well. My nipples hardened when she lifted the garment up and exposed my breast to the cool night air. She moaned with pleasure. I gently cupped her breast, taking her erect nipple between my fingers, teasing it gently. Our hips danced together. I was mesmerized watching her mouth lower to my breast.

"Harder," I begged, feeling her lips firmly attached to my nipple. I moaned with pleasure, arching my back in an effort to offer her more.

Suddenly, she stopped and pulled herself away, turning her back to me. I clasped her shoulders, turning her back around. I pulled her body toward mine. My hands resumed exploring her flesh. This time, they roamed much farther down her body. I swiftly unbuttoned her pants and lowered the zipper. She closed her eyes and pressed into me. Slowly, I slid her pants down her body. My heart raced as I realized that this was what I had been waiting for.

"No!" Alex protested and pulled herself away. "No. No drunken fumbling with a straight girl, not going to happen."

My movements ceased when I heard the first *no.* With that one word, there was no longer any room for debate. In silence, I lay there as she sat on the edge of the bed unable to look at me. The events of the evening flooded over me. Touching her had felt incredibly right. It wasn't the erotic touches. It was everything, the feel of her body lingering dangerously close to mine. The way she looked at me somehow made me feel complete. In a moment of drunken lunacy, I had discovered bliss. It ended far too quickly.

"Oh, God, I'm sorry."

For what seemed like hours, we stayed there frozen. My most recent apology lingered in the air. Finally, Alex turned to me.

"Stephanie, it's all right," she said softly, reaching down and caressing my face. "Don't beat yourself up. I bet in the morning we'll laugh about this."

"I'm the worst house guest ever."

"Oh, yeah. I just hate it when beautiful women want to make love to me."

"Then why—" I began.

"You're drunk, and there are rules about that," Alex said firmly. "And even if you were sober—"

"I see," I interrupted her explanation.

"No, you don't see," Alex spoke with a sincere gentleness. "Even if we hadn't been drinking, there's someone in your life."

"Peter." I gasped as the reality hit me.

"Peter," she repeated in a heavy voice. "The fact that the person in your life is a man just brings up a whole new drama. Frankly, I'm not up for it."

How could I ever explain this to Peter? I cheated. Not a full-fledged cheat, but what I had done most definitely didn't qualify as monogamous. How would I be able to share an office with Alex every day, not to mention live downstairs from her? I lay there on her bed and tried to vanquish all those random damnations. Hard to do when the object of your desire was staring down at you.

"What did I do?" I whispered as I ground my face into my hands. "Idiot!"

"Hey," Alex whispered softly. "Give yourself a break here. Trust me, I'm not offended. You should have seen some of the stunts my kid sister pulled when she was still drinking. Nikki could make a sailor blush. Stephanie, let it go. Personally, I won't let one night of tequila ruin our friendship. So you made a pass. Big deal. It's not like you kicked a puppy. To be honest, I would really like to forget this happened."

"Tequila, horny, and stupid."

"I warned you about those margaritas." Alex chuckled. Despite her smile, I could still hear a telltale edge in her voice. "I remember my first experience with tequila. Back at Wellesley, some of my sorority sisters were bored, so they thought it would be a good idea to introduce me to Jose Cuervo."

"You were a sorority girl?" I asked in disbelief.

"Of course," she boasted. "Sigma Kappa Epsilon. Let me guess, you were a Delta girl."

"No, I was never in a sorority." I sighed. "I was far too young to pledge."

"That must have been hard."

"At times," I confessed. "Tell me about the night you were introduced to Jose. Did you make a pass at someone, too?"

"I wish," she grumbled. "No, I climbed up on the roof of the Kappa house, took off all my clothes, and sang several choruses of *Don't Cry for Me Argentina.* They managed to get me down before campus security arrived. I spent the rest of the evening worshiping the porcelain god. So, you see, you're ahead of the game. You managed to keep most of your clothing on, you haven't sung any show tunes, or thrown up."

"Yet."

"Well, if you feel a song coming on or the bed starts to spin, just give me a shout. Good night, Stephanie."

"Good night, Alex, and thank you."

"Don't mention it." She stood to leave and instantly crashed onto the floor. "Damn it!"

"Are you all right?" I called out as I jumped from the bed and fumbled around the nightstand to find the light switch. The sudden brightness was startling but not as startling as the sight of Alex sprawled across the floor with her pants around her ankles holding her knee wincing in pain. "Alex?"

"I'm fine," she said with a miserable groan. "I tripped over my pants."

I couldn't help myself, I started to laugh. Not a tiny giggle, either, but a full-fledged belly laugh. She laughed along with me before releasing a painful groan.

"My God, you're hurt!" A modicum of sobriety kicked in, and I jumped off the bed. I wrapped my arms around her and assisted her up onto the bed.

"Ouch," she cried. "I'm such a klutz. I'm always doing this." I raised my eyebrows in question. "Let's just say that my middle name isn't Grace."

"I was afraid that you were going to tell me that you fall out of bed a lot. This doesn't look good," I said after examining her injured knee. "You need to elevate your knee. Why don't you put on something more comfortable? I'll get some ice."

"I'm fine," she protested.

"Really?" I admonished her brave attempts to hide the pain. "Do you need help getting changed?" She shook her head. "Good, then put on something more comfortable. Do you need me to get anything from your bureau?"

"No." She managed to groan. "I'll be fine." Her attempts to act as if all was well were downright amusing.

"Stop fussing." I wagged my finger at her. "Just get comfortable. I'll be right back."

I stumbled out of the bedroom and made my way into the kitchen. I teetered my way to the kitchen as a sudden wave of tequila hit me. I leaned against the doorway just long enough to allow the room to stop spinning. I fumbled around in the darkness until I finally discovered the kitchen.

When I flipped on the light, I gasped at the sight before me. It was enormous and fully equipped with everything. I couldn't help noticing that it was spotless, which was hard to believe after seeing what she had done to her office. Then again, from what I had seen overall, her apartment was very tidy.

"She really did act like a pig to irk Stan," I concluded.

After I decided that Alex was a closet neat freak, I opened the refrigerator. It was then I discovered the truth behind her kitchen's pristine condition. The interior was packed with carton after carton of every variety of takeout food. It appeared that Alex's version of cooking required the use of a telephone. I shook my head in disgust and closed the door. I opened the freezer to get what I had come in for. The contents of the freezer convinced me that the rest of Alex's culinary talents were limited to the microwave. I reached for the ice trays and discovered that they were empty.

"Apparently, she lost the recipe for ice, as well," I surmised before filling the ice trays. I grabbed the first frozen item I could find, which ended up being a handful of frozen burritos. In one of the drawers, I found a dish towel that I was certain had never been used. I pondered the possibility that Alex was unaware that her kitchen existed.

I wrapped up the burritos and made my way back into the

bedroom. I found Alex reclined on the bed clad in a T-shirt with the words *Obey Me* written across the front and a pair of boxer shorts. Gently, I raised her knee and placed a pillow under it. I placed the towel across her swollen knee.

"Ouch!" she exclaimed. "What is this?" She peeked into the hand towel. "Bean and cheese, an excellent choice."

"You're out of ice."

"Again? I'm always forgetting to fill those things."

"You might want to check out your fridge. I think something is growing in there." I searched her dresser for something to sleep in. I found a large white cotton blouse. Without thinking, I stripped off what was left of my clothing and threw it on. Although I'm certain it fit Alex perfectly, on me, the garment was overwhelming. I turned to find Alex staring at me with her mouth hanging open.

"That's cute." I pointed to her T-shirt.

"It belonged to Chris," she proudly explained. "I snagged it when I left. It was her favorite. I know that must sound petty, but I couldn't resist."

"So she got your BMW and you got a T-shirt?"

"Did I mention that it was her favorite?"

"Uh-huh." I laughed as I crawled into bed next to her. "Remind me that if I ever need a lawyer that I should call your ex-girlfriend."

I turned off the light. Alex had already started to drift off. I wasn't far behind her. Exhausted, I allowed my brain to shut off. For the moment, it was best to forget the tequila-induced chaos. My attempt at sexual exploration was over. At least for that night. Sleep, or rather passing out, was a welcome escape.

Chapter Six

The next morning, I awoke to the sweet sounds of the birds singing just outside the bedroom window. That tune felt like an ice pick piercing through my already throbbing head.

"Kill it!" I moaned as I buried my head under the pillow.

"I would if I could lift my head off the pillow." Alex groaned in agony.

Slowly, I crawled out from under my pillow to be assaulted by the blinding glare of the sun.

"I will never drink again," I vowed as I curled up against Alex, trying to hide from the offending light.

"Poor baby, come here," she whispered, pulling me into her waiting arms. "Where does it hurt?" She gently stroked my hair.

"Everywhere. How is your knee?" I listened to the steady beating of her heart. In the back of my mind, I knew I was cuddling with her. Thankfully, the thick fog muddled my mind just enough for me to ignore the obvious.

"Better. But I think the burritos are done for."

"I'm sorry about last night."

"Don't be. I wasn't exactly…unwilling."

"At least you were thinking."

"Was I?" Alex asked with a touch of sadness. "I seem to recall making out with you and ripping your clothes off. Can I ask you something?"

"Yes," I said with a hard swallow.

"Have you?" she began tentatively. "Never mind."

"What is it?" I lifted my body so I could look into her eyes. Admittedly, the small movement was painful.

"Last night, have you done anything like that before?"

"Well…" I began, uncertain as to just how I should answer her.

"Have I ever gotten so drunk that I put my hands down another woman's pants?"

The answer was no. But that wasn't the complete truth. There were times I'd have one too many and find myself making out with another woman, only to sober up quickly and go running off into the night. Then there was Gigi. Although we never made love. A part of me knew I was hiding behind a technicality. What we did together certainly went beyond the realm of friendship. Of course, that wasn't what I told myself at the time. Which begged the question of how I would answer Alex's question. There I was lying in her arms feeling more at home than I ever had with any man. I felt my world come crashing down around me.

"Stephanie?" Alex gently nudged me, alerting me that I had stalled long enough.

"Trust me, I've never done anything like I did last night," I hedged, wondering just how much I should divulge. "I have kissed a girl before."

"Uh-huh."

"Well, more than once," I reluctantly confessed. "But it never went past that, and it only happened a few times when I was—"

"When you were drunk," Alex finished for me.

"Yes," I admitted, feeling that I hadn't explained myself very well. Based on her grim expression, I knew I couldn't tell her about my teenage explorations with Gigi.

Alex didn't say a word. She released her hold on me and got out of bed and walked out of the room. Left alone with my thoughts, I started to remember poor Gigi. We were sixteen and the best of friends, even though I'd already started college and Gigi was in high school. It all started innocently enough. We were lying on my bed talking about sex. What else do you talk about at sixteen? The two main topics of conversation were boys and shopping. Since I had already begun to formulate my life plan and money was tight, very often, I had little to add to the conversation. But talking with Gigi was easier than with the other girls. There was something about her that made me feel at ease.

One afternoon, the conversation took an interesting turn. We started talking about kissing. I was embarrassed by my lack of experience, and to be honest, my lack of interest. Gigi wouldn't let it go. She was very eager when it came to the subject. Finally, I was forced to confess that I had little knowledge regarding the subject. She surprised me by confessing the same. I thought that would be the end of it, which was a mistake. Gigi kept weaving it into the conversation. Finally came the suggestion that we give it a whirl. You know, so we'd know what to do when we started dating. Always a fan of research, I agreed. Kissing led to cuddling, which led to touching. All very innocent until touching became caressing.

The caressing strayed when we discovered it was a lot more fun when we took our shirts off. The memory of our half-naked young bodies exploring was still vivid. Things were becoming intense. Too intense for me. I felt that we were about to cross a line. A part of me really wanted to go further. A bigger part of me was terrified. Suddenly, I was too busy to spend time with Gigi. Looking back, I knew I had pushed her away because I was afraid of something I didn't understand. At the time, I had convinced myself that I was far too busy with college for such idle dalliances. Gigi moved on, finding a new friend, and I pretended it didn't hurt.

All those years later, it still hurt a little. The memory of discovering how it felt to make her nipples hard with a simple touch still burned. I felt the heat in my body rising, recalling how I had asked her to touch herself. Lying there nestled against her watching. Up until my fumbling with Alex, it was the closest I had ever come to climaxing. And there I was in Alex's bed feeling like a fool.

"So now what?" For the first time, the pieces of my life were fitting together. Had Alex seen right through the lies I had been telling myself? I had been telling myself that Peter was my life. Yet I was the one who always put the brakes on when he got too close. We made love but only when it was convenient for me. He tried so hard to please me. Somehow Alex had seen through my façade. Of course, there was a part of me that was certain it was a fluke, not a façade.

She entered the room, and with one look, I felt as if she was looking right through me. I drew the bed covers around me, suddenly feeling exposed.

"I put some coffee on," she said stiffly. "I'm going to take a shower. We have a staff meeting at eleven. Then I have a class, and today is the annual butt-kissing day."

"It's what?"

"The Dean's Tea," she mumbled. "The one day of the year when everyone gathers and kisses his butt. Maybe after the gathering, we could go and pick up a futon for you." She departed the room without waiting for an answer.

I could tell by the intentional distance in her voice that despite the questions I was facing, she wouldn't be sticking around to help me find the answers. I just prayed that I had not lost her friendship, as well.

I gathered my clothing, and still dressed in nothing but Alex's shirt, I raced downstairs to my own apartment. I closed the door quickly, not wanting to meet my new neighbors while running half-naked out of Alex's apartment. Call me crazy, but I just didn't think it would make the best of impressions. Once again, my plan fell to pieces. Just as I was about to slip my key in, the front door opened, and a policewoman entered.

"Hello?" she greeted me, her voice dripping with suspicion.

"I just moved in," I feebly offered. My stomach decided to lurch at that moment. I took a hard swallow, fully aware that I didn't sound the least bit credible. My hands were shaking as I slipped the key into the lock. I knew she was waiting to see if I was lying. I couldn't lay fault with her being suspicious of a half-naked woman wandering around the building. "I'm Dr. Stephanie Grant." I nervously offered my hand.

"Shavonne Springer." She accepted my offer. I relaxed, noticing that she now appeared to be amused by my situation. "Another academic? Sweet."

"Really?"

"I'm the only one in the building who works nights. I get a lot of peace and quiet during the day. Nice meeting you," she added before heading up the staircase.

"Well, that was fun," I choked out as I ducked into my apartment.

Still feeling like my body had been run over by a tractor-trailer, I made my way to the bathroom. I picked up the dirty towel from the night before and shook it out. Not having another option, I decided that the still damp towel would have to do.

I turned on the water, allowing it to warm. I climbed into the shower wondering what I was going to do. The warm water splashed over my body while all those not-so-innocent events from my past rushed over me. The sudden realization that the female friends in my life had not drifted out of my life hit me. I had pushed them away. Because they had become too close. They say you learn something new every day. That day, I learned I had led the majority of my life as a coward.

The temperature of the water dropped suddenly, and I was forced to exit the safety of my shower. I felt numb as I dressed for the day. A new day meant a new beginning. The day before hadn't turned out the way I had hoped. My big girls' night out turned into an emotional roller coaster. I tried telling myself that none of it meant anything.

I was jolted from my battle as my ceiling began to vibrate from the music blaring from Alex's apartment. The ceiling shook violently, the sweet aroma of coffee filled the air. I needed caffeine, and I needed it bad. Big surprise, my courage failed me. After the way I had behaved the night before, how could I even think about going back upstairs? Facing Alex wasn't on my top ten list of things to do.

"Avoiding her is only going to make this worse," I reasoned with my reflection. "Okay, I'll go up and beg for a cup of coffee and hope she doesn't set me on fire. Then again if she does incinerate me, I won't have to deal with the drama."

***

I adjusted my suit and packed my briefcase. I hated facing yet another faculty meeting as the newest member of the department. It was like being the new kid in school all over again. All the moving and being smarter than most of my teachers made it hard to form any friendships. The only friends I had made in my life were Gigi and for a brief time Jenny. I managed to screw up both of those relationships. Then Peter showed up, and I had a feeling I was about to screw that up, too.

When I repacked my briefcase for the third time, it was apparent that I was stalling. The university wasn't far away, I could walk. After what had happened the night before, Alex might prefer if I kept my distance.

"Coffee?" a voice called from behind me. I turned to find Alex standing in my doorway. "It wasn't locked." She shrugged while holding out a bath towel. "You said you didn't have a clean one. Sorry I didn't bring it down on time."

"Thank you," I mumbled, accepting the towel.

She was dressed smartly in a cream-colored suit. The light from the hallway illuminated her well-defined body. She was breathtaking. "That is so not fair," I couldn't help sputtering. Having recently viewed my own reflection, I knew I possessed dark circles under my eyes and a pallor complexion. After our night of debauchery, I truly looked the part. Her eyes were slightly bloodshot, but other than that, the woman was nothing short of stunning.

"Huh?"

"I...um...nothing," I stammered. Internally, my mind was screaming, *Say something you idiot!*

"Come on." She waved to me. "If you feel half as crappy as I do, you need a jolt of caffeine."

I followed her obediently up the staircase. As we entered her apartment, I couldn't help feeling pathetic. The music was deafening, but I liked it, or I would have if my head wasn't on the verge of exploding. The steady rhythm of the guitar was intense.

"Sorry about the music," Alex shouted as she made her way over to the CD player and shut it off. "Melissa," she said as she limped slightly toward the kitchen. "It's something of a morning ritual of mine. I never realized how loud it sounded downstairs. Then again, there's something about this house that causes an echo. George never complained."

"I like it," I said with a smile. "Who's Melissa?"

"How is your head?"

"Better," I lied. "I still feel as if elves are tap dancing on my skull. How is your knee?"

"Fine," she answered with indifference. "How do you like it?"

"What?" I gasped. For some reason, my mind took a tawdry turn.

"Your coffee?" she offered in a bewildered tone. "How do you like your coffee, cream or sugar?"

"Just milk, please," I said quickly, once again feeling more than a little embarrassed.

"I think there's some in the refrigerator. I'm not positive, though. I drink mine black." I could still hear a stiffness lingering in her voice. I would have felt better if I hadn't sensed that she was trying just a little too hard to smooth over the embarrassing events we had shared the night before.

I thanked her as she placed a mug of coffee on the counter for me. I searched the bizarre contents of her refrigerator until I came upon a small carton of milk. It was hidden behind something unidentifiable. I opened the carton and was suddenly overwhelmed. I don't know if it was the stench emanating from the carton or the remnants of tequila or a combination of both. I threw the carton into the sink and made a mad dash toward the bathroom.

Upon my return to the kitchen, I found Alex cleaning up the mess I had made. "I'm so sorry." She met my gaze for the first time since we snuggled in bed that morning.

"Alex Kendell, that refrigerator is a disgrace." I tried to regain my composure.

"I know...I know." She looked down in embarrassment. "I keep meaning to clean it out. But I never seem to get around to it. Plus, I never cook, and I drink my coffee black, and...and...I'm sorry."

"Forget it. I used your toothbrush." I snarled as I retrieved my coffee from the counter.

"That seems fair."

"I just switched to black coffee, as well," I said, more than a little afraid to ask for some sugar. I sipped the coffee slowly, bracing myself for the bitter aftertaste. "Can I ask you something?"

"Sure," she said carefully.

"The music, who is Melissa?"

"Etheridge, Melissa Etheridge," she answered with a combination of shock and horror.

"Oh?"

"Don't you have lesbians in Connecticut?"

"No. We send them all to New York."

"Humor?" She snickered.

The reprieve was short-lived. We ended up just standing there sipping coffee in stony silence. Each of us seemed to be lost in our own thoughts.

"I'm sorry, Stephanie," she said finally, breaking the uneasy silence.

"For?" I responded in confusion.

"Last night...this morning."

"Why? You aren't the one who got drunk and made a pass at your hostess. Let's not forget, inflicting of bodily injury, and of course, throwing up." I felt thoroughly defeated. "Wait, I won't apologize for throwing up. That was definitely your fault. Next time, remember that they put expiration dates on things for a reason."

"Well, you can let yourself off the hook for my knee, as well," she quickly offered. "Technically, I did that to myself. At least I didn't end up in the emergency room." She laughed in a vain attempt to lighten the mood. "Could you imagine trying to explain to some poor intern at three in the morning that you tripped over your own pants?"

"The past twenty-four hours have been something of a roller coaster ride," I said absently. "I just don't understand how I screwed up so many things in such a short time. This isn't me. Everything is suddenly very confusing," I admitted finally, praying that she understood what I was trying to say.

"I don't want to cause you any more confusion." She spoke with such tenderness. I watched intently as she brushed back a lock of hair. "And I won't. I would like for us to be friends. But if my friendship is causing you problems, I could—"

"No," I interrupted, my heart beating a mile a minute. "Our friendship won't cause any problems. I haven't had very many lasting friendships in my life. I'm just starting to realize that it's my fault."

"Okay then," she offered, swaying slightly. "I need to get going. Would you like a lift? I'm driving today since there's no way I'm walking in this get-up."

And there it was. We talked, and despite her best efforts to be nice, I knew she was upset. I wanted to fix it, I needed to fix things, and I was completely confused as to what to say or do to put this behind us. Common sense said to just let it go for the moment and allow things to cool off. I didn't know how I could just back off, thank her for the coffee, and leave for work. I surprised myself by doing just that.

Chapter Seven

Along the drive, Alex complained nonstop about having to wear high heels and a skirt. As she ranted, I couldn't help noticing how great she looked. I understood why she hated wearing a skirt and heels. I also appreciated how good she looked and the way her legs just seemed to go on forever. She was ranting about the injustice of women's fashion while I sat back and ogled her. My mind kept screaming for me to stop. My body thought my mind should just shut up and enjoy the ride. As internal debates go, it was sweet insanity.

"I mean, what sick bastard invented these things? Like I'm not tall enough," Alex continued her tirade regarding her footwear. "Thank God, we're only forced to play dress-up for the start of the semester staff meetings."

My gaze drifted up as I pretended to listen to what she was saying. That was when I noticed something. Well, something other than her shapely legs. She was going to great lengths to avoid eye contact with me. True, she was driving. But in all honesty, she was a true Bostonian when it came to the rules of the road. A little glance while chatting wouldn't have been uncalled for. It was a small thing, but even during our first encounter, Alex had always maintained direct eye contact. After getting to know her since my arrival, I noticed that she made a point to look a person directly in the eyes when she spoke.

Her actions were subtle yet deliberate. I buried my disappointment even after her distant attitude continued after we arrived at the campus. We went directly to our office. How comforting it all sounded, our office, our house. That was until I reminded myself no matter how at ease she was pretending to be, Alex had pulled in the welcome mat. From the other side of the partition that separated our desks, I could hear her fumbling around. I wanted to go to her. Deciding that things were crazy enough between us, I pushed the thought from my mind.

After reviewing my options, I set about making the necessary arrangements to have my new telephone, cable, and Internet installed. Cable wasn't my top priority, but having Wi-Fi and telephone topped my list. I groaned as the woman on the other end listed my options. I tried to explain that I really didn't care how many channels I could watch. I understood that she was trying to make a sale, yet I felt she really wasn't listening to me. I jotted down my new phone number after we came to an understanding.

The problem came from trying to set up a time. With my schedule, we couldn't agree since they came between the appointed time and hell freezing over. I was frustrated, knowing that taking an entire day off at the start of the semester was very unwise. Alex finally came to the rescue when she shouted over the partition that Mrs. Giovanni could let them in. I shouted my thanks to her and set up an appointment. I knew that my meager belongings would be more than safe under Mrs. Giovanni's watchful eye. Hell, the Hope Diamond would be safe with Mrs. Giovanni. I thanked the woman when we finally wrapped things up.

"I need to buy a phone," I muttered, adding to the list I started while I was making arrangements for my phone services. "Towels, shower curtain, face cloths, some kind of bed, sheets, pots, pans, and dishes. I'm going to be broke," I grimly accepted, knowing that I hadn't even scratched the surface.

I opened my laptop and tried to get some work done. While I was pretending to be busy, I listened to Alex chatting on the telephone with someone in what sounded like French. I sat there twirling my pencil and debated on whether or not to call Peter. I knew I should call him. We had spoken so rarely since I arrived. Prior to last night, I wrote it off to my settling in and the big project he was working on. I stared at the phone. Then again, I never tried calling him on his cell. Like most people these days, he always had it on. The problem was that I had no idea what to say to him.

I was uncomfortable with the thought of talking to him. Even if I could chalk up what had happened to an innocent mistake, I had on some level betrayed him. What could I say to him? How could I tell him that I woke up that morning suddenly questioning everything? Twenty-four hours ago, my only problems consisted of finding a suitable apartment for me and Peter.

Of course, I knew who I was. I just wasn't feeling well. No small wonder since my head was still pounding. For the hundredth time that morning, I made a silent vow never to drink tequila again. I stalled a little longer, catching snippets of the phone conversation Alex was having. I felt extremely frustrated because the entire conversation was in French. The only word I managed to understand was *au revoir*.

Just who is she speaking French to? I silently questioned *Way to focus, Stephanie! Stop eavesdropping and call your boyfriend.* I dialed the familiar number, my hands shaking. Silently, I berated myself for feeling so nervous, all the while secretly hoping to get his voice mail.

"Peter Burton," he cheerfully greeted me.

"Damn! I mean hi, honey," I quickly recovered while I watched Alex make a speedy departure. She stopped at the coffee table just outside of our office. Maureen joined her, and the two began what seemed to be an animated conversation.

"Steffi, sweetheart!" Peter's voice beamed through the receiver. "It's so good to finally hear your voice. I was beginning to think you didn't love me anymore."

I knew he was teasing, but that didn't stop the guilty feeling from stabbing at my heart.

"I miss you, too," I lied. Just as I said the words, it looked as if Alex was about to re-enter the office. She turned quickly and rejoined Maureen. "I found an apartment," I continued, realizing that no matter what I did from that moment on, someone was going to get hurt. "There is some bad news."

"What is it?"

"Well, you see, it's like this…" I hesitated, unsure of what to tell him. "It's a studio. I know we had planned on finally living together, but it's much too small for two people."

"Did you sign a lease?"

"Yes."

"For how long?"

"It's a tenant at will." I struggled with each word, feeling sick. "I can give a thirty-day notice at any time."

"That's it?" Peter laughed. "I was worried that you were locked in for a year or something crazy like that. You worry about the strangest things. Look, I'll see it when I come up in a few weeks for our anniversary. If it's too small, then it still isn't a problem. We can do a serious search when I get settled. It was smart of you to take this place as a tenant at will. This way, we can take our time and find the perfect place. We should look for a place between Prowers Landing and Rhode Island. I know it will be a commute for both of us. We should think about getting you a car."

"I told the landlady that I would stay at least until the end of the semester."

"Sweetheart, that is not a problem. In fact, it gives us more time," he reasoned as the sick feeling in the pit of my stomach grew. "I still have my résumé out there. I might hook up with a company in Boston or Cambridge. There's a lot of new tech companies starting up in Lynnfield and New Hampshire, which would be closer to Prowers Landing. I should start looking there. We knew something like this could happen when you accepted this position."

"Peter, you love working for Syntax," I tried to protest.

"I love you more."

"What about your lease?"

"I told you before, I can sublet or crash with Bobby if we don't find anything by the time my lease is up. Of course, we could have talked about this if you had called my cell or gotten one for yourself. I don't understand why you're so against them. But it isn't a tragedy, it just gives us a little more time."

That was Peter, ever practical, comforting, and so willing to do anything to make me happy. I felt guilty. A part of me blamed him for making me feel that way. To make things worse, while he was chatting away, filling me in on the events of his life, I was watching Alex. I tried not to watch her. I tried to listen to Peter as he talked about missing me. Yet there she was just a few feet away talking to my boss. I couldn't take my gaze off of her.

"Can't blame the tequila this time," I accidentally said out loud.

"What was that?" Peter innocently asked.

"Nothing," I meekly responded, somehow resisting the urge to smack myself in the head with the phone.

There was something going on with me. Something I couldn't explain or understand. The best I could hope for was that my sudden bout of lunacy would pass quickly. Peter was so good, so trusting, and a good friend. I met him when we were both eighteen. I was a student teacher at UConn while working on my doctorate at Yale. We were the same age, and he needed a tutor. We became friends, nothing more. I never looked at him that way. Then my grandmother became ill. Peter was the only one there for me. When she passed away, it was Peter who held me together. He helped with all the arrangements. He looked over me, making sure I didn't fall apart. It was then that I began to see this shy dark-haired boy with big brown puppy dog eyes in a new light.

"Stephanie?" Peter's voice called to me.

"I'm sorry, we must have a bad connection," I apologized with a quick lie. "Why don't you call me tomorrow night if you can?" I rattled off my new number and ended the conversation with a quick goodbye.

Discovering that I was adept at lying was doing nothing to help my hangover. I felt like a fraud. My brilliant life plan was nothing more than a sham. Pity that I hadn't realized that you can plan all you want, life has a way of doing whatever it wants. One night of hapless fumbling, and I was disheveled. I wasn't about to make any declarations or frantic leaps. I just knew that something was wrong. For a very long time, I had told myself that I was happy.

For the first time in my life, I was questioning whether or not that was true. It had never occurred to me that the life I was living wasn't what I wanted. Things were simple when I thought I had a shot at staying at Brown. Then that didn't happen, so I accepted Maureen's offer. On paper, everything was just as it should be. A short time at Prower and I could move up the food chain. The reality was after just a few weeks at Prower, I was a hot mess.

"Stephanie?" Maureen called to me, bringing me back to reality or as close to it as I could get at that moment. "Time for the staff meeting."

I followed Maureen and Alex to Bradley Hall, which was in the next building over. This would be the only full staff meeting for the semester. Later, different groups would meet separately unless something monumental happened. Maureen had thoughtfully arranged for food services to set up an array of coffee and Danish pastries. The coffee was a welcome treat. I passed on the Danish, my stomach was still recovering. I searched for Alex, only to discover her surrounded by a large group of people.

Overcome with shyness, I took the only seat available. I sat next to Stan, who was busy adjusting his bow tie and ignoring everyone in the room. I glanced over to the other side of the room where Alex was holding court. People were laughing at something she had said. I sat there next to Stan, whose tweed suit was probably older than I was, feeling like a big dork.

Before we had arrived on campus, Alex was trying to be nice. Since arriving at our office, she seemed hell bent on avoiding me. I knew she had been upset earlier. At that moment, it appeared she had decided to stop hiding her discomfort.

"How are you surviving?" Stan questioned.

"What?" I blurted out, a bit startled that he had spoken to me. The last time he talked to me was when I borrowed his stapler. He went ballistic. Alex did apologize for putting me up to it.

"How are you surviving sharing office space with Kendell?" He snarled as he spoke her name. "She's such a fraud."

"Alex and I are getting along very well, thank you," I snapped, injured by his assessment of Alex. Of course, it seemed odd defending her when I failed to possess the courage to sit anywhere near her.

"Just be careful."

"What do you mean?"

"You never know with those people."

It was the words *those people* that left me wondering if that was what I was afraid of. Was it being labeled or ostracized?

"You know, I'm aware of the fact that your specialty is early American history, but you really should take a look at this century." I snarled at him.

"All I'm saying—" he began to argue, obviously put off by my tone.

"Stan!" I cut him off. "I'm not interested."

Thankfully, Maureen chose that moment to begin and walked up to the podium. She smiled when she was greeted with a round of applause.

"Suck-ups," she quipped.

Once the laughter died down, she proceeded to give her speech. I could tell by the looks of my fellow faculty members that this particular speech has been heard more than once. Maureen explained that this was the last time the entire faculty would meet as a whole during the semester. The department was divided by several different classifications ranging from time periods and geographical interest. Maureen went on to remind everyone of the constant crossovers that would occur within our department, as well as with other departments, and that teamwork was the key. Then she listed accomplishments of staff members who had published or received awards during the past semester. She also reminded everyone of the old academic rule of survival—publish or perish. I noticed that she was looking directly at Alex as she said this.

She continued with her talk, reminding us not to abuse the interns and teaching assistants since they were here to learn. Then she introduced me as the newest member of the department. She listed all my accomplishments and so on. Most everyone seemed to be, or pretended to be, impressed. I stood and received a warm round of applause as I was greeted by my new peers.

Maureen concluded the meeting with a reminder that the department's basketball team, the Relics, still needed positions filled. She assured us that this would be the year that we would finally beat the English Department. She looked once again to Alex, who scowled in response. After a few more words of encouragement and a few questions, the meeting came to an abrupt end.

The room emptied quickly, and Alex was nowhere to be found. Dejected, I walked back to my office alone. I found Alex and Maureen in a heated conversation. Not wanting to interrupt, I busied myself at the coffee station. I tried not to listen, but my proximity and their raised voices made it impossible.

"Alex, I want to see you make tenure."

"So do I," Alex defended herself.

"What about Stanford?" Maureen pushed. "You could still run some of your classes online."

"Nothing is definite yet." Alex sighed. "I know it would be good for my résumé. As for running my classes online, we've talked about this before. My lectures are far too interactive to pull that off."

"Think about it," Maureen pushed harder. "You need something like this. You also need to publish."

"I know."

"You could work with Stephanie," Maureen eagerly suggested. "Her specialty is the American Civil War. You've been talking about doing something on your family history."

"Stephanie must have a very full plate already."

"Is there a problem? I told you that I want the two of you to get along."

"Oh, we are," Alex replied. Her deep contralto voice sent shivers down my spine.

"She has a stellar reputation."

"I'm sure she's busy."

I decided that it was time to save Alex. I walked in pretending to be oblivious to the tension. I carried in two cups of coffee, both black, and set one on Alex's desk.

"Thanks for leaving me with Stan," I teased her in an effort to lighten the situation. I wasn't prepared for the fiery blue stare I received in return. Obviously, my attempt at humor fell short.

"You left her with Stan!" Maureen chastised her. "Didn't you just tell me that the two of you were getting along?"

"Not to worry, we've been playing nice," I tossed out in another attempt to alleviate the tension. I hated the drama that was brewing. If I was in the mood for bitter tension, I could just relive my childhood.

I was surprised when Alex turned to her desk without saying a word. I stood there gaping at her. I knew things were amiss between us. I just couldn't understand when they had turned catastrophic.

"Stephanie, do you play basketball?" Maureen asked out of the blue.

"No," I said honestly. "I like the game. Mostly because I couldn't avoid it during my undergrad years."

"Right, UConn," Maureen beamed. "You never played?"

"Sorry, like most sports, I was too young to join the team," I wearily explained. "Not to mention, making that team takes talent and having started to play the game in your crib."

"Damn," Maureen grumbled. "Alex, if you do go to Stanford, will you be back in time for softball season?"

"No," Alex responded curtly.

"Geez, how nasty is the hangover you're sporting? The team needs you." Maureen seemed determined.

"Why?" Alex laughed. "Is it the way I can't hit, throw, or run? Maureen, how many times do I have to tell you not all of us girls are good in sports? Look at you, you're a total jock and the picture of heterosexuality. Lesbians having an innate ability for sports is a myth."

"How about you, Stephanie?" Maureen innocently asked.

"What?"

"Do you play softball?" Maureen repeated.

"I played a little in a league during grad school," I stammered. "I did a little first base, and I pitched in a couple of games."

"Great, you can join the team in the spring." Maureen cheered then she bounced out of the room.

"How is our softball team?" I asked, noticing that Alex was still refusing to look at me.

"The Relics? We suck."

"Great, that would explain how I made the team." I sighed, feeling frustrated by her attempts to avoid looking at me. "Oh, well, it doesn't matter. It'll be fun. After all, winning isn't everything."

"Tell that to Maureen."

"She does seem to be a little overly enthusiastic."

"You could say that."

"So…" I stood there searching for a way to keep the conversation going. I just wanted things to be right between us again. I hated walking around feeling like a piece of me was missing. My need to fix things was in high gear.

"I need to go to the library," she said abruptly before I could conjure up something clever to say. Before I could form a response, she was out the door.

"Nice talking to you," I grumbled under my breath.

I sulked over to my desk and finished working on my syllabus for the next day's classes. I worked on the computer for what seemed like hours. I looked at my watch and realized that Alex's class was meeting. I told myself that I was going over there to listen to her theories on *The Brady Bunch*, and it had nothing to do with wanting to see her. I ran, hoping to catch the class before it was over.

I slipped in quietly and hid in the back of the room. The students were captivated as always. But it was obvious that Alex was wrapping things up. I loved to watch her in action. Maybe I could learn something from her about teaching. Maureen may have been right about Alex needing my help. Truth was, I needed hers, as well. The major stumbling block for my finding a full-time teaching position was my teaching style. Or more my lack of style. It wasn't uncommon for half my students to drop my class within the first two weeks. Peter claimed it was because I was tough, which was good. I didn't believe him. I had seen some of the reviews given by my students. I was boring. One actually said listening to my lectures would have been like watching paint dry if I hadn't been so grating. It hurt, especially since he was one of my top students.

"So what can we learn from television?" Alex asked her students. "From the facts and the distortions that the media has offered to us?"

"That most lesbians would choose Jan as their favorite Brady," one girl shouted out. The classroom erupted with laughter as I blushed.

"Yes," Alex agreed with a smile. "That's true, even though neither the character nor the actress is gay."

Alex paused slightly as she noticed me standing in the back of the room. I felt a wave of heat rush over me. Quickly, she turned away, appearing to be at a loss.

"Anyway, I-I'm sorry." She shook her head, closing her eyes for a moment, and ran her hand through her hair. She opened her eyes, fully composed, and continued. "Friday is the final. For the final, there will be eighty questions. No true or false and no multiple choice, and there will be two essay questions." There was a collective groan emitted from her students. Alex smiled at their response. "I also want you to be prepared that there will be no questions regarding television."

Her students were visibly shocked. I had to agree with them. Granted, I hadn't sat in on very many lectures, still I never heard them discussing anything but television. The first time I watched her, all they discussed was the original *Star Trek* series. Alex just stood there and smiled that all-knowing smile of hers.

"Ladies, gentlemen, and others." The students laughed, still I could hear that they were nervous. "Now before you jump out of your seats and attack, allow me to enlighten you. When you signed up for this class, you enrolled in a course offered by the History Department. I know that's easy to forget when you're talking about *I Love Lucy*. But all this time, you were really talking about American history. Therefore, I am basing the final exam on our discussions. I paid very close attention to those discussions. I'm hoping that you did, as well."

"How do we review for the final?" one panicked young man squeaked.

"Relax," Alex tried to reassure her students. "Just think about what we've talked about. We covered a great deal of history this summer. Remember the name of this course, American History a Culture in Conflict 1950 to 1980? Don't freak out! Every time I teach this course, everyone ends up in a panic over the final. Trust me. I'm certain that you all will do just fine." No one seemed to relax, even with Alex's reassurances. "I also wanted to remind all of you that I'll be teaching extra classes this fall. Because I may not be here for the spring semester."

"You're leaving?" one student said, voicing my own fears.

"No," Alex said calmly. With her response, I felt as if I could breathe again. "There's a chance I'll be away next semester. Nothing is definite."

I understood that Alex's résumé needed some padding. I hated that it bothered me. Not just bothered me, I was terrified that Stanford would offer her a permanent position. When I realized how upset I was over it, I questioned my sanity. But I had been doing that all day long, why should that moment be any different? While I wallowed in my turmoil, Alex fielded questions on the final and the courses she would be teaching during the fall semester.

"Speaking of upcoming courses," Alex's deep voice broke my train of thought. "I suppose some of you have been wondering about our mystery guest for the past few weeks." She directed their attention to me. "She's with the FBI, and you are all in big trouble for what you said about J. Edgar Hoover. Or she is Dr. Grant, who is new to the History Department here at Prower. Dr. Grant will be teaching several courses on the American Civil War and one on the history of the Free Masons. So you might want to check her out." Many of the students chuckled at Alex's blunder as she blushed. "I meant to say check out her classes, you animals. Now get out of here, and do not, I repeat do not, freak out over the final. I will see you all on Friday."

The students departed with unusual speed. I sensed that they were not heeding Alex's warning not to freak out over the final.

"Thank you for the endorsement," I said as I approached her. I secretly hoped that her generous gesture meant the awkwardness was about to come to an end.

"Anytime," Alex said quietly as she began to fill her briefcase without a single glance in my direction.

She was so sullen, which wasn't like her. Normally after one of her lectures, she was excited. Still not looking at me, she sank into the chair at her desk with a slight wince. It was the first time I had seen her use the chair. She seemed tense as she rubbed her eyes. Without thinking, I stepped behind her and rubbed her shoulders.

"Don't," she bitterly warned me.

"I'm sorry." I jerked my hands away. "I just keep stepping in it, huh?"

Once again, my body reacted before my brain had an opportunity to stop me. It seemed natural to reach out to her. Just as natural as it was to climb into her arms that morning. Had I been thinking clearly, I would have realized that I was the source of her tension. I was having a hard time reconciling her being nice one moment and kicking me to the curb the next.

"I have things to do," she muttered coldly. "See you at the Dean's Tea."

"Fine," I snapped as I spun on my heels and stormed out.

Chapter Eight

The Dean's Tea was incredibly dull. It was divided into two groups of people—those who were fighting for Dean Tanner's attention and those who were trying to avoid him. Still, everyone seemed to be very nice. There was a feeling of family among my fellow staff members. I sensed that I was going to really enjoy working with these people. All I needed to do was get past the weirdness between Alex and me. I spent the majority of the afternoon searching the crowd for the familiar tall dark figure who had turned my world spinning.

Maureen approached me and touched me gently on the shoulder. "Can I talk to you for a moment?" she said quietly so she would not be overheard by prying ears.

I nodded my consent, and we made our way down the path into the garden behind the dean's home. Once we were alone, Maureen finally spoke. "Stephanie, I'm worried about Alex."

"Why?" I asked, uncertain as to what I should and should not say regarding Alex's notable absence.

"She has been tense and flashing attitude all day," Maureen said with concern. "I know Alex has a smart mouth. Hell, it's part of her charm. But it is not like her to be such a bitch. This morning, she almost took poor Louisa's head off."

"Maybe she's just hungover from last night," I lied, hoping to offer some explanation that would ease some of Maureen's worries. "She and I really overdid it."

"I hope you're right." Maureen sighed in exasperation. "She was never a big drinker. But still, she really needs to be here, and she knows it. I think she turned her cell off, it keeps going to voice mail. I know this tea is nothing more than a dog and pony show, but Alex is in a vulnerable position right now."

I thought back to the heated conversation I overheard that morning between the two women. "Are her chances of making tenure in trouble?" I asked, worried that I had somehow let my new friend down.

"Yes," Maureen bluntly answered. "It's not fair. She's twice the teacher of anyone in the department, myself included. But she hasn't published anything in almost two years. To be honest, the works she has published are not literary gems." I felt a stab of guilt as Maureen's words hit me.

"I hate that publishing means that much." I sneered in disgust.

"Right or wrong, it's the golden rule of academics," Maureen said. "You don't have anything to worry about. With everything that you have already published and your more than impressive background, the dean thinks I scored a major coup by getting you to sign on. Even though Prower is probably just a steppingstone for you."

"How did you know?" I asked in horror.

"Don't be so shocked," Maureen said with a knowing smile. "I know Prower has a stellar reputation, and many of our instructors come here just to pad their credentials. When I first came here, I just wanted to put in my time, build my reputation, then move on to bigger and better. Before I knew it, this became home to me. When I got married, I could not think of a better place to raise my kids. Plus, being offered the department chair was a big incentive."

We stood there in an awkward silence knowing that Maureen needed to say more, but she seemed reluctant. Finally, she asked the one question I been dreading. "What happened between you and Alex?"

"What do you mean?" I choked, wondering how I was going to get around the question.

"What I mean is that last night, the two of you seemed very close. Today, it almost looked like she was trying to avoid you. Hell, she dumped you with Stan," Maureen said in a bewildered tone. "I meant it when I said I wanted the two of you to get along. It's not because she's gay, is it?"

"No." I almost laughed at the irony of her statement. "It is most definitely not her homosexuality."

"Then what is it?"

"Nothing," I lied once again.

"Stephanie, I consider Alex to be a good friend of mine," Maureen pushed forward. "Right now, something is very wrong with her, and I'm getting the same feeling that I get with my kids on report card day. I know you know what's going on, so stop hiding it and just spill it."

I was suddenly relieved that I was not one of Maureen's children. Those little buggers were never going to get away with anything. Based on the stern look I was receiving, I understood that she wasn't going to accept anything but the truth. It was time to face the music.

"Maureen…you do not have to worry about us getting along." I swallowed hard, terrified that I was about to make a huge mistake. "That's actually the problem." Maureen just stared at me blankly waiting for the rest. I had no options but to continue. "Last night, we got along a little too well." I blew out a breath and waited for everything to hit the fan.

"Well, that explains it," she said calmly.

"I wish someone would explain it to me!" I whined in despair. "Wait. You don't seemed to be surprised. Before Alex mentioned my boyfriend, did you think I was gay?"

"Yes," Maureen said reluctantly.

"Why?" I shouted in amazement.

"I don't know," Maureen said shyly. "My brother is gay, and in college, I played a lot of sports, and as a result, I have more than a few lesbian friends. Over the years, I think I developed my own sense of gaydar."

"Did Alex think I was gay?"

"Well…um…yeah," Maureen admitted. "We might have talked about it."

"You what?" I gasped in shock. "I cannot believe the two of you sat around and discussed my sexuality!"

"Hold on." Maureen raised her hands in defense. "I swear it's not what you think. After the two of you met, I asked her if she thought that you were her religion. She said yes, and that was it. Of course, I was secretly hoping that the two of you might hook up. She's been single for far too long, and I thought that you would be good for her. But she has this thing about dating colleagues."

"Really? Why is that?" I asked, suddenly intrigued about this new revelation. "You know what, it's not important. I have a boyfriend." As I heard the words come out of my mouth, I knew I sounded incredibly lame.

"So you say, yet you'd like to know why Alex has a rule about dating coworkers." Maureen's next commentary ended abruptly.

"Because Chris and I worked together, and whenever we had problems, the entire firm knew about it. In fact, most people knew about it before I did," Alex explained in a flat tone.

"Alex!" I gasped, suddenly feeling like a deer caught in the headlights of an approaching vehicle.

"Relax, you haven't done anything wrong." She tried to reassure me. "It wasn't you I've been upset with."

"Where have you been?" Maureen sternly asked before I had a chance to ask her what she meant.

"I've been making nice with the dean."

"Really?" Maureen asked her suspiciously.

"Yes, really," Alex defended herself. "I know I was late, so as soon as I arrived, I spent all my time sucking up to the old coot. I may be in a pissy mood, but I'm not an idiot."

"So is everything all right between the two of you, or am I going to have to separate you?" Maureen folded her arms across her chest, eyeing the both of us.

"Everything is fine," Alex said quickly for the both of us. "And just for the record, nothing happened last night. Although next time someone offers us free tequila, smack us before we start drinking."

"I'll be honest, I was amused watching the two of you acting like idiots." Maureen snickered.

"Next time, I'm driving, and you can behave like a jackass." Alex growled. "We'll even take pictures to blackmail you, right, Stephanie?"

"This is the strangest day," I murmured, trying to get a grasp on what was happening. "Maybe I'm still drunk."

"You're fine." Alex tsked. "We just need to talk. We can do that over lunch before we go shopping."

"You're going shopping?" Maureen gasped. "Voluntarily?"

"Stephanie, tell our boss about your coffeemaker."

"I don't have one."

"She also doesn't have a place to sleep, towels, or food," Alex expanded. "Did I leave anything out?"

"So many things," I conceded, still confused as to what was going on.

***

The three of us strolled back to the party, which appeared to be breaking up. Maureen and Alex talked by themselves. I was happy for the moment by myself; it gave me a chance to catch my bearings. The time alone did nothing to help.

Maureen waved goodbye to me and left. Alex turned to me. A tense look crossed her face as she approached me. She bit her lip as she stared at me intently. She sighed a heavy breath and smiled, looking just a little bit more relaxed.

"Come on, we need to find you some furniture," she offered in a soothing voice.

"You really want to do that?" I tried to clear my muddled mind.

"To be completely honest, I considered just loaning you my car," she confessed. "After I had a chance to think things over, I realized that I've been behaving very badly today."

"I don't get it." I tried to sort things out. "One moment, you were being nice, making me coffee, and bringing me a clean towel."

"I wasn't quick enough on that one."

"You did try," I explained. "You did all of those nice things, then after we got to work, you wouldn't even look at me."

"I was mad," Alex blew out in a huff. "At you and at myself. Both of us used the excuse of drunkenness to do what we did. I tried to let it go, then I was put off by what I heard you say to your boyfriend. I shouldn't have been. It's none of my business…it was that this morning…I…well, that is not important. I slowly realized that I need to stop overreacting to every innocent gesture. It's just that after last night, I felt confused." She seemed relieved at having explained things to me finally.

"I don't think you overreacted," I said sincerely. "Let's face it, I didn't help matters any. I'm the one who started all of this." I put my hand up, stopping her from interrupting me. "Enough. I'm sorry and you're sorry. Let's try to do what we promised each other this morning and go back to being friends. I don't know about you, but I'm getting a headache from all this drama. A drunken make-out session isn't worth all this stress."

She smiled sweetly at my declaration. We began to walk away

89

when I touched her arm. I was pleased that she didn't flinch or make any attempt to refuse my offer. "Alex, in regards to your behavior, you need to remember that I have seen you act much worse than this," I teased her.

"That's right." She laughed. "I keep forgetting that you got to see me as the lawyer bitch. Tell me something. Back then, I didn't make you cry, did I?"

"As a matter of fact, you did," I reluctantly admitted. "But I did manage to hold off until I was safely away from you. How did you know?"

"Back then, I made everyone cry, even my own mother," Alex admitted with a dejected shrug.

Chapter Nine

Alex and I drove into town to the futon shop, and I looked around. Despite my savings I had to budget everything very carefully since I would not receive my first sizable paycheck until the end of the month. A polite young salesman showed us around. I could tell by Alex's demeanor that shopping was not one of her favorite things to do. I, on the other hand, loved to explore and take my time. I curbed my usual prowling and selected a full-sized model. The salesman looked at me oddly and suggested that perhaps a queen or a king size would be more suitable. I explained that a full size was more than suitable for me, politely pointing out my height, or lack thereof.

It was when he cast a shy glance at Alex that it dawned on me that he thought we were a couple. I held back a laugh, thinking that if his assumption was correct, then yes, we would definitely require a much larger mattress. I was about to correct his error when Alex whispered to me, "How tall is Peter?"

"A little taller than you, why?" I whispered my reply, not wanting to embarrass the poor sales boy any further.

"Then I think this guy is right," Alex said. "With your build, the full is all right for just you, but what about when…you know?"

"You're right. I didn't even think about that," I confessed.

"Why would you?" Alex teased me as she patted the top of my head to stress her point.

I informed the salesman that a Queen size would be more appropriate and was relieved when he confirmed that the model I had selected was available in that size. The model I had chosen was a simple wood frame that could be pulled down easily. This way, I would not have to go to great lengths each morning and evening. With one tug, the futon snapped down into a bed, and with a push, it instantly converted back into a couch.

While the futon and its mattress were being loaded into Alex's car, the salesman suggested that we look around at some of the covers they had available. As we sorted through the various designs, I leaned over and whispered to Alex, "You know the salesman thinks we're a couple."

"I know." She snickered. "Does that bother you?"

"No," I said honestly.

"How about this one?" She held up an ivory cover with a floral design.

"Perfect, what size is it?"

"Full." She frowned, and we began searching for the correct size.

In our search, our hands touched, and I felt a spark race through my body. Neither of us moved as our gazes met, and our breathing became labored. It was the briefest of moments, but the intensity of the innocent touch was almost overpowering. Alex slowly pulled her hand away and crossed her arms in front of her. I paused for a moment to catch my breath, then resumed my search. Finding the right size, I walked over to the counter and paid for my purchases. Mentally, I tried to write off the feeling as residual emotions from the encounter from the night before.

After we departed the futon shop, we proceeded to browse through every shop Main Street had to offer. Everywhere we stopped, people greeted Alex. As she introduced me, I realized that Prowers Landing was a very small town, populated mostly by students and members of the faculty from the university. I could tell by the expressions on most people's faces that they were already assuming that Alex and I were a couple. It bothered me that people just assumed that because Alex was a lesbian and we were out shopping together that we must be lovers. It wasn't the assumption that I was lucky enough to have this woman as my lover, but it was the narrow-minded assumption that a gay woman could not be just friends with another woman.

True to her nature, Alex took every opportunity to make it clear to everyone that she was just showing her new friend around town. It was more than apparent to me that Alex had been down this road before.

"I need a break," Alex whined, holding up the plethora of bags she was carrying. "Let's go in here, my feet are killing me."

Needing relief from all the walking we had done, I saw no reason to argue with her suggestion. I waved packages I was holding toward the doorway, and we entered the ice cream parlor. Like everything else in town, it was a throwback to another era. With its Art Deco lighting and furnishings, it took my breath away. I groaned when I noticed that it was also packed with people.

"This is the only place in town to get ice cream," Alex explained, noticing my dismay. "Fortunately, it's great. Look, I think there's a booth opening up. Get ready to jump on it." We moved quickly and grabbed the booth as soon as the two young gentlemen who had been occupying it stood.

"Good work," I complimented her.

"I had no intention of standing outside," Alex griped as she discreetly slipped off her high heels. "It's not usually this busy during the week, but with classes beginning tomorrow, everyone is out running last-minute errands."

"How can there be only one ice cream place in town?" I asked in amazement.

"Prowers Landing is a small town," Alex said. "There's only one ice cream parlor, one Chinese restaurant, one bakery, one drugstore, etc. Every couple of years or so, some big chain tries to move in. They never survive. Sometimes I think this town is stuck in some kind of Norman Rockwell painting. I'm not complaining, mind you. After all those years with the hustle and coldness of living in New York City, I have really come to love the quiet of this town. If I get bored with the crickets chirping, I can always head down Route 128 and go into Boston. Of course, this time of year, a trip to Salem is always a lot of fun."

"Salem?" I could barely contain my excitement. "How far away is Salem? I'm really looking forward to spending some time there. The history is fascinating."

"Salem is only about twenty minutes away by car. I could take you there some weekend. I know which tourist traps to avoid."

"I would love that," I said gleefully.

"Unless, of course, you wanted to go with Peter," Alex added sullenly.

"Peter." I sighed. "Here we go again."

"Stephanie, don't." Alex rubbed her eyes. For the first time, I could see how withdrawn she looked. She hadn't looked so haggard that morning. The dark circles under her eyes caused my heart to drop.

"I mean it," she said firmly as she looked deep into my eyes for the first time since the previous evening. "Look, I owe you an explanation. Well, not an explanation, really, just that I should make a few things clear about myself. We have a few moments before our waiter will get a chance to make his way over here. Why don't I try to fill you in?"

"Okay."

"My parents are one of the happiest couples in the world," she casually began. "I'm not kidding, they're disgustingly happy. I get a cavity just listening to them. Yet they managed to raise three of the unhappiest children. For the life of me, I don't know how it happened. To be perfectly honest, I don't think I knew I was unhappy until I quit my job, dumped my girlfriend, and came back home. When I went back to school, something happened. I discovered something that had been missing in my life."

"What was that?"

"Me." She released a contented sigh. "Sounds strange, I know. A couple of years ago, Nicole said it was the same for her after she quit drinking and got her act together. The weird thing is, it had never occurred to me that I was just blindly following some idiotic plan I thought would lead to happiness. Ridiculous, huh?"

"Oh, I don't know."

"For me, it was. I honestly didn't understand that I was following some plan instead of living. While I was following my plan, I made some poor choices. The first was thinking being a lawyer was what I really wanted. My other errors involved poor choices when it came to my love life. You kind of know about Chris. As I said this afternoon, we worked together. What hurt me the most was when I realized that most of the people I worked with must have known that she was running around on me. To know that my colleagues just turned a blind eye to it and probably gossiped about it behind my back really hurt my feelings."

"I can understand that."

"What you don't understand and what Maureen does not know is that in the end I probably hurt her more than she ever hurt me."

"That I don't understand." Now I was really confused. Chris cheated on her, betrayed her trust, and left her open for gossip in her workplace. How could anyone hurt someone more than that?

"After we split, Chris wanted a second chance," Alex explained. "When I flatly refused, she dragged out our breakup. We had lived together, and there were details that needed to be taken care of. Chris was in no hurry to close our relationship. I don't know, maybe she thought given enough time, she could win me back. At that point, I just wanted out. Finally, one night in a moment of anger, I admitted to her that I was never really in love with her. That our getting together had more to do with timing than with passion. I know this is going to sound cold, but she simply fit into my life."

A wave of guilt rushed over me as I realized the cruelty of the situation. A cruelty that I was also guilty of with Peter. Did I truly love him or did he just fit into some ideal that I had been creating?

"It was at that moment that our amicable breakup turned very ugly," Alex went on.

"So that's how Chris got the BMW."

"And I got out," Alex admitted with a deep sigh. "I know that Chris gets a bad rap from Maureen. But you have to understand that I was never really there for her. On the other hand, she is not a monogamous person by nature. The worst part of all this is that Chris and I had been really good friends before we were lovers. It has taken a long time, but we're friends again. But we will never be as close as we once were. Of course, it doesn't help that every once in a while, she tries to hand me that 'baby, won't you please come back?' crap."

"Would you ever go back to her?" I asked with hesitation.

"No," Alex said firmly. "It would be easy to do. Life with Chris would be comfortable, you know if she didn't have the fidelity level of a Kennedy. The person I am now just wants to be in love. And I've learned you can't go looking for that. When it happens, it happens. There have been other choices that weren't the best, and they involved women I thought I was in love with, but—"

"Would you like luncheon or dessert menus, Professor Kendell?" our waiter thankfully interrupted. I was grateful for the reprieve and a moment to process what she was telling me.

"Neither, Vince," Alex said. "I'll have the aloha sundae."

"Can you really handle that after last night?"

"I think all that sugary goodness will be medicinal. In fact, Vince, I think I need extra whipped cream."

"Great," he beamed, apparently agreeing with her choice. "And what would you like, ma'am?" he asked innocently as Alex choked as I mouthed the word *ma'am*.

"What would you recommend, Professor?" I asked, hoping for some good advice.

"For you, Dr. Grant, I would have to say, you look like the kind of girl who would love the sinful chocolate boat." Alex blushed slightly as she made her recommendation. "Extra whipped cream, that makes it fresh."

"You're Dr. Grant?" Vince beamed at me. "I'm taking your course on the history of the Free Masons."

"Good for you!" Alex congratulated him. "Vince is pre-law, but what he really wants to do is become the next Jack Kennedy."

"An honest Jack Kennedy," Vince corrected.

"How was your summer in New York, other than hot?" Alex asked the proud young man.

"Great! Thank you again. I really learned a great deal from Ms. Gunnarsson," Vince gushed. "She asked about you a lot. She told me that if it wasn't for your recommendation, she would have never considered me. She runs the type of law practice that I would like to work for."

"Good to hear. Now go get our ice cream. After all the walking we did today, we deserve it." Alex shooed him away.

"Yes, ma'am."

"You know, Alex, if that boy really wants to make it in politics, he needs to stop calling every woman over twenty-five ma'am." Alex laughed at my observation. Then she seemed to drift off somewhere. I watched as she ran her long fingers through her hair. I could sense that there was something more she needed to tell me, yet for some reason she was uncertain.

"Back when I was a lawyer," Alex suddenly began to explain. I didn't miss the hint of sadness in her voice. "I worked very hard to fit that image, and I did. Except for the gay part."

"Did you ever try to hide it at work?"

"Never, that was just something I never would do," Alex said firmly. "Chris and I started at Wainwright and Griggs at the same time, and she was all hung up on people not knowing. But that was the one thing I refused to compromise on. Granted, I didn't rent a billboard in Times Square. I just never felt a need to lie about my homosexuality. When I left, I was on my way to becoming a named partner. I never kidded myself. Deep down, I knew it was my name more than my talent. Maybe that's why I wasn't afraid of being out in a very conservative law firm."

Listening to her, I could only imagine what it felt like to be that free.

"It was nice of you to help Vince out." I tried to keep the conversation going. I knew there was something she wasn't telling me. It amazed me that after such a short period of time, I felt as if I really knew this woman.

"He's a good kid," Alex said. "I just wanted to see him start off on the right track. Jessica's firm is a good place to start. She does a lot of pro bono and women's rights cases, not to mention her constant battles with the slum lords in New York. Firms like hers will help him keep focused." She paused for a moment and swallowed hard, and I felt that she was about to tell me what was weighing so heavily on her. "Stephanie, there's something else I need to explain to you...about why I was—"

"Alex!" an overly cheerful voice called out to her.

I turned to see an older woman from this morning's staff meeting approaching us. I couldn't help thinking that this town was just way too small.

"Hello, Ruth," Alex greeted the woman warmly.

I, on the other hand, just sat there quietly thinking, *Go away! Go away! Go away!*

"Look at the mob in here, can you tell the semester is about to start?" Ruth laughed as she looked around at all the people crammed into the ice cream parlor. "Hello, we haven't had a chance to meet. I'm Ruth Steiner." She offered her hand to me.

"Stephanie Grant." I accepted her hand, all the while thinking, *Now go away!*

"Ruth's specialty is the effects and defects of the American Constitution," Alex explained to me before turning her attention back to Ruth. "How's Emily?"

Please don't let Emily be her daughter! I silently pleaded while contemplating plunging head first into my ice cream.

"She's good. Right now, she's at a conference in San Diego." Ruth sighed sadly.

I smiled, not stopping to think of how I knew she was a lesbian. Instead, I sat there grinning like an idiot as Ruth went on about missing her girlfriend who was due home in a few hours. At some point, I had lost interest. Mostly because I wanted this woman to leave so Alex and I could finish our conversation.

Thankfully, Vince arrived with our ice cream. Alex's sundae was a mountain of whipped cream and pineapple. My fudge boat was just that—a very large boat of chocolate also laden with a mound of whipped cream. I doubted that I would ever be able to finish it. Then I sampled my first bite and released a gluttonous moan.

Given the recent twists and turns in my life, I pondered the possibility that chocolate might be all I really needed.

"Oh, my!" Ruth exclaimed as she eyed our decadent excuse for lunch. "I'm impressed. When I saw you at the staff meeting this morning, I was a little worried about you."

"What do you mean?"

"Well, Alex, you looked a little..." Ruth hesitated. "Worse for wear."

"Thank you?" Alex snorted. "I'm fine, I just had a late night."

Ruth flashed a knowing smile in my direction, which I'm certain Alex caught. Before she could correct her, Ruth quickly said her goodbyes and was on her way. Alone once again, silence overcame us. This time, it wasn't awkwardness. This time, it had to do with the mounds of ice cream in front of us. To my surprise, both of us managed to eat every last drop.

"I may never eat again." I groaned miserably as I rubbed my stomach. Alex began nervously tapping her foot. "Either your sugar rush kicked in already or you want a cigarette."

"No, I'm good," Alex lied as she nodded.

"We probably have some time before Vince makes it back over here with the check," I offered, not believing that she didn't want to run outside and light up. "I can take care of it while you get some fresh air."

"No, no" came her terse answer. "I'm fine."

"Okay," I gave in, not believing a word she was saying. "Why don't you finish telling me what you were going to say?"

"Oh, right," she reluctantly agreed. "Well, it's like this. Chris and I were friends before we were lovers, and we worked together. After that ended as an utter fiasco, I vowed that I wouldn't ever make those mistakes again."

"Mistakes?"

"Dating a friend or coworker."

"Oh?" I'd be lying if I said I wasn't disappointed. I couldn't justify my feelings, yet there it was.

"And—" she nervously began.

"And?" I repeated, thinking, *Oh, goodie, there's more!*

"Before my relationship with Chris, there was someone else." Her voice trembled. She paused for a moment and collected her thoughts. Finally, she cleared her throat and began her story. "When I first moved to New York…I met this woman at a local bar. Jessica Gunnarsson. Jessica was older and really fascinating and the kind of lawyer I should have been. It was wonderful until eight months into our relationship, I discovered that she had one major character flaw."

"Which was?" I pushed, once again not certain that I really wanted to hear about this woman.

"Jessica had a memory problem." Alex sneered. "It seems that she kept forgetting that she had a husband. I was furious when I found out. When I confronted her, she confessed that it was the truth. The kick in the pants is her reaction was, 'Didn't I tell you that?' To top it off, much to my disappointment, she had no intention of leaving him for me because she was not a lesbian."

"Seriously?"

"To her, I was just someone she cared about." Her voice turned bitter. "Even though I was just one of many women in her life, according to her, she's straight. This woman cruises gay bars and keeps an apartment in the city where she can spend time with her lovers. When I finally accepted the truth, I was devastated. I really thought I was in love."

"Wow! So last night when I got all grabby, I really hit the trifecta." I couldn't help feeling miserable.

"We work together, we're on our way to becoming friends, and you're straight," she carefully laid out for me. The only thing holding me together at that moment was that next to Jessica Gunnarsson, I was a rank amateur.

"Wow, when I made a pass, you must have wanted to douse me in holy water."

"Trust me, that is not what I wanted to do with you," Alex teased. "Stephanie, this isn't about you. Last night just brought back a barrage of memories. Ones that I thought I had dealt with. None of this is your fault. But I have been down this road twice already, and I have no intention of treating myself like that again. Been there, done that! I like my life, I love my job, and yes, I would like to meet someone, but I will not lose my self-respect again."

"I appreciate your honesty."

"Now as your friend, I think that I should take you to the grocery store," Alex said, suddenly avoiding eye contact. "Since we both know you cannot rely upon my cooking."

"You know where the grocery store is?"

"I think so." She laughed.

***

After a brief discussion, Alex allowed me to pay the check. I wanted to thank her for all her help. We strolled down to the local market. As we shopped, we shared a cart. I couldn't help but notice the looks we received. We strolled up and down the aisles and went over a list of what I needed. I felt oddly comfortable with her as we argued over what to buy. I tried to convince Alex that fresh fruits and vegetables were a good idea. She in turn extolled the virtues of Pop-Tarts and coffee. When I mentioned that I would need a table for my computer, she questioned me as to where I would put it.

"I should be able to squeeze something in," I protested, knowing that she was right.

"I have a suggestion," she said. "My apartment was at one time two separate apartments. I took over the upper floor when the old tenants moved out. I pay more, but I needed the space for all my books and stuff. I have a spare room upstairs that I originally planned on turning into a guest room. I never got around to it. You could use it as a study if you'd like."

"Are you sure?" I asked her as I wondered, *Just how does someone take over a second apartment and convert it? Most people would just move to a bigger place. Yet another mystery.*

"It's just sitting there empty. I'm only using it for storage. The good news is that there's already a desk in there. The former tenants left it."

"Why?"

"It won't fit through the doorway. Believe me, I've tried," Alex said. "I think it has been up there for years, and somewhere along the line, someone changed the doorway. Probably when the house was converted into apartments. Someone just forgot to remove the desk. You could just bring your laptop up. I do find it interesting that you have a state-of-the-art laptop, but you won't get a cellphone."

"The laptop is a necessity."

After I agreed to think about her offer, she decided to fill me in on our neighbors. Mine was the only apartment on the first floor since the entryway was so large, which was typical of the architecture of the time. Behind her apartment on the third floor was Hal. He was a physics professor at Prower and a transvestite, so I should not be surprised to see a man wearing a dress wandering the hallway. On the second floor behind Alex's apartment was Shavonne, the cop I met that morning when I was running around half-naked. After she filled me in on the neighborhood gossip, we paid for our purchases and drove home.

***

Alex helped me unload my groceries, and I kept mulling over her offer. I really needed the space, and I would love an excuse to spend more time with her. Having a friend was such a delightful gift, I just didn't want to push any harder than I already had.

"Alex, are you certain my using that room won't be an inconvenience?" I asked as we tried to find places to put my new purchases. "I don't want to invade your privacy."

"Please." She scoffed. "I lead a nun's life. It'll be nice having some company."

"Why don't you use the desk or the extra room?"

"I set up my office in the room across the hall, which is big enough to house the multitude of bookshelves I needed. The room I'm offering you isn't very big, and I've been using the same writing table since I was a teenager." She looked for a place to put the can goods I purchased. "Then again, we may need that space for all the food you bought. Stephanie, I wouldn't have offered it if I didn't want you there. It's just going to waste."

"Tell me what is so special about the writing table that you use." I relieved her of the cans of soup she was holding.

"It was my great-grandmother's," she said proudly. "Actually, she was my great-great-grandmother. The extra great just sounds a little silly."

"Haley Ballister?" I gaped in wonderment. "You do your work on Haley Ballister's desk!" The historian in me was drooling at the thought.

"Yes, it was hers," Alex confirmed, giving me a curious look. "I'm still amazed that you know about my ancestors. I'm also curious as to why. It's not like I'm related to one of the more known people from that era."

"It's an interesting story," I argued. "A gentleman from the upper levels of New Orleans high society chooses to enlist in a company full of immigrants and drunkards. I've always been curious as to why he chose that route."

"You've studied up on it, I'm guessing you have a theory."

"Yes."

"And your theory is?" She neatly folded the paper bags.

"You won't like it."

"Give me a try."

"He was not your great-great-grandfather," I said, hoping I hadn't overstepped. "Excuse the extra great and any implications against your family name."

"Please." Alex scoffed. "You don't even want to know how the Kendells made their money. As for the Ballisters, they were plantation owners in the Deep South. I do not have to explain to you what that means. They made their name off the backs of people they enslaved. Not a very proud history if you ask me."

"Is that why the family won't show the diaries?" I began to wonder if I was on the right track with my theory.

"No," Alex said with a smile. "Haley wasn't like the others. Truth be told, we have shown the diaries. I just think no one wanted to tell the true story. I get back in the day, but now I don't see a reason to keep it quiet."

"What was in those diaries?"

"Haley led a very interesting life."

"Is there something the family would be ashamed of?"

"Not in my opinion." Alex sighed deeply. "You know that Maureen is pushing me to publish."

"I heard," I said quietly, trying not to get my hopes up.

"Oh?" Alex smiled with a cocky grin. "My previous books were well...Let's just say, they had a lot of pictures in them, and they look good on a coffee table. Your books, on the other hand, are brilliant. Is there any chance you would consider cowriting Haley's story with me?"

I wanted to leap into her arms and not just because she had just offered me the opportunity of a lifetime. I really needed to find some way of controlling my emotions.

"Are you certain?" I asked carefully. "After last night, do you think you can trust me?"

"Last night was last night," she said in a deep soothing voice. "You are a brilliant writer and a dedicated scholar. Just because you found me attractive while under the influence of tequila is no reason not to trust you. After some ups and downs, we did manage to get through today. I'm thinking it was just the tequila talking."

"And if it wasn't?" I asked, instantly embarrassed when I had spoken out loud.

"Peter," she responded flatly.

"Do you find it strange that you mention his name more than I do?" I said quietly. "I'm starting to realize that I might be doing to him what you did to Chris." I was startled by my bold admission.

"We make our own choices," Alex said sadly. "I would like to make one suggestion. Perhaps the next time you kiss a woman, you might want to try it sober."

There was something cruel in her voice that made me shiver. Jessica Gunnarsson's wound may have healed, but she definitely left a scar. Her suggestion that I try kissing a woman while not inebriated lingered in my mind. There was something about the suggestion that made me feel slightly unbalanced. A part of me wanted to hunt down Jessica Gunnarsson, rip out her heart, and scatter it to the four winds. I was forced to abandon my thoughts of revenge when Alex suggested that we bring the futon in and get it set up.

Chapter Ten

After we unloaded the car and set up the futon, Alex and I proceeded to move some of my books and papers into the upstairs office. She gave me a brief tour of the space. Next to the office was what had been a kitchen. Alex had converted that space into a laundry room. Her office was across the hall, and there was a sitting room. I just couldn't figure out how someone convinces her landlord to convert two apartments into one.

After we finished moving some of my stuff upstairs and setting up the last of my things in the apartment, we decided to relax. I knew Alex was tired and her knee was still hurting, although she tried to play it off.

We sat out on the balcony of Alex's apartment and looked at the stars. Alex opened a bottle of wine, a very nice New Zealand sauvignon blanc. She gave me a glass after I pledged Scout's honor not to let it go to my head. I knew she was teasing, yet I was also aware that there was a hint of truth in her joking. A part of me was hurt, and a part of me was offended. How could I be feeling so many conflicting emotions at once? As I stared at the stars, I wondered if I had really been living my life of just simply walking through it.

"Can I ask you something?" She sounded nervous.

"After everything you told me today?" I was surprised by her apprehension. "This isn't about why I don't have a cellphone again, is it?"

"No, I don't think I'll ever understand that."

"What would you like to know?"

"I'm confused," she tentatively began. "You and Peter were living together, weren't you?"

"No." I rolled my eyes at the thought. "This was to be our first place together."

"Oh?"

"What?"

"Based on what you said last night, I got the impression that the two of you have been together for a while," she tried to explain.

"Almost five years now," I said after quickly doing the math. "Well, on and off."

"Don't like to rush things?"

"Something like that." I groaned, fully prepared to list the litany of reasons I had used over the years. "You said your parents are phenomenally happy. To put it mildly, mine were the complete opposite. I wish I knew your parents' secret."

"Me too" came her quiet response. "They said it was just meeting the right person. Growing up, I thought it was that simple."

"It should be," I absently noted before taking a moment to breathe in the night air.

Once again, we fell into a silence. This time, it was comfortable. We just sat there sipping wine and gazing at the stars. I couldn't remember the last time I felt so relaxed.

Alex excused herself for a moment, and upon her return, she handed me a leather-bound journal. I ran my hands over it as if it were the Holy Grail.

"I've read all of them. If you want to do this, you have some catching up to do," Alex said with a smile. My heart skipped a beat at the sight of her standing there in the moonlight. "This is the first one, it covers the war years," Alex went on to explain, apparently unaware of my staring. "If we're going to this, we might consider doing a trip to Louisiana."

"I cannot believe I'm holding this," I gushed like a lovesick schoolgirl.

"I'm going to bed." Alex yawned. "Stay if you like. I often come out here to read when the weather is nice. There's something about the stars and the faint smell of the ocean. I find it peaceful."

I thanked her as she went off to bed after I decided to stay and read. For the first time in my life, I was not looking forward to sleeping alone. Normally, I hated when Peter and I slept together. I did not treasure the intimacy the way he did. That night, I wanted to lie beside Alex as we had that morning, all warm and close, snuggled up in the feather bed safe in her arms. Just as easily, I dismissed the foolish notion. I promised myself I would read for a short while, then go downstairs to my apartment and sleep on my new futon. I sipped my wine and opened Haley Ballister's journal. My heart skipped a beat as the musty scent from the pages surrounded me. I had dreamt of this moment for years. Nothing could have prepared me for what I was about to discover.

***

June 10, 1862

It feels good to finally have the time to put my thoughts on paper. My old journals are forever lost since my banishment over two years ago. I am a Yankee trapped in a world that I do not understand. I will never return home. Home? I must learn to accept that I no longer have a home.

I was a happy child living with Ma and Pa on our farm not far from Lowell. I will never utter the name of that hateful place again. The good God-fearing church folk sent me away and told me that I could never return. My family made no valiant effort to save me from the disgrace. For I have shamed them in the eyes of the Lord. Now I live in another small town somewhere in Virginia. The town is called Haverstone. I'm not entirely certain as to where in Virginia it is. Haverstone is where I stopped. I had been traveling for so long. I walked into Haverstone as I had walked into so many towns. One looking like all the others I've seen in my travels. I look for work, but it was the same as everywhere else. I have no skills or references. I'm a young girl traveling alone, which to many means one thing.

With the war, there is very little work for those who live here much less for a strange Yankee girl. I remember thinking that perhaps I should travel back North. There must be some work in New York. But I tried New York once before, and the only offers I received were indecent. My first day in town had been a disappointment. When night fell, I made my way to the stables. I have found that by going there late in the evening, I could sometimes find an empty stall and sleep there. It was risky, but I knew I could not trust the openness of the streets. I cried myself to sleep, not for the first time. I was awakened by the sight of a very large man standing over me. Fearful, I tried to run, but he caught me easily. I struggled to free myself.

"It's all right," he reassured me. I've heard those words from men before. The end was always the same. They would provide me with safety only if I gave myself to them. I'm ashamed that I have allowed this transgression to occur.

My fortune changed when this man turned out to be different from the others. He told me of a woman who would take me in for the night and feed me. No questions asked and no payment required. I still did not trust him entirely. But the thought of a bed and food was far too tempting. I could not remember my last meal.

He took me to a grand house just outside of town. He led me around back, so I would not be confused with one of the working girls. My stomach lurched as I realized where he had brought me. I assumed that he would receive some kind of payment for his new find. I had heard the women in town cackling about this place. Mrs. Moorehouse's whorehouse. To my surprise, my savior delivered me and told me to take care, then left.

I turned to run out the door when I was greeted by a gentle lady. Anna Moorehouse turned out to be the kindest soul I would ever meet. She took me and fed me without asking for anything in return. She only offered me a place to stay and a job as a cook. I failed terribly in the kitchen. Anna patiently tried to teach me. She made it clear that I would not become a working girl. I was no cook and I was no fool, everything in life has a price. Yet she seemed determined not to ask anything of me. I could not live off this woman's generosity. I needed money, and it was I who offered my services to the house. Anna was disappointed and tried to talk me out of it. I explained that it would not be the first time I earned my way in this manner.

I saw true sadness in the older woman's face upon hearing these words. Finally, she accepted my offer. Anna explained that if I did go to work for her in that manner, I would not be allowed to stay on. She told me to earn the money I needed, then I was to go and start a new life and forget this place. I quickly learned that this was Anna's policy. She helped all of her girls get back on their feet and build a savings, then gave them a little something extra and helped them relocate and start a new life.

Over the next few months, I learned how this fine lady came to be a madame. She was living in Savannah with her husband and child. Her husband was a doctor, and her life was very proper. Until the unthinkable happened. The good doctor abandoned her and her child. Instead of receiving kindness from her neighbors, she was shunned. Disgraced in the eyes of proper society. Funny, her husband was a cad, yet she and her child paid the price for his misdeeds. She was left with the good doctor's debts and no skills. A marked woman, much like myself, with nowhere to turn. Finally, she sent her daughter away when she lost their modest home. Then she was turned out onto the streets and began the only trade available for a woman on her own.

Some years ago, Anna's daughter, Sarah, died from pneumonia. Anna was forever grateful that young Sarah never learned of her profession. I found myself trusting her so much. Though she never asked, I told her my own story. I told her how a beautiful young girl who came from the upper levels of my town's society charmed me and took me to her bed. Catherine and I found pleasure with each other for almost three years before our secret was revealed. Since Catherine was from a good family, I must have been the one who had led her down this evil road. She never defended me or our love. She lied, saying that I had been the one who seduced her into committing unnatural acts. I begged her to speak the truth and tell them of our love. She turned her back on me, and I was driven out of town and told never to return.

Now here in this distant land I sit, finally having the time to write down my thoughts. As of late, the days are slow. Saturday nights are when we really have to work. Haverstone is out of the way, so Mrs. Moorehouse's little hideaway just outside of the neighboring towns is ideal for discretion. Many of the men we entertain travel in groups. I soon discovered that many of them were not really interested in coming to a whorehouse, but it was what is expected of them.

Men are such unusual creatures. Many of them are happy if you just sit and talk to them. They marry women for business reasons and not for love. Now they find themselves alone with no real companionship. This does not mean they don't want me to touch them. So many of them seem to enjoy the conversation more. Of course, it doesn't matter if they do or do not touch me. The moment they depart my chambers, they are boasting to anyone who will listen about their grand exploits. Those who have no desire to converse are at least quick about their business. For this, I am grateful. I have no desire to share my bed with them any longer than necessary.

With the war coming closer and closer, even our Saturday crowds have dwindled. Often we spend most of our time waiting for the soldiers. The soldiers are trouble, but thankfully, they are eager, which leads to very limited time in my company. Many of the girls have left knowing that they can make more money by following the troops. I know this upsets Anna. Unlike the others, I prefer to stay. I enjoy Mrs. Moorehouse's company, and I feel safe here. Anna and I spend our days just talking, dreaming of the day when she can turn this house into a real inn. This, of course, is just a dream.

I must confess, even though I do enjoy Anna's company, I have enjoyed a few evenings with some of the other girls who have chosen to stay on. I do not apologize for my actions. The company of men is not something I seek. I wish I could feel something more than desire or friendship for the ladies with whom I share my favors.

***

I put down the journal briefly. "So Alex's great-great-grandmother was a working girl and a lesbian. No small wonder the family kept the story quiet." I took one last sip of wine. In this day and age, this was hardly scandalous. Still, I could understand why prior generations didn't want the truth getting out. For me, I found it sad. I couldn't help but feel sympathy for Haley. She was trapped in a cruel world forced to sell her body to survive. But given what I just learned, it did beg the question of how she met and married Stephan Ballister. Despite the lateness of the hour, I opened the diary and kept reading.

Chapter Eleven

June 11, 1862

We have received word that some soldiers are coming to call on us. I was mildly excited knowing that their arrival would mean money. As much as I was enjoying the quiet, we needed money. One of the girls said the boys were from New Orleans, and they warned me that they're a rowdy group known for their drunkenness.

Another girl was upset because the company was filled with foreigners. I didn't care. Men are men, none are to be trusted. Sharla told me to go after the men in the gray uniforms if I can. She said the ones wearing gray were the officers. I find this puzzling. Don't all of the rebs wear gray? Sharla explained that in this company they wear a more colorful uniform with striped pants and straw hats. How unusual. Can you imagine straw hats in battle? The more Sharla and the others tell me, the more I become concerned.

These boys from Louisiana have an unsavory reputation. Of course, I know from experience that talk can be just that. But still I'm worried. I expressed my concerns to Anna while we were unloading the fresh shipment of spirits. Anna quieted my fears. She knew her girls and would select their companions carefully. Admittedly, some of the girls do like the wild ones. Anna knew me, and she knew people. She could size up a man's character in the blink of an eye. A skill she claims to have learned after her husband left her high and dry. She has assured me that my companion or companions for the evening would be gentle or fast. Still I am relieved to hear that she has hired on some extra help for the evening. Some local boys who are big and strong.

Before the war, Anna had been hiding runaway slaves. Some of them have stayed on to work for her fixing up the house and keeping the peace. Anna has strict rules for the patrons. For a price, you can drink as much as you can handle and keep company with one of her girls. But any man who raises his hand in anger will find himself tossed out into the street wearing nothing but a promise that he would never enter her house again. As unsavory as our trade is, Anna tries to maintain some dignity. Not one of us has chosen this path. The rules of proper society have left us no other choice. Someday, Anna promises that we will no longer have to sell our bodies. I want to believe her.

Sometimes, I find it difficult to understand this woman. Before the war, I know she helped runaway slaves. But now she uses her house to gain information to help the Confederacy. When I questioned her about this, she shook her head and explained that she is a Southern lady, and that was that.

***

June 14, 1862

I'm still reeling from the events of last evening. The boys from Louisiana arrived and brought with them many surprises. Sharla had been truthful about their strange attire and fondness for the bottle. More than one of the lads found himself thrown out into the street. Anna pulled me aside to tell me that she had found my beau for the evening. He was a sergeant and a gentleman from a fine New Orleans family. When I looked at him, I was shocked. He was nothing more than a boy. How could someone so young fight much less hold such a high rank? There was something about his slight stature that I found attractive. I've never looked at a man in that manner before.

Anna explained that it was his birthday, and his men had paid for his present. His present, of course, was to be me for the entire evening. I immediately became fearful at the thought of spending an entire evening with someone. Anna calmed my fears, explaining that his comrades told her that they feared the poor boy was a virgin. He was young, and if he was indeed a virgin, it would be an easy night for me. As Anna escorted me across the room to meet my new beau, I barely caught his name over the noise. His name was Stephan Ballister.

He stood before me tugging his cap down, probably to hide the blush clearly written on his face. I took him by the hand and led him upstairs while his company cheered him on. As they shouted their encouragement, I noticed that a smile never crossed his face. Although it was difficult to see since he kept his hat pulled down so that it cast a shadow over his features.

Once we were alone, I went to touch him, but he refused. I tried to encourage him. He still refused. I remember thinking that this was going to be the easiest money I ever made. I explained that my services had been paid for and he could have a warm bath that, based on his odor, he was in much need of. I also offered him my bed to sleep in. He could tell his buddies in the morning that he showed me the time of my life.

"Why would I lie?" he asked in the softest, gentlest voice I had ever heard.

I told him that he should lie since his friends were convinced that he was pure, and if he refused me, they might think that he did not care for the company of women. I silently feared that this might be the boy's problem. It was a problem I understood far too well.

He laughed heartily. "So this is why they've chosen such an odd present for me." He smiled, and I have to admit that I liked his smile. "I do like women, and I have known the pleasure of their bodies. I just don't believe that a woman should be forced to sell herself."

In anger, I told him that I had no choice.

"I know," he said with such sweet sincerity that it almost broke my heart. I thanked him for his kindness. He was a real gentleman, and I have not met many in my life. Seeing him standing before me refusing my favors on sheer principle was something new to me. I told him he should at least enjoy a bath and a good night's sleep. Suddenly, he seemed to become very uneasy. I tried to explain that he could not return downstairs before dawn or his troops would lose respect for him. I also stressed that he certainly would not be sleeping in my bed smelling the way he did.

"You smell like a pig sty," I said as I removed his hat and ran my fingers through his hair.

There was a sadness in his eyes that captured my heart. I kissed him, and he returned my kiss with such passion that I have not felt in a very long time. His kiss also told me that he had been truthful, he had known the touch of a woman before. When our lips parted, I was left wanting more. For the first time in my life, I wanted a man—I wanted this man. I looked into his deep blue eyes, and suddenly, I knew. I could not believe that I had not seen it before. How had so many others missed it? Stephan was not a man.

God had smiled upon me and sent me this dashing woman who now stood before me. The sight of her set my body on fire. I ran my fingers down her long neck and kissed her again. This time when our lips parted, it was she who was breathless.

"How could I have not seen it before?" I asked her.

Her face changed quickly as the words escaped me. She was afraid. I quieted her fears as I kissed her again. I told her that I would never reveal her secret, but I did want her to accept her birthday present. She protested that she still did not believe that I should have to sell myself. She also informed me that it wasn't really her birthday, it was Stephan's. I didn't care if it was Robert E. Lee's birthday! I wanted her.

"Think of it as a gift for me then. It has been so long since I have known the pleasure of a woman," I whispered in her ear. It wasn't entirely the truth, still I just couldn't quell my desire.

"Then you're like me?"

"Yes, we are the same."

***

"I did not see that coming!" I blurted out, looking around to see if anyone had heard me. I was left with so many questions. I wanted to read the entire diary, yet I was overcome by weariness and could not read any further. Reluctantly, I closed Haley's journal and retreated downstairs. Curled up on my futon, I could almost hear Haley's words *Yes, we are the same.* I fell asleep with the image of these two women. One in uniform while the other explored the secrets that lay beneath.

My last clear thought was, "Yup, this is helping with my confusion!"

***

I was awakened by the sounds of Alex's morning concert. That day, I was greeted by Cher. I groaned as I rolled out of bed. The futon was comfortable but not as comfortable as the feather mattress in Alex's big brass bed.

I took a deep breath and vowed that I was going to get over my feelings for Alex if it killed me. "And it just might!" I shouted for no other reason than I was a bundle of frustration. There I stood, and my first thoughts of the day were of Alex. *Yes, we are the same* echoed in my head. Granted, not the most poetic way to say it, but still, it was so simple and honest.

I was tempted to skip going to campus so I could stay home and read more of Haley's story. "Get it together, Stephanie," I chastised myself, grabbing one of my new towels. I took a long shower while relaxing under the steady stream of water. I realized that I had forgotten to put on a pot of coffee.

"I'll get some at the dining hall," I promised myself as I dried off.

I tossed the towel in the bag I had been using for my dirty laundry. "I need to go to the Laundromat." I grimaced, thinking about how much I hated doing laundry. I picked the white dress shirt up off the floor. "I should wash this before I give it back to her." For the strangest reason, I didn't put it into the bag. Instead I held on to it before folding it neatly and placed it carefully on my futon. The truly odd thing was I hadn't bothered to make the bed, yet I took the time to fold her shirt.

I glanced up at the throbbing ceiling and wondered what Alex was doing. Then I realized that I was behaving like an idiot. I set about getting ready for my first day of classes. As I checked the lines of my skirt, I wondered if maybe I should dress more casual, more like Alex did. Perhaps the students would be more at ease with me, and I would be more comfortable.

After I finished getting dressed, I grabbed my briefcase and picked up the diary. I headed upstairs and knocked on Alex's door.

"I wonder if she's hard of hearing," I pondered as I rapped louder on the door.

The music ceased just before the door opened. "Sorry. I forget about the volume. Come in. Have you had your coffee yet?"

"No, but I would love a cup."

"Help yourself."

"I wanted to leave this with you," I held up the diary while putting my briefcase on the sofa. "I don't feel comfortable leaving it at my place."

"You can leave it in your study." She pointed to the second floor.

"My study?" I wanted to chuckle; instead, I allowed her to pour me a cup of coffee while I went upstairs. I put the diary in the desk drawer and headed back downstairs. My heart skipped a beat when I saw her standing on the landing with a mug of coffee. As I got closer, the warm feeling fled when I got a closer look at the beverage. "Oh, my God, you put milk in it?"

"Fresh milk," she defended herself. "You were with me when I bought it."

Recalling her purchasing a fresh carton calmed my fears, and I accepted her offer. "I enjoyed Cher this morning."

"Crap, I'm sorry."

"No need to apologize," I tried to reassure her. "Who doesn't like Cher?"

We went out on to the balcony and sipped our coffee. Alex made some comment about it turning into an Indian summer and how she could never live in the Midwest. I agreed. After a few weeks at Prower, I knew I could never live that far from the ocean again.

"I can't believe it's the first day of classes," she said absently.

"Why are your summer courses still going?"

"Don't get me started on that snafu." She snarled. "My summer course load was supposed to have ended two weeks ago. Then some genius decided to fix up the dorms the second the students moved out after the spring semester wrapped. By the time it got straightened out, we were behind schedule. I know the dorms need work, but students are not permitted to live off campus until their junior year."

"Do things like that happen very often?"

"No," she reassured me. "Here at Prower, things tend to run very smoothly."

"Good to know, I was worried for a moment."

"What did you think of my great-great-grandmother's diary?" Alex asked me slyly.

"I wish I could have stayed awake to finish it." I sighed. "I have so many questions."

"I bet you do," Alex said knowingly. "Before I answer your questions—and I will not answer all of them—I want to know what it is about my ancestors that interested you in this story."

"I've already told you."

"Tell me again."

"Fine." I shook my head. "When I first came across Stephan Ballister, I began to question his identity."

"Why?"

"Because he was a proper gentleman from New Orleans who opted to serve in a unit filled with immigrants," I explained. "No one from his station in life would have done so. And from what I have learned about him prior to the war, it was not in his character to do so. Plus, he was already enlisted in a unit more appropriate to his station. He was a corporal in a rifle company along with many of his school chums."

"True, his rank was earned solely by his station in society, and no, he never would have associated with anyone he felt was beneath him."

"It begs the question as to why run off and join Company D?" I went on, getting more and more excited. "A man in his position would have stayed with his peers. He joined Company D in the middle of the night. I never believed the story that he was eager to join the battle. Everything I read about his life prior to the war indicated that he was not that kind of man. Granted, it makes a great story, but somehow, it doesn't ring true. Here was a guy who leased his slaves out to farmers in Texas because he knew the war was coming. He wouldn't take the chance that his slaves would be freed, and he had business dealings in England. My initial research revealed that he sold equipment and supplies to the North just to make a buck. Which is why I think when faced with the very real prospect of having to fight in a real battle, he hightailed it to England."

"All true," Alex confirmed.

"All of it?" I eagerly pried.

"The great old Southern tale is nothing but a very well fabricated web of lies," she proudly answered. "Stephan was not enraged by the act of Northern aggression. He did not tell his sister to be brave while he went off to fight the great fight."

"His sister just seems to get lost." I shook my head. "I know she was a school teacher. Some of the work I've read claims that she died during Sherman's March. Other claims have her dying when the Union burned down the family plantation, and still other reports claim she passed away before the war began. The only thing scholars agree on is that she died. Mostly, her history never seemed important."

"Because she was a woman." Alex scoffed. "Eleanor was indeed a school teacher, a spinster school teacher. Even if she was around when Stephan joined the fight, I doubt he would have taken the time to tell her to be brave. I get the feeling that they got along about as well as Newt and Candace Gingrich. Historically speaking, she just wasn't that important."

"Based on what I've read so far, your family history is—"

"Entertaining?"

"Amazing," I retorted before I took one last sip of coffee. "Stephan Ballister is not your great-great-grandfather."

"Sure he is."

"What?"

"We'll get to that," she quickly silenced my question. "First things first, see that box on the sofa?"

"Yes." I glanced over at the slim box.

"It's called a television," she gloated. "And it was just sitting upstairs still in the box."

"I have a television."

"Yes, but this one was made in this century and will probably be a lot easier for the cable guy to hook up. That other thing you have is a thirteen-inch relic."

"No," I flatly refused. "You can't just keep giving me stuff. The television I have now is just fine."

"When it dies, which I suspect will be soon, you'll need a special permit to have it picked up." She sounded horrified. "Seriously, how old is it?"

"I don't know, it belonged to my grandmother." I groaned, knowing that I was about to lose this argument. "I don't watch that much television."

"Really?" She seemed shocked.

"Yes, really. Based on the large flat-screen down here and the even larger one in your sitting room, I get that you enjoy television. We need to get going or we'll be late for class. Which would be bad since we're the teachers."

"Will you take the TV as a loaner?" she persisted as we gathered up our things.

"Fine," I conceded, picking up the lightweight box. "If you promise that you'll let me do something for you."

"Okay," she said. "Let's go. Do you mind not walking since I'm stuck in heels again? The good news is I won't have to drag these puppies out again until spring."

"How did you survive in the corporate arena?" I laughed as we locked up her apartment before stopping at mine so I could put the TV inside. "If it's any consolation, you look terrific."

"Running late, as well, Alex?" a voice called out as we made our way to the parking lot.

"Yes, Hal," she brightly answered. "Dr. Harmon, have you met Dr. Grant?"

"Hal."

"Stephanie," I returned his offer of a handshake. I studied the tall middle-aged man clad in a tweed suit. I couldn't help wondering what his other persona looked like.

"Need a lift?" she asked him.

"Thank you, no," he answered, his British accent showing. "I'm driving, as well. I won't be returning until quite late. I'm meeting with my new doctoral candidates after my lectures."

"Don't you just love the start of the year?" Alex teased as she unlocked her car and held the door open for me.

Hal laughed in response while she and I buckled up.

"So your great-great-grandmother was a lesbian prostitute?"

"You've been dying to say that all morning, haven't you?" She snickered.

"Honestly, yes!"

***

"She was an abolitionist, wasn't she?" I asked Alex after we had arrived at our office.

"Eleanor? Yes," Alex said while furiously typing on her laptop. "You certainly have studied this. Eleanor worked for the

Underground Railroad prior to the war. I have a feeling she wasn't very popular with her family or anyone else in New Orleans. Do you want to do dinner tonight?"

"Sounds good," I accepted all the while thinking that all I wanted to do at that moment was talk about her ancestors. "Can we talk about your family over dinner?"

"Sure, Mom and Dad are lawyers," she taunted me. "My kid sister is a doctor."

"Funny." I grunted as I shut down my laptop and began to prepare for my first class. "Wait, Nicole is a doctor? Like a doctor, doctor?"

"I take it that you met her years ago, as well." Alex sighed heavily. "Like me, she's changed. After she quit drinking, she really pulled it together."

"Good for her," I said honestly. "Over dinner, maybe we could discuss your ancestors and not your immediate family? Or do you just want to keep yanking my chain?"

"I thought I'd yank your chain for a little while longer, but if you insist, we can work over dinner."

I glanced up at the clock and was surprised. "Almost time for my first class." I blanched as Alex crossed over to my side of the office.

"You look nervous."

I was just about to answer that yes I was nervous when Louisa entered our office carrying a bouquet of roses. "For you," she said brightly. Alex just looked at the arrangement nestled in a rose-colored vase. She pursed her lips before turning and retreating to her side of the office. I didn't need to look at the card to know they were from Peter. I thanked Louisa, who waited for me to look at the card.

"My boyfriend," I mumbled as she smiled. I thanked her again before she returned to her duties. I didn't miss the fact that Alex seemed content hiding behind her laptop.

The card was typical of Peter. *Good luck on your first day. I miss you and cannot wait to see you. Love, Peter.* Granted, he was no poet, but he could still pull at my heart strings. If only I could feel for him what he apparently felt for me. My life would be so much easier if I could just feel something—anything—remotely close to romantic.

I called him to thank him for the flowers. The sound of his voice left me feeling flat and devoid of emotion. "I have to go," I finally ended the call, much to his disappointment. "This sucks," I whimpered after I hung up. I heard Alex grunt from the other side of the partition that separated our desks. Before I could think of something to say, she got up and stormed out of the office.

"Nice flowers."

I looked up and found Maureen standing in front of my desk.

"Peter."

"You don't sound happy," she said. "Most women would be showing them off. I know I would if my husband sent me flowers."

"I need to break up with him."

"No kidding," she grimly agreed. "Sorry, but the other night when you talked about him, you used words like nice, dependable, efficient, and hardworking. Honestly, that's the way I describe my dishwasher."

My shoulders slumped as I was filled with a sense of dread. "I'm not being fair to him," I finally managed to say. "Things were so much easier before I made out with Alex."

"You what?"

"Oh, God, I said that out loud." I smacked myself in the forehead. "Is there any chance you could just forget I said that?"

"Not a chance," she gloated while I buried my face in my hands. "Okay, fine. For the moment, I'll let that slide. Can you email me your syllabus for your 101? It seems to have vanished."

"I'll get it to you by the end of the day," I meekly offered, lifting my head. "Is there anything else?"

"Oh, yeah, maybe we can grab a bite tonight and discuss—"

"No." I blushed as I scrambled to gather my notes for my class. "Besides, I'm having dinner with Alex tonight."

"Really?"

"I'm going to be late," I blurted out, making a mad dash for the door.

"Was it good?" she called after me.

"Hell yes," I whispered, hurrying down the hallway.

Chapter Twelve

My classes went the way I had expected. The usual grunts and groans when I explained the workload. The usual scrambling for pen and paper when I began my lecture. I tried to relax and make things light and fun the way Alex did. But as I faced the same blank stares I had faced so many times before, I knew it was useless. How did Alex do it? I reviewed the final exam for her summer course, and based on the questions, she did manage to cram a great deal of history into those six weeks. Somehow, she made it fun. I was encouraged when I noticed one young man in the front paying close attention to me. Until I realized that he was interested in me and probably had no clue as to what I was saying. Now if my legs and breasts could give the lecture, this guy would pass with flying colors. The poor thing left at the end of the lecture with his textbook carefully placed in front of himself.

I felt defeated when I dragged myself back to my office. I stopped in the doorway when I discovered Alex sitting on the edge of my desk sporting a troubled look. I closed the door and braced myself.

"You didn't by any chance tell our boss that we sucked face, did you?"

"Kind of," I sheepishly confessed, making my way across the room. "It was an accident and only after she compared my boyfriend to a kitchen appliance."

"Excuse me?"

"She noticed the flowers." I flopped down on the sofa feeling thoroughly exasperated. "I said something about needing to break up with Peter, and without meaning to, I mentioned kissing you."

"Oh?" She seemed to be mulling over what I had just said. "I'd like to say that what you just said made sense, but no, not so much. I do feel a need to warn you that Maureen can be like a Rottweiler with a pork chop. When she sinks her teeth into something juicy, she won't let it go. She's not a gossip, but she does enjoy a good story."

"You don't seem bothered by any of this." I tossed my briefcase next to me. "Why is that?"

"I'm not the one having a crisis of faith."

"Let me guess." I rolled my shoulders in an effort to alleviate the tension that had been building. "Been there, done that, and have the T-shirt."

"Yes, it's a great T-shirt, by the way. I got it at my first Pride," she teased. "Doesn't really fit me anymore, but at one time, I looked stunning in it."

"You're just a little crazy, aren't you?" I couldn't help smiling at her attempt to make me feel better.

"A wee bit." She shrugged. "How did your classes go?"

"Ugh." I snarled, allowing my head to fall back.

"Now how could that question be worse than the one I greeted you with?"

"I'm not you."

"Okay?"

"You light up a classroom." I finally lowered my head. "My students are usually in a coma by the time class is over. I'm just awkward, always have been. Oh, God, I need to email Maureen." I grabbed my briefcase and made my way over to my desk. Alex slid off my desk. "My 101 syllabus is missing. This is why I hate technology." I groaned when I powered up my computer and opened my email. "I never sent it. For some reason, it's still in my drafts. There, sent."

"Next time, just print it out and hand it to Louisa," she said, gathering her stuff. "Trust me, it'll never get lost that way. Power down, stuff your laptop in the bag, and let's go. Do you like Chinese?"

"Yes." I complied with her instructions.

We made our way out of the building and headed toward the parking lot. "What did you say to Maureen?" I asked, more than a little curious about what had happened.

"I pretended not to know what she was talking about," she explained as she unlocked her car. "Then when that didn't work, I pretended that there was big-ass spider on her shoulder. Then I ran like hell and hid behind the library for about a half an hour chain smoking."

***

The restaurant was nice. We ordered tea and hot and sour soup to start. I took a notebook out of my briefcase eager to get started on our project. It wasn't just my excitement over the pending project. The truth was, I needed the distraction. Alex sat across from me looking nothing short of amazing. Images from the other night kept creeping up, the memory of how right it felt to hold her, kiss her, and the other things we had shared. It was distracting, to say the least.

"How did you first hear about Sergeant Ballister?" she asked after we placed our dinner order, agreeing to share a couple of entrees.

"It was a letter one of my professors at UConn showed me," I began, helping myself to more hot tea. "It was from a fellow named Carsen Ellison. He was originally from New Orleans, and the letter was to his wife. In the letter, he talked about his day-to-day life, which in itself I find fascinating. That's what my professor wanted me to see. Also in the letter, he mentioned Ballister. Ellison had known Ballister from New Orleans, and he claimed that the man he met at the Battle of Cross Keys was much smaller and younger than Stephan Ballister. He suspected that he was a boy who was too young to enlist, so he stole Ballister's name. He also went on to say that he would not expose the young man since despite his youth he was one hell of a soldier. That's how I got hooked. From that moment on, I wanted to know who this soldier really was. Never in my wildest dreams did I suspect that Stephan James Ballister was a woman."

"No," Alex corrected me with a cocky smirk. "Stephan James Ballister was a man. Master Sergeant Ballister was a woman."

"Who was she?"

"Keep reading," she taunted me.

"Brat." I growled in frustration.

"Come on, where's your sense of adventure? This way, you'll enjoy the mystery more," Alex challenged. "You're so very close to the truth."

"I think I know," I said. "I just can't understand how it happened. It never ceases to amaze me how history can be distorted so easily. Stephan Ballister is remembered as a brave soldier of the Confederacy who ignored his station in life to fight for his home. He will always be remembered as a fallen hero."

"Not when we get done with him, he won't," Alex said bluntly. "Ballister was a piss ant who bought and sold human beings because he thought it was his right to do so. You know that we're going to take a great deal of heat from the Southern historians."

"I know." I sighed. "None of my books has been a source of controversy before. What the hell, if I'm going to shake up my life, I might as well go full throttle. It just bothers me that historians have been extolling Ballister's virtues for over a century. Then again, these are the same historians who have been writing that Anna Moorehouse was a widow who ran a nice little inn. Based on what I read last night, that isn't quite accurate."

"According to history, Haley was a simple farm girl who bravely carried on her husband's memory," Alex added. "Although by the end of the war, the whorehouse was in fact an inn. But they washed away the fact that it was originally a house of ill repute, and the noble Mrs. Ballister had been a working girl."

"Speaking of which…" I began with hesitation. "Are you certain that you want to expose your great-grandmother?"

"Of being a prostitute or a lesbian?" she asked pointedly.

"Either." I swallowed hard as I answered her.

"She wasn't ashamed of her homosexuality," Alex said firmly. "She was always very honest about what society had forced her to become. She had no options. It was either sell herself or die. I think she must have possessed amazing courage to survive everything that she did. Her story was never hidden away from us like some deep dark secret. It was politely suggested that we not share her story."

"I can feel her strength as I read her words," I said. "I just can't figure out how she managed to marry a woman and have a child by her. After all, this was long before the days of the turkey baster babies."

"Now where did a nice girl from Connecticut learn about that?" Alex teased me. "Stephanie, you are so very close to the answers."

"How can I figure out Haley's life when I can't figure out my own?" I said absently.

"Are you really going to break up with him?"

"I think it's for the best," I said. "It hit me when the flowers arrived. Instead of being happy, all I could think about is how unfairly I've been treating him. I think if someone sends you flowers, you should at least smile."

"I'll have to think twice the next time I'm tempted to send a woman flowers." She laughed, and I smiled. I smiled because the sound of her laughter warmed me. The food arrived, and we dug in while I tried to clear my thoughts.

"Food is good," I finally managed to say. The food was good, it was just sad that it was the only thing I could think of to comment on.

"It does amaze me that with the limited choices in town that almost every restaurant is truly amazing," she said brightly. Once again, I sat there unable to speak because of her smile. "You know what book of yours I loved?" She disrupted my staring. "The one on Gardner's Island and Captain Kidd."

"Got a thing for pirates?"

"Who doesn't?" She sounded overjoyed. "You penned a couple of books based on pirate ports along the East Coast, but that one was my favorite. You must have had a blast researching those."

"I did." I finally relaxed and smiled. "You wouldn't have any pirates in your family tree by any chance?"

"Not that I'm aware of," she said. "A couple of crooked politicians on the Kendell side, not nearly as interesting. Your area of expertise is amazing, not to mention vast. You specialize in colonial to post-Civil War. That's a broad range."

"I just can't stop with one era. Each has its own amazing aspects," I gushed. "I'm really looking forward to working on this project. For me, reading Haley's diary is like being given a winning lottery ticket."

"I love your enthusiasm."

"Speaking of which, I have some reading to do tonight," I beamed as I flagged down the waitress for the check. "My turn." I grabbed it and slapped my credit card down. I was thrilled when

Alex didn't put up an argument.

"Let's head home," she suggested after I had taken care of the bill.

***

Later that night, I was sitting in my studio thinking about everything. It was shocking to think how quickly I had come to the conclusion to end my relationship with Peter. Just a few short days ago, I was apartment hunting for the both of us. One bouquet of flowers later, and I was ready to call it a day. I knew it was the right thing to do. The man sent me flowers, and I felt sad. Alex smiled, and I felt amazing, which was not a good sign. It didn't seem fair. I felt completely at home in my studio, and Peter was back in Rhode Island thinking I was waiting for him.

I got up and puttered around. As much as I wanted to immerse myself in Haley's diary that night, I thought taking a moment to think about my life was more important. I unpacked the slim flat-screen television. It was small but considerably bigger than what I had been using. After everything that happened a couple of nights ago, I was still amazed how gracious Alex could be.

"Crisis of faith, huh?" I muttered out loud as I set up the television, knowing that the cable guy was coming the next day. "That's one way to put it. Alex, what is it about?"

I kept unpacking things until everything was in its place. I blinked with surprise when I looked at the clock. I had been up all night organizing my new space while my mind kept screaming at me. I knew I had to break up with Peter, and I knew that I needed to do it in person. He deserved that much. The other thing wearing on me was my undeniable attraction to Alex.

Chapter Thirteen

The next few days weren't any easier, mostly because I found it difficult dodging Maureen's questions. I tried to make it clear that I didn't want to discuss my misstep with Alex. She'd let it go for a good minute or two before finding a not-so-clever way to bring the subject up again. Alex, on the other hand, managed to avoid all of Maureen's questions.

I wasn't sleeping well, either. Each time I fell asleep, I dreamed about a certain brunette with amazing legs. Each morning, I awoke feeling agitated and extremely frustrated.

The other troubling part of my first week of classes revolved around my classes. For the life of me, I just couldn't understand why I couldn't get through a lecture without inciting a massive case of boredom. After a couple of my lectures, I seriously considered changing my specialty to sleep studies. The only thing I had managed to accomplish was avoiding Peter's phone calls. By the middle of the week, I was looking forward to spending the weekend alone with Haley Ballister's diary.

There was one other thing I needed to accomplish. I needed to cook something special. I returned home and began to fix dinner. I decided to make a home-cooked meal for Alex. A thank you, I lied to myself, for all her help. I changed into a pair of old blue jeans and a tattered Yale T-shirt and breaded some fresh chicken cutlets I had picked up at the meat market. I was just about to start frying the chicken after I stirred the sauce I had made the night before when the telephone rang.

For a brief moment, I was excited, hoping it was Alex. My heart sank, and my stomach felt uneasy when I answered, and it was Peter. We talked casually as I prepared Alex's dinner. I kept things decidedly evasive while we chatted. He seemed so happy to catch me. He wanted to know everything from how my first day went to life in Prowers Landing.

He seemed disheartened when I told him that my lectures were the same as always. He was so sweet and supportive and told me not to worry. As we talked, I quickly mentioned that perhaps we could get together before our anniversary. There was no way I was dumping him on our anniversary. His excitement over my suggestion filled me with even more guilt. Poor Peter, he deserved better than what I had to offer him.

***

Peter and I talked for over an hour while I cooked. On the one hand, it felt good to talk to him, and it reminded me why he was my friend. On the other, there was the constant feeling of guilt knowing that I wasn't in love with him. It bothered me that it took this move to make me realize that we both deserved more. I just wished I could feel something deeper for him. The oven timer pinged, alerting me that the chicken parmesan I had made from scratch was ready. I pulled it out to cool while I said my goodbyes to Peter. I set it down wondering when was the last time I had cooked for Peter.

I went to my bathroom and checked my appearance in the mirror. I combed my hair and brushed my teeth. When I looked up into the mirror, I saw something reflected in my eyes that I never saw there before…desire. I brushed the thought aside and headed out to my kitchen. I grabbed two potholders and retrieved the chicken and made my way upstairs to Alex's apartment.

***

Alex smiled when she opened the door and discovered me standing there. "Food!" she exclaimed happily as she ignored me and stuck her head down to inhale the fragrance of the fresh-baked meal.

"And Stephanie," I teased.

"Yeah, yeah. Now bring the food in," Alex insisted.

Alex let me in and ran to fetch some plates and forks. We settled in and ate our meal. It was so comfortable. After dinner, Alex cleaned up. I had offered to help, but she insisted. "No way. You cooked, I'll clean. Coffee?"

"Sounds good." I rubbed my sated stomach.

After the coffee was brewed, we sat closely on her couch. But not close enough to touch. With our legs tucked under ourselves, we sipped our coffee as I told Alex how my first week was going.

"They never expect a lecture the first class." Alex sighed, shaking her head. "I don't care if they're freshmen or seniors, it always comes as a complete shock."

"So you lecture on the first day?"

"Of course," she said. "This isn't junior high."

"I wish I could get my students involved the way you do," I said with regret.

"I'm sure you can do it," she said. "Your books are exciting, and you're a bright, intelligent woman. I'm sure you'll get through to them."

Alex stood to refill our coffee cups, and I watched her as she moved. There was something about this woman's presence that made me insane. Maybe it was her long dark hair or the way she would tilt her head just slightly when she was about to say something. Then again, maybe it was the baby doll T-shirt that was clinging to her breasts.

"I have got it bad."

"What?"

"Speaking of books…" I quickly shifted gears as she re-entered the room, hoping to distract myself. "Thank you again for Haley's journal."

"You're welcome."

"I spent years dreaming of reading this woman's diary."

"I'm surprised you haven't finished it."

"I've had a lot on my mind," I confessed as she sat next to me. "I don't know what's happening to me. Normally, I'm organized and in complete control. Since arriving in Prowers Landing, I feel like I've lost my footing. Maybe there's something in the water."

"Maybe it's just your time."

"For?"

"You." Her response was simple, yet it confused me to no end. "From what little you've told me, you've had a hard go of it. Starting college at twelve, when did you have time to be a kid?"

"I…" I couldn't think of an answer.

"That's what I thought." She jumped on my lack of response.

"We need to make a list."

"Of?"

"Things you need to do," she exclaimed with gusto.

"I have my planner." I was lost. At times, Alex was more than a little difficult to follow.

"Not that kind of list," she chided me. "A list of things you never did as a kid. Things most kids do at least once. Think about it. When most kids were out riding their bikes, you were locked up in a college library preparing for your physics exam."

"Okay." I groaned, unable to think of anything I had missed out on. "I'll try."

"I'm serious," she stressed. "Think about it, have you ever gone to a carnival, had a sleepover, spent a sunny afternoon Rollerblading, and what about playing hooky?"

"Why would I want to do any of those things now?"

"Because they're fun." She looked exasperated.

"I just feel like the moment my IQ was revealed, I was destined to be a dork."

"You're not a dork, people don't get historians." She sighed wistfully. "People think all we do is lock ourselves up in a library studying what is already accepted as the truth. They don't get that we're looking for the truth, just like a good mystery, and we need to know the answers. I'd bet you'd wet yourself if you had proof positive what happened to Amelia Earhart."

"Well, yeah," I said with excitement. "Who wouldn't? Wait a second, how did we get here? I swear I'll never understand how your thought process works. How did we get from Haley Ballister to carnivals and Amelia Earhart?"

"Sorry about that." She laughed. "My mouth and my mind just never seem to be on the same page."

"Good to know for the next time you ask me a question that is out of left field." I stretched my arms over my head. "I should grab the diary and try to get some work done before you ask me another random question."

"Well, thank you for dinner," she offered as I stood.

"My pleasure, I just wanted to thank you."

"For?"

"Everything." I blinked with surprise, confused by the curious look she was giving me. "Can I ask you something? How did you deal with reading about your great-great-grandmother's love life?" I was pleased when she chuckled.

"I always found the romance to be sweet. Admittedly, I'm always grateful she never got graphic. On some level, it's like thinking about my parents doing it." Alex shuddered at the last comment.

"Come now, Professor Kendell." I couldn't help laughing. "How did you think your parents got you?"

"Don't! My parents never had sex."

"Alex, your parents had three children."

"They never had sex," she insisted.

"You go with that." I rolled my eyes. "I'll go down to my place and read about your ancestor getting it on with her dashing girlfriend."

Then it happened. She ran her fingers through her hair while her eyes fluttered shut. In just a couple of weeks, I had learned that was her way of avoiding something. "I need to get some sleep," she threw out, leaving me wondering what it was she really wanted to say.

"We just drank a pot of coffee."

"Amateur."

Chapter Fourteen

After I left Alex's apartment, I cleaned up, put on my comfy clothes, and sat on my futon with the diary sitting in my lap. For a brief moment, I pondered taking the time to photocopy the pages. I was more than a little worried about damaging the diary. But that wasn't what was keeping me awake and unable to focus on my work.

Something had happened when Alex and I were talking. I just didn't know what it was. I also couldn't understand why it was extremely hard for me to leave Alex's apartment. No, not her home, it was leaving her. I would have been happy just sitting up all night talking to her.

"Come on, pull it together," I chastised myself when a knock on the door disrupted my thoughts. "Now what?" I got up and peered through the peephole. My heart skipped a beat when I spied Alex standing on the other side. I threw the door open before I stopped to think about the fact that I was wearing nothing but an oversized T-shirt and a pair of boxer shorts.

"Hi."

"Hi," she stammered slightly, holding out a glass baking dish. "Your baking dish," she nervously explained as she handed it to me.

"Thank you."

"I washed it." Again, she sounded nervous.

We just stood there in the foyer looking at each other. My mind was telling me to thank her and say good night. I couldn't. The front door opened, and Shavonne rushed in.

"Good evening," she greeted us with a knowing smile.

"Shavonne," Alex greeted her casually. "This is—"

"We've met," I interrupted with a blush. "And once again, I'm half-naked."

"What?" Alex squeaked.

"I was wearing your shirt," I feebly began, not realizing that I was just making things worse. "I mean…"

"Good seeing you again," Shavonne said with a sly grin. "Sorry I keep meeting your girlfriend this way, Alex."

"She's not…" Alex nervously began.

"Have a good night, ladies." Shavonne ignored her attempt to correct the situation. "I need to grab something to eat before my break's over."

"Come in." I tugged Alex inside while Shavonne hurried upstairs. Once inside, I realized that we were holding hands and had been when Shavonne entered the building.

"Doesn't that bother you?" she asked as I reluctantly released her hand.

"That people keep assuming I'm your girlfriend?" I turned to put the baking dish away before I crossed the room to ensure that my door was locked.

"No, that you're gay," she sounded angry. "It ticks me off when people assume I'm straight."

I turned to her, feeling completely adrift. "Are you saying that I should be bothered?"

"No. I mean, yes, maybe a little," she fumbled once again, running her fingers through her hair.

"Did I do something wrong?" I tried to look her in the eyes, yet my gaze drifted to the sight of her nipples straining against the thin material of her white cotton T-shirt. The sound of her clearing her throat alerted me to my erroneous actions. "Never mind. I think I just answered that question." I felt my body shaking. "I'm sorry." I stumbled over to the futon and flopped down.

"You have nothing to be sorry for," she tried to calm me as she tentatively sat next to me. "I'm just confused. You tell me you have a boyfriend, then we make out. You said you think sex is tedious, and that is *not* the impression I got the other night. I'm really confused—"

"You're confused?" I barked, not knowing whether to laugh or cry. "Tedious?" I repeated, thinking that the brief moments I had shared with Alex were glorious. "When did you come out?"

"Not going to answer the tedious question?" She tried to sound whimsical. I didn't know if she was trying to put me at ease or avoiding my question.

"For the first time in my life," I carefully began, "I've been looking at my life as if I hadn't lived it. For the past week, I've realized that there have been more than a few women I had obvious crushes on. Shouldn't I have questioned this before now? That's why I'm curious as to when you came out."

"Which time?"

"What do you mean?" I asked in bewilderment.

"First, there was this girl in high school," she admitted shyly. "While we were together, I came out to myself and my sister. Then after we stopped messing around, I managed to convince myself that it was just her, and I started dating this boy named Kenny."

"You're kidding?" I was shocked. Alex seemed so at ease with her sexuality.

"I have the prom pictures to prove it." She gave my shoulder a gentle nudge. "The summer after high school, he came out. Then I went out with another guy Ralph. I think he was seeing Kenny on the side. Then there was Paul, and he also turned out to be gay. Then I went to college."

"Wellesley."

"Nothing but women," she happily offered. "After half a semester of trying to convince myself that I hadn't met the right guy, I had an affair with this girl, and that was when I finally came out. To myself and my friends and family. I've been with women ever since."

"Were there many?" I asked, not really wanting to know the answer.

"Yes," she said honestly. "Before New York, I played the field. Which is funny because when I was dating guys, I managed to keep my virginity."

"That's because they were all gay." I couldn't help laughing. "And correct me if I'm wrong, but hadn't you already lost your virginity to that girl in high school?"

"True," Alex confessed. "The subconscious is an amazing thing."

"Tell me about it," I agreed with a heartfelt groan. "I'm with

135

Peter because he's safe. My father ran around on my mother, and I knew Peter would never chase after another woman. I never stopped to think that I might. Why did I never let myself see myself?"

"Are you sure about this?" Alex asked in a very serious tone. "It seems so sudden."

"It isn't." I reached out and let my hand rest on her knee. For a brief moment, she smiled, and it warmed my heart. Just as suddenly, the smile vanished, and I removed my hand.

"Stephanie…" she began as she closed her eyes once again. "I think it's great that you're coming to terms with everything …"

"But." I knew it was coming.

"But…there's still a guy out there sending his girlfriend flowers," she finished bluntly.

"I know," I grimly accepted as I stood, wanting nothing more than a little distance. "Thank you again for washing the baking dish."

"Sorry about bringing it down in the middle of the night," she said sheepishly as she stood. "I just…well, I just wanted to see you again. I'm kind of lame like that."

"It did give me a chance to flash our neighbor again," I tossed out, feeling slightly better after hearing that she wanted to see me. "I've only been in town for about a month, and already I'm getting quite a scandalous reputation."

"Just wait until we hit a carnival."

"How much trouble could I get into?" I teased, guiding her toward the door. "Never mind, don't answer that."

I opened the door. She leaned against the wall and parted her lips. I held my breath waiting for her to say something. My focus seemed to be locked on her lips. Her tongue peeked out as she wet them. I released a needy gasp and blushed the moment I realized what I had done. I stepped closer, my body tingled as I felt her lean toward me. I moved closer to her. I could feel my heart beating out of control. I never wanted to kiss anyone so badly. I felt her strong fingers caressing my cheek. I tilted my head up as she leaned down toward me. I could feel her breath on my face. I swallowed hard knowing what I wanted.

For the first time in my life, I needed to be kissed. She was so close I could feel the heat emanating off her body. I could feel my heart beating, my body tingling, then there was a loud thump. Another thump, thump, and thump. Instantly, we separated from the loud sound crashing down the staircase.

"Really?" I gritted my teeth, looking over her shoulder at the offender. "Officer Springer? Finished your dinner, did you?"

"Have the two of you moved?" she teased with a huge smile before she caught the murderous gleam in my eyes. "My bad," she blurted out before making a quick exit.

"Was she wearing combat boots?" Alex blew out.

The tender moment passed, leaving us standing there in an awkward silence. Alex blew out a terse breath before saying good night and heading back to her apartment. I watched as she ascended the staircase. The subtle sway of her hips mesmerized me. I lingered for a moment before retreating back inside my apartment.

"I hate my life." I snarled before I retreated to my bed and to the only woman I was going to be with that night—Haley Ballister. I picked up Haley's journal and started to read where I had left off. It was June 14, 1862, and the war was raging, and a young Haley had just met a beautiful woman in uniform.

***

I unbuttoned the jacket of her uniform and thanked God for sending this vision of beauty to me. I removed her jacket slowly and unbuttoned her shirt. Beneath her garments, I discovered bandages that she had wrapped tightly around her bosom. I unwrapped each one, and I felt the excitement of a child on Christmas morning. Even now as I sit here writing these words, my body tingles as I recall the sight of her nakedness standing before me. I poured a hot bath. Anna had instructed me to prepare the hot water for my special guest earlier. At the time, I had no idea just how special my guest would be.

I lowered my beauty into the bath. Her face glowed. After all that she has endured, the hot water must have felt like walking through the pearly gates. While she soaked in the warm water, I gathered up her clothing and raced down the back staircase. I gave them to Sam, one of the handymen. I paid him what little money I had to have him clean and stitch the uniform. I know that washing the uniform of a Southern officer was not a pleasure for Sam. I had to plead with him to do it. Finally, he agreed. Washing the clothing of any white man was the last thing Sam ever wanted to do again. But for me, he did it and refused to take my money. In a few days, Sam was to be heading north. I know that I'll miss him, and I was truly sorry for what I had asked him to do. But I could never tell him my true reasons why.

Upon returning to my room, I found my sweet angel just as I had left her. I washed her back and gently scrubbed her hair. With each touch, I felt my heart beating faster and faster. After bathing her, I stood beside the tub and disrobed. I stood there exposing all that I am. She smiled at the sight. I climbed into the bathtub, offering myself to her. With each touch, I could hear her pleasure. She pulled me to her body and kissed me as I had never been kissed before. As she released me, she asked me to take her to bed. How could I refuse? I obeyed without protest.

I dried off my soldier and led her to my bed. I pulled back the bedding and lowered her onto the bed. We lay together, our bodies touching. I kissed her neck and tasted the sweetness of her shoulders. I looked into her eyes and swept the hair from her face. I kissed her again and again before I asked her name. She did not answer.

"Tell me your name. Before I give myself to you, I must know who you are. Your secret will be safe with me. But I must know who has captured my heart." Never had I needed to hear anything so desperately.

"Eleanor" was all she said before taking my body.

We loved until the call of the rooster disturbed our bliss. We pulled the bedding around us and held each other tightly. Each of us knowing that this could be the last time we would ever see the other. I asked her where she had come from before finding herself here.

"We just finished outrunning the Yankees in the Shenandoah Valley. We walked for days. I thought we would never stop walking. Old Jack got us into trouble, and we had no choice but to keep moving ahead of the Yankees." I was amazed by the courage that my love possessed. Yes, I think of her as my love. Perhaps this is presumptuous of me, but I cannot help myself.

I asked her why she was pretending to be a man. She explained that Stephan was her brother and that she knew the Yankees were approaching and New Orleans would more than likely fall. Stephan had sold off everything he could not carry with him, then he ran to Florida. Eleanor thinks he may be in England by now. I was stunned. I asked how he could just leave her behind. She explained that Stephan was a coward who did not care about their home. She laughed as she told how because of her actions in battle Stephan would be remembered as a hero while everyone thinks she died in the fire that claimed the family plantation.

I had so many questions for my lady. Eleanor answered as many as she could. Before the war, she had been a school teacher in Savannah. After the incident at Fort Sumter, she returned home and continued to run slaves to the North. She had been involved with helping free slaves for many years. Home was a large plantation in New Orleans, which her brother controlled. According to Eleanor, he was a scoundrel. He had sent their parents to Newport, so he could take over the plantation in their absence. Now they were trapped in Rhode Island, and he had taken the family fortune. This bastard even tried marrying her off to an elderly neighbor. Stephan had hoped to gain control of the neighboring plantation.

When word reached New Orleans of the Yankees' approach, most of the troops left to fight with General Lee. The Southern Navy would never hold the Union Army on the Mississippi. Stephan fled, and Eleanor took his place and raced down to Natchez and joined Company D. Because of Stephan's social standing, she was made an officer. She wasn't afraid of dying, and she had killed others in battle. She was afraid of being captured or discovered. Her fear was that she could not rely on her captors to behave like gentlemen. She made it clear to me that she was not fighting because she believed in slavery. She did not. She was fighting because New Orleans was her home. She told me that even though she was a woman, she did understand that this war had nothing to do with slavery. I do not understand what she means by this.

When she left my bed this morning in her freshly pressed uniform, I was breathless. She promised to return to me if she could. Until then, I will have my memories of her touch, the sweetness of her taste, and how I held her body. Unlike Emily, this woman gave herself freely and took only what I offered. I was so taken with her that I offered her everything.

June 25, 1862

I find myself unable to perform for my guests. My only thoughts are of Eleanor. Is she safe? She promised to write, but she needed to be cautious with her words. Each day, I pray to hear something. I need some sign that my love is alive and will return to me.

August 4, 1862

More of the girls have left, as well as most of the hired hands. Still no word from Eleanor. Anna and I busy ourselves with the much-needed repairs to the house. I no longer wish to entertain gentlemen. Anna has agreed that it is time to close the business and convert the house into an inn. Our carpentry skills are lacking, and the roof will not stop leaking.

August 13, 1862

Anna has received some news. There was a battle at Cedar Mountain a few days ago. Our boys rallied, and Jackson led them to victory. Strange that I now think of the rebs as our boys. Many of the boys fell, but Anna has heard that my young sergeant is alive and well. Thank you, God! I pray for her continued safety so that someday she may come back to me. It is strange the war is all around us, yet it can take days, or sometimes weeks, for us to find out what's going on. Where are you, Eleanor?

August 15, 1862

I am truly blessed. Eleanor and her unit returned. They could not stay long. Many of them were disappointed that there were no longer women to entertain them. Anna offered them food, baths, and a dry place to sleep. This pleased the weary men. I could barely hold back when I saw Eleanor walk through the front door. I grabbed on to her and rushed her upstairs. After we made love, I returned downstairs and helped Anna care for the others. When they were finally settled down for the night, I returned to my room and Eleanor's waiting arms. What I shared with this woman was more than passion. I gave her my body, my heart, and my soul. She left me before dawn. She promised to return as soon as she could. I begged her to stay. She refused, explaining that they had a truce with the Union Army so they could bury the dead.

August 20, 1862

I praise Jesus for Anna's unknown sources. For they have set my mind at ease once again. It seems that the truce was not honored. More fighting broke out. But Eleanor's unit was not involved. They were engaged in a small skirmish elsewhere. Fortunately, it was not serious. Each day, I look out over the hills that surround this small town. I know that just over those hills somewhere is the one who has captured my heart. Each dawn, I look for her to come back to me.

***

I finally closed Haley's journal for the night. After reading everything that this woman endured so bravely and without question, I suddenly felt like a wimp. Here I sat in my comfortable home, lacking the courage to break up with my boyfriend. Disgusted with myself, I turned off my reading lamp and crawled under the covers and drifted off to sleep.

Chapter Fifteen

I walked into our office. Alex had departed quietly in the morning without her usual fanfare. I found her sitting at her desk working intently on her computer. I could smell cigarette smoke in the air. I walked over to her and gave her a knowing glare. I looked behind her file cabinet and discovered what I was seeking. There nestled behind the cabinet was a pack of Merits. Without a word, I retrieved the half pack of cigarettes and brushed past her. I cracked open the side window behind her and unceremoniously tossed the cigarettes out the window.

"Brat." She growled. "I can't believe you did that. Ah, saved by the bell," she announced when her cell rang. "Professor Kendell...What do you want?" she hissed.

I was stunned by her venomous tone. I brushed past her without bothering to comment and proceeded to my desk. I placed my briefcase on my desk while I tried not to listen to her conversation.

"That's not my problem, Chris!" she barked as I found myself suddenly very interested in the conversation. "I don't understand," I heard Alex protest. "Well, you're the lawyer, you take care of it...I know I still am, but only in the technical sense. I told you last night I'm not getting involved with this mess...It's not my problem!"

I felt guilty listening to the heated conversation. I got up and quickly made my way to the coffee station. I hung out there, hiding until I heard Alex utter a curse and slam her phone down. I wanted to give her space, so I continued to hide by the coffee maker.

"It's safe," she called out. I peeked my head into the office to ensure that she was talking to me. It seemed safe, so I strolled back in holding my coffee mug, silently asking if she wanted one. "I'm good," she answered my unspoken question. "Before you ask, I don't want to talk about it." She returned her attention to her laptop.

"Okay." I glanced at my desk. The sight of the roses made me feel queasy. I scooped them out of the vase, cracked open the smaller window on my side, and tossed them out, too. It felt oddly cathartic. Granted, the poor flowers hadn't done anything to warrant such treatment, but it felt good.

I slumped down onto the couch and adjusted the pleat of my skirt. "I missed my morning concert."

"Things to do," she said without looking up.

"I can see that."

If she didn't want to talk, I wasn't going to force her. We continued to sit in an uncomfortable silence. The only sound was the constant clanking of Alex's keyboard. It was hard for me to fathom that just the evening before, I was a hair's breadth away from kissing this woman, and this morning, I was being treated like a redheaded stepchild at a family reunion.

I sat there sipping my coffee until the typing stopped. "I can't believe you threw my cigarettes out the window." Alex finally looked up.

I laughed as she tried to intimidate me with her classic scowl. I shot her a look that said *nice try*. She just flashed me a cocky smirk.

"It's for your own good," I said calmly.

"Ladies?" Louisa chose that moment to pop into our office. "I just got off the phone with security. They've requested that we stop throwing things out the window."

"It was only a pack of smokes," Alex argued.

"And a dozen roses," I reluctantly added.

"Oh?" Alex was clearly surprised. "What did they do?"

"They were mocking me."

"Okay, then." Louisa was clearly flustered. "Can I have your word that there will be no more projectiles?" We nodded our compliance as she rolled her eyes. "If I have to talk to security again, the two of you will have a hard time accessing anything. I'm serious. You won't be able to find a coffee cup, never mind trying to access your email."

"Damn, she's pissed," Alex said after Louisa stomped off.

"What are you working on?" I asked, needing to change the subject.

"Notes for our book," Alex offered blankly as if nothing had happened between us. I didn't know if I should be angry or relieved.

"Great," I said with enthusiasm. Relief was the option I selected mainly because door number two would involve explaining why I felt a sudden need to throw flowers out a window. "So it was Eleanor, what an incredible story."

"It's going to upset people," Alex said.

"Do you care?"

"No," she said firmly. "Now that you know everything, ask me anything."

"Anything, huh?" I said before I thought better of it. There were many things I wanted to ask her, like if she could ever love me. I quickly rejected that question and decided it was safer to stick to the book. "I take it Stephan made it to England?"

"Yes," she said. "He did return briefly near the end of the war. He had changed his name to Arthur Fennamore. He sailed back when he heard that the Confederacy was certain to fall. I can only assume that he was concerned about his investments. The moment he arrived, he began to buy up property from the war widows."

"Sleazebag." I choked on my coffee. "First he runs away, then he comes back and takes advantage of those who stayed and lost everything. I mean, if he had some moral objection to the war, I could understand his leaving."

"He had no morals." Alex shook her head with disgust. "While he was hiding in England, he was selling arms to both sides. Just as everything is about to come to a close, he hopped on the first ship heading to the States. Then he buys up land dirt cheap. It gets better." Alex sneered. "While traveling through the South ripping off widows and orphans, he hears about a young sergeant from New Orleans."

"Oh, no!"

"Yes," Alex confirmed. "I don't know if it was curiosity or his oversized ego, but he decided to pay a call on the widow Ballister. Haley's diary is a little sketchy on the subject. I get the definite impression that he blackmailed her into sleeping with him. The timing was just close enough that everyone assumed that it was her husband's child."

"Nice guy." I blanched. "And Eleanor died in battle."

"No," Alex teased. "The end of the war was approaching. Eleanor sensed that the Confederacy was about to surrender, so she deserted. She was terrified of being captured."

"Since she could not rely on the Union soldiers to behave like gentlemen," I cut in, recalling the words from Haley's journal. "A great many women were discovered passing as men, and they were treated very well."

"She couldn't have known that," Alex added sadly.

"When did Eleanor and Haley get married?"

"Just after Eleanor returned from Gettysburg," Alex said. "She had been wounded. Though it wasn't serious, she became concerned that she may not live until the end of the war. They were very much in love, and Eleanor knew that by marrying Haley she could give her respectability. With one simple ceremony, Haley went from fallen woman to an officer's wife."

"Well, this certainly explains a lot," I said absently, lost in thought. The historian in me was thrilled beyond belief. "In Haley's diary, she said Mrs. Moorehouse's daughter Sarah had died in childhood. That confused me since I remembered that my earlier research led me to believe that when Mrs. Moorehouse and Haley and her son moved up North, Sarah Moorehouse had traveled with them."

"It was easy enough to pull off," Alex explained, knowing that I had figured out how Eleanor stayed with them. "After the war, everything was in upheaval with no birth or death records. While they were still in Virginia, Eleanor kept out of sight. If anyone asked, they explained that she was Sarah Moorehouse. No one in the area ever asked Mrs. Moorehouse about her past. Those who had known her before she became a prostitute knew that she had a daughter who had been sent away."

"Whatever happened to Stephan?"

"He returned to England, and from there, I have no idea what happened to him."

"I'll research that." I volunteered.

"Great," Alex said, finally sounding relaxed. "There are some more papers and Eleanor's journal at my parents' house. I'll get them when I go home for Thanksgiving, or as we call it in my family, Football Day."

"Why Football Day?"

"Because my grandmother is a Native American, and if you mention anything at all to do with the Pilgrims, she gets a little testy, and my Dad lives for football." Alex laughed.

"I can understand where she might have a problem with that," I said. "I can't believe that after all these years I finally know the truth," I said with joy, knowing that I wasn't just referring to the mystery of Stephan James Ballister. "I'm looking forward to working with you, Alex. I hope after the past few nights that we still can."

"Don't be silly," Alex said. "Sorry I was a jerk this morning, it was the phone call. It was from Chris. She called last night, as well. It seems that my old law firm is being investigated. Some of my old cases have come into question. She wants me to go down to New York and work on the case."

"Will you?" I asked, suddenly frightened by the thought of Alex leaving to work with her old flame.

"No." Alex snorted dismissively. "I'm not a lawyer. Even though I still pay my bar dues. But I only do that to keep my parents happy. The only time I practice law is when I do some pro bono work for a woman's shelter in Boston. Chris may have been a lousy girlfriend, but she's a damn good lawyer. I'm certain that she can straighten out this mess without my help. I'm not worried. I may have been a complete bastard, but I never broke the law. Bent it more than a few times but never broke it."

"What made you leave New York?"

"I—"

"If you don't want to talk about it—"

"No," she interrupted. "Like I said, I bent the law more than a few times. My firm was doing work for a big real estate developer. I was the key litigator, which was common for me at that point. The developer wanted to revamp a dilapidated neighborhood, which on paper sounds like a good thing. The only thing standing in their way was the owner of this little bodega. It was my job to clear the way by any means possible."

"What does that mean?"

"It means calling the health inspector, checking everyone's

immigration status, and looking for anything that might cause trouble." She looked sick as she explained her duties. "They were nice people, husband, wife, three kids, and the wife's father. The grandfather wasn't in the best of health and up in years and living here illegally. It would have tied up the family with litigation trying to keep the store and trying to keep Grandpa here to live out what little time he had left with his grandchildren."

"You didn't?"

"It wasn't any worse than anything I had done before," she continued, clearly ashamed of what she was saying. "But no, I didn't. I was sitting in my office knowing all I had to do was call immigration and earn a whole lot of money. I kept thinking about my parents and how ashamed of me they must be. If they were involved with this case, they'd be on the other side. It turns out that the lawyer working that side of the case was a former mentor of mine. I called her and brokered a deal. The owner of the bodega was paid a great deal of money for his shop."

"That's good."

"Not really," she grumbled. "For them, yes, but not for the dozens of other families we had already kicked to the curb. Now, instead of that nice little neighborhood shop, there's a Starbucks. The upwardly mobile types that live there now love it. And there was the little matter of the more than six figures I had just cost my firm. I finalized everything before anyone knew what I was up to and went straight to my boss's office and quit before he could fire me. I cleaned out my office and headed home to my loving partner. There were candles, takeout cartons from a very expensive restaurant, and a girl in our bed. It got really ugly, more so after I started throwing her things out the window and told her why I had come home early. I don't know what upset her more, that I had finally caught her or that I had quit my job."

"Your job and your girl all in one day. What did you do?"

"Came home," Alex said brightly. "I moved back in with Mom and Dad, went back to school, and started over again. I'm finally happy. It's amazing how your life can change so quickly. That's my sad story, or my happy story, depending on your point of view."

"I feel like such a weenie," I confessed, much to her confusion. "Compared to you, Eleanor, and Haley, I'm a complete and total weenie. I mean, Eleanor and Haley could have been beaten, jailed, or even hanged just for being in love. Here I sit all pouty because I didn't get my morning dose of Cher. It's not like you were inviting Cher over to give me a personal concert."

"Now how cool would that be?"

"I'm serious."

"So am I," she protested. "A personal concert with Cher! Oh, come on, Stephanie, you are *not* a weenie. Let's be honest, the main reason I told you my deep dark secrets was a way to avoid talking about how much of a weirdo I am for the way I acted last night. I don't know why I was possessed with an overwhelming desire to return your baking dish."

"Maybe we're both weenies?"

"Well, this weenie has a lecture to give." She closed her laptop and gathered her belongings. "I also have an overwhelming desire to chain smoke. Sadly, some wench threw my cigarettes out the window." She stopped to close the window I had left open.

Per usual, I watched her walk out of the room. I honestly did not know which I preferred more—watching her enter a room or leave it. I glanced over to my desk at the empty vase sitting there. I had indeed felt as if the hapless flowers were mocking me and my inability to do what I knew needed to be done.

Chapter Sixteen

The rest of my day went the way of the previous. All day, I fought against a gnawing in the pit of my stomach. My troubles dogged me throughout the day. First was knowing I was going to hurt Peter. Then there was the incredible way I was drawn to Alex and the painful knowledge that Alex wasn't the first or only time I had felt that way.

I found myself in my last lecture of the day, and I was not looking forward to returning home. I was about halfway through my lecture, and it was clear that my students were bored. Most of them were looking at their watches instead of the notes I was scribbling on the chalkboard. A part of me wanted to scribble an apology for boring the crap out of them when I saw a familiar face hiding in the back of the lecture hall with her head resting in her hand.

"Am I keeping you awake, Professor Kendell?" I boldly asked, much to the surprise of my students.

They turned, surprised by my outburst. Many of them sought out Alex. Most seemed amused by her presence. After all, Alex was one of the most popular instructors on campus. She just flashed that cocky grin of hers in my direction.

"So, Professor Kendell, what's your opinion of the Free Masons?" I challenged. No way was I letting her off the hook.

"A bunch of white guys creating a secret society?" She had the bad manners to yawn. "What is so special about that?"

"Oh, man," I heard Vince sputter, one of the few faces I knew. "This is going to get weird."

The look on my face must have been priceless. *Is she challenging me? The nerve of this woman.* I was possessed with an overwhelming desire to kick Alex Kendell's arrogant ass.

"Tell me, Dr. Grant, why do you find this subject interesting?"

She was challenging me! I could not believe the nerve of this woman coming into my classroom and challenging me in front of my students. Based on the shocked expression my students were sporting, they couldn't believe it, either. Then she did it, she had the bad manners to flash that cocky smirk that I was becoming accustomed to. That did it. There was no way on God's green earth I was going to allow her to get the better of me.

I squared my shoulders. Glaring at her, I prepared for battle. "Well, Professor Kendell, since you are so interested in the subject, allow me to enlighten you." Full of fire, I began, fully prepared to let her have it with both barrels. "The very beginnings of this country were formed by Free Masons. If I'm not mistaken, some of them are your ancestors. The Free Masons started out with very noble ideals. Today, the organization tries to reflect these ideals and offers a more inclusive membership. In the beginning, the structure of the society was very exclusive. Not intentionally, but when you form a secret society, these things happen. They drew the guild practices from the medieval stonemasons. The first Grand Lodge was organized in London in 1717. During the American Revolution, the Masons were active in the Revolution and continued as a force in later politics. George Washington is known to have been a member of the society, along with Benjamin Franklin. It's rumored that Washington's life was spared during the war when the British discovered he was a mason."

"And?"

That did it, I began reciting every interesting fact I knew about the Masons, some of which did not shed a positive light on the organization. I spoke about the intricacies and history of the Free Masons and the rumors. For the first time in my teaching career, my students were asking questions. When it came time to dismiss the class, many students approached me with more questions. I gave them some references and explained that I didn't want to get too far ahead on the first day. Some of them seemed disappointed and wanted to know more about the infamous murder I had mentioned.

Finally, I managed to clear the classroom. I approached Alex, who was still sitting in the back looking very pleased with herself.

"For the first time in my teaching career, my students were

paying attention, and not because the final was coming up. Thank you."

"You love what you teach," Alex offered. "They don't need to love it, as well. Just let them see why you do." She placed her hand over her heart. "Make it personal, teach from here."

"I don't know how I can thank you."

"Buy me dinner," she eagerly suggested.

"I just made you dinner last night," I pretended to fuss.

"Oh, did you want me to cook?"

"No, thank you," I blurted out, slightly terrified by the offer. "I'm buying you dinner, just name the place. I've already seen the Jade Garden and the ice cream place. What's left?"

"Sadly, very little. We want to avoid the burger joint and not just because I don't eat red meat," she began.

"Not any good?"

"It's good." She chuckled. "However, it's the first week of classes and rush week, the place will be packed with students. I love the little darlings but not enough to endure waiting at least an hour to be seated in a noisy diner. There's a Greek place that's amazing and a little more upscale, which keeps the students at bay most of the time. They have an excellent wine list and a vegetarian moussaka that is to die for. It's also close enough to walk to."

"Everything is."

***

The food at Athena's was amazing. By the time we finished a shared order of baklava, I was ready to explode. Over dinner, we talked nonstop about everything. I was mesmerized by everything Alex had to say. I found myself staring at her neck and the slight hint of cleavage her blouse exposed. Alex had unlocked so many doors for me.

Walking home was a welcomed experience. Thankfully, Alex hadn't driven to work that day. Between the food and a few glasses of wine, the evening stroll in the crisp autumn air was just what I needed. Paying close attention to the path ahead helped me not stare at Alex and her cleavage. It did nothing to stop me from thinking about her cleavage and various other parts of her anatomy.

"I think you're right," she said, her rich voice disrupting my lurid thoughts.

"Of course I am," I said, shifting the shoulder strap of my briefcase. "Just out of curiosity, what am I right about?"

"Eleanor and Haley," she said. "They really were heroic on so many levels. Everything they had to endure didn't seem overwhelming to them. I freak out if my cable goes out."

"I'm sure you do." I couldn't resist teasing her. "But you're right, their story is amazing. Such an incredible love story. I'm humbled to be able to tell it. Strange, really, theirs is probably the most romantic story I've ever heard."

"Why is it strange? Because they're women?"

"No." I stopped walking. Thankfully, she did, as well. She turned to me, capturing me in a smoldering gaze. "Strange because of the timing. If I had read their story when I first tried to, I might have just shrugged off the details as interesting. Now…"

"Now?" she eagerly prodded.

I stood there trying to organize my thoughts and tumultuous emotions. To her credit, Alex stood there patiently waiting. "Now…" I carefully began, only to have my words cut off by the quick blare of a police siren. The both of us jumped, turning to find a very amused Shavonne waving to us. "I'm beginning to hate her."

***

The following day, I completed the first week of classes and felt amazing. I was teaching, not just informing my students of the facts as we know them. I knew I had Alex to thank. In fact, I did try to thank her. She shrugged it off while playing with what appeared to be a Barbie.

"Okay, what's with the doll?"

"It's Wonder Woman," she beamed, turning it around so I could see it.

"I can see that."

"It's for one of my lectures today."

"Uh-huh?" I stood there stupefied. "Which class?"

"American history." She shrugged as if that explained everything. "The history of the United States post World War II."

"So why the doll?"

"Have you read the Wonder Woman comics or any comic book?" She held up the doll once again.

"No."

"Of course not." She shook the doll again. "I'm adding that to the list."

"The list?"

"The list of things you missed." She twirled her doll. "DC Comics introduced Wonder Woman in 1941. She was created by William Moulton Marston, a psychologist, lawyer, and inventor. Wonder Woman, aka Diana Prince, was kickass fighting evil alongside the likes of Batman. Until the war ended and Marston died. Then she was relegated to fighting for the lovelorn. In some episodes, she actually worked as an advice columnist. It was all about girlie things, and of course, Steve Trevor, her love interest. Women worked during the war, then it was over, and they were told it was their duty to go home, make babies, and clean the house. In the fifties, the Comics Code Authority was under fire by Fredric Wertham, who was convinced that there was a direct link between comic books and juvenile delinquency. He felt that Wonder Woman, who at one time fought for other women and hung out with all of her female friends back on Paradise Island, promoted lesbianism. So she turned into a bigger femme until she was on the cover of the very first issue of Ms. Magazine. The feminists who used her iconic image weren't aware of her transformation. In fact, by the seventies, she no longer had any powers and ran a boutique. Occasionally, she went off on a mission, very Cold War inspired. Thanks to Gloria Steinem and others lobbying, she got her powers back and returned to her former kickass glory. Forever securing her place as a feminist icon."

"Wonder Woman is a media reflection on women's roles in society from the war to today." I was truly impressed. "I don't get how people thought just because Wonder Woman fought for and empowered other women that she was a lesbian. It also doesn't explain the dolls you're hiding back there."

"That one," she pointed to a blond doll. "That is Jamie Summers." I just stared blankly at her, not having the slightest clue as to who she was talking about. "The Bionic Woman, then we have Xena, Buffy, no wait, that's Faith. Buffy is the blonde next to her. I'm using them in future lectures. Not Faith, she's just cool."

"Interesting," I praised her. "Who knew comic books could

actually be educational? Just out of curiosity, these are your own personal dolls, aren't they?"

"Maybe. I need to get to class." She blushed, shoving Wonder Woman in her briefcase.

"That's what I thought," I quipped as my phone rang. "Dr. Grant," I greeted the caller. My stomach churned when I heard Peter's voice. "Hi." My body stiffened as I returned his greeting. He began to ramble on, enthusiastically asking me questions. I kept my responses to two words or less, until he informed me that he was unable to come for a visit as we had planned.

"What do you mean you can't come up?" I blurted out before I could stop myself.

I didn't listen to his explanation, only catching that he had a project that needed to be worked on. I was far too busy watching Alex stomp out of our office. "No, that's okay," I finally managed to utter, feeling like a horrible person. The feeling only grew after I hung up. Poor Peter, he had kept apologizing for canceling, not realizing that I wanted to see him in person so I could end our relationship.

***

A week later, I returned to our office after teaching one of my classes. Alex wasn't there; instead, I walked in to find a woman searching the contents of Alex's desk. My first instinct was to grab the still empty vase on my desk and try to use it as some form of protection. Instead, I opted to find out who she was first. After all, this was a college campus. I held serious doubts that a nefarious character slipped by Louisa.

"Hello?"

Her head jerked, and I was greeted by a familiar smile and cocky grin. "You're not Stan," she coyly observed.

"What was your first clue?" I couldn't resist playing along.

"No bow tie, and you have much nicer legs."

"Ah, that Kendell charm." I sighed.

"What can I say?" Nicole continued to tease me.

As she stood, I noticed that Nicole was a few inches shorter than her sister. "Why do I get the feeling that when the two of you were growing up, nobody's sons or daughters were safe?" She just laughed at my assessment. "Stephanie Grant." I extended my hand, knowing that the chances of her remembering our first encounter were slim to none.

Nicole accepted my hand. "Nicole Kendell, but you already knew that," she added in a questioning tone.

"We crossed paths years ago," I said hesitantly.

"Oh, dear, what did I do?"

"How do you know you did anything?"

"Law of averages," Nicole said flatly. "Come on, fill me in on just how big of a jackass I was. Use specifics. To be perfectly honest, most of the nineties are a bit of a blur."

I was more than a bit surprised by this woman's candor. "Well..." I stammered. "We had a lunch meeting. You pretty much drank your way through it, then stuck me with the check."

"Sorry, that really doesn't narrow it down for me." She shrugged. "Tell me, princess, there's more, isn't there?"

"It's not important."

"Why do I doubt that? Thing is, I take my steps very seriously," Nicole added. "One of the twelve steps is that I need to apologize for the transgressions I committed while I was drinking. Needless to say, I've been extremely surprised that no one set me on fire. What did I do?"

"You agreed to arrange a meeting with your sister so I could view the Ballister diary."

"I what? Seriously?" She was shocked before she seemed to think about what I had said. "No, I did—. I kind of remember you. I excused myself to call Alex under the guise of setting the meeting up."

"Yes."

"Yeah, what I really did was hit the bar again." She cringed. "Banged back at least two more drinks, added them to your tab. Alex must have been pissed when you showed up."

"To say the least."

"I am so sorry," she said sincerely. "Given Alex's personality back then, she would have eaten her young. I vaguely recall that you were a student of some sort. How much?"

"How much?" I repeated, feeling as if I had missed something. In many ways, it was like having a conversation with her sister. The difference being that I wasn't thoroughly enthralled by her.

"The bill," she clarified with a warm smile. "I set you up and took your money. For which I am truly sorry. So how much was the bill?"

"I don't remember. Besides, it's water under the bridge," I attempted to brush it off.

"More like gin under the bridge," Nicole countered with a smirk. "I don't want to make you uncomfortable. I'm a drunk, and I've spent far too many years behaving like an entitled asshole. Now that I'm sober, I would like to at least try to make amends."

"I appreciate that," I said warmly, noting that this was definitely a different woman than the one I had met almost a decade ago. "Your apology is more than enough. I am curious as to why you're ransacking your sister's desk."

"I need a smoke or three," Nicole said as she resumed her search. "What can I say? I traded one vice for another. I had the train ride from hell on the way up here. There was this kid behind me who only stopped coughing and sneezing long enough to kick the back of my seat. His mother was too preoccupied with chatting on her cell to notice him or his screaming sister. I swear, that family follows me everywhere."

She was so much like her sister, I couldn't help but smile. "I hate to be the one to break it to you, Alex is trying to quit smoking."

"Yeah, yeah." Nicole snorted with amusement. "I'm very familiar with how the Amazon tries to quit smoking. She always keeps a pack hidden away for emergencies."

"Oh? Umm…she did have a pack tucked behind the file cabinet." I grimaced, recalling my actions the week before. "Sadly, they met with an unfortunate accident."

"Get away from my desk." Alex's voice boomed from the doorway.

"Whatever, Amazon." Nicole grunted at her approaching sibling. "Where are your cigarettes?"

"Someone threw them out the window." Alex growled as she cast an accusing glance in my direction.

"Seriously? Got her trained already." Nicole snickered. "Good for you! Don't you take any crap from the Amazon here.

Sometimes, she is just too butch for her own good."

"Nikki, stop," Alex cautioned. "We're colleagues, that's all."

"Right." Nicole waved her off. "She threw your cigarettes out the window and is still breathing. If that's not lo—"

"Nicole!" Alex shouted, holding up her hand. "Let it go."

"What? I'm wrong?"

"Yes, per usual, you're wrong."

"*Quelle dommage.*" Nicole cast a sad glance at Alex.

"Oh, good now I'm going to need subtitles," I blew out heading toward my desk, finally knowing who Alex had been speaking French to on the phone.

"No, that would be rude of us," Nicole said. "Alex is buying me lunch, why don't you join us? We're going to need to stop and buy cigarettes."

"No!" Alex blurted out.

"But I really need a smoke," Nicole whimpered.

"Yes, on the smokes." Alex groaned, running her fingers through her hair.

"Oh, my God, you're playing with your hair. This can't be good."

"Nicole, I asked you to visit so I could discuss something with you," Alex said, looking suddenly embarrassed.

"Okay," Nicole began slowly. "So you want to talk about Stephanie when she isn't in the room?"

"*Couillon!*" Alex spit out.

Nicole's jaw dropped. "I'm telling Mom," she threatened with a wag of her finger. "Stephanie, it was a pleasure meeting you. I'm sure we'll meet again." Alex started to push Nicole toward the doorway. "Hold on, Alex." She slapped her away. "Stephanie, I want to apologize again for what I did to you before."

"What did you do now?" Alex flared angrily.

"I'll tell you at lunch, now feed me," Nicole demanded. "Hey, you're the one that sent me a text saying you needed to see me."

I watched them arguing their way out of the doorway. They exchanged a few more phrases in French, which I was quite certain should not be translated in public.

"Their mother must have the patience of a saint. Maybe the brother is normal."

***

Later that evening, I returned home alone. Just as I stepped up onto the porch, I could hear the Kendell sisters bantering just outside of Alex's apartment door. I was quickly learning that the odd echo in our building could be very educational.

"Nicole, did you listen to anything I said at lunch today?" Alex's voice rang out in frustration.

"Yes," Nicole said calmly. "Did you?"

"What is that supposed to mean?"

"I let you rant and rave about this tired-ass list you have for why you should stay away. Frankly, if you believed any of it, you wouldn't need to keep saying it. I would like to add that maybe you need to have an operation to remove that stick that is so firmly shoved up your—"

"Nicole!"

"The truth hurts," Nicole added gently. "Alex, I love you, but you're driving yourself insane over this. I listened to all your excuses. I also saw the way you looked at the girl."

"News flash, little sister. I'm a lesbian, she's an attractive woman. I checked her out. Big surprise!" Alex argued.

"That wasn't lust I saw in your eyes," Nicole countered. "Well, not just lust. You're very lucky she had her back to you when you entered the room. I never thought I would see you look at someone like that. I'm happy for you. Why can't you allow yourself to be happy, too? I understand your track record hasn't been great."

"Better than yours," Alex shot back.

"Liz Taylor had a better track record than I do," Nicole teased. "Of course, she was married fewer times than I was. Stop taking care of everyone but yourself. You have worked so damn hard to get to this point in your life. Take the next step. She isn't Chris or Jessica, and she's certainly not Brenda, and honestly, not one of those bitches deserved you. I like this girl, and so do you."

I was touched by Nicole's endorsement. Granted, I was only assuming that it was me they were discussing. I became uncomfortably aware that I was once again eavesdropping. I stepped into the hallway and made my presence known.

"Hi," I called out sheepishly to the approaching pair.

"Hi," Nicole said in a surprised tone.

"Hey, are you just getting home?" Alex asked, seemingly nervous.

"Wait, you live here?" Nicole laughed uncontrollably until Alex jabbed her with her elbow. "What? You going to call me a filthy name again?"

Alex held up a finger in warning, effectively silencing Nicole. "I'm going to drive this idiot to the train station," Alex said. "Unless you want to change your mind and let me drive you home."

"The train is fine."

"You know, if you let me help you get your driver's license back, you wouldn't need to take the train," Alex pushed.

"I don't know," Nicole began hesitantly. "That judge was very clear that he would see to it that the commonwealth would never grant me another driver's license while I was still breathing. At least I think that's what he said. I was pretty loaded during my hearing."

"I'm sorry I missed that one." Alex groaned.

"Well, my DUI hearings were like my weddings. If you missed one, you could always catch the next one."

"Nikki..." Alex began sadly.

"Hey, I need to face what I did." Nicole suddenly looked much older than her sister. "You can't save me. I'm the only one who can. This is the way the program works."

"I hate it," Alex grumbled.

"I know." Nicole sighed. "Now if we're done sharing with the neighbors, I have a train to catch."

"Come on," Alex conceded.

"Bye, Stephanie," Nicole addressed me. Then she pulled me aside and whispered, "Good luck. Just remember she isn't as strong as she thinks she is."

"Thanks," I whispered in response as she pulled away. Alex looked at us suspiciously. "Come on," Nicole ordered.

I watched the siblings bickering as they strolled over to Alex's car. Suddenly, I was relieved that I had been an only child. I don't think I could have survived that kind of stress on a day-to-day basis. Two things were clear. One was that deep down, Alex and Nicole adored each other. The other was that Nicole was definitely in my corner. The only question was...would Alex listen to her and who in the hell was Brenda? I was exhausted. Normally, I would have waited for Alex's return. That night, I thought she might need time alone. I showered and put on my favorite flannel pajamas and crawled into bed. I was fast asleep before I knew it. Like most nights since moving into my studio, my dreams revolved around Alex.

Chapter Seventeen

September passed slowly, and with autumn approaching, the leaves were turning. Fall in New England—there was nothing else like it in the world. You could smell the changing of the season in the air. It would soon be October, and I had been working side by side with Alex mostly in silence. That was when she was there. Most times I'd come into the office, she'd greet me, then within a few moments, her cellphone would ring, and she'd excuse herself and disappear for the rest of the day. I tried to engage her at work or at home. Every time she would open up, she would retreat further back. I knew that a part of it was that I had yet to break up with Peter.

I made plans with him, even told him that there was something important I needed to talk to him about. It never happened. The project he was working on was do or die. Apparently, there was a breach at his company, which was incredibly bad since his company designed firewalls. They needed to fix the problem, find the source, and ensure that it never happened again, all the while needing to keep it quiet. Needless to say, he needed to work or lose his job.

I felt horrible knowing that I was trying to schedule time with him so I could dump him. How do you break someone's heart while he's trying to save his career? To make matters worse, he kept apologizing for not getting together with me. He was worried about his future and me. I was trying to figure who I was.

It was the weekend, and I was alone. Alex had been absent over the past couple of weekends. I missed her. I did manage to keep myself busy with laundry, work on the book, and cooking. I was in the middle of baking an apple pie, which I had hoped to take up to Alex. That was until I realized that she had taken off Friday night. It was early Sunday, and she was still away.

It bothered me that she wasn't around. It bothered me more that I was focused on why she wasn't around. I just couldn't help wondering if there was someone she was meeting. I kept reminding myself that it was none of my business. I rolled out my dough, perhaps a little too roughly. Disgusted, I started over again.

"Come on, Stephanie, the pie didn't do anything," I chided myself. I floured the counter again in preparation to roll out another crust. A knock on the door startled me. Thinking it might be Alex, I rushed over with my hands covered with flour. I flung open the door without bothering to check to see who it was. "Hal?" My voice dripped with disappointment. "Sorry," I quickly apologized. My eyes widened as I took in his appearance.

Before me stood a six-foot, middle-aged man clad in a flowery housecoat and fluffy slippers. "Come in," I offered, unable to tear my gaze from the sight. I knew that Hal was a cross dresser, I just hadn't seen him wearing anything other than men's clothing.

"I'm a mess, I know," he said with a shy smile. "I hate to disturb you this early on a Sunday. I'm making dinner for an amazing woman I met in my Aikido class. Do you by any chance have cinnamon?"

"You're in luck." I smiled as I closed the door. "I'm in the middle of baking some pies, and I just finished with the cinnamon. What level are you at?"

"With Julie?" he teased as I handed him the tin of cinnamon. "Early days."

"Actually, I meant your Aikido."

"I earned my black belt last spring," he said shyly. "When you parade around in women's clothing, it's best to have a skill. Although living here has been glorious, my last apartment was a tad close to fraternity row. Now I live in a nice house with three lesbians. I'm the luckiest girl in the world."

"Shavonne's gay?" I asked, not feeling a need to correct him regarding my sexuality. Then again, I wasn't entirely certain he was wrong.

"Oh, yes," he said. "Thank you again." He held up the tin. "I knew not to try Alex since I never see her carrying groceries, but I've seen every restaurant in town delivering food to her door."

"I don't think she's home," I muttered. "But you're right about her lack of skills in the kitchen."

"That's our Alex." He chuckled as we made our way to the door. "On the weekends, she is either out the door before the sun is up or locked up throwing herself a movie marathon. I can hear her talking back to her television."

"Why does that not surprise me?"

"Stephanie, may I ask you something?"

"Sure."

"Are you and Alex—"

"No," I tersely cut him off. "We're just colleagues."

"Oh? I thought you might be together, but then with you living down here and her up there, it didn't make sense. Then again, Mrs. G doesn't rent to unmarried couples. I hope I haven't offended you."

"No, I've been getting that a lot lately."

"The two of you do seem to have a connection," he said. "I need to go. I still need to start on my dinner preparations. Not to mention that it will take me hours to make myself pretty."

"Have fun tonight," I said as he made his departure.

I pondered Hal's situation for a moment. He liked to dress as a woman, but he was straight. Oddly enough, I found his life far less complicated than my own. In need of a distraction, I went back to my pies. I ended up baking three in all. One I would keep, one I left with a note outside of Alex's door, and the last one I decided to take to work the next morning.

"Now what?" I groaned after I had left the pie for Alex. I wished that I owned a glass pie plate so Alex would have an excuse to come visit me when she got in. I stood there looking around my home. The studio was comfortable, more comfortable than anywhere else I had ever lived. So why was I on edge? "There is the little matter of being thirty and just realizing that I'm gay." I felt light-headed making the admission.

I wandered into the bathroom and splashed my face with cold water. I stood there looking at my reflection in the mirror. "Would that be so awful?" I asked myself as my heart raced. "I'm a lesbian," I told my image. Something happened in that moment. I knew what I had just told myself was the truth, and I hadn't changed. Nothing terrible happened, the sky didn't fall, and I hadn't imploded. I stood there for a moment longer as I contemplated my next step.

"How does one leave their longtime boyfriend because they've come to terms with their latent homosexuality? I don't think Hallmark has a card for this one."

Peter was one hurdle I was facing, then there was, of course, my overwhelming attraction to Alex. Since the night of the tequila-inspired groping, I found that I was noticing women. It hadn't taken me long to realize that I had been noticing women my entire life. Which brought me back to Alex. I hadn't simply noticed her, I was filled with a constant need to be near her.

"Okay, food shopping, laundry, baking pies, and coming out of the closet. Whatever shall I do with the rest of my weekend?" I pondered out loud as I also wondered just when it was I began talking to myself. I glanced at the television Alex had loaned me and quickly dismissed the idea of spending my Sunday watching something mindless. Left with only one option, I picked up Haley's diary.

I had finished reading it a couple of weeks ago. Still I found myself rereading Haley's words.

Her life with Eleanor was captivating. Eleanor had served bravely at Gettysburg, and after being wounded, the two married. A bold decision but one that did provide Haley with respectability. They saw little of each other during the war, but each time was memorable. As I read of their endless devotion and love, it would fill me with desire. I often found myself lying awake at night wondering what would happen if I dared to climb up the staircase to Alex's door. Would she be there with open arms or would she slam the door in my face?

I thought it didn't matter since Alex seemed determined not to be near me if she could avoid it. I spread out my notes and opened the diary, determined to get work done. I always found the passages from Gettysburg enthralling, so I settled in and began with those.

***

July 4, 1863

We have received word of a bloody battle on a farm in Pennsylvania. Many lives were lost to the Union and Confederacy. I sit here and wait for some word. All I know is that Eleanor's unit was involved. Please, God, let my love come home to me.

July 7, 1863

Still no word. Mrs. Whitman, who has the farm down the road, has received word that her boy Beau has fallen. He was all she had left, and Anna has offered for her to come and stay at the inn until she can reach her sister in Richmond. Where are you, Eleanor? The waiting is driving me mad.

July 8, 1863

Panic filled my heart when there was a knock on the back door last evening. I have learned that no good news comes at that hour of the evening. This time, I was mistaken. There she stood, her arm wrapped in a sling. Eleanor is alive and well. Her wound, thank the good Lord, is not serious. She feared being exposed more than the bullet that grazed her shoulder. In Mrs. Whitman's presence, Eleanor was kind enough to keep up her charade. Mrs. Whitman doted on the poor girl. When we were finally alone, she told me what she could of the events in Gettysburg. I was horrified as she explained that the smell of blood was everywhere. Eleanor claimed that it filled the earth and the air. She feels that the smell will haunt her for the rest of her days. I begged her to stay with me. Once again, she refused. She could not abandon her men now that they had lost so much. She tells me that I cannot imagine the horrors they witnessed with the coming of each dawn. I knew that the words she spoke were the truth. I could never understand what she has seen. For three days, Eleanor and the others that endured the battle vowed that they would continue to fight until the war was over.

I could still see love and warmth in her blue eyes, yet now they are clouded with sadness, as well. Then she asked me to grant her a favor. I agreed without asking what it was. She smiled and asked me for my hand. I was confused. How could we?

"Marry me," she insisted. Eleanor calmed my fears by explaining that with the exception of Mrs. Moorehouse, the world outside thought of her as a man. No one will question our marriage. "Marry me, and I promise that I will return to you. I promise that we'll both live to be very old and die in each other's embrace long after this century has past."

How could I refuse her? We were wed this very morning. Our neighbors came out to witness our union as old Reverend Stamford gave us his blessing. One of the ladies from town was kind enough to allow me to wear her wedding gown. She explained that she had no daughters to pass it along to, and she could not think of anyone finer to wear it. Strange how war changes things. Not more than a year ago, these same people all but shunned me. I must admit that Eleanor in her freshly pressed dress uniform and I all in virginal white made a striking couple. After dancing into the late hours of the evening, we went up to our room and began our honeymoon. With my neighbor's blessings, I took this wonderful woman to my bed.

***

I sighed deeply as I wondered what Haley's neighbors would have said if they knew the truth. In one brief moment, Haley was transformed from fallen woman to the wife of a prominent New Orleans gentleman. I almost wept as I read her words. I prayed for the day that I would promise the woman I loved that I would grow old with her and would only leave her side when I departed from this earthly plane. I flipped through the journal until I found another set of passages I was fond of. These events occurred a few year later.

***

April 4, 1865
Petersburg and Richmond have fallen! It is unthinkable. The Yankees are approaching, and there is no word from my beloved. I saw her briefly a few weeks ago. There is something else troubling me. A man has arrived in town by the name of Fennamore. I don't like him. He is an unsavory Englishman who has been buying everything he can get his hands on. He has been asking a great many questions regarding my husband, as well. He frightens me. He also seems strangely familiar. Is he one of the many faceless gentlemen I entertained in the past? I will do my earnest to stay away from him, which is difficult since he has taken up lodging here. Anna is keeping a watchful eye on him.

April 5, 1865
It is with a heavy heart that I write these words...my love has

died in battle. A cannon ball ripped her poor body apart. A blessing I am told since it is unlikely that she suffered as life passed from her. I am thankful for this and that the manner of her death made it impossible for her true identity to be discovered. But how could she leave me? How dare you break your promise to me, Eleanor? You promised me that we would grow old together. I am forced to wait to join you, and I am tempted to cut my time away from you short. Something is holding me back from joining you, my beloved.

April 6, 1865

Shame has befallen me. Mr. Fennamore was not who he pretended to be. He is in fact the real Stephan James Ballister. He confronted me only hours after hearing of my beloved's death. He laughed at the thought that someone had died a hero's death for him. Then he joked that he should thank the chap. Then he...I cannot say what he did. I regret that I allowed him to be alone with me. Stephan is not the gentleman his sister is. To protect her memory, I gave into this snake's blackmail. When he finished his business—rather quickly, I might add, proving that he is certainly not the lover his sister is, either—he informed me that it was an adequate down payment.

"Burn in hell" were my only words to him. He just laughed cruelly.

His laughter was cut short as my bedroom door crashed open. Stephan was dragged from the bed and slammed onto the floor. A boot was planted firmly across his throat, and a pistol placed against his temple. "Still chasing after my women, are you, Stephan!" a familiar voice growled. I do not recall who was more shocked, me or the unfortunate Mr. Ballister. He trembled and begged for his life. "Still the coward?" Eleanor scoffed as she ordered him to leave. He left with his life and a promise that if he ever came near Eleanor's family again, she would be feeding his sorry carcass to her dogs. She dragged her brother from my room without ever glancing at me.

April 7, 1865

I did not sleep. I waited for her to return, but she did not. My only companion is my journal. Finally, Eleanor came back. She greeted me wearing one of Anna's old dresses. I tried to explain everything to her and begged for her forgiveness. But she silenced me with a kiss. "I trust you, and I know him. You did nothing wrong, this I know in my heart." How could she forgive me so easily? I looked into her eyes for what seemed like an eternity. Finally, I raised the two questions that plagued my thoughts—how is it that she is alive and why was she wearing a dress? She laughed at my curiosity over her attire. Then she explained that the war was over and the South was finished. She could not risk capture, so she boldly exposed herself to Jack Hammstead, her corporal. After he recovered from the shock, he helped her run away and faked her death in such a manner that no one would ever know the truth.

During the night, she and Anna cooked up a scheme. Anna was out spreading the news that her daughter, who had been living abroad, somehow made it through enemy lines and rejoined her. They both agreed that Eleanor would take Sarah's name and stay close to the inn away from prying eyes.

My love kept her promise, and I know that we will be together always. Although in some way, I am going to miss that uniform. God has smiled upon this lost soul.

***

It amazed me how much these two women truly loved each other. How dangerous it must have been for them. Every waking moment threatened them with exposure. After the Ku Klux Klan began to make its presence known, they decided it was time to leave. Along with their young son and Mrs. Moorehouse, they made their way to Boston, then traveled north. Finally, they settled in Salem, Massachusetts, where they opened a small inn. There they lived out the rest of their lives. Eleanor was finally free to go outside and into town. They lived happily until the day Eleanor finally did break her promise to Haley. In the winter of 1899, she died. The war had left many scars on her body and mind. Haley forgave her for leaving her far too soon. Haley lived out her remaining days, as she put it, "with the memories of the sweetest love anyone could have known. She left me, but she will always be with me."

Chapter Eighteen

"No dolls?" I greeted Alex as I entered our office a couple of weeks later.

"Oddly enough, they don't make a set for the Bay of Pigs," she quipped while she typed. "Or do they?" She stopped typing and looked up.

"Really?" I gaped at her. "You know what, they probably do. Paulette Kwan is very impressed with our book," I took a seat on the sofa.

"That's great." She perked up. "Who is Paulette Kwan?"

"My editor," I offered, secretly thrilled that she was smiling. "My publisher wants to offer us a contract, providing we can get a first draft to them by the end of the year."

"When did this happen, and why didn't you tell me?"

"I haven't seen you," I bluntly told her. "Not here, not home. Did I do something wrong?"

"No," she sputtered. "I'm sorry, it's the kerfuffle at my old law firm. The problem isn't going away as quickly as I had hoped it would. When I'm here, I'm stuck texting and emailing Chris constantly. I've had to fly down to New York every weekend. It's making me crazy. Why didn't you text me about the book? Oh, sorry, I forgot you don't have a cell. How is that possible? Did I thank you for the pie?"

"How much coffee have you had today?"

"Just a pot or two."

"It's not even eight in the morning."

"How are your classes going?" She ignored my concerns.

"Great, thanks to you." I blinked as she began tapping her fingers against her desk. "You were right, all I needed to do was show why I loved what I teach. When was the last time you slept?"

She scrunched up her face, "Well, I got in late last night."

"Didn't you sleep on the flight?"

"No, I like sleeping when I fly." She yawned. "Sadly, it is not so joyous for my fellow travelers. I snore. Apparently, really loudly."

"I didn't notice," I confessed, taking in her ragged appearance. "Then again, I'm fairly certain we passed out that night."

"I've been told that it's disturbing." Alex yawned again as I listened to an odd noise going on just outside our office.

"Martha Dayton is your TA, isn't she?" I asked, ignoring the noise. "You should let her cover your lectures today and go home. You need sleep."

"I'm fine," she lied, her head drooping slightly. Just as the words came out of her mouth, her cellphone chimed. I recognized the tune, it was the same one that had been driving her out of the office for the past couple of weeks. "Damn, that's Chris again." She growled, picking up the phone.

"Is that the theme for the Wicked Witch from *The Wizard of Oz*?" I reached over in an attempt to grab her phone.

"Yes." She giggled, jerking the phone out of my reach.

"Don't answer it," I pleaded as I stood and leaned over, taking the phone from her grasp. Thankfully, she was sleep-deprived and didn't put up much of a fight.

"I need to take that call."

"No, you don't," I argued, tucking her phone in the pocket of my blazer. "What you need is sleep."

"Stephanie," she whined, which I ignored, making my way toward my desk. "Gimme," she demanded, her hands grabbing at my blazer.

"You need—" I turned toward her in an effort to deflect her hands. My words were cut off as her search became more persistent. Her hands slipped beneath my blazer, tickling my ribs. "Stop." I laughed as she guided my body against the desk. I gasped when her roaming hands brushed against the swell of my breast. "It's not there," I panted, her body pressing against my own.

I was lying slightly on top on my desk while her search turned to tickling. "Stop." I laughed, squirming against her body. My senses were on overload as I secretly enjoyed her search. I pushed against her, not hard enough to get her off of me. Her hands glided along my torso, and my hips thrust forward. I hadn't meant to do it, yet my body had other ideas.

"I need my phone," she hotly purred into my ear, sending delightful shivers down my spine. I wanted to respond, but words failed me. Instead, I planted my hands on her hips.

She moved slightly, and her thigh slipped between my legs. I forgot why we were wrestling as she tilted her head. The smoldering look in her eyes left me breathless. My heart hammered against my chest as she inched closer.

At that moment in time, nothing mattered until the sound of the phone on my desk chose that moment to ring. "Ugh." I growled. My hand slipped from her body and reached out.

"If I can't answer mine," she taunted, reaching out to stop me.

"Stop it." I giggled, managing to grasp the receiver. "Dr. Grant," I panted while Alex tried to search my body. I gasped, my body reacting to her touch.

"Stephanie?" I heard him say, his voice filled with confusion.

I froze for a moment before I could make an effort to greet him. "Hello," I said with a hard swallow as Alex ceased her exploration. "I'm sorry, what did you say?" I stammered, realizing that Peter had been talking.

"Tell *him* I said hi." Alex sneered, climbing off of me.

I was only half listening as I watched Alex storm out of the office. "This isn't a good time," I interrupted whatever he was saying. I froze when I heard a bloodcurdling scream. "I have to go!" I shouted into the receiver before slamming it down. I jumped off the desk and dashed out of the room.

Maureen was standing there pleading for Alex to calm down. Alex just stood there pointing at the coffee station. I looked down and instantly understood what was going on. The condiments and mugs were sitting in their usual place. However, the coffeemaker, pots, and coffee were notably absent.

"Alex, just take a breath," Maureen tried to reason with her.

"Gone," Alex choked out, looking as if she was going to cry.

"Maureen?" I looked to her for help as I wrapped an arm around Alex's waist.

"We're replacing the old pots with a Keurig," Maureen explained. "I know it was voted down for environmental reasons, but it will be cleaner and more cost-efficient."

"See," I said slowly, fearful that I might startle her. "The coffee is coming back. Right, Maureen?"

"Yes," she reassured Alex, who still looked shell-shocked. "The machine and K-Cups will be here by midafternoon."

"They took the coffee." Alex turned to me.

"It'll be back," I promised, hugging her a little tighter. "If you're not going to call Martha, we need to get to our classes."

Miraculously, I managed to send Alex off to give her lecture and arrived at my class just in time. I was in the middle of my lecture, which led to a debate regarding Sherman's March.

"Was it necessary to burn everything?" I posed the question just as I felt a strange vibration. Before my students could answer, the theme music for the Wicked Witch of the West was blaring from my jacket. There were snickers and laughter from my students, probably because cellphones, along with other gadgets, were strictly forbidden during my lectures.

"Ben," I addressed one of my students as I reached into my pocket and extracted the phone. "You're always trying to text in class, could you turn this thing off?" He looked as if he was going to argue; instead, he accepted the phone.

"Um, Dr. Grant, why is Satan calling you?" he sheepishly asked, showing me the front of the phone. According to the ID and the demonic image that went along with it, Satan was indeed calling. "I'll just shut it off." He quickly backpedaled. "Here, it's off." He handed it back to me.

I stuffed the phone back in my pocket, taking a moment to regain my bearings. "William Tecumseh Sherman, brilliant leader or pyromaniac? What are your thoughts?"

"Since I grew up in Savannah…" Hilary, who sat in the front row, began. "I'm guessing that was him calling you just now."

"He was a brilliant strategist," Ben argued.

"Hilary, you first, why do you think Sherman wasn't a nice guy? Calm down, Ben, you're next," I encouraged with a smile.

***

After back-to-back lectures, I returned to my office. Alex was sitting at her desk, her face resting in her hands as she stared off into space. I didn't question it since I noticed that the new coffee maker had yet to arrive.

"Can I have my phone?"

"You'll just play Candy Squash all night," I teased, retrieving it from my pocket and handing it back to her.

"Crush, Candy Crush," she corrected, tossing the phone on her desk.

"So your nickname for your ex is Satan?"

"Nicole did that." She chuckled. "They don't like each other. I never got around to changing it. Crap that means she called again." She moved to pick up her phone.

"Don't," I softly pleaded. "Is the world going to stop spinning if you don't turn your phone on until tomorrow?"

"No." She pouted, opening the middle drawer of her desk. I sat on the couch watching curiously as she slid an envelope over. "I meant to give that to you sooner. It's from Nicole."

I opened it and gasped when I saw what was inside. "Um, this is money, a lot of money."

"Very good," she quipped with a shy grin. "Nicole took into account that you're the type that would tip."

"Of course I tip," I sputtered, counting out three hundred dollars. "I can't—"

"It would mean a lot to her," Alex cut me off. "If you don't want it, give it to charity. Something occurred to me when I found the pie outside my door. I offered you a space to work in but not a way for you to get in." She slid a shiny new key over. I opened my mouth fully prepared to explain that I wouldn't feel comfortable just letting myself into her home. "Don't say no," she pleaded. "You're doing all the work on our book. Besides, the next time you bake, you can bring it inside."

"You liked the pie?"

"Very much." She smiled before releasing a yawn. "Speaking of our book, I'd like to work with you. How about tonight?"

"Tonight?" I gaped at her. "You can barely stand up."

"I'm fine." She yawned once again. "I can't put my name on it if I haven't held up my end. I'll order some takeout."

"I'll cook," I countered. "That way, I'll have a chance to shower and get my notes together. But if you yawn again, the deal is off."

"Or," she interjected. "You cook, I clean, we get some work done, and we don't stay up too late."

"Fine," I caved, checking my watch.

"I thought you had told *him*," she whispered as she diverted her gaze. "When the vase disappeared, I thought maybe…"

"Not yet," I said. "He has this thing at work that's almost literally do or die. I can't right now."

"Oh?" Her voice was somber. "I have class, see you tonight about seven? Oh, and I should let you know that Eleanor kept a journal, as well. Any chance you'd want to read it?"

"Yes." I gulped.

"It's back home with my parents." She gathered up her things. "I don't know when I'll have a chance to get it. I think I can convince my Dad to scan some of the pages."

"Thank you." I shook my head as she walked out the door.

***

That night, we shared a nice meal and managed to get some work done. The mood was awkward, to say the least. She was beyond exhausted, and her phone kept ringing. I flinched each time, recognizing the ringtone. I was jealous knowing it was her ex-lover, and I felt guilty knowing that I had yet to settle things in my life. Later that week, we got together when she was more rested, still the mood was the same.

***

It was yet another weekend alone. I found myself sitting in Hal's apartment sipping coffee and giving him fashion advice.

"So you kissed this woman, whose name you won't tell me?" Hal eagerly asked as I sat at the breakfast bar that connected his kitchen to the living room.

"We were drunk," I tried to clarify as he held up a sparkling blue dress. "That's a bit much for brunch," I offered my humble opinion.

"Thank you." He smiled before offering me a tray of muffins. "Just out of the oven."

"Thank you." I plucked one off the tray. I took a bite and moaned with delight. "You need to give me the recipe."

"I will if you tell me what happened next."

"She asked if I had kissed a woman before," I shyly continued before taking a sip of coffee. "I told her I had but always when I was tipsy."

"Oh?"

"That's kind of the reaction she had." I sighed. "She told me that the next time I make out with a girl, I should try it sober."

"Can't say that I blame her," he said. "So have you?"

"No." I groaned. "Not for a lack of trying. We almost did more than once, but we keep getting interrupted. The last time was because a phone call from my boyfriend killed the mood."

"Boyfriend? I could have sworn that you're—"

"I am," I confessed, feeling just a little freer. "I'm only just realizing it. This woman is all I can think about. And now that I've allowed myself to think about things, I mean really think about things, I couldn't lie anymore. Do you know what I mean?"

"Trust me, I do." He gave a sympathetic smile. "Every time I meet a woman I'm interested in, I wait for what seems like an eternity before I tell her about myself." He held up a simple green dress.

"No, the color is all wrong." I regretted shooting down his choice. "How do the women in your life take the news?"

"Most of them assume I'm gay." The smile slipped from his face. "Then I'm faced with the agonizing chat about the differences between a transvestite and a drag queen. Others just walk away before we get to that point, thinking I'm some sort of pervert. It's arduous at times. I've served my country, I'm a respected member of my field, and I'm happiest when dressed in women's clothing. Everyone thinks it's sexual. Like your situation, it's about following one's heart. Speaking of which, what are you going to do about your boyfriend? Tell me he's some awful brute, and leaving him will be a relief."

"He is one of the nicest, sweetest, hopelessly devoted, and kindest spirits I have ever known. He sent me flowers, and it hit me like a ton of bricks. All of a sudden, I understood how unfair I was being to both of us."

"Oh, dear." He patted me on the shoulder. "Pity. If he was a jerk, you could just send him an email and be done with it. Go and see him and do it."

"I would, but he's dealing with this major clusterfu— Um, problem at work," I whined, picking at my muffin. "If things go wrong, he could lose his job. It's just not the right time."

"I doubt it ever will be," he annoyingly pointed out, holding up a blue dress.

"Maybe. I'd have to see it on. I'm worried about your shoulders."

"With my size, they are a problem. Just let me try it on and be honest."

I promised that I would be, returning my attention to my muffin. When he stepped out of his bedroom, I applauded the look. "The wrap makes it."

"Thank goodness." He smiled. "The really good news is I already have shoes and an adorable clutch that match. Now that my crisis has been resolved, let's focus on you. First, you're handling the hardest part being honest with yourself. No small task, trust me, I understand. However, until you're honest with the boy and this woman, nothing is going to change. I won't lie to you, it took me a very long time before I met someone like Julie who I care for and cares for me, despite the fact that I possess a better sense of fashion than she does. As for you, free yourself from these complications, then kiss the girl. If it was meant to be, you'll know it."

"Thank you, Hal." I smiled, snagging a second muffin. "For later," I teased. "I need to go so you can get ready. Thanks again."

"Good luck," he called after me as I made my way out the door.

After spending the morning with Hal, I changed and made my way to the train station. It was time for me to get out and enjoy my life. I took the train into Boston, stopping at the local gay bookstores. Much to my surprise, a woman approached me. The conversation began innocently enough, until I realized that she was flirting with me. I was flattered, and despite her good looks, which I did appreciate, I politely declined her offer to join her for a cup of coffee. After purchasing a few titles that intrigued me, I headed over to the Gardner Museum. I got lost in the beauty and returned to Prowers Landing late. Much to my disappointment, Alex's car was still missing.

Chapter Nineteen

On October 28, I found myself working in Alex's apartment again. Several times during the evening, I tried in vain to get her to laugh, but nothing seemed to be working. I finally gave up and focused on our book. As we went over the mundane details of the book, I forced myself to maintain a professional atmosphere. We were getting very close to finishing. Everything was coming down to rechecking dates and information. All I needed to do was read Eleanor's diary. Alex had filled me in on the content as much as she could, and her father would often fax or email passages to us. But I needed to see the journal for myself. With all of Alex's traveling, she did not have a chance to visit her parents. I would just have to wait until she returned from the Thanksgiving holiday to see it.

"Where is Eleanor buried?" I asked as I watched her stoke the fire. I inhaled, loving the smell of the fire.

"Huh?" she mumbled. Her tone was all business. There were times I wondered if she even knew I was there. She stood from her duties at the fireplace. The glow of the fire illuminated her features, making my heart race. Her beauty never ceased to amaze me.

I couldn't take my gaze off her. She looked at me, and I could feel the heat, and it was not emanating from the fireplace. There was something in the way she looked at me. The kindness and joy I hadn't seen in her for a long time seemed to return. Standing before me was the woman I had first fallen for. The flames let out a loud snap, and we were both brought back to reality. She closed her eyes, ran her fingers through her hair, and she was gone again.

"What was I saying?" She rubbed her eyes.

"Eleanor's grave," I prompted her with regret.

"Right." She opened her eyes and looked back up but not in my direction. "She's buried in Salem. In fact, Eleanor, Anna Moorehouse, and Haley are all buried in the same cemetery."

"We should include a picture of their headstones in the book if we can," I said. "Your family doesn't have one by any chance?"

Suddenly, Alex was laughing. "Uh, no. Not exactly something you put in the family album."

"Maybe I could go down to Salem sometime and get one," I offered carefully, not wanting to jolt her out of her happy mood.

"We could go now," she suggested enthusiastically.

"Are you serious?" I cautiously asked. It had been far too long since Alex had suggested that we do anything together, but a trip to a cemetery? Not what I had been hoping for.

"Why not?" she asked. "It's still early enough. If we hurry, we can just make it before it gets dark. Please!"

"You're serious." I shook my head in disbelief. "Won't the cemetery be closed at this hour?" I wanted to spend time with Alex, but it was late and cold, and this was a cemetery, for pity's sake!

"This little graveyard is locked up constantly," she answered plainly.

"Oh, so now it's a graveyard? I so do not like where this is going!"

Alex just looked at me pouting. "Come on, Stephanie. What could be more fun than breaking into a graveyard in Salem three nights before Halloween?"

"I don't know...gum surgery?"

"Please, if I don't get out of here and do something fun soon, I'm going to snap," Alex begged.

"Alex..." I could think of a thousand reasons why this idea was completely ludicrous. I had to admit, though, deep down, I wanted to go. I'd never done anything like it before. I was always the voice of reason or the wet blanket, depending on your point of view.

"Chicken," she taunted me.

"Okay, so now it's a dare! Well, that changes everything!" I finally caved. "I'll go only if you leave your cellphone home." That was all it took. I jumped off the sofa and grabbed my shoes. "Come on then!" I demanded, meeting her challenge. "Put the fire out and get your keys, Kendell."

On that note, I raced downstairs. As I waited for her, I quickly checked my reflection in the side mirror. I looked good, and my blue jeans and turtleneck should be fine for the trip. I ran my fingers through my hair in an effort to make myself more presentable. I took one last look before racing out to her car.

She met me at the car carrying a long wool coat, her digital camera, and a flashlight.

"Come on, Kendell, daylight is burning," I hollered after her. She laughed at me as she climbed into the car.

"You'll need a jacket," she said.

"I'm fine," I argued as I climbed into the passenger seat.

Salem was a short twenty-minute drive away, but twilight was approaching quickly. The traffic was insane. I did not think it was possible, but the drivers in downtown Salem were actually worse than those in Boston. The quaint streets, which twisted and turned for no apparent reason, were jam-packed with people.

"Tourist season," Alex said with a snarl as she drove like a woman on a mission. I thought I would like to come back someday and see some of the sights that were whizzing past us. She turned the car onto upper Essex Street and found a parking space in front of a white colonial style house. A sign in front informed me that it was the Ropes Mansion.

"It's our lucky day," Alex boasted. "Parking around here can actually be worse than downtown Boston. Especially this time of year." As she locked up the car, Alex told me that the Ropes Mansion, like many homes in Salem, was rumored to be haunted.

I chose to ignore her comments and endless ghost stories as we made our way down the cobblestone sidewalk. "This entire area was known as Flint's pasture." Alex pointed to the end of the street.

So what happened there—a mass murder? I wondered as we continued our journey.

"That big red house at the end was built in 1706. During the eighteen hundreds, it was part of the Underground Railroad. In the nineteen thirties, it was a tea room, then at one point, an inn."

"And now?" I asked with enthusiasm, grateful that there was no creepy tale connected to the quaint home full of history.

"Apartments, mostly college students."

"Is it haunted, as well?" I couldn't resist teasing.

"Of course," Alex said seriously, making me regret that I had asked. "This is Salem, Stephanie. If you don't have some kind of specter running loose in your abode, the neighbors will talk."

"You really get into Halloween, don't you?"

"I do," she gushed. "Next to Christmas, it's my favorite time of year. Over there, they say you can see a woman in the window," she added, filled with glee.

I ignored her attempts to frighten me as we made our way up the street. "Here we are!" Alex announced as we approached a large wrought-iron gate. I looked at the padlock securely in place and grimaced. I looked through the bars at the graveyard with its small headstones. The sight was strangely out of place on this residential street. Someone had kept up the lawn, but it was painfully obvious that teenagers liked to hang out there, as well. I contemplated just how we were going to make our way into the graveyard shivering from the cold.

Without a word, Alex removed the long wool coat she was wearing. I looked at her, questioning her action. "Aren't you going to be cold?"

She just shrugged as she draped the camera around her neck and tucked the flashlight into the back pocket of her black jeans.

"Would you like to go first?" She cautiously scanned the quiet street.

"How?" I asked. My question was answered as she cupped her hands together and offered me a boost. "You're not serious?"

"Come on, you need to hurry before anyone sees us."

I don't know what came over me. Perhaps it was the challenging look in her eyes. I wrapped her coat around me and stepped into her waiting hands. I grabbed onto the gate and allowed her to help lift my body up. I climbed up the gate, stopping only for a moment when I reached the top. I checked to make certain that I wouldn't catch the large coat on anything. I jumped down with a thud, tumbling to the ground. I scrambled to my feet, pretending that I had stuck my landing.

"Good job," she complimented me, handing me the flashlight and camera through the gate.

I looked around the graveyard as a chill ran through my body. This time, it wasn't from the cold. Night was falling, and hanging out in a graveyard wasn't the place I wanted to be.

Alex made her way over the gate with ease until she hit the ground, literally. I helped her stand before handing her the flashlight and camera.

"Thanks." She smiled as she pulled the coat tighter around my body. "I think it's close to the far corner."

"Of course it is because right up front would be too much to ask," I grumbled, noticing that the sun had all but vanished from the sky. I strained to see where Alex was going, "Yup, most definitely a graveyard." I shivered, making my way around the fragile gravestones and gnarled trees.

Alex headed off to the far corner, which was shaded by two large oak trees. Beneath the trees stood three weathered gravestones side by side. *Anna Moorehouse died February 16, 1872, Sarah Moorehouse died February 11, 1898, and Haley Ballister beloved wife and mother born January 18, 1844, died October 28, 1929.*

"What do you think—black and white, color, or both?" Alex readied her camera. "I'll do both. We can decide later what we like."

"Haley died today." A shiver ran through my body.

"I think I got some good shots, we can check them on the computer when we get home," Alex said as if she had not heard me. Then suddenly, her eyes flew open as my words hit her. "I'm sorry, what did you say?"

"October 28, she died today."

As the words escaped my mouth, a branch above us snapped and fell to the ground in front of us. I jumped into Alex's arms, thankful when she held me tight. Alex clicked on her flashlight and looked around.

"It got dark very fast," I said with a shiver.

"Well, you know…fall in New England…maybe we should go," Alex offered in a frightened tone.

"I think you're right." I pulled myself away from the comfort of her body. Something occurred to me, and I grabbed her arm.

"Jesus, don't do that!" She jumped slightly. "I'm sorry." She placed a comforting hand on my shoulder.

"Alex, do you think that maybe Haley doesn't want us to write this book?" I pointed to the fallen tree branch.

"Well, I'm not waiting around to find out," Alex asserted with a slight tremble. "This is getting a little too creepy."

"We should," I said firmly. "We're about to reveal the most intimate details of these women's lives. Maybe, just maybe, they don't want us to do that."

"Okay," Alex said slowly. "Go ahead."

"What?"

"Go ahead and ask them."

"Me?"

"It was your idea." Alex gave me a slight nudge.

I paused for a moment, wondering if Alex had thought that I had lost my mind. She reassured me with a smile and an encouraging nod.

I knelt before Haley and Eleanor's graves. "Ladies, is it all right with you that we do this?" I asked quietly. Alex and I listened to the eerie quiet. Thankfully, nothing happened. "Well, they didn't say no." I chuckled as I stood and rejoined Alex. "Now let's get the hell out of here," I added fearfully.

"Okay then, I just want to move that branch off of their graves." She handed me the flashlight. She pulled the heavy branch up easily and tossed it away. "What the—" she uttered in surprise. "Stephanie, could you shine that light down here?"

"What is it?" I stammered as I shined the light to where she directed me.

Alex was pushing away at the soil between the headstones. "Look." She pointed toward the ground. "The branch must have dug it up."

I looked down at the spot filled with curiosity and fear. My heart stopped for a moment when I saw it. Nestled between Eleanor and Haley's gravestones was a small rectangular stone engraved with two cherubs embracing with the word *Forever* inscribed on it.

"Thank you," Alex whispered as she replaced the soil.

We understood that the marker was never meant to be seen. We accepted it as an encouraging sign as we made our departure. I climbed back over the gate first and was greeted by a very unhappy-looking police officer. Alex failed to see him until she was landing on the cobblestone sidewalk.

"Oops," she whispered, realizing that we were busted.

"Ladies." The officer shined his flashlight in our eyes. "Do you mind telling me what you're doing here?"

"We can explain, Officer," I stammered out.

"I see," he said indulgently.

"It's really quite simple," Alex said as she placed her hands gently on my shoulders.

"Alex?" he said with surprise.

"My God, she knows everyone," I mumbled.

She looked down at me in confusion and shrugged. Then she peered more closely at him. Which was easier to do since he immediately extinguished his flashlight. Her eyes flew open, and she captured him in a big hug.

"Roger!" she loudly exclaimed.

As they exchanged pleasantries, I got the full story. Roger, it would appear, had once dated Alex's sister. He asked how Nicole was doing and seemed relieved that she was on the wagon.

"Would you like to explain what it is you're doing breaking into a graveyard?"

"Research for a book we're working on. I have a couple of relatives buried back there. It was a last-minute decision, and I didn't have time to get the key from the caretakers."

"There's a key?" I whispered to her.

"Same old Alex." Roger chuckled.

After Roger made his departure, we both exploded into laughter. Without thinking, we fell into each other's arms and giggled uncontrollably. Instantly, I became acutely aware of the closeness of Alex's body. I wanted to touch her and to run my hands up under the thick white fisherman's sweater she was wearing. The laughter waned as we stood there holding each other.

I could feel her breathing becoming labored. My body was awakened by the subtle scent of her perfume. I felt her body when I glanced up at her. She released a heavy sigh as she smiled back at me.

"Hungry?" she asked. "We can walk to the wharf, catch a bite, maybe a glass of wine?"

"Sounds good," I agreed, slipping a hand from her body and into the pocket of the coat. Thankfully, her arm remained around my waist as she guided me along the narrow streets.

The crowd grew as we neared the wharf. Alex kept a tight hold on me as we weaved in and out of traffic. I looked out over the ocean and inhaled the aroma of the autumn air. A beautiful fall evening with a lovely woman at my side, who could ask for anything more? We ended up at Victoria's Station, which seemed to have the shortest waiting list. We managed to get a table by the window. The food and bottle of wine we shared were wonderful. For just one evening, all pretense between us had vanished. There was something about the romantic atmosphere that made me feel like I was on a date with Alex.

Chapter Twenty

The following morning, I popped a K-Cup into my Keurig before padding off to the shower. I hummed along to the Beatles. I felt on top of the world. The Beatles were singing, coffee was brewing, and the night before was amazing. I stepped out of the shower, dried off, and poured my coffee. I knew I was smiling like an idiot. Everything felt right...until the music abruptly stopped.

I shuffled to the door to listen. I recognized Alex's gait instantly. I strained just to be certain it was her. When she tripped slightly on the third step, I knew it was her. It was an odd thing, she always tripped on the third step coming down and the fourth step going up. I felt strange standing there naked with my ear pressed against my front door until I heard her exit the building.

"Okay, I'll just see her at work," I reasoned as I dragged myself away from the door and began to get ready.

A truly odd thing happened. I never saw Alex that day. In fact, there weren't any signs that she had been in the office at all. I wrote it off as a fluke, I just couldn't help missing her. I missed her so much that when my phone rang, I almost collided with my desk rushing to answer it. Naturally, it was Peter. Finally, good news—the crisis at work was over, and he was driving up on Friday.

I felt like a jerk knowing he was gearing up for a romantic weekend while I was planning on a very short visit. I managed to make it through the rest of my day without seeing Alex. When I returned home, I was more than a little disappointed that her car was gone.

Still not comfortable with just letting myself into Alex's apartment, I spread out my notes and settled down. I stopped long enough to shower and eat.

It was well after three in the morning when I heard the front door close. I knew by the sound of the footsteps that it was Alex. I was so familiar with her, I even knew that she was wearing her old worn-out leather boots. "Maybe I could just pop into the hallway pretending that she had awakened me." I instantly scolded myself at the suggestion.

It was then that I noticed that Alex's footsteps had paused just outside my door. I jumped off the futon and made my way to the doorway. Before I could reach the handle, I heard her moving away and heading up the staircase. I listened as she paced around in her apartment. Finally, a familiar pattern emerged as she went to the kitchen, then to the bathroom, and finally to her bedroom. The sounds ceased, and I knew she was in bed for the night.

By the time Alex's morning concert began Friday the 30th, I had already watched the sunrise. I listened to Diana Ross and The Supremes while plopping a K-Cup into my machine. After a quick jolt of coffee, I showered and dressed quickly. Before the concert ended, I was halfway to campus. I left early in hopes of catching her even for a few moments.

There I was sitting alone in our office chewing on the end of a pencil. Everything seemed to be coming to a head. Peter would be arriving later, and more than likely, Alex would leave for New York after her classes were over. For the first time since they had begun, Alex's trips out of town were a blessing.

I had just about chewed my pencil in half as I contemplated just how things might go with Peter. "Face it, this is going to suck!" I groaned as I tried to prepare what I was going to say to him. I was beginning a new life, yet I was still somehow trapped in my old existence.

To move on, I had to sit Peter down the moment he arrived and tell him everything. I just needed him to arrive after Alex made her usual weekend departure. I had no intention of the two of them meeting each other. Somehow, I doubted that I'd survive the awkwardness of such a meeting.

All day long, I kept telling myself to stay strong. That and wondering where the hell Alex was hiding. I also was wondering why everyone I ran into greeted me with, "I'll see you tonight." By the time my day was ending, I was ready to explode. Between nervous energy and copious amounts of caffeine, I was a hot mess. I was looking at my laptop wondering why my email looked like gibberish when Alex finally arrived.

"Is it possible to overdose on coffee?"

"Not in my world," she muttered before retreating to her side of the office.

"Alex," I carefully began, needing to know just why she had decided to avoid me after a fun night together.

"Hey, gang!" Maureen popped in, cutting off my question. "Anyone willing to babysit tomorrow night?" She tried to make it sound like fun. The fake smile she was sporting quickly vanished. "Come on, my sitter just canceled. If I don't get a chance to go out with my husband, I will go postal."

"Sorry, no can do," Alex quickly dismissed her request.

"Not New York again!" Maureen groaned. "What about tonight?"

"Calm down," Alex said in a reassuring tone. "There's no way I'm spending Halloween in New York. Tonight will be the same as every year. As for tomorrow night, I'm going to The Galaxy."

"Skip The Galaxy," Maureen begged. "You can go there anytime. Come on, do an old married woman a favor and watch my kids."

"Watching your kids on a sugar high on Halloween night? A tempting offer, but I have a date," Alex said in her own defense.

"Are you kidding?" Maureen asked in amazement as she looked at me. I think she could tell by my suddenly pale features that I was just as surprised as she was.

"I do date," Alex said sharply.

"Since when?" Maureen asked, again looking toward me for some sort of answer. I had none to offer. "Stephanie, any chance you would be available?" She quickly shifted gears.

"Sorry, I have plans, as well," I said bitterly.

"Well, damn. I guess I'll see you both tonight then," Maureen said with disappointment.

Maureen left in a bit of a huff, chasing after her next victim Louisa. I slammed my laptop shut while my mind screamed, *Alex has a date. Isn't that just dandy?* I had heard about The Galaxy from Hal. It was nightclub in Boston that catered to an extremely diverse community. Hal claimed it was the only club he truly felt comfortable in and suggested that I might check it out. He suggested that I go on a Thursday since that was gay night.

The sudden realization that was where Alex was the night before was giving me a headache. I tried to calm down, reminding myself that I had no say over Alex's personal life. Alex had repeatedly let me know that she wasn't an option. I just had to accept the facts, and it didn't change how I felt about Peter and me. It did, however, mean that she was going to be around that afternoon when Peter arrived.

"Crap!" I shouted, startling myself and apparently Alex.

"Are you okay?" She rushed over to my desk.

"There's something going on tonight." I ignored her while trying to figure out if the mysterious event could prevent Peter and Alex from meeting each other. "What is it?"

"It's nothing, really," Alex said quickly. "Just a little gathering I kind of host every year on the night before Halloween."

"I see," I said slowly, hurt by the knowledge that she had failed to mention a gathering that almost everyone on campus was talking about.

"Stephanie, it's just…" she nervously began when Stan popped his head into the office.

"Alex?" he called to her in a surprisingly friendly manner. His tone was not only friendly, but he addressed her by her first name, something he never did. "Should I bring *The Legend of Sleepy Hollow*?"

"Of course, Stan, the little ones love it," Alex said warmly.

"Great!" he gushed. "The boys are really looking forward to coming."

"Don't forget your pumpkins," Alex gently reminded him.

"Just one this year. Richard feels that he's too old for pumpkin carving," Stan added sadly.

"Some of the students are planning on doing some tie-dyeing in the upstairs' kitchen that I use as a laundry room. Perhaps he'll enjoy that?" Alex said.

"He might if he can do it in black. It's the only color his mother and I can get him to wear these days." Stan chuckled. "I'll pick up some T-shirts on the way. Thank you for the suggestion. I'll see both of you tonight." Stan waved and left.

"Did I just enter the twilight zone? Or maybe the pod people had finally taken over?" I sputtered, pushing past Alex and flopping down on the sofa. "Stan is coming?"

Just then, a young student I recognized entered the office. "Same time this year, Professor Kendell?" she asked brightly.

"Yes," Alex said uneasily. "Carla, could you close the door on your way out?" Carla smiled brightly and closed the door. As the door was closing, Alex approached me. "Stephanie, I never invite anyone over for this."

"I see," I said bitterly.

"It's the truth!" Alex said with exasperation. "The first year I was teaching here, I told this outrageous ghost story in class. It's just something I like to do. Like the way I teased you in Salem. When the class was over, everyone wanted to hear more and share their own spooky tales. I forget how it happened, but everyone ended up at my apartment for an impromptu party. We decorated the porch and Mrs. Giovanni's porch. We carved pumpkins, and someone brought a horror movie. The whole thing just snowballed. Now every year on the night before Halloween, people just show up. For the kids that aren't pledging, it's a nice alternative."

"Why didn't you tell me about this?" I felt the walls closing in. "This is a small campus, Alex. Everyone knows where I live. I feel like an idiot. Just when were you going to mention this? Were you waiting for when a hundred-some odd people showed up on our doorstep? You could've said something when we went to Salem!"

"I'm sorry. It...it's just that..." Alex was stammering like an idiot.

"Why today?" My head was spinning. "How in the name of all that is sacred am I going to tell him with a house full of people carving pumpkins and telling ghost stories?"

"Tell him?"

"I wanted to catch him before he had a chance to take his bag out of the car," I started rambling,, unaware that she had sat next to me. "I figured that you'd be gone and now that his work problems are over, it's the perfect time."

"For?" she encouraged, taking my hand.

"Telling Peter everything." I struggled to breathe, and there was a strange tightness growing in my chest. "You know, someone should write a book explaining the dos and don'ts of coming out."

"Coming out?" Her jaw dropped.

"Yes, coming out." I leaned forward, burying my face in my hands. "I'm gay, happy now?"

"Yes." She sounded thrilled. "When did you—?"

"I admitted it to myself a couple weeks ago." I found it harder to speak as I tried to catch my breath. "I told Hal, the cashier at Calamus Books, and the guy who sold me my ticket at the Gardner Museum. Although I don't know why I felt a need to tell the last two."

"Calamus, the GLBT bookstore in Boston?"

"That would be the one." I gasped. "I can't breathe."

"It's okay," Alex rubbed my back. "I think you're hyperventilating. Lean forward and try to relax. Do I need to get a paper bag?"

"No," I squeaked.

I'd lost track of time as she held me. Finally, I could breathe normally. Alex continued to hold me as I lifted my head. "I should have told you sooner." I blew out.

"How could you?" She winced, still stroking my back. "I haven't been around. It's getting late, we should go."

I had no idea how long we had been sitting there. It must have been quite a while since the sun had begun to set. Alex stood slowly and gathered our things. Then she held out her hand to me and helped me stand. Without a word, she placed a comforting arm around my shoulders and led me to her car.

Upon arriving home, I saw that our front porch, as well as Mrs. Giovanni's front porch, was covered with people. There were pumpkins everywhere, along with various ghosts, skeletons, and a few Frankensteins to boot. The crowd consisted of students, faculty, and many people I had never seen before. There was one tall figure with dark puppy dog eyes who stood out. He was busy helping string orange lights across the porch and laughing without a care in the world.

"Is that him?" Alex asked quietly, putting her car in park.

"Yes, that's Peter," I responded painfully.

"It's going to be all right." Alex wiped an errant tear from my cheek.

"Liar," I whispered.

I inhaled deeply and braced myself as Alex caressed my thigh. I was still upset with Alex for not telling me that half the campus was showing up at our home.

After taking several more deep breaths, I steadied myself enough to exit the car. Peter ran over to me with a huge grin plastered on his face. Alex walked past him without a second glance. Peter threw his arms around me and held me tight.

When he pulled back, the smile left his face instantly. "Are you all right?" he asked, hugging me furiously.

"Fine," I lied. "Just a bad day."

"You can tell me all about it later." He squeezed my shoulder reassuringly. Before I could react, he bent down and claimed my lips passionately. I stiffened when his tongue tried to enter my mouth.

"Not now," I choked, pushing him away.

"It's good to see you, sweetheart." He smiled hopefully. "I feel like we've been separated forever."

I offered a weak smile, fighting against the urge to wipe my mouth. His kiss made me feel the same way it always had—empty. I looked up into those trusting brown eyes and quickly turned away. I was unable to face him due to the overwhelming guilt that engulfed me. I felt someone watching me. I turned and found Alex staring at us with an icy expression. She held my gaze for a brief moment before turning away.

"Okay, everyone!" she shouted without missing a beat. "Now everyone knows the rules, right?"

"Yes," the crowd responded.

"Okay then, what are they?" Alex asked them like a drill sergeant.

"There's hard cider and alcohol-free cider," a few voices volunteered.

"And who can drink the hard cider?" Alex drilled them.

"Anyone over twenty-one," someone answered.

"Excellent, now who's on key duty?"

"I am," a voice answered.

"Good for you, Vince." Alex patted the boy on the shoulder.

"Just remember, no drinking, and you must take everyone's car keys as they enter the party, and they can't have them back if they're unable to drive. So what's the movie tonight?"

"*The Shining*," a couple of people answered.

"The original," someone else supplied before Alex could ask.

"Excellent! Just remember—"

"No one under seventeen in the living room while the movie is playing," Carla cut Alex off.

"Okay!" Alex clapped her hands together. "The houses look great. I think this is the best decorating job yet. Now let's get this crap upstairs and start this party."

"Peter," I tried to get his attention.

"This is amazing," he gushed, ignoring me and tugging on my sleeve.

The crowd began to head into the house. Someone called out to Peter, and he waved to whomever it was before looking back at me.

"This is so much fun," he exclaimed. "Your neighbor certainly knows how to have fun."

"You have no idea," I said absently.

"Let's go then." He bounced up and down like a little kid.

"Peter, we have to…" I stammered.

"Come on, Peter," one coed called after him.

"This is great, let's go!" He guided me toward the house.

"I have to change."

"I could help you," he playfully suggested.

"No!" I snapped. "I mean, why don't we go inside so we can talk?"

He wrapped his arms around me. "Talking sounds good." He purred again. I pushed him away.

"Go join the party," I told him, feeling defeated. "I'll see you upstairs."

He kissed me again and ran off to join the others. I made a mad dash into my apartment and slammed the door behind me. Mentally kicking myself was the first thing I did. If only I had felt something when he kissed me. "Why didn't I just tell him?" I berated myself while grabbing something to wear. I knew that I had panicked, and now it was too late.

It was obvious that the party was going to go on all night. I would have to wait until the morning, which led to a new problem— Peter would expect us to sleep together. "No, I need to get him away from the party and tell him." I tugged on a pair of jeans and my Yale sweatshirt. I just needed to find an excuse to get him to leave the party, hopefully before he and Alex met.

I made my way upstairs, stumbling past students who were hanging out on the stairwell. I was promptly greeted by Vince. He asked for my car keys, then quickly apologized when he realized who I was.

"I'm sorry, Dr. Grant, I guess you won't be driving tonight."

I smiled and pushed my way inside. The apartment was filled with people on both floors, and more were entering as I searched for Peter. I needed to pull him aside and get him downstairs. The thought of him and Alex talking suddenly bolstered my courage. I had to get him out of there and fast. I spotted his lanky frame sipping a bottle of cider. He seemed to be in a deep conversation with someone. I pushed my way through the crowd. My heart stopped when I saw just who it was Peter was talking to. Alex stood there nodding and smiling. She looked over his shoulder and captured my gaze. She smiled sweetly enough, but her eyes seemed to be pleading for help.

I made my way over to him and placed a gentle hand on his shoulder. He turned to me with a bright smile.

"Hey, honey, I was just talking to—"

"Alex," she supplied.

"Peter, we need to—" I firmly began since the situation was already far too weird for my taste.

"This is just great, isn't it?" Peter slurred slightly.

"Yeah, right." Alex groaned, then quickly bit her lip and grimaced.

"I know that being alone would have been nice," Peter continued, oblivious to what was happening. "I've been locked in my office for months, everyone worrying that we were going to get canned. This party is just what I needed." He gave me a quick peck on the lips and took another swig of his cider. "Thank you, darling, this is a great surprise. Plus, we have the rest of the weekend for just the two of us." He winked at me playfully.

"Peter, we need to—" I began once again.

"Hey, the movie is about to start!" He informed us as he wrapped his arm around my shoulder. "Come on, I'll hold your hand during the scary parts." He winked again.

"Great." I groaned. "But we should—"

Before I could finish my sentence, he was dragging me toward the second floor stopping to grab himself another Angry Orchard Cider. I turned to find Alex grinning at me like a Cheshire cat. "Thank you again." He sighed, releasing his hold on me so he could crack open his bottle of cider.

"Peter—"

"I know you don't like these kind of movies," he cut me off.

"Save me a spot," I blurted out, knowing that this was my chance to make a break for it. He kissed me once again and headed upstairs while I nudged my way through the crowd. I squeaked when I literally ran into Alex.

"Drink?" she asked in a strained voice.

"Yes, thank you," I said in relief, accepting her waiting hand.

Alex pulled me into the kitchen. I released her hand only when we encountered yet another crowd of people.

"Where are they?" Alex grumbled as she searched her kitchen cabinets frantically. "Come on, where did I hide you?"

I made my way past the bottles of cider sitting in ice in the kitchen sink and went directly to Alex's refrigerator. In a brief moment, I realized just how familiar I was with Alex's kitchen. I grabbed a bottle of Kim Crawford.

"Corkscrew?" I reached in the upper cabinet and retrieved two wine glasses.

"Screw top."

"I'll never get used to that." I grunted. "Did you find them?" I asked impatiently.

"Bingo!" She held up a fresh pack of cigarettes. I reached back into the drawer and snatched a book of matches and tossed them to Alex.

I peeked out through the kitchen door and spotted Peter chatting with a group of people. "He couldn't stay upstairs?" I whimpered as Alex placed her hand on my shoulder. "He's having a great time," I said sadly as I turned back to Alex.

"Now what?" She frowned, looking at the swarm of people that surrounded us. I stepped over to her and gently placed a hand on her hip. I leaned up and whispered, "My place."

Without hesitation, we pushed our way through the crowd and ducked outside to the back staircase. We crept downstairs to my apartment, pausing once or twice to listen to the sounds of the party emanating from her apartment. I reached into my pocket and retrieved my keys and opened my back door. We stumbled through the darkness and made our way to the futon, which I had left open that morning. I placed the wine and the other items I was carrying carefully on the coffee table.

"Can I have the matches for a moment? I don't want to turn on the lights," I explained. She handed me the matches, and I lit the large three-wicked candle I kept on the coffee table and returned the matches to her. Alex lit herself a cigarette. "Light one for me," I requested as I opened the wine.

Alex handed me the cigarette she was smoking and lit another for herself. I took a deep drag and went in search of something I could use as an ashtray. I settled on a small plate, which I placed on the table. I placed the spent matches on the plate as Alex poured the wine and handed me a glass.

"You'll have to excuse the mess," I apologized as I settled down next to her. "I had been planning on cleaning up for Peter's visit. Then I thought that he wouldn't be staying, so why bother."

"No chance of that now." Alex groaned. "He's having a grand old time."

"I know." I sighed in desperation.

"How weird is this?"

"Oh, this?" I laughed. "Let's see, my boyfriend of the past five years, who I've been avoiding for the past couple of months, is upstairs in your apartment. While I'm hiding down here with the woman I made a pass at."

"So nothing out of the ordinary?"

"No, not at all," I jested before taking a sip of wine. "Considering a few hours ago I came out to you. Not that it matters since you've made it clear that I'm not the girl for you."

"Stephanie," she began slowly. "I want to make something

clear."

"Stop," I pleaded before I took another drag off my smoke.

"Wait." She extinguished her cigarette. "I just want you to know...well...I..."

"What?" I snapped, impatiently waiting for yet another lecture on how we could never be more than friends.

"It's just that you seem to be under the impression that I'm not attracted to you," Alex blurted out. "If that was the case, trust me, the last few months would've been a hell of a lot easier on both of us."

"So you're attracted to me?" Mentally, I was having a hard time keeping up.

"Haven't you ever looked in a mirror?"

I looked over at her. The candlelight made her face glow. I'd never wanted anyone the way I wanted her. My hands were shaking from the smoldering gaze she offered. Somehow, I managed to look away and put out my cigarette.

"I know that I've been putting off breaking up with Peter," I tried to explain my reluctance. "It's just that there was that problem at his job and now his birthday is coming up."

"There's never going to be a good time to break his heart," Alex said softly as she rubbed my arm. "No matter what you say or when you say it, he's going to be hurt."

"I know." I leaned into her touch. "I just wish there was some way I could avoid hurting him."

"Then stay with him," Alex said.

"I can't." I sighed, curling up against her. "Now that I know what I want and who I am, I have to let him go. It's the right thing to do."

We sat there silently sipping our wine, each lost in our own thoughts. I placed my glass on the table and leaned back into Alex's body. My hand absently traced a pattern across her white cotton blouse. I could feel the taut muscles of her abdomen through the material. She kissed me gently on top of my head. Then she sat up and placed her glass on the table next to mine. For a brief moment, I thought she was going to leave. Instead, she leaned into me and caressed my face. It was all the encouragement I needed. I slipped my hand over her broad shoulders and tenderly ran them down the front of her blouse. I gasped as I felt her nipples harden from my touch.

My heart was racing as she lowered her head and captured my lips. I kissed her gently in reply. She leaned away slightly. I reached up and laced my fingers through her hair, pulling her toward me. Her lips were so soft and inviting. I felt as if I could lose myself within her or die trying. I felt her tongue teasing my bottom lip. Eagerly, I invited her in.

The sensation of her explorations was overwhelming. I lost all sense of reason. I wanted more. I pressed my body into hers, and my fingers began exploring the front of her blouse. I unbuttoned her shirt. I felt her powerful hands pressing against my back, drawing me closer to her. With the last of the buttons freed, my hands took control, feeling the taut skin of her abdomen.

Our lips parted as the need to breathe overtook us. I kissed her cheek, then my tongue trailed down her neck. She released a needy moan when I sucked on her neck, feeling her heat beneath my lips. I felt her hands beneath my sweatshirt. I was trembling as her hands freely explored my body. I needed her more than I needed to breathe.

I pushed her down so that she was now lying beneath me. I straddled her hips and began a slow and steady rhythm swaying against her body. I cupped her breast, molding it into my hand. I lifted my head and nibbled on her earlobe. She gasped as my tongue found its way into her ear.

"Is this what you want?" I growled in a voice that I didn't recognize.

"Yes!" She moaned deeply as she clutched my backside, pressing us closer together.

The steady rhythm of our bodies crashing together was driving me to the brink of insanity. Unable to contain my desire, I reached down and lowered her bra, exposing the breast I had been caressing. The sight of that beautiful mound shimmering in the candlelight with her rose-colored nipple erect forced me to ride harder against her. My body was throbbing. I bent my head down and allowed my tongue to circle her nipple. Her body arched as she pushed herself closer to me. Fueled on by her response, I captured her nipple in my mouth and suckled it greedily. I was lost in her. The taste of her skin, the feel of her hands exploring my body was driving me insane.

My pulse was racing as I pressed my center against hers. My body was reacting of its own will. I tore my mouth from her breast, and she groaned with disappointment. I raised my body from hers while still straddling her hips. No longer able to contain the desire, my hands frantically unbuttoned her jeans. I felt her hands working the zipper of my jeans. Soon we were each struggling to yank each other's pants down. I pressed the length of my body against hers and reclaimed her lips.

I slipped my tongue between her lips, our bodies rocking in a needy rhythm. Our hands exploring, each gasping for air when our kiss came to an end.

"So wet," she whispered hotly in my ear.

"Alex, I need you." My voice trembled.

"Yes," she hissed as her hands firmly clutched my bottom, driving farther into her.

"Take me," I pleaded.

She responded by flipping me over and capturing my mouth in a searing kiss. I felt her thigh slide between my legs. I eagerly accepted her offer and began to thrust against her firm thigh. In the distance, I heard a pounding. I ignored it, assuming that it was the beating of my heart. Alex broke away from me and looked down with a curious expression. "What the—?" she panted as the pounding grew more insistent. "Someone's knocking," she whispered, her body tensing.

"Why does this keep happening?" I whimpered.

"Stephanie?" he called out.

"It's Peter," I whispered in shock as Alex and I remained frozen.

We remained locked in the same pose for what seemed like an eternity until we heard his footsteps walking away. I raised my hand to my mouth to stifle the sob that threatened to escape. Alex pulled away from me and lay beside me as I tried to calm myself. I could feel her body slip away. I watched as she climbed off the futon and fixed her clothing.

"Come on," she whispered as she bent down and caressed my

cheek. "You don't want him to find out this way."

"I'm sorry." I sobbed quietly as I adjusted my clothing.

"I'm not."

"Liar." I accepted her hand, allowing her to lift me off the futon.

"Let's just go back upstairs, he'll never know." She gathered up the wine glasses and cigarettes. She walked over to the back door and turned to me. "You should fix your bra before you go back up." Having said that, she left my apartment. I felt my sweatshirt and blushed when I realized that she had somehow managed to undo my bra without my knowledge. I hooked the garment and tidied up the apartment and made my way out to the backyard. I started up the wrought-iron stairs that led to her apartment.

I saw her standing there talking to a couple of students. "No breaking the law," she softly cautioned the duo. "Put it away and smoke it in your dorm room like a normal college student," she was saying as I made my ascent.

By the time I reached the top, the students were gone. I rested my hand on her hip. She turned to me, and in the darkness, I could still see the silly smile she was sporting. I wrapped my arms around her waist. I found myself gazing into her eyes. At that moment, I realized that I had found something I never knew I was looking for.

She looked as if she was going to say something; I didn't give her the chance. I reached up and cupped her face with my hand. My heart swelled when she leaned into my touch. Unable to control myself, I pulled her closer. I quickly claimed her lips, instantly becoming lost in the searing kiss. I was breathless when it came to an end.

I bolstered my courage and stepped inside. Based on the curious looks we were receiving, I could only assume that we had been seen. "So?" Maureen stepped in front of me.

"Hi," I stammered. "I didn't know you were here."

"Just leaving. The party is getting a little rambunctious for the kids," Maureen slyly explained. I shifted nervously. The way she was looking at me made me feel uncomfortable. Alex brushed past us. "Interesting gathering this year. Just a moment ago, I saw two of my teachers snogging. Which is interesting since I met a drunken fellow in the living room who claims to be your boyfriend."

"He's drunk?" I groaned, slapping my forehead. "Isn't that just great."

"Yeah, good luck with that." Maureen patted me on the shoulder before disappearing into the crowd.

I shoved my way through the kitchen, making my way into the living room where I discovered a very drunken Peter. I couldn't be certain, but he appeared to be playing or trying to play a game of beer pong with some of the upperclassmen. Alex was nowhere to be seen.

"There you are," Peter slurred just as Alex made her entrance.

"The game is over," Alex announced, effectively scaring the players.

"I needed some fresh air," I lied to Peter, who I was trying to help to his feet. "Peter, did you eat today?" I asked him in a motherly fashion.

"I probably shouldn't have added shots of Fireball to my cider," he choked. "Tasted good."

"Did you eat today?" I sternly repeated.

"No," he slurred, slumping slightly.

"I think that maybe we should put you to bed."

"I've been waiting months to hear you say that!" he shouted, snaking his arm around my shoulders. I wanted to cry as I led him through the crowd and out the front door.

"He's not driving, is he?" the every diligent Vince asked as he opened the door.

"No." I snarled, cursing my bad luck as I went to close the door behind us. I caught a glimpse of Alex among the crowd. The dark expression clearly written on her face broke my heart.

Somehow, I managed to get Peter downstairs. No easy task since his hands began to wander. Taking his suit off proved to be no problem since he was more than eager to undress for me. Getting him to go to bed became a test of wills. He kept trying to grab me for a kiss. It was a struggle, but finally, I got him tucked into the futon where he quickly passed out. I had never seen him so drunk before. It broke my heart when he was trying to kiss me. "I love you so much, Stephanie," he kept repeating. As he snored in his drunken slumber, I sat on the edge of the futon and finally released the tears that I'd been fighting since I heard him knocking on the apartment door.

I ended up spending the night in the beat-up armchair in the corner of the apartment. Above me, the party lasted until the wee hours of the morning. Despite the ruckus going on above, Peter failed to move. He just lay there snoring. I cried until my body had nothing left to offer.

I could have easily crawled into bed with him and tried to sleep, as well, but I felt that I had betrayed him enough for one evening. As the sun began to emerge, I lifted myself out of the armchair. My body ached from sitting there all night. I dragged myself into the shower and tried to lose myself under the steam.

After I had showered and dressed, I waited and waited for Peter to wake up. The waiting was driving me insane. Finally, I gave up and brewed a cup of coffee as I debated on sneaking back upstairs to see if Alex was awake yet. As the coffee was just finishing to spit out the last few drops of caffeine, I heard Alex moving around upstairs. Since Peter showed no signs of life, I decided to wait until Alex finished her shower and was dressed. I needed to see her. To be with her. I needed to explain just what last night had meant to me. What she meant to me. It was time to tell her everything, to tell her that I had fallen for her. For me, the night before wasn't just physical. Although the physical was pretty damn nice.

Right on cue, I was jolted out of my thoughts by the blaring sound of Alex's morning concert. It was Melissa, which was not a good sign since she was playing the same CD the last time something like this happened.

"What the hell is that?" Peter bellowed, pulling the covers over his head.

"Alex."

"Does she do that every morning?" He groaned, daring to peek out from under the comforter.

"Most mornings," I mumbled. Taking a sip of coffee, I set my mug down.

I listened to his grunts and groans while fetching a mug and setting up the Keurig for another round.

"God, how do you put up with that noise?" He struggled to sit up. "Is that coffee I smell?"

"Yes," I curtly answered while I searched for sugar for his

coffee. "I used it all on the pies," I mumbled, recalling how I made another round of pies for Hal, Shavonne, and Mrs. G just the other night when I couldn't sleep. It never occurred to me to buy more for his coffee since I hadn't planned on him staying overnight.

"I'm sorry, I seem to be out of sugar."

"That's okay." He smacked his lips and scratched his head. He wrapped the blanket around himself and stumbled into the kitchen. "Man, I feel like someone scotch-taped my tongue." He bent down and gave me a quick peck on the cheek before taking the cup I offered to him. "When did you start drinking your coffee black?"

I didn't answer his innocent question. What could I say—I changed my tastes after I got loaded one night with Alex and she failed to have any milk that wasn't toxic? Not stocking sugar for his coffee was such a small thing, yet it spoke volumes.

"Peter, we have to—" I began, fully prepared to just be done with it.

"Stephanie," he cut me off. "I'm sorry about last night. I hate getting drunk. I should've eaten something, not to mention doing shots. I don't know what I was thinking. But I'm going to make it up to you. Let me hop in the shower, then I'll take you to breakfast."

He kissed me gently on the cheek and asked if I could grab his bag from the car. I nodded mutely as he made his way into the bathroom. I went outside in the crisp morning air and retrieved Peter's bag. As I pulled the bag out of the car, I found myself repeating, "I'll tell him over breakfast. Just like kicking a puppy." As I stepped up onto the porch, I was startled by a young woman. She seemed to be checking the names on the doorbells.

"Can I help you?" I asked her sternly.

"Hi," she beamed. "I'm looking for Alex Kendell."

"I bet you are. I mean, come on in."

We stepped into the foyer, and I wasted no time sizing her up. She was young and very attractive with long chestnut hair. She was also very skinny and seemed to possess a bubbly personality. I hated her immediately. Just as I was about to grill her about just what the hell was she doing on my front porch, my apartment door swung open, revealing Peter wrapped in nothing more than a small bath towel and an embarrassed expression.

"Oops," he quickly said.

I was about to hand Peter his bag when I spotted Alex descending the staircase carrying two large trash bags. She looked past the youngster and directly at Peter. Her icy gaze diverted to me. There was no mistaking the look in her eyes, it screamed of betrayal. I stood there trying to formulate a plan when she finally noticed the youngster.

"Courtney?" she blurted out.

Good heavens, even her name is cute. I could just throw up.

"Hey there, Alex." She giggled, further bolstering my need to throw up.

"I was just about to call you," Alex said.

"I know I'm early, but it's a beautiful morning, and I couldn't wait to see you," little Miss Perky explained. "There's supposed to be this great place around the corner for breakfast."

"The Java House?" Alex and I responded in unison.

"Yeah, that's it." Courtney nodded enthusiastically. "Hey, why don't you two join us?"

"Sounds great," Peter chimed in. "We were just going to grab a bite. I'm Peter, by the way."

"Courtney." She extended her hand, then withdrew, realizing that Peter needed to keep his towel in place. She giggled, and I rolled my eyes. I glared at Alex, who seemed to take a sudden interest in the wallpaper.

"Peter, I don't think—" I began in a panic.

"Come on, sweetie, I'm dying to get to know your new friends." His excitement was a tad overwhelming. I couldn't say anything. I stood there staring at him. "Good, it's settled then," he gushed. "Uh, Stephanie, could I have my clothes now?"

I tossed the bag at him as I glared at Alex with a pleading look. She just stood there with her jaw hanging open. Somehow, Peter managed to catch the bag and keep his towel in place. He muttered his thanks and retreated into the apartment.

"Do you need help with those?" Courtney motioned to the trash bags in Alex's hands.

"I'll help her!" I snapped, grabbing one of the bags and digging my nails into Alex's arm with my free hand. I dragged Alex out the door before anyone could voice an objection. We went around back, leaving a stunned Courtney in the foyer. Without a word, we deposited the bags in the barrels. "What the hell just happened in there?" Alex said wildly.

"Well, it seems that we're going on a double date." I snarled.

"No," Alex said firmly while shaking her head.

"Yes," I hissed.

"No," she repeated more strongly.

"Then what are we supposed to do?" I pleaded with her. "Tell me, I'll do it."

I could see the wheels turning in Alex's head. Finally, she released a groan. "There's nothing we can do. We have to go," she conceded. "This sucks. I was just about to call her and cancel. Who knew she would show up ten hours early for our date? Who does that?"

"Children," I answered bitterly.

"Hey!" Alex snapped.

"Oh, come on." I snapped back. "How old is she?"

"Old enough." Alex snarled.

"For what?" I hissed, invoking a harsh glare from Alex. "I see," I responded coldly. We just stood there like a couple of idiots shivering in the cold. I had enough, firmly convinced that the situation was bordering on ridiculous. "I didn't sleep with him last night," I explained quietly.

"Was I that transparent?"

"Yes," I answered her gently but honestly. "Seeing him standing there half-naked couldn't have looked good."

"My fault," she confessed. "I was just thrown by it."

"He passed out," I tried to explained. "I just sat up all night crying. I thought about coming upstairs. But I was afraid that we might...you know."

"Sleep together," Alex stated simply.

"Yes," I confessed with a blush. "But with him downstairs, it wasn't the right thing to do. I just wanted to make a clean break, you know?"

"If he ever gives you the chance," Alex said sharply.

"What do you mean?"

"Stephanie, I must have watched you try to get him out of the party at least a dozen times," Alex said. "You start by saying Peter, we need to...then he stopped you. He knows."

"About us?" I gasped, not realizing what I was implying.

"I don't think so." Alex shook her head. "But he knows something is up. Face it, no good conversation starts with 'we need to talk.' I think he knows that you're leaving him, and he's doing everything he can to prevent you from finishing that sentence."

"What do we do now?"

"I guess we go to breakfast," Alex said grimly.

"This should be fun," I tried to joke. "Just like having my teeth drilled or being audited. Fine, we'll eat, then I'll bring Peter back here and sit him down and tell him the truth. I can't put this off any longer."

"Tell me something?"

"It's because I don't love him and because I'm gay," I said with confidence.

"That's not what I was going to ask you. I just wanted to know what we did wrong in a past life to be going through all of this now."

"I wish I knew. From the moment I got to town, I feel like I've been trying to juggle a pack of porcupines. Whatever we did prior to this lifetime must have been extremely evil." I tried to make sense out of the mess that was our lives. "Your turn."

"What?"

"Just when and how did you undo my bra last night?" I asked with a blush. "If you hadn't told me, I would have walked into the party with the girls exposed." Alex wiggled her eyebrows in response. "Whatever," I scoffed.

"Do you think if we just hide out here long enough they'll go away?" Alex asked in an almost serious tone.

"Not a chance."

We waited for a few more moments before the cold became unbearable. Reluctantly, we returned to the house. Just as I had predicted, we found Peter and Courtney eagerly awaiting us. Alex and I retrieved our coats and rejoined our dates in the foyer.

"I can't wait to see the rest of this house!" Courtney purred as she took Alex by the arm and led her out the front door.

I swear if Peter had not taken my hand and led me outside, I would have smacked the youngster in the head.

"Are the two of you related?" Courtney asked.

"No." Peter laughed at the question. "Well, not yet. Stephanie is my girlfriend."

"Really?" Courtney cast a curious glance in my direction.

I understood the look, she knew. I shot her an angry glare. She responded with a weak smile that reeked of pity as she tried to drape her arm around Alex, who brushed off her advances.

We made our way down the street, and I was filled with an uncontrollable desire to shove Courtney into oncoming traffic. When I realized that someone would have noticed, I dismissed the notion. Peter tightened his hold on me, which made me flinch. I reminded myself that it was just breakfast, then I would finally sit him down for our long overdue chat.

Chapter Twenty One

Upon reaching the Java House, despite the early hour, we found it crowded. I wasn't surprised by the crowd. Early on, before Alex grew distant, we had eaten there a few times. Due to the line, we were forced to wait outside in the cold for a table. Courtney and Peter chatted away while Alex and I pretended to listen. Alex was bouncing nervously; I knew it meant she was craving a smoke. Finally, we were seated in a booth at the back of the restaurant.

"Professor Kendell, I haven't seen you in a while," Betty, the waitress, greeted us. "I see you brought Dr. Grant back. Nice to see you again." She cast a confused look at Courtney snuggled up to Alex. Then she cast another confused glance at Peter sitting next to me.

Alex and I quickly requested a round mimosas and a pot of the house coffee. I looked over at Peter's strange expression. I proceeded to order omelets for Peter and me since he had grown strangely quiet upon Betty's arrival. Alex and her spunky little playmate followed suit, each ordering cheese and mushroom omelets. I fought the gnawing in my stomach when Courtney decided to have whatever Alex was having. Alex just rolled her eyes at me. Betty returned quickly with our beverages.

"Perhaps this will help my hangover," Peter joked as he sipped his mimosa. "That was some party last night."

"Thanks," Alex mumbled, strumming her fingers on the table. "I need a smoke," she grumbled, extracting a pack from the inside pocket of her coat.

"I didn't know you smoked," Courtney said with a hint of disgust.

"I'm trying to quit," Alex snarled and reluctantly returned the pack to the pocket of her camel hair overcoat.

"When did you score another pack?" I shook my head before taking a sip of my drink.

"When you weren't looking," she bragged, ignoring the fact that only she and I were amused. Our companions just sat there staring at us. "So what's up, Pete?" Alex asked tersely. "You've become awfully quiet all of a sudden."

Her shortening of his name did not escape my notice. It also hadn't escaped my notice that Courtney was practically sitting in her lap.

"I'm just putting something together," he said absently as my body stiffened. "Alex Kendell?" he said slowly.

"Yes?" she responded with a warning tone.

"Alex as in Alexandra? That Alex Kendell?" he squeaked out, tightening his grip on my hand.

"I hope so, I'm wearing her underwear."

I almost spit out my mimosa, thinking her response was typical Alex. What I couldn't figure out was what in the world Peter was doing.

"The lawyer?" he spat out.

"Peter," I cautioned, suddenly understanding what was going on.

"I thought you taught history," Courtney said in confusion.

"I do." Alex looked at me for help.

"Peter, it was a long time ago." I was hoping to calm him down, remembering how upset he was after my first encounter with Alex. To his credit, he did everything he could to cheer me up, including calling Alex some not-so-nice names. I couldn't believe that he was just putting it together. Sometimes, his timing just sucked.

"What?" Alex held up her hands in confusion.

"Our previous encounter," I offered as an explanation.

"Just what did I do to you?"

"I'll tell you what you did," Peter shot out in anger.

"Peter, enough!" I snapped, not liking the look in his eyes. "Let it go."

"This woman," he fumed as if he was marking his territory.

"You know what, Pete?" Alex snarled. "I was a lawyer, and it's true I was the one who made your girl...who made Stephanie cry. Not that it's any of your concern, but I've already apologized. I wasn't a very nice person back then. Wainwright and Griggs is better off without me."

"None of my business," Peter shot back in a protective manner.

"Peter, it's in the past." I gritted my teeth. "Alex and I have already talked about this. She's my colleague and a friend." I watched him hang his head in embarrassment. He looked like a child who was being punished.

"Oh, boy." I heard Alex sigh as she poured herself a cup of coffee.

"I'm sorry, Alex," Peter sheepishly offered. "I just remember how much Stephanie had been hurt at the time. Forgive me?"

"No worries," Alex muttered.

"So are you a lawyer or a history professor?" Courtney asked with confusion.

"I'm a history professor who used to be a lawyer. Can we drop this now?" Alex groaned.

"You were with Wainwright and Griggs? That's so funny." Courtney had the bad manners to giggle.

"Hysterical," Alex responded flatly.

I hoped that Courtney would just keep yakking. If she did, Alex might dump her perky ass before the check arrived. The thought made me smile.

"Kind of, yeah." Courtney giggled once again. "Firms like Wainwright and Griggs are the reason I went to law school."

"You're a lawyer!" Alex choked as she spit out her coffee, which managed to just miss hitting Peter.

"Not yet," Courtney said. "I just graduated from Suffolk. I still need to pass the bar. But it was the firm of Wainwright and Griggs that inspired me to get into law in the first place."

"Oh, this is too good to be true," I whispered.

"Please, tell me you're joking," Alex pleaded.

"No," Courtney boasted. "Those bastards stole my grandparents' property. They spent their savings trying to stop them. I decided to become a lawyer to make sure that didn't happen to someone else."

"Thank God," Alex blew out with relief just as Betty arrived with our food.

Eager to avoid any more conversations or confrontations, Alex and I ate quickly while Peter and Courtney chatted away like old friends. Occasionally, one of us would answer a question or nod in agreement. I had no idea what they were talking about; I was relieved that the meal was almost over. As our dates continued chatting, Alex and I drained the pot of coffee. Betty brought another round of mimosas that I had no idea who ordered. Alex reached for her coffee, and Courtney reached for the inside of Alex's thigh. In a sudden surge of jealousy, I made a quick sweeping motion as if I was reaching for something. My aim was dead on, and Courtney's crotch was wearing her mimosa.

"I'm so sorry! That must be cold," I feigned embarrassment.

"It's okay," Courtney squeaked before she raced off to the ladies room.

"How clumsy of me." I tried to sound believable. Alex curled her lips and shook her head while Betty rushed over and cleaned up the mess with Alex's assistance.

"Thank you, Betty," Alex politely offered. "It seems Dr. Grant has lost control of her senses." She shot me another angry look. I shrugged off her accusation. "Could we have the check when you have a chance?"

Courtney rejoined us with a half-hearted smile and a pair of very wet jeans. "Oh, Cory, I'm so sorry. That looks terrible." I gasped, trying not to sound snarky.

"Courtney," she growled before plastering a fake smile on her face. "Not a problem, accidents happen. I have another pair of jeans in my car." She began to caress Alex's arm. "I can change at your place before we go." She smiled to Alex.

"She brought a change of clothes?" I hissed toward Alex.

"Go?" Alex gaped at me.

"What? Go where?" I added, equally confused.

"Weren't the two of you paying attention?" Peter asked as the check arrived.

"Of course," Alex lied, snatching up the check.

"We better hurry if we're going to beat the traffic," Courtney said, feeling the need to keep rubbing parts of Alex's anatomy.

My blood boiled. If not for the warning look Alex flashed in my direction, I would have jumped up and throttled the spunky little urchin.

"Unless you don't want to go to Salem. We could just stay in," Courtney added with a purr.

"No," Alex said quickly as she pulled away from Courtney's touch. "Salem at Halloween sounds like fun. Crowded, noisy, and fun. Perhaps you and Pete would rather be alone?" Alex suggested.

"We have all day tomorrow for that," Peter said with a smile. "Isn't that right, sweetheart?"

"That's right," I replied quickly. Had I been thinking clearly, I would have bagged out on the field trip, so I could do what I had been trying to do the night before.

My head was spinning as the four of us left the restaurant. I yelped when Alex grabbed hold of me and pulled me aside while motioning for our dates to go on without us.

"What in the hell are you thinking?" she spat out once we were alone.

"If you think I'm going to leave alone with Lolita there, you are sadly mistaken."

"What's it to you? I'm not your girlfriend," she flared.

"No, you're right, you're not my girlfriend," I shot back. "I'm not anyone's girlfriend."

"Well, that'll be news to Pete." She snarled.

"His name is Peter," I foolishly argued. "And I'm going to tell him the truth."

"When? After the two of you are married and have twelve children?"

"Today!" I shouted as I closed the distance between us and poked her in the chest. "I'll tell him everything today."

"Do what you want," she shot back, snagging the appendage I was poking her with.

"I will," I spat back. "Shouldn't you get back to your date before her curfew kicks in?"

"Very clever, Dr. Grant. You do know that none of this is any of your business."

"You're right, it's none of my business." I growled, not liking the surge of jealousy raging through me. "Do what you want. Date her, fuck her for all I care. Like you said, I'm not your girlfriend. If I was, you wouldn't have been out the other night picking up women."

"You don't understand," She suddenly sounded lost.

"You're right, I don't." I sniffed, leaning against the brick wall of the store we were standing in front of. "But I'm new in town."

"Stephanie…" Her voice trembled, her eyes fluttered shut, and I knew I had gone too far. "You really don't understand."

She leaned closer, clasping my hips and drawing me to her. I was about to pull away until I felt her strong thigh slide between my legs. Out of instinct, I clutched her hips and thrust against her. All I wanted to do at that moment was to ride her thigh until I found the release I so desperately needed.

"Does he make you feel this way?" a cruel voice whispered hotly in my ear.

Feeling ashamed, I pushed her away and stomped off, fighting back the tears. I could feel her following behind me as I walked back to the house.

"Hey, there you two are," Peter called out as we approached.

They were smiling and waving as they stood next to Courtney's aging Volvo. Courtney had already changed into a fresh pair of blue jeans and was holding the car door open. Peter took my hand, and before I realized it, I was sitting in the backseat with him. Alex climbed into the front passenger seat and slammed the door.

***

The trip was long and strenuous. Peter and Courtney chatted away, discussing everything, including the insane amount of traffic and the weather. We ended up parking in a makeshift parking lot next to what had been a gas station at one time. Alex hid behind her dark Ray-Ban sunglasses, and we kept our distance. I could feel her anger emanating from her. I ground my teeth and stewed in my own anger.

We wove in and out of the crowd that seemed to be growing with each passing moment. I did try to get Peter's attention more than once. He was too excited by the festivities to listen. I tried repeatedly to get him alone so we could talk. Alex was right. Peter did everything he could to avoid being alone with me. He was, however, determined to show me a good time. He had taken my hand on the drive up and refused to release it during the entire outing. I noticed several women eyeing him. I silently wished that he would notice them.

Instead, he and Courtney decided to play tour guide, dragging us to one flashy attraction after another. More than once, I looked at my watch, trying to determine what would be the right time to suggest leaving the merriment. I saw the opportunity when the skies turned dark, and the crowd turned to alcohol. Everyone agreed, and we headed back to the car.

"Hold on," Alex spoke for the first time. "I'll be right back." She slipped her sunglasses off before darting into a comic book store.

"I can join—" Courtney volunteered too late. Alex was inside before she could catch her. "Never mind," she added with a pout.

True to her word, Alex was in and out in record time. "Here." She handed me a bright yellow plastic bag. Everyone was looking at me as I held it in my hands. "You don't have to open it now," she said before encouraging us to keep moving toward the car.

***

On the drive back, Alex grew anxious, worried that she wouldn't get back in time to hand out candy.

"What did she give you?" Peter sounded uncomfortable.

"What?"

"Alex, what did she buy at that store?"

Curious, I looked inside the bag and found a shirt. I slid it out and laughed. "Perfect." I smiled, looking in the rearview mirror, catching Alex's shy smile. "It's a Wonder Woman T-shirt," I told Peter before carefully slipping back inside the bag. "Thank you, Alex."

"Every girl needs one." She smiled once again. Oddly enough, no one else said anything; instead, we fell back into the uncomfortable silence we had endured since leaving Salem.

I could feel the tension growing as we approached our house. Upon arriving, Alex and Courtney left us. They were going to hand out candy, then off for a night of dancing. I hated that they were going out, but I was elated with the knowledge that Peter and I would finally be alone and I could sit him down.

Upon entering the apartment, he excused himself to the bathroom. I sat on the futon and waited for him. I was confused when I awoke several hours later covered in a blanket. The emotional turmoil and lack of sleep must have caught up with me.

"Come on, sweetheart." Peter nudged me.

"What?"

"It's a surprise." He seemed excited. "We have plans to meet up with Bob at a club. I can't remember the last time you and I went dancing."

"What?" I repeated, still lost in a sleepy haze.

"You need to get dressed," he sweetly instructed, helping me to my feet.

I think I mumbled okay or something similar as I stumbled toward the bathroom. I was still half asleep when I climbed into the shower. I showered and dressed on autopilot. It wasn't until we were heading out the front door that it hit me. I was going out with Peter!

"How did that happen?" I sputtered as he opened the car door.

During the drive into Cambridge, I made several valiant efforts to talk to him. But he kept changing the subject. He was very excited about the place we were going. He and Bob had made plans to celebrate not losing their jobs. So much for being alone.

"I can't wait to get you out on the dance floor," Peter said as we walked from the parking garage on Green Street.

"About that, Peter," I began as we approached the large black building with a huge crowd milling about. Most of the patrons were in costume or very revealing leather outfits, eagerly waiting to show their IDs so they could enter. The sea of leather distracted me from what I was about to say.

"There's Bob." Peter waved excitedly to his friend.

Bob was a well-built tanned blond surfer type. He was talking to or at least was trying to talk to a familiar raven-haired beauty.

"Wow, for a second, I thought that was Alex." Peter gasped.

"Close." I shook my head, noticing the bored expression she was sporting.

We approached the pair. Bob noticed us and waved like a lunatic.

"Hey, stranger," Nicole greeted me with a warm embrace.

"You know each other? That's great!" Bob was practically panting. Nicole, on the other hand, rolled her eyes. "So now that you've met my friends, maybe you'll let me buy you that drink?"

Nicole shot her elbow back and connected with his rib cage, leaving Bob gasping for air. "I told you before, buddy, I don't drink." Nicole growled.

"I see that the Kendell charm is in full swing." I couldn't resist the pun.

"Speaking of charm, where is that Amazon sister of mine?" Nicole asked. "Don't tell me she made you wait in line by yourself. I'm going to have to teach that girl some manners."

"Date, she's on a date," I choked out.

"Hi, I'm Peter," he suddenly introduced himself, holding out his hand. "Stephanie's boyfriend," he clarified when her eyes widened with surprise.

"Nicole Kendell," she managed to say, finally shaking his hand.

"So are you related to Alex?" Peter asked uncomfortably, draping his arm around my shoulders.

"Yes, she's my older and seriously misguided sister," she said wryly. "So what brings you kids to The Galaxy?"

"The Galaxy?" I gasped. "Damn it!"

One of the doormen requested our IDs while waving for Nicole to head on in. She took my hand and led me in the doorway. "She's with me," she explained, leaving Peter and Bob dumbfounded. When we reached the front of the line, our hands were stamped without question. Then without skipping a beat, we breezed past the cashier.

"You don't pay?"

"No, I'm on the guest list." She shrugged. "Back when I was drinking, I think I dropped a good chunk of my trust fund here. So Peter's cute, and I'm guessing completely clueless."

"You want him?" I offered hopefully, glancing at the red neon sign with the words *The Galaxy* emblazed across it. "I can't believe he brought me here. This is where your sister is coming."

"Not with you?" She shook her head, completely confused. "What happened?"

"Everything and nothing," I tried to explain. "Then everything again and back to nothing. Now she's out on a date with some perky little thing."

"This should be fun."

"Fun it is then!" Bob exclaimed, rushing over to us.

"Listen, Bubba…" Nicole scoffed.

"Bob," he happily corrected, not getting the hint.

"Whatever." Nicole snarled, then she leaned over and whispered to me. "This jerk has been hitting on me since I got in line."

"Hey, Nicole," a voice called out.

"Sorry, that's my friends." She waved back at a group of people. "I hate to ditch you, but we're all from the program. We kind of like to keep an eye on each other in places like this." With that, she gave me a quick hug and waved to Peter before joining her friends.

"I think she's into me," Bob boasted.

I chose to ignore his delusions and look around the expansive nightclub. It was an impressive place. To my left was a room with a large dance floor blaring retro music. The lights pulsated to the music as two disco balls glimmered above the sea of bodies dancing to *YMCA*. I couldn't help but notice the diversity of the crowd. It was a mix of Halloween, goth, quite a few PVC fetish outfits, and folks wearing basic club clothes. There were men and women dancing together, men and men dancing together, and women and women dancing together. No one seemed to mind the differences of the people they shared the dance floor with.

Peter and Bob followed me as I passed by the first room and entered a much larger dance room with a stage at the far end. Spread out around the room were dance floors and bars. "How can anyone hear in here?" I couldn't help asking.

"We can hang in the lounge while you get your sea legs," Bob offered. "And I can look for that hot brunette."

I followed after Bob and Peter into yet another room. This room was decorated as a lounge area, and a long bar covered the length of the back wall. The room also had velvet couch and several armchairs. It possessed two old-time video games and a pool table. That was when I saw them. Alex was bent over trying to make a shot while Courtney was trying to feel her ass. My chest tightened while I mentally reminded myself that I had no right to be upset.

I stood there with Peter's hand resting on my arm. I knew I was smiling, all the while internally, I was plotting Courtney's death. I clenched my teeth when Alex bent over once again to make a shot and Courtney once again reached for her ass.

Just as I was about to storm over and break up their little party, I felt a hand on my shoulder. I spun around to find Maureen smiling back at me. I buried my anger and made the proper introductions. She in turn introduced us to her husband, Mort. Peter, Bob, and Mort offered to check our coats.

"Come on, let me buy you a drink," Maureen offered as she led me back to the room we had just exited.

"What's with the phone booth?" I asked when I noticed a British-style red phone booth tucked in the corner.

"That's so you can make a request from the DJ in this room," Maureen said. "They were playing some really great industrial earlier."

"I like new wave," I said as we nudged our way through the crowd.

Behind the bar was a tiny woman with platinum blond hair dressed in a flowing black dress. I wondered how she could move so well in such an outfit. As she approached us, I noticed that both of her wrists were tattooed in a floral pattern, and her nose and lip were pierced.

"What can I get for you ladies?" she asked brightly.

"Captain and Coke," Maureen ordered.

"Something strong." I shrugged.

"Red Death." The bartender seemed excited.

"We don't want to kill her," Maureen interjected. "How about a Cuervo sunrise?"

"No tequila." I blanched, still feeling worse for wear from my last experience. "Double Jameson, rocks. I can sip that."

"So how old is that child with Alex?" Maureen shouted after the bartender spun around to make our drinks.

"According to Alex, old enough," I bitterly supplied.

"For what? Never mind. I heard the four of you had just a super day!" Maureen teased with a wide-eyed expression.

"Who said that?"

"The teenager," Maureen said sarcastically. "Look out, here comes trouble." Maureen looked over my shoulder. I steadied myself and was relieved to find Nicole approaching us. She waved to the bartender, who just nodded.

"Ladies," she greeted us as the bartender returned with our

drinks and a bottle of Poland Springs water for Nicole.

"I have this," I volunteered, pulling money out of my purse.

"Thanks," Maureen and Nicole accepted.

"Just make you sure you tip Teresa well," Nicole cautioned. "Rumor has it that she once killed a coat check girl."

"What do you mean, rumor?" Teresa laughed as she accepted my money.

"Keep the change," I quickly offered.

"Thank you, miss." Teresa smiled and went off to wait on more patrons.

"So what are you gals talking about?" Nicole asked.

"I was just going to ask Stephanie here where she and Alex disappeared to last night at the party," Maureen said smugly as she sipped her cocktail. "'Cause I could have sworn that I saw two women that looked just like them making out on the back stairwell."

"Do tell?" Nicole encouraged. "Now if that's true, why are they here with different people?"

"I don't want to talk about it," I said.

"Come on, Stephanie, share," Maureen pushed. "It's not the first time the two of you have sucked face. What's going on?"

"Who knows?" I said with a hint of defeat in my voice.

"Look, there's that idiot again." Nicole groaned, pointing toward Bob, who was at the other end of the bar trying to talk to the women gathered there. "Look, he's chased them off already."

"And now he's chasing off the rest of the women at the bar," I noted as the three of us tried to hide.

"Teresa isn't going to like that," Nicole noted as the bartender approached Bob and began to shout at him. "I almost feel sorry for him. My God, he's trying to flirt with her. What is wrong with him?"

I watched with some degree of amusement when Teresa hurled a whole lemon at Bob. "Wow, got him right between the eyes."

"Well, it got rid of him." Nicole seemed pleased as we watched Bob stumbling off. "So back to what is really important, why aren't you dating my sister?"

"There's nothing to say."

I sipped my Irish whiskey and pretended that the two of them weren't staring at me. "I don't want to talk about it," I said finally as I slammed my plastic glass down on the bar. I looked at Maureen, who was standing to my left, she just smiled. I turned to Nicole, who was standing on my right with her arms folded across her chest, giving me the same knowing look. I was trapped. "It's the truth. I don't know what's going on." I received two disbelieving glares.

"There you are," Mort called out as he approached Maureen. He placed a tender kiss on her cheek. "Everyone is looking for the two of you. Hey, Nicole, how are you?"

"No complaints, Mort, good to see you."

"We'll catch up with you in just a second, Mort," Maureen said. "We were in the middle of some girl talk."

"Please hurry." Mort sounded desperate. "Peter is nice enough, but that Bob guy is driving me crazy."

"Bob?" Nicole groaned.

"Yeah." Mort sighed. "If we don't get back there, they might just come looking for us."

"Gotta go." Nicole spit out quickly and disappeared into the crowd.

The three of us followed Nicole's lead and made our way back into the lounge area. At the bar, we found Peter and Bob. They weren't alone. Courtney had joined them.

"Look who I found!" Peter said brightly.

"Hey, there." Courtney giggled as she waved to us. "We were just going to do some shots."

"Maybe you could fix her up with Peter," Maureen slyly whispered to me.

I laughed, thinking about how well the two of them got along. It would be the perfect solution. Just then, a tall beautiful blonde approached the bar. Everyone with the exception of Maureen turned and watched her as she ordered and got her drinks. Maureen just glared at Mort. The rest of the party, including me, watched the blonde as she walked away. Safe to say, Peter was definitely not Courtney's type.

"Mort, you're a pig." Maureen growled at her husband, who was now hanging his head in shame. All eyes turned to me expecting me to do the same to Peter. I couldn't very well scold him since I had also checked out the woman's attributes. I just shrugged, catching a knowing smirk from Courtney.

"How many kamikazes?" the bartender asked.

"None for me," Maureen said quickly. "This is my last drink since I'm driving."

"Darling?" Peter asked.

"No, thank you." I waved off the offer, knowing the last thing I needed was to get drunk.

"Five then," Courtney ordered.

"Five?" I questioned.

"Yeah, the four of us and one for Alex," she said brightly.

"She won't drink that," I supplied knowingly. Courtney just glared at me.

The bartender skillfully lined up and poured the five shots.

"I won't drink what?" the deep alto voice said from behind me.

"We're doing kamikaze shots," Courtney said.

"No thanks," Alex said bluntly as Courtney pouted. "Ginger, you can have my shot. I'll take a bottle of water."

"Ginger?" Peter asked in confusion.

"Yes?" The bartender winked at Peter.

Peter's face turned pale as he wrapped his arm around me and pulled me closer. Ginger just laughed, sliding the shots over along with a bottle of water. Alex paid for the round and tipped the man generously.

"Thanks, Ginger." Alex smiled as he downed the shot that had been meant for her. Our four companions downed their shots and proceeded to order another round, along with beers. The four of them continued to drink while Alex, Maureen, and I talked about school. The three of us passed on all offers for alcohol. Courtney seemed disappointed that Alex wasn't joining in on the festivities.

Nicole approached quietly and pulled Alex aside. The two of them walked to the other side of the lounge and began a very animated conversation. I caught one or two words that they were saying. Unfortunately, they were speaking French again.

"What the hell?" Courtney growled, catching sight of the two of them. "Now what?" Courtney slurred as the Kendell sisters rejoined us. I felt no need to inform Courtney that Nicole was Alex's sister. Apparently, Maureen agreed with my choice as she stood there smirking. "This has been happening all night," Courtney slurred again.

"Imbecile!" Nicole snapped at Alex as she shook her head in disgust. Alex held up a cautioning finger in Nicole's face. Courtney strutted over to Alex and placed a possessive hand on her arm as she stood toe to toe with Nicole. Courtney raised a warning finger and was about to poke her in the chest when Alex stopped her.

"Tread carefully, little girl," Nicole warned before redirecting her attention toward Alex. "*Ivre?*" Nicole asked, looking at Alex, then casting a disgusted look at Courtney.

"*Oui.*" Alex nodded.

"Listen, you Euro trash..." Courtney began to sputter.

"Down, Courtney." Alex stepped in. "My sister is a black belt."

"Sister?" Courtney blushed. "I'm sorry, I didn't know."

"Yeah, like she couldn't look at them and figure it out," Maureen discreetly whispered to me.

"Uh-huh." Nicole waved Courtney off with indifference before resuming her conversation with Alex, once again opting for French, clearly not wanting anyone to know what she had to say.

"*Arret!*" Alex shouted, holding up her hand.

"Do you know what they're saying?" I whispered to Maureen.

"From what I can catch, Nicole just called Courtney stupid and a little girl," Maureen whispered back with a smirk.

At this point, Nicole pushed past Alex and Courtney to join us. Bob rushed over. Alex quickly followed.

"Glad to see you came back," He leered. "You're sure I can't buy you a drink?"

"She doesn't drink." Alex fiercely growled.

"Alex." Nicole waved her off. "I can handle this ass hat. Listen, Bert."

"Bob." He happily bounced, somehow thinking that her not remembering his name was some form of endearment.

"Whatever, Skippy," Nicole rolled her eyes. "For the last time, I don't drink. Not ever. I can't, I'm in AA."

"Huh?"

"I'm an alcoholic," Nicole spelled it out for him.

"Oh." He finally caught on. "Well, how about a dance? You don't have any rules about that, do you?"

"Not in this lifetime or the next," Nicole brushed him off.

"Why?" He seemed confused. "Are you…well, you know, like your sister?"

"You mean a lesbian?" Nicole laughed. "Hell no, I just think you're obnoxious."

"Right." He laughed. "So about that dance?"

"You're a couple clowns short of a circus, aren't you?" Nicole concluded as her cellphone vibrated. "Kendell?" she answered the call. "On my way," she said before hanging up. "It's the hospital, I can always count on being called in on Halloween. It's been a pleasure, everyone, except for you, Brad." She snarled at Bob. "Alex, I love you, but you're an idiot, and we *will* talk later. Stephanie, I'm sure we'll be seeing each other again." With that, she smirked at Alex and left.

"Nice meeting you," Courtney called after her. Nicole never turned around. "So your sister is a doctor?"

"Yes, she practices emergency medicine at MGH," Alex said.

"I wouldn't mind playing doctor with her." Bob was drooling.

"Excuse me!" Alex snapped. "You wouldn't be making any unwanted advances toward my baby sister, now would you?"

"That woman was seriously hot," Bob continued, completely unaware of the danger he was in.

"Bob," Peter cut in, placing himself between Alex and Bob. "Dude, shut up now," Peter warned him. Bob just got that faraway look in his eyes. "Hey, you know the bartender in the disco room said you were cute."

"Really?" Bob preened before he strutted into the disco room.

"Thank you." I took Peter's arm, breathing a sigh of relief that no blood had been spilled.

"No problem," Peter said. "He's not a bad guy. He's just a little bit of a …"

"Dumbass," Alex cut in.

"Basically," Peter agreed.

"You do know the bartender you sent him to is a lesbian?" Alex asked.

"Yes, I do." Peter smirked knowingly.

Everyone laughed, easing the tension for everyone, with the

exception of me. I found myself standing there with my hand on Peter's arm. It was such a small gesture, but I understood the implications. It somehow said that I was his. I slipped from his embrace just as Courtney announced that it was time for more shots.

"No more, please," I pleaded with him. I couldn't risk another night of him being far too inebriated to understand what I was trying to tell him.

"What, no one is going to join me?" Courtney fussed.

I pulled him over to me and leaned up and whispered in his ear. "Peter, we need to talk." I'd finally said it, and now was the time to get him out of there to finish what I had started.

"Okay," he said loud enough for everyone to hear. "But first, you owe me a dance." He brushed off what I had just said. "What do you say, dance with me?" Everyone was looking at me with the exception of Alex.

Against my better judgment, I allowed him to take my hand and lead me into the front dance room. Peter and I had always danced well together until tonight. Perhaps it was the guilt, but every time he touched me, I pulled away. I survived dancing to three songs before I could pull him off the dance floor.

As we were exiting the dance floor, I saw Alex and Courtney dancing very closely together. Alex looked incredible with her tight black jeans and red silk blouse. Watching her sway to the music was thrilling. But it broke my heart to see another woman touching her.

Peter and I rejoined the others. Bob had returned from his quest, apparently shot down by the bartender. Everyone was deep in conversation. What they were talking about was a mystery to me. I failed to join in. I just watched the dance floor, trying to catch glimpses of Alex and Courtney. Someone said something to me, but I failed to respond. I was far too busy looking for a certain dark-haired beauty until she disappeared into the crowd. Peter slid his arm around me, and out of habit, I placed my hand in his. It was a familiar yet empty gesture. Just as it had always been.

"Stephanie?" a voice called to me.

"Huh?" I was shaken from my thoughts as I realized that it had been Peter talking to me.

"I asked if you wanted something to drink," he said.

"No thanks. We should get going soon." I looked back toward to the dance floor.

"Not yet," he pleaded with a sad little smile.

Frustrated and feeling a little bit like a stalker, I excused myself and went downstairs to the ladies room. It was crowded, and to my surprise, the long line of people included men. Granted, most of them were wearing dresses, but for a girl who grew up in Connecticut, it was a bit of a shock. No one else seemed to notice. I looked around at the young faces and suddenly began to feel self-conscious. I was definitely overdressed in my black dress and heels. Not to mention my matching purse.

Standing in line gave me time to think. The events of the day had been so surreal. I could have stopped most everything from happening. All I had to do was break up with Peter. I could have done it the night before or that morning. Instead, jealousy won out, and I spent the day touring Salem. There was no way in hell I was going to leave Alex alone with that girl. If only I had trusted Alex and done what I knew I should do. Look where it got me. Peter was doing everything he could to avoid talking to me alone. Alex was pissed off because I was allowing him to get away with it. Courtney was doing everything she could to get Alex into bed. At this rate, if I didn't pull myself together, I was going to end up as a flower girl at their wedding.

I left the ladies room deciding that hiding there was not going to solve anything. As I stepped out into the dark hallway, I felt a familiar hand on my arm. Gently, she pulled me around away from prying eyes. I knew her touch instantly. I pulled her close to me and held her tightly.

"Alex," I whispered.

"How are you holding up?" she asked gently, stepping slightly away from me.

"Not very well," I said honestly. "I'm sorry about today. I shouldn't have gone."

"No," Alex said firmly. "This is my fault. I had no right telling you what you should do. This is none of my business."

"None of your business?" I answered sadly. "So last night and this morning meant nothing to you? It meant something to me. I don't go around just kissing anyone." There was no harshness to my words, just honesty.

"Of course, it meant something to me." Alex looked deep into my eyes. "That's what you don't understand. It means so much to me that it's scaring the hell out me. Stephanie, you have no idea of the power you hold over me. Last night, this morning, and right now."

"Right now?" I moaned as she lowered her head and ran her tongue across my lips. Her lips brushed mine gently as her tongue begged for entrance. I parted my lips and allowed her in. I pulled her closer, and our kiss deepened. I felt my legs opening slightly as her thigh slid between them. Our bodies melded together. I could feel my legs tremble as I became aware of the wetness between my legs. I shivered as I felt a hand making its way up under the hem of my dress and caressing my cheek.

I felt lost, not knowing where I stopped and she began. A sudden coldness overcame me as she pulled away. I opened my eyes as I felt the coldness of the basement wall I was pressed against. Only moments ago, I was on fire. Her touch alone had burned me, and now I was freezing.

"Not like this," she said tenderly as she brushed her hand across my face. "We'll talk later." Her other hand retreated from under my dress. I nodded to her as I straightened my clothing. She brushed my arm, then walked away. Her departure wasn't like the other times. Alex was not running away. I stood there for a moment as she went to the coat check, her gaze never leaving mine as she received the coat and departed. I gave her time to make her departure while I collected myself.

Once I had returned to the lounge, I touched Peter on the arm, and with a newfound sense of strength, I whispered to him, "We should go."

"But it's still early," he protested.

"You're not leaving, too?" Bob piped in. "First Courtney and Alex and now you two."

"It was past Courtney's bedtime," Maureen added snidely.

"I just can't believe that those two beautiful women are lesbians," Bob added in disbelief.

"Oh, please." Ginger scoffed from behind us. He just smiled and pretended to be busy.

I shot Bob a cold look, suddenly wishing that Peter had allowed Alex to kill him. I grabbed Peter firmly by the arm. "Excuse us." I dragged Peter away from the others. "Peter." I spoke firmly as I placed my hand over his mouth to stop him. "We have to talk and not here. Get our coats," I demanded.

"Fine," he conceded sadly. Then he turned back to the others as I walked over to the bar. "We're taking off," Peter announced with a false joyous tone.

"No," Bob argued.

"Bob, what would you do?" Peter teased him. "Stay here and look at your ugly mug or go home with her?"

Bob laughed and slapped Peter on the back before saluting him with his bottle of Rolling Rock. Ginger and Maureen just cast a knowing look at me. Peter went downstairs to get our coats, and I ordered a bottle of water from Ginger. As I paid for the overpriced water, Ginger leaned over and quietly said, "Girl, you're going to break that boy's heart."

"I didn't know that it showed." I placed a tip on the bar.

"You know you might want to come in on a Thursday night," Ginger suggested softly.

"Thursday?" I asked. "Isn't that gay night? Oh…how did you know?"

"Oh, please, honey." Ginger scoffed. "You're not fooling this queen with those Doris Day looks of yours. Of course, from what I heard about Doris."

I just laughed as I sipped my water. I only had the one drink that night, but I wanted to be completely lucid for my talk with Peter. He returned with our coats, and we said our goodbyes. I took his keys from him, and we stepped out into the cold autumn air. Neither of us spoke as we walked back to the parking garage. The drive home was silent, as well.

It wasn't until we crossed over the Prowers Landing town line that Peter finally spoke. "Is there someone else?" he asked in a strained voice.

"No and yes."

"What the hell does that mean?" he snapped.

"I have met someone," I tried to explain. "But that isn't why

I'm…"

"Leaving me. That is what you're doing, isn't it? You're leaving me, aren't you?"

"Peter, I'm sorry."

"I don't understand, Stephanie." His voice dripped with resentment. "Are you…have you slept with him?"

Of course, he would assume it was a man. Life can offer you so many options to a situation. Now I could have just told him everything right then and there and let everything hit the fan all at once. Or I could do what I did. Not lie but not tell the entire truth. Somehow, I thought it would be easier on him if I just skipped over the most important reason I was letting him go.

"No," I said with some degree of honesty. "The truth is that I'm not in love with you."

"Don't say that!" he shouted.

I was thrown by his anger. As we pulled up in front of the house, I received a second shock. Courtney's car was parked in front. Peter and I just sat in the car, each of us lost in our own thoughts. Finally, he ripped off his seat belt and sprang out of car, slamming the door behind him. I jumped out, too.

"Peter?" I pleaded.

"What!" he shouted.

"Please, don't," I begged him.

"Don't be angry!" he bellowed.

I just stared at him. "Let's go inside and talk, okay?" I offered as calmly as I could manage at that moment. He slumped his shoulders and nodded mutely. We entered the building and were greeted by the obvious sounds of someone having sex.

"Well, at least your friends are having a good time," he spat out.

"What do you mean?"

He just gave me a knowing look and pointed to the ceiling. The sounds were most definitely coming from above. The exact location was unfamiliar to me. I tried to make sense of it as I unlocked the door to my apartment. The sounds grew more urgent with each grunt and gasp. All I could think about was the fact that Courtney's car was parked in front of the house. I tried to dismiss the sounds as Peter shrugged off his coat. I just stood there with my hands in my pockets, unable to focus on the events unfolding around me. I was jolted out of my musings by the sounds of laughter coming from Alex's apartment. That time, I was certain that it was Courtney's annoying giggle.

"I'll make us some coffee," I offered weakly.

I removed my coat and went into the kitchen. As I prepared the coffee, I was relieved that the sounds from upstairs had ceased. While I fired up the Keurig, I couldn't stop asking myself if Alex was some kind of twisted player.

"Stephanie?" Peter's voice brought me back to reality. "Please tell me what I did to make you fall out of love with me."

I turned to him slowly. "Oh, Peter, it's nothing you did," I said gently. "The truth is that I was never in love with you." I swallowed hard as I watched his face turn pale.

"What?" He gasped as he sat on the futon. He looked as if someone had just kicked him in the face or perhaps somewhere much lower. "That's a lie," he said in a daze.

"I'm sorry," I said softly. "It's the truth. I've loved you as a friend, a good friend. I never should have let it go beyond that. This is my fault, and for that, I'm truly sorry."

"Never?" Peter said absently.

"I'm sorry," I repeated over and over again. My heart was breaking for what I was putting him through. But I knew that if I stayed with him that I would be doing something far crueler than what I was doing now.

"Was it the sex?" he asked sincerely. "You never seemed comfortable with it. Was that it?"

"No," I lied, and I told him the truth. How could I explain to him that I spent my entire life thinking that sex was not something that interested me? Now just one look from Alex and I felt alive. "I just thought that the friendship we shared was enough, but that isn't fair to you."

"When did all of this happen?" He was still shell-shocked. "I knew that something was wrong. You kept blowing me off, and I had to chase you down just to get you to talk on the phone. When we did talk, you were so distant. I thought maybe I was smothering you, then I thought maybe you were feeling neglected. I've been struggling for months trying to figure out what the hell I was doing wrong. Stephanie, when did I lose you?"

"I knew how I really felt not long after I moved here." I handed him a cup of coffee before starting another for myself.

"I don't understand," he stammered. "Then why did you wait so long to tell me?"

"I didn't want to hurt you."

"You didn't want to hurt me?" he asked in a bewildered tone. "The only way you were going to do that was by not doing this. This is breaking my heart."

"I don't want that. I never wanted that."

"Stay with me, we can work this out," he begged.

"No, I can't."

We talked for hours while Peter made a few more attempts for a second chance. When the sun came up, we were both exhausted. When it was time for him to leave, I hoped that he had finally accepted that it was over between us. I had explained that I was afraid that I would lose his friendship. He told me he needed time to work this out. Reluctantly, he left my apartment just before seven a.m. I stood in the driveway and waved goodbye to him. I prayed that it would not be the last time I saw him.

I turned to go back into the house when I was greeted by Courtney bouncing down the staircase with a giggle. I decided at that moment that it wasn't normal for a person over the age of five to giggle so much.

"Morning!" she greeted me, and yes, she giggled again. "Rough night?" She pointed to the dress I was still wearing from the night before. I tried to ignore her as I went to my apartment door. "So where's Peter?" She smirked.

"He's gone."

"I see. Well, I'm off. I guess I'll be seeing you around."

I spun around and gave the child an icy glare. "What's that supposed to mean?" I snapped.

"What do you think?" she purred and nodded toward the upstairs, then cast a wink in my direction. "We should be quiet, Alex is still sleeping. I'm afraid we didn't get much sleep last night."

"Bitch," I muttered under my breath and tried to retreat into my apartment.

"Really?" she responded coolly, having caught my comment.

"I'm a bitch. Forgive me, but I wasn't the one drooling over someone else's date yesterday. Tell me something, Stephanie, did your boyfriend take off because he finally figured out that it was Alex you wanted?"

"Where do you get off?" I snarled.

"Listen, lady." Courtney cut me to the quick. "I don't know what your deal is, and I don't care. All I do know is I'm the one who spent the night with Alex. By the way you were acting, I thought I should seal the deal as quickly as possible. Seriously, what did you think would happen? That maybe she'd be willing to date you and Peter?"

"Peter and I aren't together anymore," I shot back, clueless as to why I was telling her this.

"Well, isn't that convenient." She mocked me. "Whatever. Like I said, I'll be seeing you around. I'll just make sure I keep plenty of clothes here just in case you decide to toss another drink at me. I didn't miss a thing yesterday. So just back off, Blondie." Having made her position clear, she bounced out of the front door and was on her way.

Chapter Twenty Two

I stormed into the apartment and slammed the door behind me. I leaned against the door holding myself. I tried to calm down, reminding myself that Courtney was a snarky little juvenile delinquent. "Sealed the deal," I spat out with disgust. "Who talks like that?" I stood there until my knees were ready to give out. I decided that I needed to tidy up my humble abode if for no other reason than to distract myself.

I yanked the sheets off the futon and tossed out the bottle of wine that was still sitting on the coffee table. Both were remnants of the night of the party. I washed out the coffee mugs, my shaking hands reminding me that I was out of K-Cups. I gathered the dirty laundry and shoved it in the hamper. I put fresh sheets and blankets on the futon and folded it into its upright position. I dusted, vacuumed, and stripped off my dirty clothing, tossing it in with the rest.

The good thing about living in a studio was it didn't take long to clean up. The bad thing about living in a studio was it didn't take long to clean up. I took a long hot shower hoping that it would clear my mind. It didn't help. It did, however, give me a new project. After tidying up the bathroom, I had exhausted all options.

The only thing I had left to do was to get dressed. I smiled when I spotted the bright yellow bag from the day before. I pulled the T-shirt out and held it up. There was Wonder Woman in all her glory on a navy blue shirt. I threw on a pair of jeans and my new shirt, grabbed the laundry and a jacket, and headed out. I paused for a moment and listened.

"Okay, she's sleeping in," I blew out, still not believing Courtney's version of events.

I headed to the Laundromat, not the best choice on a Sunday

morning. The only thing working in my favor was the night before was Halloween. Alex wasn't the only one who was sleeping in. Other than a couple of other lost souls, I had the place to myself. I finished my laundry and returned home.

I looked at the clock, noticing that it was after one in the afternoon and Alex was still wasn't around. "She's sleeping in," I reasoned while putting away my laundry. "Doesn't mean that snot-nosed little twerp was telling the truth." I knew I was being more than a little bitchy, but then again, I hadn't slept in a couple of days.

I thought about sleeping, but it just seemed like a waste. This was the first day of my life. Granted, I was starting that day tired, cranky, and in a generally clueless state of mind. I grabbed my jacket and once again was out the door. With no destination in mind, I just started walking. I ended up in one of the last places I thought I'd be in—a cellphone store.

"Dr. Grant?" Ben, one of my honor students, greeted me. "Some party the other night."

"Yeah, that was…" I hesitated for a moment. "Weird actually."

"Okay," he drew out the word, probably not knowing how to respond. "So here to upgrade your phone?"

"I don't own a cellphone."

"Okay, I guessed that the one you had in class the other day wasn't yours."

"Why?"

"You didn't know how to turn it off."

"Truth is, I've never owned a cellphone."

"Are you punking me?"

"No." I yawned. "Sorry, I've come into some extra cash recently, and everyone in the universe seems to think I need a cellphone. I'm still not sure I do."

"Um, okay," he shook his head. "Why don't I show you some options? I'm guessing that the basics are probably what you're looking for."

"Something that makes phone calls would be good."

"Even the basic models these days can do that and so much more." Ben looked more and more afraid with each comment I made. "GPS is one of the features that this phone includes."

"I don't own a car."

"Are you Amish?"

I had to laugh because he was sincere. "This would be a wild Rumspringa, but no, I'm not Amish," I finally answered. "Just a little overly practical having lived in areas where higher education is prevalent, which usually means a halfway decent public transportation system. If not, there's always one bus that goes to the nearest major city."

"Okay, good. I just didn't know what to think. I mean, I had a guy in yesterday who was ninety, and he was upgrading his iPhone."

"I'm really out of touch," I blew out. "I used to date someone who was very tech savvy, but other than my laptop, I never felt the need to join the tech circus we live in." It was strange to say *I used to date* given that my relationship ended a few short hours ago.

"The good news is that you won't be locked into a contract," Ben began his spiel. "None of the major carriers want to do that anymore. The other good thing is if you have an emergency, you can get in touch with someone. I'm sure that friends and family have already pointed that out to you."

"Maybe once or twice," I grumbled.

"Watch this." He pulled his own cellphone off of his belt. "Who is Samuel Mudd?"

"Samuel Alexander Mudd, born December 20, 1833, died January 10, 1883, was an American physician who was imprisoned for conspiring with John Wilkes Booth in the assassination of U.S. President Abraham Lincoln," a mechanical voice informed me.

"Before you say it, no, it does not eliminate the need to do research," he quickly explained before I could say it.

"Good because there's a whole lot your phone didn't mention that's going to be on your final."

"Good to know." He smiled. "Okay, let me show you the basic 3Gs that will allow you to make phone calls, send texts, and take pictures."

"I need to do all that?" I scoffed.

"Maybe, maybe not, but these are features that come with the simplest models," he said. "And this way, you can give Professor Kendell her phone back."

"How did—" I started in a panic before realizing that probably at least half of my students saw me and Alex making out the other night. "Never mind. Just show me a phone that won't break the bank and doesn't take a degree from MIT to operate."

Picking out a phone wasn't difficult since Ben kept it simple, but the poor misguided lad made the mistake of trying to teach me how to use it. Over the course of the three hours it took to get me up to the beginner level, he kept repeating, "It's okay, it's never busy on Sundays." Which proved to be true since no one else came in while I was there, but I still felt bad for the poor kid. To his credit, I think he would have kept trying to teach me if closing time hadn't sneaked up on us.

I felt pretty good as I walked home. It was almost five, which meant that Alex was more than likely awake, and I felt fairly confident that I could convince her to go out to dinner with me. That was until I got to our house. Sitting out front was an aging Volvo, the same dilapidated car that left early that morning.

"Are you kidding me?" I stomped into the house. Above me, I could hear the distinctive sounds of laughter. I jabbed my key into the lock and stormed into my apartment, releasing a stream of curses as I kicked the door shut. I tossed the bag with my new phone onto the counter before I shrugged off my coat. I was muttering to myself as music began to play. "Adele, that's just freaking great," I hissed as I began to pace.

* * *

After a good hour or so of pacing while Adele sang, I decided that I needed to handle things the way I've always handled things. I needed to do some research. I plugged in my new cellphone when I remembered that Ben instructed me to charge it before trying to use it. Then I opened my laptop and began my quest. I was a little shaky at first, only because I made the mistake of checking my email, finding it loaded with messages from Peter.

After reading a couple of them, which consisted of Peter begging for another chance, I deleted all one hundred forty-seven of them. Then I set about educating myself. After being duped into opening websites that were nothing more than porn, I found the local LGBTQ sites.

The Internet turned into a cornucopia of information. There

were support groups, dating services, social groups, Facebook pages, and something I didn't know still existed—chatrooms. And that was where I found myself spending my time. Somehow, I ended up in a conversation with a woman named Rita who wanted to meet. Against my better judgment, I agreed to meet her for coffee Tuesday. I think I only agreed because Adele was still singing, and Courtney's car was still parked out front.

"What did I just do?" I questioned my sanity as I shut down my laptop. I glanced at the clock and was shocked to see that it almost nine o'clock. Deciding that going days without sleep was catching up with me, I changed into a comfortable T-shirt and lounge pants before lowering the futon.

I was just about ready to climb into bed when there was a gentle knock on the door. I went to the door realizing that the music had stopped. I opened the door and found Alex looking extremely anxious. Suddenly, I felt sick.

"Are you all right?" she asked tenderly.

"I'm fine," I lied as I wondered why she hadn't come down sooner. Then again, she might have if not for her houseguest. If she came down to see me, I doubted that I would've made a date with another woman.

"Are you sure?" she asked me in disbelief, reaching out.

I jerked my hand away, unable to stand the thought of her touching me. "I said I'm fine," I snapped bitterly. Her eyes widened in shock at my outburst.

"Stephanie?" She reached for me once again. I pulled away from her touch. "What is it?" she asked in a fearful voice.

"Look, I just want to be alone right now," I flared. My heart skipped a beat as I saw the pain reflected in her eyes. "I broke up with Peter last night," I explained, hoping that she would just leave. I couldn't deal with the whirlwind that happened whenever we were together.

"Is there anything I can do?" she offered. "Do you want to talk?" She reached out to me again and tried to step into the apartment. I blocked her way without allowing her to touch me.

"I just want to be alone right now," I repeated as I clenched my fists.

"Are you sure?" she asked with such sweetness that I almost

believed her.

"Yes," I answered firmly.

"Well...all right then," she said hesitantly. "I'll be upstairs if you need anything." Reluctantly, she turned from my doorway and walked away. I slammed the door behind her. I tried to hold myself together, but it was useless. I sobbed and crawled into bed, letting everything that had been building loose. This time, there was no stopping the tears. I hated myself for being so weak; I hated her for making me fall in love with her. I know that the road to true love can sometimes be a rocky path. But this was getting ridiculous!

Chapter Twenty Three

Over the course of the next few weeks, I felt as if I had lost all sense of reality. It all began the following day. In my defense, I was so worked up, I failed once again to sleep. Alex had been very friendly that morning. She knocked on my door and offered me a cup of coffee and a ride to work. Since my emotions were still on edge and my ego was bruised, despite the frigid temperatures outside, I declined. Alex seemed hurt by my indifference. While she was offering coffee, I was mentally calculating how many hours I'd been awake. If my math was correct, it was somewhere near ninety-seven.

I walked to work shivering with each step and thankful that the campus wasn't far away. I skipped going to my office and opted for a jaunt to the library instead. Somehow in my sleep-deprived state, I had decided that mooning over Alex was not helping my situation, and it was time that I put some distance between us.

By the time I found myself standing in front of my last class of the day, I was ready to drop. It didn't help that apparently no one had done the reading. "Come on." I yawned. "Didn't anyone read Mary A. Livermore's memoir? I'd think you'd jump at the chance since it's one of the few books on the reading list I didn't write." This comment did earn me a laugh. "You had all day yesterday to recover from Halloween, but since I'm still shaking out the cobwebs, as it were, this is your lucky day. I expect everyone to be caught up by Wednesday's lecture. If anyone blabs, I will continue lecturing and throw in a pop quiz. Now go before I change my mind."

I flopped down into my chair and put my head down on the desk. "Interesting approach," I heard Maureen say. I tried to pretend that I was alert when I snapped my head up. "Oh, don't bother." She scoffed at my attempt. "Not to be rude, but when was the last time you slept?"

"I woke up at about six in the morning." I yawned once again, not missing the scowl clearly written on her face. "On Thursday." I blinked rapidly in an effort to stay awake.

"Thursday!" she shouted, scaring the bejesus out of me. "Why?"

"Friday, I was dealing with Peter and the debacle at the party," I tried to explain. "Saturday night after we left the club, I broke up with Peter. Oddly enough, he wanted to talk. It took all night."

"What about yesterday or last night?"

"I was pissed at Alex."

"Because?" she prompted.

"Courtney spent the night Saturday." I struggled with the words. Just saying them made me feel sick. "Then she came back yesterday afternoon."

"Oh?" I could see that she was just as confused as I was. "There's probably a good reason—"

"I'm sure." I snarled. "Spending the night, coming back, and hanging out for hours listening to Adele sounds perfectly innocent to me."

"Adele?" She cringed.

"I know, right? I think if they'd been listening to the Beatles, I probably wouldn't have made a date with a woman I met in a chatroom." I felt slightly numb. "I bought a cellphone."

"Okay, I'm hoping you're delusional." She seemed frightened. "Just to be on the safe side, I'm driving you home now. You're going straight to bed."

"Okay," I agreed, struggling to stand. "Promise me that you won't say anything to her. I mean it, promise me," I added when it appeared that she was about to object.

"Fine." She grunted and grabbed my briefcase. "Did you really make a date with a complete stranger you met online?"

"Yes, and I bought a cellphone," I continued, blindly following after her. "Don't know what I'm going to do with it. So far, I've only learned how to charge it."

***

After Maureen dropped me off, I let myself into my apartment, stripped off my clothes, and climbed into bed. I was fast asleep not long after my head hit the pillow. I slept so soundly that I missed hearing my alarm. If not for the frantic knocking at my door, I might have slept through the entire day. I stumbled out of bed and opened the door. Alex stood there clearly confused.

"Are you all right?"

"I'm good," I lied, rubbing the sleep from my eyes. "I must have overslept. I'll see you at the office."

"I can wait," she volunteered.

"No, you go ahead," I quickly dismissed her offer.

"Stephanie—" She sounded nervous.

"Alex," I cut her off. "Go on, I'll see you at work." I tried to ease my tone. She frowned before turning and heading out the front door.

I scrambled to get ready, just making it to my first lecture. Things went better. Having finally slept, I felt more centered. I don't know what happened when I found myself alone with Alex. I was more than a little distant. Alex made every attempt to talk to me. She played it safe by throwing out mundane questions. I was hurt, and despite knowing that I held no claim on her, I felt betrayed.

"Would you like to do dinner tonight?" Alex asked while I was packing up for the day.

"Sorry." My shoulders slumped, thinking of course she'd ask about tonight. "I have plans." Plans I wished I hadn't made, but I did, and a part of me really needed to go. It was my first date with a woman, and I was terrified.

Alex mumbled something to the effect of have a good night as I made my way out. When I got home, I had to rush, not wanting to miss the 6:05 train into Boston. I dressed casually in a pair of black jeans and a teal blouse. I grabbed a jacket and my wallet and rushed outside. I spied a familiar aging Volvo rounding the corner. I hurried to the train station, just catching the train. The trip into the city was short, but it felt like forever. I just kept thinking about Courtney and wondering if she had visited last night, as well.

I arrived right on time at the coffee shop on Newbury Street. I wiped my sweaty palms on my jeans as I looked around for Rita. All I knew was she was about my age and blonde. I spied a well-dressed woman who matched the description sitting at a table in the back.

The anxious look she gave me alerted me that this might be my date.

I felt weak in knees as I made my way over. "Rita?" I squeaked out, thankful when she stood and offered her hand.

"You must be Stephanie," she said with a shy smile.

"Yes," I nodded, shedding my jacket. "I'm not late, am I?"

"No, like myself, you're early." She offered me a seat. "Can I get you a coffee?"

I thanked her, telling her how I liked my coffee and sat down. I tapped my foot nervously as she went to the counter. I looked around at the quaint setting. The laid-back crowd did nothing to calm my nerves. Rita returned with my coffee, and I thanked her as she sat.

"I have to be honest, I don't usually meet women in chatrooms," she nervously confessed.

"Neither do I." I laughed lightly. "To be honest, I didn't know that chatrooms still existed."

"My good fortune." She smiled. "You said you've recently moved to the area. Where were you before?"

"I was working in Providence for a while," I said, not wanting to go into a lot of detail. Rita seemed nice enough, but we did meet online.

We fell into an easy conversation while drinking far too much coffee. Rita owned a boutique just down the street, which was why she suggested meeting at the coffee house. She was intelligent, easy to talk to, and I did find her attractive. There was just one little hiccup. As attractive as I found her, there was something missing, and it wasn't who she wasn't. Despite her attributes, there wasn't a spark between us.

"Are you involved with someone?" she asked me suddenly.

"No," I answered truthfully. "But..."

"You're just getting over someone," she finished for me.

"How did you know?"

"Story of my life," Rita said casually. "So what happened?"

"It's complicated," I replied with reluctance.

"Always is. I'm here to listen if you want."

"Okay, you asked for it." I sighed. "First I need to explain that this is all very new to me. Up until very recently, I had a boyfriend."

"Excuse me? You're joking, right?

"No, I'm afraid not."

"I'll be honest. Normally, I do like a challenge," she confessed with a mischievous smile. "But even though I find you very attractive, intelligent, and everything I'm looking for, there just isn't—"

"A connection," I concluded with relief. "I thought it was just me."

"Thank you," she blew out, seemingly just as relieved as I was. "Which sucks because on paper we're perfect for each other. Well, except that you just came out. You are out, aren't you?"

"I am, which feels so good to say. I just wish I had figured it out sooner."

"There isn't a rule book," she teased.

"There should be," I playfully argued. "I blew into town in August, and everything I thought I knew about myself turned out to be a lie. When did you come out?"

"It was my second semester in college." She sighed. "I met the woman who I mistakenly assumed was the love of my life."

"What happened?"

"They legalized gay marriage," she wryly explained. "We had been sharing our lives ever since that first kiss on the ski slopes in Vermont. Suddenly, she didn't want to rush things. We owned a house together, had three dogs, and were talking about adopting a baby, but she didn't want to rush things. I thought fine, we didn't need a piece of paper. I told her there was no pressure, and she told me she needed space."

"How much space?"

"It required her getting a passport." She snorted with disdain. "She did return long enough for us to sell the house. Despite everything, I'm still convinced that the right woman is out there. Now tell me about this woman who was foolish enough to let you get away."

"We work together," I began my tale of woe. "Which she has a rule about. She also has rules against dating someone who is straight or involved."

"Not bad rules, but still you've since come out and gotten rid of your boyfriend," she pointed out. "That just leaves work, and if that's what's keeping you apart, then she's an idiot."

"You don't want to date me," I teased her.

"Which is a shame because we would've had great-looking kids."

"I don't know if it is work," I grumbled. "I think I just took too long. She's dating someone else, someone young and perky."

"Ouch!"

"Ouch indeed," I agreed. "I can't compete with that."

Rita offered her opinion, which was quite an unflattering assessment of Alex's character. I was thankful that I hadn't mentioned Alex by name just in case the two ever met. We talked for another hour or so covering a wide range of topics. It was a nice night. Sadly, I finally had to leave or risk missing the last train back. Rita and I exchanged phone numbers and agreed to get together again. It felt good having made another friend.

***

The good feeling lasted until I approached the house only to discover that Courtney's car was still parked out front. "I hate her," I muttered, stomping onto the front porch just as Shavonne was making her exit. Her hours were so odd I never knew if she was coming or going.

"Whose piece of crap is that?" She shook her head. "Damn thing has been parked in front of the house all week."

"It belongs to Alex's new girlfriend," I reluctantly said, digging my keys out of my jacket pocket.

"I thought you were Alex's new girlfriend."

"Not so much."

"If you want, I can give her a ticket," she whispered, shifting her utility belt.

"Is she parked illegally?"

"No." Shavonne smirked. "But look at that thing. There has to be a code violation in there somewhere."

"That's sweet of you, but no."

***

After surviving my first date with a woman, I decided to take another bold step. I went to The Galaxy. Rita was meeting me there to act as my wingman. I took the train into town and arrived very early. The place was deserted, which was surprising since less than a week earlier, it was mobbed. I checked my coat and headed to Teresa's bar. I sipped my Jameson wondering if I was wasting my time. Rita made it in not long after I had settled in.

"I love that you run early. I thought I was the only one," she said before ordering a white Russian. "Speaking of early, I should warn you that things don't start to pick up until after eleven. It's kind of a Boston thing."

"Don't the bars close at two?"

"Yes, I didn't say it made sense."

"I don't know how late I can stay tonight. I don't want to miss the last train," I explained, thinking that it was okay since I only wanted to check things out. I spotted a few of my students. "No wonder they're always tired on Friday mornings!"

"Who?"

"I just spotted a couple of my students."

"What about her?" Rita nudged me, pointing toward a woman about our age dressed in chinos and a blue dress shirt.

"For me or you?"

"Me." She moved slightly away from me. "I don't want her to think we're together. But keep talking to me."

"Okay." I shook my head. "What would you like to talk about?"

"How is it going at work, you know with the girl?"

"She invited me to dinner tonight." I sighed. "That's twice this week. Both times I had plans with you."

"Good, make her think about things."

"I think maybe she's just trying to stay friends," I reasoned. "I just wish I could stop thinking about her."

"Normally, I'd tell you that what you need is to get back on the horse," she advised me. "But you haven't even seen the stables yet."

"Funny." I snarled. "Your new girlfriend is heading this way. Should I leave?"

"No, just move down a stool."

I moved away and watched Rita trying to get the other woman to notice her. She finally did, and they began talking. While they chatted away, I amused myself by watching the crowd. I glanced over to see Rita and her new friend hitting it off, or at least, I hoped they were hitting it off. When I turned back around, a young woman with dark hair and thick black glasses was standing next to me. She asked me to dance, and I politely declined. She proceeded to offer to buy me a drink. Although I admired her boldness, once again, I declined. She finally took the hint when I ordered another Jameson.

I sensed that if I hadn't been blunt, she wasn't going to give up. Rita was still busy chatting while I sipped my whiskey. The club was quickly filling up, so much so that I was jostled more than once. Eager drinkers didn't seem to care if they bumped into me, with one notable exception. Her name was Josie. She had curly brown hair and a great smile. We ended up talking for a bit. She appeared to be very nice and well grounded.

I lost track of how much time had passed until Rita interrupted, offering me a ride. I made my excuses, not one to turn down a ride back to Prowers Landing.

"How did it go?" I asked once we were on the road.

"Her name is Kathy, and she seems very fixated on my income." She shivered. "Once I clued into that, I decided that you shouldn't be taking the train home."

"Good call." I laughed.

"How did it go for you?"

"Her name is Josie," I nervously started. "She seemed nice. We're going out on Sunday afternoon. Rollerblading along the Charles. Which means between now and Saturday, I need to buy a pair of Rollerblades."

"Do you even know how to Rollerblade?"

"Nope," I sheepishly confessed. "I probably should have mentioned that."

"You think?" She chuckled. "I have to hand it to you, Stephanie, you've been out of the closet for what—a week, two weeks—and you've already scored two dates."

"Yeah, now if I could just get over the woman who pushed me out of the closet, life will be good."

***

It was after midnight when I returned to Prowers Landing. Upon approaching the house, I spied Courtney's Volvo pulling away.

"Oh, goodie. Junior's just leaving," I snapped.

"Junior?"

"The new girlfriend," I spat out. "Sorry, I can't help it."

"You live in the same building?"

"Yes." I sighed. "Which is an added joy."

"Have you thought about moving?"

"Briefly, but I love my studio, and it's only four hundred a month."

"Shut the front door!" She gasped. "Four hundred? In Prowers Landing? Are there any openings in the building?"

"You work in Boston."

"I'll commute," she said. "That is insane. What's wrong with the place?"

"Nothing except for her living one floor above me, and no, all the units are occupied," I said, her disappointment clearly showing. "Thank you for the ride. Call me when you get in."

"I will, call me and let me know how Saturday goes. Maybe you'll get to see the stables."

"Good night."

I waved to her once I opened the front door. I opened the door to my apartment feeling completely spent. It had been a long week, yet I was proud of myself for surviving. I showered and threw on some comfortable clothing. I settled down, and for the first time since moving in, I flipped on the television. Alex was right about one thing—my old television sucked in comparison. Rita called, saving me from a rerun of *The Nanny*. During the call, my phone beeped alerting me that I had messages.

After I ended the call, I checked my voice mail. I had two messages, the first from Peter asking how I was doing. He stammered nervously as he prattled on about how he was just calling to say hello.

The second message threw me for a loop. It was from Alex wanting to know if I would consider changing my mind about dinner. She also wanted to know if I was all right. I couldn't help wondering if Courtney had been her plan B for the evening. I told myself that it didn't matter, but that didn't stop me from listening to her message several times before erasing it.

Chapter Twenty Four

I was more than a little tired the next morning. I brewed my cup of coffee while listening to Joan Jett, which I thought was a nice choice. While preparing for work, I decided that I should walk to campus with Alex. I was finally working things out in my life, except working on saving our friendship. Sadly, the music stopped, and she was out the door before I had a chance to catch her.

"I have to fix this," I vowed before finishing up and heading out. I did stop and grabbed my cellphone, thinking it was time for me to start using it.

I almost ran right into Shavonne as I raced out the door. "Sorry," I quickly apologized as she laughed. "Now I don't want to get a ticket, Officer," I played along.

"Speaking of tickets…" She smiled brightly. "Guess who ran a stop sign?"

I stared at her for a moment before I realized that she was talking about Courtney. "You know, that kid isn't nearly as charming as she thinks she is," she told me. "She tried flirting with me. When that didn't work, she felt a need to point out that I lived in the same building as her girlfriend. She must have seen me coming or going at some point. I thought Alex had better taste than that. And now I've depressed you," she added, noticing my sullen mood.

"No, I'm good," I lied.

"Uh-huh, we should play poker together some time."

"I think I'll pass." I tried to sound upbeat, but I could tell by the dubious look on her face she wasn't buying it.

***

"Oh, my God, is that a cellphone?"

It was midway through my day, and I was sitting at my desk when Alex decided to finally come into our office. I felt a painful

246

stab when I looked up at her. I froze for a moment before I set my new phone down.

"Can I see it?" She bounced up and down.

"You're a tall child." I handed her the phone.

"It's true." She smirked as she started playing with my phone.

"What are you doing?"

"Programming in my number," she blithely explained. "Next to Josie and Rita. Oh? Well now, we can text each other."

I let her play with my phone, not missing the surprise in her voice when she discovered two women's numbers already programmed in. "Having fun?" I finally asked when she kept playing. I was already adept with it after reviewing the instruction manual. To be honest, I hadn't used it other than to program in the two phone numbers.

"Not so much." She sounded grim, finally handing my phone back. "I need a favor."

"Anything," I reassured her.

"Tempting," she quipped, offering that all-too-familiar cocky smirk. "I have to go back to New York again."

"When?" I was disappointed, hoping that perhaps her jaunts were done.

"In just a bit."

"Today?"

"Sadly, yes." She tucked an errant lock of hair behind her ear. I found the movement absolutely adorable. I was surprised when she handed me her car keys. "On the weekends, I take Mrs. G grocery shopping. With this crap I've been dealing with, I haven't had the chance. Can you take her for me? She likes to go early on Saturdays to Market Basket and the meat market on Maplewood. You can use the car for whatever you want the rest of the weekend."

"No problem," I readily agreed. "Do you need a lift to the airport?"

"No thanks, Maureen is taking me."

"I have to pick up my in-laws at the airport," Maureen groused as she entered the office. "Are you ready, Alex?"

"She doesn't look happy." I noted the scowl on Maureen's face.

"Oh, I'm not." Maureen growled. "I love my husband, but his mother and I do not get along. That woman will find any excuse to nitpick. Like being late picking her up. Come on, Alex."

***

"I think it's very important work," Josie said enthusiastically. "We have to stop her."

"I don't understand." I shrugged as I tried to urge my Rollerblades to speed up so I could gain some distance from Josie. "What do you have against *Judge Judy*?"

"The show is the dumbification of America," Josie asserted just before I admitted that on occasion I'd watched the show. Truth be told, I love when Judge Judy cuts someone to the quick for being a dumbass.

"Dumbification?" I questioned. "Is that a word?"

Josie just stared at me blankly. It would appear that Josie had "issues" with the show. I wasn't surprised at this point. It seemed that Josie had "issues" with just about everything. There were her abandonment issues, her issues with her parents, the government, the environment, Starbucks, and everything under the sun, including M&M's. I was having a real problem with that one. In the twenty minutes since I met up with her and began our skate on the bike path that ran along the Charles River, Josie had explained in painful detail her issues. If that wasn't enough to ruin my afternoon, it seemed that she also belonged to every self-help group imaginable. Self-help groups are admittedly important for the people who needed them. But Josie seemed to be a professional joiner.

"But couldn't you simply just not watch the show?" I tried to argue. "Television shows rely on ratings to stay on the air. If you don't like a show, don't watch."

"Oh, I don't own a television," Josie happily explained. "I've had a major issue with it since I came to the realization that *The Facts of Life* was an excuse to exploit Tootie."

"So how many people are in this Stop Judge Judy Campaign?"

"Right now, there's just me and Sara," Josie beamed, mistaking my question for interest. "We met in our WATI support group."

"WATI?" I asked before I could stop myself.

"Women Against the Internet," she proclaimed proudly. "You do realize that this whole Internet scam is just one more way that Big Brother can track us," she cautioned me. "You could meet with us if you like. We discuss the whole issue online every Wednesday night. WATI has a great chatroom set up."

"Chatroom? Like an online chatroom?" I spun around on my skates in shock. Unfortunately, I should have paid more attention to my actions. My feet became tangled up, and suddenly, I was lying on the bike path in agony.

After a short debate, I allowed myself to be taken by Josie across the footbridge to Mass General Hospital. The emergency room was swamped. I gave the triage nurse my information while Josie remained glued to my side. My only desire at that moment in time was getting rid of Josie. We were instructed to wait, and I was given an ice pack for my knee.

I tried to convince Josie to leave; she instead fussed and fumed about the delay. I tried to reason with her as I pointed out that there were people in greater need of medical attention than I was. When she announced as loudly as she could that we were being made to wait because we were lesbians, I wanted to climb under my chair. Mostly, I wanted Josie to just go away. Gay, straight, or indifferent, Josie was just a really bad date. Finally, we were shown to an exam room. I looked at the cotton Johnny and panicked.

"Would you like me to help you with that" Josie offered. I shook my head sharply in refusal. There was no way I was taking my clothes off in front of this woman.

"I'm fine. In fact, why don't you get going? I'm sure you have a meeting." I hoped she would take the hint and just go.

"Oh, baby," she said softly. "I'm not leaving your side. In fact, I'm calling my father's driver to come get us when this is over." With that announcement, she whipped out her cellphone.

"I thought you weren't speaking to your parents." I was dumbfounded.

"I'm not. But I have use of their driver, which makes sense since I won't go see them to pick up my weekly check," Josie calmly explained. "They just send the driver over with it to the town house they bought me."

"Excuse me?"

"Well, I need it to get around to all my meetings." Josie was so sincere and so delusional.

"Your parents support you?" I was at a complete loss.

"Of course. I couldn't very well be expected to have a "job," not with all the important work I have to do!" Josie said with a smile. I was bothered by the way she said job as if working for a living was beneath her.

"Put that away," a very familiar alto voice commanded. I snapped my head around to see Nicole dressed in pale blue hospital scrubs and a long white lab coat with her hair pulled back in a French braid. "The cellphone," Nicole insisted. "Turn it off. Apparently, you missed the signs hanging everywhere explaining the dangers of using a cellphone in a hospital. Now put it away before you kill someone." Reluctantly, Josie complied as she gave Nicole an icy stare. Nicole was unaffected; she simply smiled at me. "Ms. Grant, I'm Dr. Kendell." She smiled.

"I'm Josie Stendorf, Stephanie's partner," Josie announced boldly.

"No, you're not," I shouted, completely flabbergasted. "This is our first date." I looked to Nicole for help. Suddenly, I reached up and grabbed her by her lab coat and drew her down to me. "Make her go away. Please, she's crazy. Nicole, please, she has issues," I pleaded.

"Tell me again why you're not dating my sister." Nicole chuckled softly as she pulled herself away.

"Ms. Stendorf," Nicole began in a very professional tone. "I'm familiar with Ms. Grant, and she needs to do this on her own." Josie opened her mouth to speak, but Nicole quickly cut her off. "She has issues with privacy and apparently self-assertion." At the last part, she cast a glance in my direction. Turning back to Josie, she touched her gently on the arm. "You understand that it's very important for her to do this on her own?" Josie's eyes widened with a sudden understanding.

"Oh, yes, of course." Josie leaned over me and patted my shoulder in sympathy. "Call me. I have some groups that could help you."

Then Josie was finally gone—for good, I prayed. I breathed a sigh of relief. "Okay, one scary date taken care of. Now let's take of you." Nicole smiled brightly. "First I need to ask you something…"

"I swear she seemed perfectly normal when she asked me out," I protested.

"That's not what I was going to ask you." Nicole laughed as she shook her head. "I was going to ask you if you would feel more comfortable with another physician."

"No," I answered honestly.

"Good." Nicole smiled. "Now put on the Johnny, and I'll be right back."

"But..." I began to protest.

"No buts," Nicole chastised me. "Put it on, and I'll be right back."

"Rats," I grumbled.

***

Once I was clad in the flimsy hospital gown, Nicole returned carrying a clipboard. "Okay, what happened?" Nicole placed the clipboard down and put on a pair of rubber gloves. She gently removed the ice pack and examined my knee. "We were Rollerblading along the Charles when Josie said something stupid. It caught me off-guard, and I fell."

"Hmm," Nicole said thoughtfully. She opened the back of the hospital gown and examined my back, then took a quick look at my head. "Did you hit your head at all?"

"No."

"Lose consciousness at any time?" She cleaned my knee with disinfectant.

"Ouch. No."

"Raise your leg." I obeyed. "Wiggle your toes." I followed her instructions. "Any nausea?"

"Nope."

"Dizziness?" She shined a penlight in my eyes.

"No."

She returned the light to the pocket of her coat and retrieved her clipboard. "Are you on any prescription or nonprescription drugs? Any allergies?"

"No and no." I snarled.

"Did you drink any alcohol today?"

"Not yet."

Nicole chuckled at me. "All right. We're almost finished. It looks pretty superficial. We need some X-rays just to be on the safe side."

"Oh, man." I groaned.

"Just a precaution, Stephanie." Nicole was very reassuring. "I need to ask before you go down, and they'll probably ask you again, but is there any chance you could be pregnant?" I just rolled my eyes and stared at her in disbelief. "I have to ask."

"Well, let's see in the past three months, I have only come close to having sex with one person, and although your sister claims to have many skills, I doubt that's one of them," I teased, causing Nicole to blush. "And before you ask, no Peter and I hadn't been intimate in a very long."

"I see." She cleared her throat. "I'll leave it to you to break the news to her on that one. Speaking of which…" I held my breath as I waited for her to finish her thought. "I can't tell anyone about this. As your doctor, I cannot even mention that you were here. Not to my sister, not to anyone. As a patient, you have rights. So this entire afternoon is *entre nous*." I stared at her blankly. "Between us," she explained. "Anything you tell me is confidential. I just needed you to know that." Her pager went off, and she looked at it and scowled. "I'll see you when you back from X-ray."

"Thanks, Nicole."

***

I returned from having my knee X-rayed from every possible angle. I quickly got dressed and waited and waited, and waited and waited some more. Nicole finally returned.

"Well, it seems that all you have is a really big boo-boo," Nicole coyly offered. "Just sign here and take these to the front desk, and you're free to go. For the next few days, just remember RICE. Rest, ice, compression, and elevation. Do that and take it easy, and you should be fine."

"Thank God." I sighed as I signed the paperwork and accepted my copies. "So is boo-boo a technical term?"

"Absolutely," Nicole brightly confirmed. "Just remember when you get home, RICE. Speaking of which, how are you getting home?"

"I have Alex's car."

"That's right, she's in New York again," Nicole added without missing a beat. "Take it easy, and I'll see you on Thanksgiving."

"Excuse me?"

"Don't tell me she hasn't invited you?" Nicole groaned. I just shook my head in response. "Big dumb Amazon. Well, I'm inviting you."

"Nicole, I don't want to make your sister uncomfortable," I said. "Things are a little tense between us. I also don't want to see her at a holiday gathering with her new girlfriend."

"Her new...fine," Nicole conceded with a groan. "Oh, by the way Thursday is—" Just then, her pager went off again. "Damn." She snatched up the offending object. "I have to go."

Chapter Twenty Five

I was sore, but thankfully, I had taken Mrs. G to the market earlier in the day. Upon returning home, I went up to Alex's apartment to drop off her keys. I felt a gnawing in the pit of my stomach when I spied a backpack sitting by the sofa. It was rumpled with pins from bands I had never heard of. I was willing to bet it wasn't Alex's backpack.

I tried to ignore it and went upstairs. I went over the chapters Alex had left on my desk. Then I did what Nicole had instructed me to do—I sat back and propped my leg up. Before making myself comfortable in the upstairs sitting area, I took a moment to peruse Alex's collection of DVDs. It was an eclectic collection of documentaries and television shows. She owned complete sets of shows I had only a passing knowledge of. *Xena: Warrior Princess*, *Buffy the Vampire Slayer*, *Remington Steele*, *The Bionic Woman*, *Star Trek*, *Perry Mason*, *Game Of Thrones*, and *The Twilight Zone*. There was also every movie Jodie Foster had ever made.

As interesting as her taste in entertainment was, I needed to get some work done. I returned to the large leather sofa, propped my leg up, and began to review the paperwork Alex had left for me. Just when I got comfortable, my cellphone rang. It was Rita wanting to know how my date went.

"Oh, where to begin." I chuckled, finally seeing the humor of the situation. "Let's just say, there won't be a second date." I told her about my date from hell, skipping over some of the details. She had the bad manners to laugh at my plight. We made plans to go dancing at The Galaxy on Thursday. Even though there was no sexual tension between us, I really enjoyed spending time with Rita.

After I hung up, I sent a text to Alex asking if she needed me to pick her up at the airport. I checked my phone repeatedly during the night but never heard back. Filled with good intentions of simply doing a little work before retiring to my apartment, I managed to fall asleep. I awoke at sunrise, comfortably nestled on the sofa with a quilt covering my body and a pillow under my head.

A warm fuzzy feeling encompassed me. I burrowed beneath the quilt ready to fall back asleep. The loud cawing from a seagull disrupted my attempt to remain in my warm cocoon. I felt safe, warm, and completely at home. Blinking my eyes open, I remembered that I wasn't home. I climbed off the sofa and folded the quilt before gathering my belongings.

I made my way downstairs, catching a glimpse of Alex sound asleep in her bed. She looked positively adorable. "Wow, she really does snore." I was amused by the loud sounds echoing throughout the apartment. It was getting late, and I knew I should be heading to my home to prepare for the day. Instead, I went into the kitchen, which was as pristine as ever. I poured water in the coffee maker and ground some beans.

I smiled thinking how nice waking up Alex with a fresh brewed cup of coffee would be. Then I spied the backpack. My heart sank. I stood there wallowing in my misery when there was a shy knock on the door. My misery increased when I spied through the peephole and saw Courtney standing on the other side. I tried to bury my anger, I just couldn't. I grabbed her backpack, opened the door, and tossed it at her. She started to say hello and explain how much she needed her backpack. I didn't let her finish, I slammed the door in her face. It felt good to throw something at her while she was yammering on. I may not be an expert when it comes to dating, still I found it odd that she didn't seemed bothered by the fact that another woman was answering her girlfriend's door first thing in the morning.

"Morning," Alex croaked out from behind me.

"Morning." I gulped, slowly turning toward her. "I was just about to brew a pot of coffee."

"You're a goddess."

"Thank you." I blushed and returned my attention to the task at hand. "Another late flight back?"

"Yes." She yawned. "I can't wait for this mess to be over with."

"You didn't call for a ride." I handed her a cup of coffee.

"It was late," she blew off my question, inhaling the coffee.

"I need to get ready for work," I excused myself, noticing the disappointed look on her face.

"Thanks for the coffee," she grumbled while I gathered my things and made a hasty exit.

***

I was more than a little confused. I had planned on visiting Alex that evening, yet once again, she failed to return home. It was well after midnight when I decided to go to bed. I received a surprise when I entered our office the next morning. Alex was stretched out on the sofa sound asleep. Maureen walked in as I was standing there watching her sleep. She was covered in what appeared to be paperwork.

"Not again." Maureen scowled. "Alex, wake up!"

Alex grumbled loudly as she shifted on the couch in an effort to raise herself up. As she lifted her body, the books and papers that had been covering her toppled onto the floor. "*Merde*." She bent down to clean up the mess. I put down my briefcase and knelt to help her. Maureen muttered something unintelligible as she stomped off.

"What is all of this?" I asked as we gathered up her work.

"Just getting ready for midterms," she grumbled once again. "I finished the work on chapter ten, as well. It's on your desk...I think." Alex scratched her head aimlessly. It was more than obvious that she was not fully awake yet.

"Why are you working here?"

"Tired of getting the cold shoulder," she muttered and suddenly snapped her head up and stared at me with surprise. "I'm sorry. Did I just say that out loud?"

"Yes," I said harshly.

"Forget I said anything," she tried to apologize. "Look, I'm just trying to do the right thing here," she said as she hurried to clean up her mess.

"I'll get this," I offered in confusion. "You'd better hurry home and shower." She stared at me helplessly. "Go on," I insisted.

Alex thanked me and rushed out of the room. Something was happening, and I was completely clueless as to what it was. Nothing seemed to make any sense. Later that day, Alex did explain that she had forgotten to charge her phone and didn't get my message. That night as I walked home, I was determined to sit Alex down and have a very long talk with her. As I approached our house, I discovered Courtney's Volvo parked out front. It appeared that there was nothing for Alex and me to discuss after all. The rest of the week was more of the same. Further confusing me since I was convinced that there was something I didn't know.

***

The next day, I was in Maureen's office going over some paperwork. I tried to focus on the matter at hand, but I was distracted by a nagging question. "Maureen, can I ask you something?"

"Of course." She peered over her reading glasses.

"Back before you were married—" I tried to gather my thoughts.

"Yes." She slammed down the papers we had been going over. The eager look in her eyes made me nervous. "Is this about Alex?"

"Kind of," I stammered. "I'm just curious about something. If you showed up at your boyfriend's apartment early in the morning and another woman answered the door, would you just let it go?"

"Hell no!"

"So—"

"Again, hell and no," she said. "What is this about?"

"I don't really know."

Chapter Twenty Six

On Thursday morning, I was greeted by yet another surprise as I entered my office. Alex's desk was covered with several flower arrangements. The office was empty, and after a quick check into the hallway, I dashed over to Alex's desk. As I peeked at the cards, I asked myself, *At what point does this become stalking?* There were roses from her parents, irises from Nicole, and more roses from Chris. The cards all conveyed the same message. It was Alex's birthday. That was what Nicole had meant to tell me at the hospital.

Without a second thought, I made certain that the cards were all returned to their proper positions. I was tempted to toss Chris's contribution in the trash. Realizing that would be petty, I dismissed the idea. I crossed back over to my own desk and snatched up the local directory and placed a call. I had a surprise of my own coming for Alex. Yes, it was true that I was angry with her. But it was also true that my anger was born out of my feelings for her. I couldn't allow her birthday to pass without doing something. As I finished my call, I could hear familiar footsteps approaching. I could tell by the self-assured stride that it was Alex. I threw open my briefcase and pretended to be working.

Alex entered our office, took one look at her desk, and asked dryly, "Who died?" Her eyes suddenly widened as a snarl crossed her face. "Ah, crap," she spit out as she dropped her briefcase. Just then, Maureen bounced in waving a card around.

"Happy birthday!" she shouted joyfully. Alex groaned in response. "What?" Maureen laughed.

"I forgot," Alex said grimly.

"That's not like you," Maureen said in surprise. "You usually live for this stuff."

"I guess I'm just not in the mood this year," Alex said as she accepted the card and retrieved the briefcase. "Thanks for the card."

Just then, Alex's phone rang. She rushed over to answer it as Maureen waved her goodbyes. "Professor Kendell." She spoke in her professional voice. "No...no...please, Mother, no! Don't sing!" Alex pleaded as she slumped into her chair and banged her head on her desk. "Please stop," she implored her mother. "No, not Dad, too!"

I started to laugh as my telephone rang. "Dr. Grant," I greeted my caller with a chuckle.

"Well, you seem to be in good spirits, Blondie," Nicole responded. "How's the knee?"

"Fine," I shouted over Alex's fussing.

"What the hell is going on there?"

"Your parents are torturing your sister," I explained as Nicole laughed.

"Let me guess, they're singing?" Nicole laughed hysterically.

"From what I can gather."

"I guess this call is a bit late then. I forgot to tell you the other day," Nicole explained.

"No problem. I've got it covered."

"Good. Feel free to torture her, she loves that," Nicole teased.

"Yeah, right." I couldn't help laughing. "Thank you, Nicole," I said loudly to be heard over Alex's grousing. Unfortunately, I said it a little too loud. Alex's head shot up over the cubicle wall, and she glared at me.

"Why is Nicole calling you?" Alex asked in desperation. "Not you, Mom," she said into the receiver.

"None of your business." I couldn't resist teasing her. I could hear Nicole laughing on the other end.

"Stephanie." Alex growled.

"Yes, oh cranky one?" I taunted her.

"What?" she barked into the telephone. "No, Mom...we work together." Alex sounded exasperated. "No, you can't talk to her. I have to go," Alex said. "Thanks for the flowers. Love to both of you." Alex ducked down long enough to hang up her telephone. Her head popped up, and she glared down at me again.

"Is she staring at you?" Nicole asked.

"Of course," I replied.

"Let me talk to her." Nicole sighed.

I stood and handed Alex the receiver. "Play nice," I warned her.

"Why are you calling Stephanie?" Alex snapped. "I am not old and cranky." I snorted at the comment. "Yes, I got them. They're beautiful. Yes, thank you." Alex relaxed slightly. "So why are you bothering my coworkers?" Alex listened for a moment. "Why can't you tell me? What are you two conspiring?" Alex demanded as she glared at me. "Well, if it's nothing, then you can tell me," Alex pushed. "Fine," she conceded. "Thanks again for the flowers. Talk to you soon, Nikki." She handed the phone back to me and ducked back to her side of the office.

I hung up and began to chuckle. "You laugh?" Alex growled. "Trust me, the Kendell clan is not musically gifted."

"What's the matter—feeling old?" I teased.

"Bite me." She snarled. I listened as she slammed the drawers on her desk. I knew instantly what she was searching for.

"You threw them out," I sang cheerfully.

"I did?" She groaned. "Why would I do that?"

"Because you want to quit." I turned on my computer.

"Oh, yeah." She sighed. "That must be why I threw out that pack I had hidden at home."

"When was the last time you smoked?" I asked as I logged on.

She paused for a moment before answering. "Halloween." I could tell by her tone of voice that she was telling the truth.

"Good for you. Now isn't this a great way to kick off a new year?" I encouraged her.

"*Mangez moi,*" Alex muttered just loud enough for me to hear.

"Now why do I think that wasn't a thank you?" I retorted.

"No, it wasn't." Alex snorted with delight. "But I would certainly enjoy it."

I reached into to my briefcase and retrieved a book I had checked out of the library on one of my late-night work sessions. I quickly flipped open the copy of *Beginner's French.* "Now let's see," I spoke aloud as I flipped through the pages. "*Mangez.*"

"What are you doing?" Alex gasped as she raced over to my desk. "Stop."

"Here it is." I smiled. "*Mangez* means eat, and *moi* means me. I see." I blushed as I spoke. "I must say, you Harvard girls certainly have an elegant way of expressing yourselves. You know, when it comes time to return this to the library, I might just go out and buy a copy. You just never know when it might come in handy."

"I…I…I…" Alex stammered.

"Give it a rest, Harvard." I laughed, deciding to let her off the hook. "Since it's your birthday, I'll let it slide." Alex sighed in relief. "Oh, and thanks for the offer," I added with a wink. I doubted that I had ever seen anyone turn that particular shade of scarlet before.

For a brief moment, it was as if the past few weeks hadn't happened. No sexual tension, just the two of us joking as friends. I had to admit, it felt good. Alex returned to her side of the office and began working on her computer. I decided to check my email; there was the usually university mailings. Some from my students regarding finals. There was also one from Peter. His made me slightly uneasy. He invited me to join him and his family for Thanksgiving dinner. Thanksgiving was just a week away. I couldn't help wondering where the time had gone. I emailed Peter back and thanked him for his offer, but I had to decline. Since we were no longer together, I wouldn't feel comfortable.

Seconds after sending my message, I received a reply from him. It was very sweet, and he invited me once again. I wrote back and used as much tact as I could muster and politely declined. There was no way I was going to get his or his family's hopes up by attending the holiday gathering. I would just spend the day alone. Maybe Alex would let me use her kitchen so I could cook something up for myself and make a day of it.

"Stephanie?" Alex called out from behind the wall. "I need to drive down to the Cape this weekend so I can lock up my house in Provincetown. Would you like to join me? I could show you around Ptown," she offered hopefully.

"I…um…" I stammered while my mind screamed, *Yes!* I paused for a moment, trying to calm myself so I wouldn't sound like a complete dork.

"Never mind," Alex said grimly. "Forget I asked," she added with false cheerfulness. Then she strolled out of the office and went off to her morning class. Once I was certain that Alex was out of earshot, I banged my head on my desk repeatedly, calling myself a moron.

***

Later that day, I found myself rushing toward Alex's classroom. It was her last class of the day, and I knew my surprise would be arriving soon. As I sped down the hallway, I spotted my present strolling toward Alex's classroom. She was an attractive blonde, dressed in a tuxedo and carrying an enormous bouquet of balloons. I followed her into the classroom and hid in the back. Ignoring the obvious stares from the students and instructor, the woman strolled down the aisle and walked right up to Alex. Poor Alex looked like a deer caught in oncoming headlights.

"I'm here to wish you a very happy birthday, Professor Kendell," the blonde purred as she handed Alex the balloons. Then she did something I had most definitely not requested. She leaned over and kissed Alex on the cheek. The room exploded with hoots and hollers from the students. A chorus of *Happy Birthday to You* began as the blonde made her departure.

I grabbed her by the arm, instantly recognizing that she was gay. "I didn't pay you to kiss her, penguin," I growled menacingly into her ear.

"I guess I just blew my tip?" she responded with a smirk. I just glared at her coldly and opened the door for her to leave. "Oh, well, it was worth it." She sighed and winked at me before making a hasty exit.

The students were just finishing their second chorus of *Happy Birthday to You* while Alex read the card attached to the balloons. She smiled sweetly.

"All right, enough!" Alex chastised them, the smile never leaving her lips. "Thank you, Dr. Grant," she said without looking up at me.

"You are most welcome, Professor Kendell," I replied, rather pleased with myself. *So you knew I was here.*

"I told you they were together," I heard one student whisper to another. I chuckled softly to myself at the thought that Alex and I were already part of the small-town gossip mill.

"Okay, settle down, everyone," Alex repeated over the chatter.

"Now let's get back to reviewing for the midterm." The response was a collective groan from the students. Alex just shook her head, and she looked up, capturing me with her dazzling baby blues. "The hell with it," she announced. "There are only a few minutes left, and it's my birthday. Go on, get out of here." The classroom cheered as the students quickly gathered up their belongings. "If anyone has any questions, just stop by my office during posted hours," Alex added as her students fled.

Alex was now sitting on her desk rubbing her eyes as I approached her. I gave her a playful nudge as I sat next to her. "Happy birthday," I whispered softly.

"Thank you," she said without meeting my gaze. "How did you know that I love balloons?"

"Because you are basically a really tall child." I gave her another playful nudge.

"Ah, so you have uncovered my secret at last." She chuckled lightly, still unable to look at me.

"I also noticed that you have a thing for white roses."

"Champagne," she said. "They're actually off-white with a touch of pink on the tips of the petals. Those were from my parents and Chris. It's funny, really, Chris couldn't remember to come home at night, but she still remembers what my favorite flowers are. Women." She scrunched up her face in a mocking grimace.

"Tell me about it," I teased in return.

Alex barked a laugh and began playing with the balloons. "Hmm, there are certainly a lot of them." She smiled absently. "Are you busy tonight? Would you like to go out for dinner?" she added hesitantly.

"Yes," I responded before I had a chance to think about it. Then I remembered my plans with Rita. "Wait, I have plans."

"It's okay." She sighed dejectedly.

"But it's your birthday," I protested.

"No worries. I have a ton of work to do anyways," she lied.

"Alex—" I began to protest.

"Stephanie, really, it's fine," she interrupted me. "Thank you again for the balloons." She finally looked over at me.

Our gazes met, and there it was. I suddenly understood why it was so hard for her to look into my eyes. I felt it instantly. That look! My knees felt weak, and I couldn't breathe. I leaned over to her and whispered, "Happy birthday, Alex." Our faces were a mere breath apart. I looked at her full lips as I licked my own. I began to close the slight distance between us, giving into what my body and heart were crying out for. At the last moment, I pulled away as the image of Courtney flashed through my mind. This was killing me. For the life of me, I just couldn't understand how could she have chosen that child over me. I looked back toward her, and my resistance instantly vanished as I reached for her once again.

This time, it was Alex who broke away suddenly. I was surprised at first, then once I managed to catch my breath, I reminded myself that Alex already had someone in her life. Without looking at me, she casually offered me a ride home.

"Sure," I accepted her offer.

"Good, then you can grab the balloons," she teased me.

***

It was a struggle to get all the balloons into the car.

"Why did I order so many?" I grunted as we fought to get them into the Subaru.

"Because I'm cute." Alex pouted.

"No, that's not it," I teased as I managed to get the back door closed. I watched as she continued to pout. "Nice try. Come on, let's get your flowers." We returned to the office and gathered up the floral arrangements and cards and the rest of our belongings. On the drive home, neither of us spoke. I was secretly pleased with myself for not mentally berating myself for my earlier actions. I knew that Alex felt it, too. There was no need to beat myself up for making a pass at her. I had finally accepted that whatever was happening between us was not one-sided.

***

When we returned home, I took the flowers upstairs to Alex's apartment while she struggled to get the balloons out of the car. As I reached the porch, I saw that Alex had managed to free the balloons safely. Mrs. Giovanni was standing there holding a pie as she wished Alex a happy birthday.

"Hello, Mrs. Giovanni," I greeted her.

"These are beautiful, Stephanie." She pointed to the balloons.

"That was so nice of you." She smiled. "Isn't she nice, Alex?" Mrs. Giovanni pushed.

"I'll take the balloons, you can take the pie," I said.

"She's such a good girl," Mrs. Giovanni went on. "Not like that Chris."

"Zia Maria," Alex snapped suddenly and pulled Mrs. Giovanni aside.

I struggled with the balloons as they whispered to each other. Alex's slip had not escaped my notice. I placed the balloons in her living room and looked around. The one little slip had shed light on something that I had been curious about since I moved in. I turned as I heard Alex entering the apartment.

"I didn't know that you spoke Italian," I tried to maintain a casual tone of voice.

"I don't," Alex said absently.

"Really?"

"Mrs. Giovanni may have taught me a word or two."

I knew she was lying. My only question was whether or not to confront her with my suspicions or to just drop the whole thing. It had been bugging me for months, and the clues just kept piling up. There was the way Alex treated Mrs. G and my apartment.

"The two of you must be very close," I carefully began. "I don't know much Italian myself, but I do know that Zia Maria translates into Aunt Mary." I tried to sound indifferent. "I think it's sweet the way you look after her. You do her shopping, take care of her bills, some nights, you even tuck her in and make certain that her house is locked up. Is that why she let you convert two apartments into one?"

"Ah…well, it's complicated," Alex hedged.

"Alex, are you my landlady?" I finally asked straight out. It wasn't the first time I suspected it. Alex was the one who called the repairmen, and I saw her on more than one occasion writing a check for their services. I also noticed that the tax bills were addressed to Alex.

"I am not your landlady," Alex flatly denied.

"But you do own this house."

"No." Alex seemed to be frustrated as she tried to explain. "I own my apartment."

"And Mrs. Giovanni is your aunt." Again, it was not a question.

"Why the big secret?"

"Because she's embarrassed," Alex said. "When my Uncle Joseph passed away, both houses were paid for, but there was the upkeep to contend with. Plus the taxes, water, sewage, and on and on. It was too much for her now that she was living on one Social Security check. She hated to raise the rents because the tenants were like family to her. I finally got her to raise them, but then she got sick, and the cost of maintaining her own home was too much. So I just…"

"Did what you always do," I added with a smile. "You stepped in and helped her. Just like you always have, like with your grandfather's debts and your sister's drinking. Is that why I got such a great deal on my rent?"

"It's not what you think," Alex said. "You were in a bind, and I wanted to help out. I did not have any hidden motives. I was just trying to be a friend. For the record, I have no idea what you're paying. Mrs. G owns your apartment."

"Four hundred."

"What? Holy crap! That is way below what she's supposed to be charging you," she sputtered. "I need you to know that there wasn't an ulterior motive."

"I know that." I scoffed at the implication. "You're a big dumb Amazon with an interesting memory. If you recall, I'm the one who keeps—I mean, I was the one who kept—trying to get you into bed, not the other way around."

"Hold on a second. Just what is going on with you and my sister?"

"Huh?"

"The two of you are up to something." Alex wagged her finger at me. "Nikki is the only one who calls me an Amazon. Then she called you this morning. What are the two of you conspiring?"

"Nothing," I said honestly.

"Then what gives?" Alex pushed, not fully convinced of my innocence, or perhaps it was Nicole she didn't trust. It was hard to tell. "Why couldn't she tell me why she called you? If the two of you aren't plotting something, the only other reason she couldn't tell me would be if the call was for professional reasons… Alex's face went pale. "Stephanie, is everything all right?"

"Yes, I'm fine." I groaned. "She called to tell me that it was your birthday. She meant to tell me last weekend when I ended up in the ER at MGH. Nicole was the doctor who treated me, and before you ask, I really am fine. That's all there is to it."

"But if that's all it was, why didn't she just tell me?"

"Excuse me, counselor?" I almost laughed. "I don't really need to explain the law to you, do I?"

"No." She pouted, and I had to admit she was damn cute when she did that. "Are you sure you're all right?"

"There you go again. I scraped my knee, that's it." I didn't feel the need to add that I wouldn't have sought out medical attention if my date hadn't been such a complete wacko.

"Wait, does this have anything to do with the pair of Rollerblades I found in my laundry room?"

"Um, yes, feel free to keep them," I said. "Alex, about tonight—"

"Don't worry about it," Alex cut me off. The dejected look on her face was something I had become more than a little familiar with over the past month.

I took a deep breath and calmed myself before proceeding to talk to this stubborn woman. "I was just going to offer for you to join us."

"Us?" she asked me with surprise.

"Rita and I," I carefully explained. "We're just going dancing at The Galaxy. You and I could have dinner first and head into Cambridge."

"Dancing at The Galaxy with Rita?" Alex said absently as she processed the information, running her fingers through her hair. "I don't know, I would hate to feel like a third wheel."

"You wouldn't be," I said quickly, hoping to extinguish her fears. Judging by her stunned expression, I was failing miserably. "Rita is a friend and not in the frisky way you and I started out. We went out once, and there was no chemistry between us."

"Does Rita know this?" she asked me harshly.

"Yes," I strongly answered her accusation. "We talked about it, and now we're just friends. We go out dancing together and scope chicks."

"Excuse me?" Alex roared with laughter. "You have been busy during my absence, haven't you?"

"I needed to start living my life," I said honestly.

"And so you have," Alex conceded.

"Well, I see that Aunt Mary still hates me," a sultry voice boomed from the doorway. Nothing in the world could have prepared me for the sight I found standing in the doorway. She was as tall as Alex with a well-toned and very beautiful body. Not to mention long sandy brown hair and legs that went on for days. My mouth just hung open, overwhelmed by her presence.

"Can you blame her? This is what I get for leaving the door open," Alex responded dryly to the striking woman. "What are you doing here, Chris?" Alex asked her suspiciously.

I felt ill hearing the question. This stunning woman was Chris, the same woman Alex once lived with and was now spending almost every weekend with. For a brief moment, I pondered crawling under the sofa.

"Alex, it's your birthday." I cringed at the sultry tone Chris used. "You sounded a little down on the phone." She smiled at Alex as her gaze scanned her body. "Besides, it's raining in New York."

"Well, it's not raining here," Alex shot back smugly.

"Pity." Chris drawled as she continued to leer at Alex in a lecherous manner.

Alex just returned her gaze with an icy glare. I wanted to waltz over to Chris and wipe that smug expression off her face. But judging by the size of her and my own shortcomings, I assumed that she could probably mop the floor with me without even breaking a sweat. I opted for plan B and cleared my throat very loudly in an attempt to end their staring contest. Chris turned to me and captured my gaze with lustful hazel eyes.

"Well, hi there," she purred.

"Chris!" Alex snapped.

"Hmm?" Chris hummed as her gaze scanned my body, making me feel exposed.

"Chris, no!" Alex commanded. There was something in her tone of voice that reminded me of someone trying to train a naughty puppy. I wouldn't have been surprised to hear Alex command her to sit or fetch.

"Sorry," Chris apologized to Alex. "Hi, I'm Chris," she said to me in a much more civil manner as she offered me her hand.

"Stephanie Grant." I returned her strong handshake.

A single thought ran through my mind as she released my hand. *Wow!* Chris then removed her overcoat, and I was impressed all over again. The woman was clad in a tight pair of black leather pants and a midcut black tank top, which slightly exposed her well-defined abs. I couldn't help thinking when they were a couple, they must have been the poster girls for drop dead gorgeous lesbians.

"This isn't very nice of you, Alex," Chris's deep voice cooed. "I flew all the way up here because I was afraid that you were going to be all alone on your birthday. And here I find you all cozy with this cute little thing. Now why didn't you tell me you were seeing someone?"

"I'm not seeing anyone." Alex was firm as she blew out an exasperated breath.

I couldn't help wondering if Alex was lying. Which begged the question, just where was Courtney anyway? It wasn't like her to pass up an opportunity like Alex's birthday. Clever thing that she was must have known that it would allow her to one-up me yet again. There was something missing here. From the tone of Alex's voice, I knew she was telling the truth. Could it be that Courtney was finally out of the picture? My heart did a double backflip at the very idea that Courtney had been given the heave-ho. But it would explain why her only concern the other morning was retrieving her backpack.

"Really?" Chris responded coyly to Alex's denial as she allowed her gaze to wander over my body. Without thinking about my actions, I took a step toward Alex. Chris was nothing short of stunning; however, the way she was looking at me was making me uncomfortable. Alex must have agreed. Protectively, she moved in front of me and held a cautioning hand up toward her ex-lover.

"I said behave."

"Make up your mind," Chris taunted her. "If she's not yours, then she's fair game."

"Hey!" I piped up, insulted that I was being treated like the last slice of pizza in the box.

"Chris, I'm warning you." Alex growled. Chris threw up her hands in a mock surrender. "I see you brought your briefcase," Alex noted. "Is that my present—a night poring over old case files?"

"You seem surprised?" Chris tried to laugh it off. "Hey, what can I say? I thought we could slip some work in, and I could bill the firm for my hours and the flight up here. I also thought we might slip something else in, but I guess that's out of the question now." She looked directly at me with an accusing stare.

Sorry to ruin your plans, stud, I thought with self-satisfaction.

"Some things never change," Alex muttered as she headed for the kitchen.

I was left alone with Alex's larger-than-life ex-lover. Suddenly, I wasn't feeling so cocky. Chris was once again eyeing me up and down. This time, however, there was nothing lustful in her gaze. This time, I felt as if she was sizing me up the way a fighter would size up his opponent.

"Nice balloons," Chris called nonchalantly out to Alex.

"Thank you, they're a gift from Stephanie," Alex said brightly from the kitchen.

"Very nice," Chris offered in a congratulatory tone. "Relax, kid, despite what you must have heard about me from Alex's friends and neighbors, I'm not the devil herself. A close relation perhaps." She smiled warmly and patted me gently on the arm. "I was in love with her, and I'll always be jealous of anyone that is special to her. Trust me, I don't bite," she whispered to me in a friendly manner. I sighed with relief as I understood what she had been doing. Chris had flirted with me to see how Alex would react. Then she made an attempt to scare me off. "So has Alex told you that I'm a womanizing jerk yet?" she asked me loudly.

I stood there with my mouth hanging open, uncertain as to how I could respond to her statement. Chris ignored my discomfort and made herself at home by plopping down on the sofa.

"Oh course, I did," Alex said brightly as she returned from the kitchen with a tray of coffee cups.

"Don't worry," Chris reassured me. "We can finally joke about it now. I was a jerk and I lost her, no one to blame but myself. But you didn't have to toss my entire wardrobe out the fifth-floor window."

"You deserved it," Alex said bluntly.

"True," Chris admitted. "But my best Vera Wang did not."

"Speaking of clothes, Stephanie found one of your T-shirts." Alex placed the coffee cups on the table and motioned for me to join them. I took a seat at the far end of the sofa and accepted the mug of black coffee she offered to me.

"Which one?" Chris asked her enthusiastically as she reached for her coffee.

"Hold on." Alex retreated into her bedroom, returning with the black T-shirt with the words *Obey Me* printed across the front. Alex tossed it to Chris, who snatched up the garment happily.

"I knew you took this, you fink." She smirked. "Wait a second. What do you mean Stephanie found it? What's the deal with the two of you anyway?"

I couldn't help but blush at her question as I recalled the night I first saw the T-shirt. I turned to Alex for help, only to find her blushing, as well. "Uh-huh" was Chris's only response. Alex, in typical fashion, shut her eyes and rubbed them. "Ugh, don't you just hate that?" Chris groaned as she looked directly at me.

"As a matter of fact, I do," I confessed.

"What?" Alex snapped as she glared at both of us.

"That whole shutting the world out thing," Chris explained bitterly. "It's like if you shut your eyes to the situation, it will just go away. It used to drive me insane. Oh, and what about her morning concerts?" Chris directed her question toward me.

"I kind of like that."

"What?" Chris snorted with delight. "How could anyone enjoy having their living room turned into Woodstock every morning?"

"I still enjoy it, but then again, I don't live here," I tried to explain.

"I see," Chris said slyly. "Then how pray tell do you know about her morning concerts?"

"Because my apartment is directly below this one." I hoped to nip her suspicions in the bud.

"How convenient, is that how you two gals met?"

"No." I was losing ground fast, and Alex appeared to have been stricken mute. "We work together."

"So you're a history professor, as well?"

"Actually, I'm a PhD," I corrected her without boasting. At least I hoped I wasn't boasting.

"So it's Dr. Grant then," Chris complimented me. "Hey, that means she outranks you, Alex."

"Just where did you get your law degree? Doctor of Jurisprudence? Any of this sound familiar?" Alex grumbled. "Whatever, I don't know why I bother."

"I'm hungry," Chris announced, ignoring Alex. "So are you going to allow me to take the two of you out to dinner?"

"Stephanie has plans," Alex blurted out.

"Not until ten o'clock," I spoke up, not eager to just hand Alex over to Chris. "I'm meeting a friend at The Galaxy for some dancing. I was just trying to coax the birthday girl into joining us when you arrived."

"Dinner and dancing, now that sounds like a plan," Chris said eagerly. "Why don't you gals go get changed? We can eat at that Mexican restaurant that Alex is so found of. If I remember correctly, it isn't too far from the club."

"I don't know," Alex hesitated.

"I know, tequila," Chris slyly stated. "It could make things more interesting. So what do you say, birthday girl, a little TexMex and dancing?"

I was miffed that Chris was offering Alex what I had planned on doing, and she was doing it really well. Alex stood there sporting a blank expression.

"Alex, is there a problem?" Chris asked her in a serious tone.

"No," Alex muttered as she turned back to us.

"Then lighten up," Chris pushed. "It's your birthday, and two beautiful women want to take you out on the town. I should be so lucky."

"Fine, I'll get ready," Alex gave in and stomped off into her bedroom.

I excused myself and followed Alex into the bedroom. "Are you okay with this?"

"Yes," Alex said. "I really wanted to have dinner with you tonight. Chris can be somewhat of a steamroller at times."

"I've noticed. She isn't what I expected."

"I told you that Chris gets a bad rap."

"Well, I think she's nice," I admitted. "She's also very—"

"Attractive," Alex finished for me. "Yes, Chris is a beautiful woman. Unfortunately, Chris is all too aware of that fact."

"Hey, what's with the sad look?"

"Nothing." Alex pouted, something I found positively adorable.

"I am not interested in your ex." I sensed that my comment might have made her uncomfortable.

"Am I really that easy to read?"

"Sometimes, yes, you are." I smiled.

"I didn't like the way she was flirting with you," Alex confessed.

"That's why she did it."

"Huh?"

"Forget it." I sighed, not wanting to explain my suspicions. "Get dressed so we can take you out for your birthday. Don't forget, it's your night, so anything you want."

"Anything?" she coyly asked with a gleam in her eyes that made me quiver.

It was far too tempting to resist. I stepped closer to her and leaned into her firm body.

"Anything," I said seductively. "What is your wish, birthday girl?"

"Just this." Alex cupped my face in her hands and lowered her lips to capture my own. The kiss quickly deepened as I felt her tongue brush against my lips. Instinctively, I parted my lips and allowed her to enter my mouth. I moaned from the feel of her tongue worshipping my mouth. I could feel my body being lowered onto her bed.

"Hey, what's taking you two so long?" Chris shouted from the other room.

We groaned in unison as we broke apart and climbed off the bed. "Now I hate her," I groused before I stomped off without looking at Alex. A part of me wanted to rip Chris's head off. Instead, I muttered something about being back soon. I went downstairs and caught my breath after entering my apartment. I showered quickly. I pulled on a new pair of black jeans as I tried to forget what had occurred in Alex's bedroom. I then put on a new silk camisole that matched the teal silk blouse that I purchased recently. I looked good, I told myself, as I checked myself one last time in the bathroom mirror.

I raced back upstairs eager to see Alex and put some well-needed distance between her and her ex-girlfriend. I was just about to open when the door when I heard shouting coming from within.

"Why not?" Chris asked anxiously.

"It's complicated," Alex said in exasperation.

"Alex, not again," Chris chastised her. "It's always something, isn't it? Stop being such a coward. Or just keep doing what you're doing, and we can ditch the kid."

"Did you fly all the way up here just to give me a lecture?" Alex argued with her. "Or was it to hit on me?"

I decided that my newfound hobby of eavesdropping needed to come to an end. I knocked on the door and entered. I felt my breathing halt suddenly. Alex had changed into a pair of faded blue jeans and a white tank top. She was standing with her back to me. There was something about the sight of this woman's backside wrapped in well-worn denim that was my undoing. I shifted my gaze from her well-defined butt, only to find myself drooling over the sight of her back. I flushed as I leered at her back. It didn't help matters that I was thinking about the kiss we had shared earlier.

"This is going to be a long night," I couldn't help muttering, thankful no one heard me.

I was relieved as Alex put on a black men's blazer. Now I could make it through the evening without staring at her back like some lecher.

"Hi," Alex said as she turned to me. "You look great." A slight blush crept across her normally dark complexion.

"Back at you." I noticed how absolutely adorable she looked.

Unfortunately, I wasn't the only one who noticed. Chris stood and quickly moved beside her and adjusted the collar on her jacket. Then she caressed Alex's face. "You look beautiful," she whispered sweetly, and I clenched my fists in anger.

"Thanks," Alex muttered as she took a slight step away from Chris. I looked at the two of them standing next to each other. My early bravado vanished. I felt like one of the ugly stepsisters from Cinderella.

Pitifully, I slumped down onto the sofa and wished that I could disappear. I looked at the coffee table that was now covered with a stack of papers. Something caught my eye, it was a date. One that was all too familiar to me. Chris crossed over and gathered up the papers.

"Chris, it doesn't matter," Alex said abruptly. "I trust Stephanie." My heart warmed slightly with her declaration. Granted, she wasn't pledging her undying love to me, but it was a nice gesture just the same.

"Are you certain?" Chris asked her in a professional manner. "No offense, Dr. Grant," she added halfheartedly as she shoved the papers into her briefcase and snapped it shut. Chris then crossed back over to Alex and touched her on the arm.

"None taken," I said honestly as I understood that she was only doing her job. "I understand." Truth be told, I didn't care if Chris out and out accused me of spying. Hell, she could have accused me of kidnapping the Lindberg baby…just as long as she stopped touching Alex.

"Chris, I've nothing to hide from Stephanie," Alex added in a harsh tone as she once again stepped away from Chris's grasp. "I've been accused of bribing a jurist," Alex said to me.

"Excuse me?"

"Alex!" Chris harshly cautioned.

"Let it go, Chris," Alex hissed. "I trust her."

"All right," Chris grumbled.

"Alex?" I voiced my concern over the seriousness of the situation.

"Don't worry, they can't touch her," Chris added in a serious tone. "First off, the statute of limitations has run out."

"No," Alex cut in. "First off, I didn't do this."

"I know," Chris reassured her.

I realized at that moment despite some of her personal shortfalls Chris was a very good lawyer. Watching the way she handled herself when she wasn't flirting, Chris proved to be quite an impressive figure. There wasn't a doubt in my mind that she could sell ice to an Eskimo. Of course, there was one little problem with

Chris, and that was Alex. I hated the ease between the two. The little intimacies that showed that they had once been a couple. I knew it was a fact of life; just the same, it worked my nerves.

"So then why are they bothering with this?" I asked in hopes of drawing out Chris's instincts as a lawyer. Perhaps that would keep her from touching Alex.

"The ADA is using the RICO statute. He's claiming that the firm was involved in a string of illegal activities." Chris approached me. "If he can prove this, then he can turn it into a federal case. So far, most of his accusations aren't holding water. We've managed to clear away most of the charges. With the exception of the one against Alex."

"If that's the case, then how is he hoping to prosecute Alex?" I asked. "RICO implies an ongoing racketeering case, right? If the other charges have been dropped and the statute of limitations of bribery has expired, he can't bring charges against Alex. Am I right?"

"Very good." Chris seemed impressed. "However, Alex doesn't want the case to be dismissed."

"I'm not going to have people think that I did this," Alex fumed. "Chris, you know as well as I do that people will always assume that I'm guilty and I simply used my name to get out of it. Plus, I could still be disbarred. That would kill my parents. I need to prove my innocence."

"It's a moot point,." Chris shot back. "He can't proceed with it."

"I didn't do this!" Alex said angrily. "Hell, I didn't have to. That case was garbage. Even if it wasn't, I would never break the law. My name is on the line, and I'm not letting Simon Brenner drag it through the mud! I want it in writing that I didn't do it, end of story."

"That and get one up on him," Chris shot back.

"Who is Simon Brenner?" I asked innocently. Something told me I shouldn't ask, but it was too late.

"Jessica Gunnarsson's husband," Alex said bitterly.

"I guess you two really don't have any secrets," Chris snarled, apparently not happy that I was privy to Alex's secrets.

"It's not like he knew," Alex said with disgust.

"He might not know that you slept with his wife," Chris began slowly. "But every time you went up against Simon in court, you made a fool out of him."

"So I'm petty." Alex sighed. "But I never broke the law."

"You do have an alibi for the night of the twenty-second." Chris pointed out. "That alone could end this. I mean, if this bozo is lying about one of the dates, it casts doubt on the rest of his story."

"I can't use Higgins." Alex groaned in desperation. "I've already explained that to you. If the judge or Brenner questions him about what we were doing together, he'll have to perjure himself."

"So?" Chris shot back.

"Counselor, may I remind you that suborning perjured testimony is a crime?" Alex shot back. "I can't go to a judge and tell the truth about what I was doing with Higgins. Somehow, I don't think that telling a judge that I couldn't have possibly been bribing a juror on that day since I was busy committing a different crime would help my cause any."

"Excuse me?" I asked her.

"Higgins is a professional deprogrammer," Alex wearily explained. "I was meeting with him all day and night making plans to have my brother snatched from the cult he joined."

"Isn't it an alibi?" I asked, confused by how that would be a bad thing.

"It's also kidnapping," Alex replied grimly.

"I guess I never looked at it that way." I sighed. "I suppose legally trying to save someone from a bad situation doesn't count if they're there by choice. I could help you."

"That's sweet, but only the truth can help me."

"I can help you, and I can do it without lying." Alex and Chris looked at me strangely. "I couldn't help but notice the dates written on one of the sheets of paper. One of them caught my eye. On the seventeenth of May, you were standing on the sidewalk in front of your office building yelling at me."

"What?" Alex gasped.

"What time was that?" Chris asked with enthusiasm.

"I don't know the exact time. I know that Alex had just exited the building," I said. "But I distinctly recall that I caught the 6:20 train back to New Haven. I arrived at the station not long after we had a disagreement over why I was there and you tried to steal my cab."

"How can you be so certain about the date?" Chris pushed in full lawyer mode.

"How could I forget? It was my birthday, and I was in tears." I had never intended to let Alex know that her actions that had hurt me so deeply happened on my birthday. But if telling her helped her out of this mess, I had to do it.

"You made her cry?" Chris shot out at Alex. "Hey, this helps," she said suddenly. "Your secretary has you leaving the building at 5:15, and your time prior to that is accounted for. It isn't enough, but it definitely closes the gap. Stephanie, would you be willing to give a deposition?"

"Of course," I said without a second thought. I looked over at Alex and was surprised to see the sullen expression on her face.

"Great." Chris was almost cheering with joy. "Now if we could just figure out where you were for the rest of that evening and the following one, this will all be over."

"I was probably with you, Chris," she said.

She's lying, I thought to myself.

"No, you weren't," Chris said in a crisp professional tone. "I've already checked my old appointment books, and we did not start seeing each other until the following week."

Alex glanced over at me. Her sullen expression had grown darker. "I can't believe I made you cry on your birthday. God, I'm such an ass."

"Alex, it was over ten years ago." I groaned, rolling my eyes. "Let it go. Speaking of birthdays, this is no way to spend yours. You've been promised dinner and dancing, now let's get going. The only legal talk I want to hear for the rest of the evening is whether or not we should risk parking in a tow zone, got it?"

"Fine by me," Chris readily agreed. "But in light of this new information, dinner is definitely on Wainwright and Griggs."

We gathered our coats, and I caught Alex smiling out of the corner of my eye. I let Chris exit the apartment ahead of us. I quickly pulled Alex aside. "And just what are you smiling at?"

"I remember," Alex spoke softly, forcing me to lean in to hear her words. "Not everything, mind you, but I remember you. I was supposed to meet Nikki, or so I thought. When I found out my meeting was with some college kid, I was furious. I remember you standing on that sidewalk all flustered, your long blond hair seemed to glow in the sunlight. I also remember thinking that you looked incredibly hot and if only I wasn't involved."

"What?" Now I was confused. "Chris just said the two of you weren't together yet."

"Oh, right," Alex answered a shade too quickly. "Maybe I don't remember everything. If I could, I wouldn't be in this mess."

"Uh-huh," I grunted as I wondered why she was lying. "I was still hot, though?" I couldn't resist teasing.

"Oh, yeah," Alex said with a deep sigh just as Chris bellowed for us to hurry. "You still are," she added in a hushed whisper.

I spun around quickly, causing her face to turn a deep shade of crimson. "Good," I retorted with a wink and turned away from her and headed down the staircase before she could see the blush racing across my face.

Chapter Twenty Seven

I drove us to the Church Street Café, and Sara was once again tending bar. I was pleased to find her behavior much more professional this time. Of course after the last time, I doubted that she would still consider Alex being swayed by her charms. Chris, on the other hand, flirted with the girl outrageously. This made me very happy. If she was flirting with Sara, it meant she wasn't flirting with Alex. During dinner, I limited myself to just one margarita. With Chris's encouragement, Alex had three and was just a little tipsy. At the end of the meal, the servers sang *Happy Birthday to You* to Alex as the entire restaurant cheered. When we left the restaurant, I insisted on driving.

We arrived at The Galaxy a little after ten, and I checked our coats quickly as I was not eager to leave Chris alone with Alex. I found Alex and Chris seated at Teresa's bar ordering another round of drinks. I opted for spring water. I searched the crowd and found Rita. As I crossed the room to greet her, I glanced back at the bar to find Chris caressing Alex's shoulder. Then she bent down and whispered something in her ear, which caused Alex to laugh brightly.

I just stood there watching them, feeling like an idiot. It wasn't until I felt a hand touching my shoulder that I stopped staring. I spun around and found Rita smiling at me.

"There you are," she exclaimed. "I was beginning to think I had been stood up."

"Sorry I'm late. I ended up having dinner with one of my colleagues for her birthday," I explained. "I hope you don't mind, but I invited her and an old friend of hers to join us."

"The more the merrier. Is she cute?"

"She's…beyond words," I answered absently.

"Uh-huh."

"Come on, I'll introduce you." I took Rita by the arm and led her back toward Alex and Chris.

As we approached the giggling duo, Rita's jaw dropped.

"Alex?" she exclaimed cheerfully.

"Rita?" Alex greeted her with a warm hug.

"My God, she knows everyone," I sputtered while wondering if there was a hole I could crawl into.

Alex made the introductions, explaining that she and Rita had attended Wellesley together.

"I hear it's your birthday, Alex. That calls for a round of drinks." Rita waved Teresa over and ordered a round of margaritas. I politely declined, explaining that someone had to drive. I listened to them chatter about the old days, and I was suddenly the odd woman out again.

"Do you remember that time during finals?" Rita asked Alex. "What was it, freshman year?"

"Sophomore," Alex corrected her.

"You really shocked everyone." Rita laughed.

"Oh, please, our dormitory floor was the queerest on campus." Alex scoffed.

"You two aren't going to believe what the prim and proper Ms. Kendell did," Rita began to explain as Alex blushed. "It was during finals, and everyone was so stressed. So Alex in her infinite wisdom decided to relieve the tension, as it were. She streaked down the hallway screaming, 'Come out, come out, wherever you are!'"

"Streaked?" Chris leered. "Do you mean that you...?"

"Yes, I ran buck naked down the hallway," Alex shyly confessed. "Hey, I was nineteen," she added defensively.

"Well, it certainly lifted everyone's spirits," Rita added.

"I bet it did," Chris said as she licked her lips.

I thought I was going to be sick. Just then, Rita touched me on the arm. "I hear that new Cher song playing in the other room, let's dance," she asked me sweetly.

"I'll go," Chris offered a tad too quickly.

"Maybe later," Rita said coolly. "Stephanie owes me a dance." Rita dragged me off before I could respond. Much to my surprise, Rita led me into the lounge instead of the front dance room. "Alex Kendell?" she asked quickly. I just stared at her blankly. "Alex Kendell?" she repeated. I was still at a loss. "Stephanie, is she the one you were telling me about?"

"Yes," I admitted reluctantly.

"I knew it. I could tell by that goofy look on your face."

"Hey!" I shot back indignantly.

"I'm confused," Rita blurted out.

"Why are you confused?" I asked in bewilderment. "I'm not the one speaking in code. Then again, you did refer to Alex as prim and proper. I doubt that's the same woman who the other day gave a lecture on the Cold War using Mork and Mindy hand puppets. Granted, she needed to explain to me who Mork and Mindy were. I still don't get the correlation."

"Focus."

"I'm trying to."

"First, I need to explain a few things to you," Rita started. "Years ago, there was this women's bar in the Financial District called Somewhere Else. It burnt down a long time ago. But in its heyday, Alex's reputation would walk in about ten minutes before she did."

"Great."

"Relax," Rita tried to reassure me. "It was a long time ago. Personally, I think a lot of women lied about being with her. Once she got into Harvard, she calmed down a lot. Her only interests were in her studies. Then she went off to New York and left a string of broken hearts behind her."

"I know all of this," I butted in. "New York was where she met Chris. New York was where she had a life long before she ever laid eyes on my sorry ass." My pity party seemed to be in full swing.

"What you don't know is that since she came back to Boston, that everyone—and I do mean everyone—and their sister has been trying to get up close and personal with her. I mean, she's beautiful, successful, and rich. Alex is quite the catch."

"Is this supposed to be cheering me up?"

"Yes," Rita said with a cocky smirk. "You told me that you were trying to get over someone that was involved."

"That's because she is or was, I'm not really sure anymore," I tried to explain.

"No, she's not, and there isn't a chance in hell she'd take Chris back."

"I know that," I snapped. "She's seeing this youngster named—

"

"Courtney," Rita cut me off. "A little brunette about yea tall." She held her hand up at the appropriate height. "A little too perky for her own good."

"That would be her."

"They're not together, and they never were," Rita asserted. "They had one date, and Alex shot her down."

"What are you talking about? I've seen her leaving Alex's apartment."

"Stephanie, I ran into Courtney around the beginning of the month, and she was with someone else. Not only that, she was bitching about how all she got from the high and mighty Ms. Kendell was the cold shoulder."

"I don't understand," I exclaimed in frustration.

"Don't you?" Rita scoffed. "Courtney set you up, so she could keep you away from Alex. Stephanie, trust me on this. If Alex Kendell had a girlfriend, I would've heard something."

"How?"

"Stephanie, sweetie, Boston may be a big city, but in many ways, it's a very small town," Rita explained. "I'll prove it to you. Chris is Alex's ex-lover. They lived together in New York for a couple of years. They met while working at the same law firm. They split up because Chris was cheating on her. Alex caught her in the act when she came home unexpectedly one night."

"Okay, that is spooky."

"Not really," Rita said. "When Alex blew back into town, who do you think were the people she called first?"

"Her old college friends." I smacked myself mentally at the realization.

"Of course," Rita confirmed. "That's half the point of attending the colleges we did, the connections. Alex came home and was forced to start all over again. Being the bright girl that she is, she called on her old cronies to help her get re-established. Both socially and professionally."

"Then why is Courtney at her apartment constantly?" I asked absently as I tried to piece together the events of the past few weeks. "I had a feeling they weren't together. Yet Courtney told me that they had, you know, and she's been spending a lot of time at Alex's place late at night."

"You're not spying on her, are you?"

"No, of course not," I said quickly, understanding Rita's concerns. "I live in the same building."

"That's right," Rita said with sly look. "Again I think that it must be very handy."

"Everyone seems to think so but not so much."

"Stephanie, trust me. Alex is single," Rita reassured me with a slight squeeze on my shoulder. "Think about it, if there was someone special in her life right now, then why isn't she here on her birthday?"

"This is driving me insane." I growled. "None of this makes any sense. Come on, let's dance before my head explodes."

Rita just laughed and led me onto the dance floor. I was enjoying dancing with Rita, happy to be lost in some pleasant thoughts. Out of the corner of my eye, I caught a glimpse of a very startling sight. Alex and Chris were dancing together. It pained me to admit it, but they looked good together. They moved in perfect harmony with each other. Why wouldn't they? After all, they used to be lovers. I wasn't the only one who noticed the two. Men and women alike were staring openly at the attractive couple.

Silently, I couldn't help asking myself how in the world I could compete with a woman like Chris. Then I realized that I don't need to. After all, I was the one Alex was kissing in her bedroom earlier. I continued dancing with Rita and tried to relax, but thoughts of the kiss kept running through my mind. I lost sight of Alex and Chris. Unaware that I was ignoring Rita, I kept searching for them.

"Come on." Rita finally groaned as she grasped my hand and led me off the dance floor. "God, you've got it bad." She dragged me over to the bar in the front room and ordered a couple of woo woo shots. I downed mine without even thinking. The liquor tasted so sweet it was hard to believe there was alcohol in it.

"I can't leave you alone for a minute, can I?" a soft contralto voice whispered in my ear as two familiar hands caressed my shoulders.

I leaned back into Alex's body, glancing at our companions, Rita grinning and Chris scowling.

"Does anyone want another drink?" Chris offered with a hint of harshness to her voice. I waved off her offer as Alex wrapped her arms around my waist.

"Just a bottle of spring water, I think I need to sober up a little," Alex said.

"I'll have another one." Rita smiled up at Chris.

Chris returned Rita's smile and ordered their drinks. "Oh, no." Rita groaned as she accepted her drink from Chris. We all looked at her oddly.

"What is it?"

"Issue girl at twelve o'clock, and she's heading this way." Rita sighed.

"No, tell me you're joking." I dropped my head, knowing it had to be true.

"Sorry, Stephanie, she's already seen you."

"Alex, would you do me a favor?" I asked as I looked up into a pair of very confused blue eyes.

"Anything," she said honestly.

"Kill me now."

"Huh?" Alex pulled me closer and shook her head.

"Who is issue girl?" Chris, clueless to the situation, asked.

"Stephanie's date from hell," Rita tried to explain as I felt Alex stiffen from behind me.

"You mean the good-looking woman heading this way?" Chris asked. "What's wrong with her?"

"She's not that good looking," I heard Alex mutter as she turned to see Josie blazing a determined path toward us.

"She has issues," I said bluntly.

"Oh." Alex and Chris groaned in unison.

"But still, she is good looking, and everyone has baggage." Chris was grasping at straws.

"With Judge Judy, M&M's, the Internet, and television?" I tried to explain.

"Now that's just un-American." Alex snorted.

"She's beyond freaky. I checked myself into the ER just to get away from her."

"Stephanie?" Josie called out to me in an accusing tone.

"Hello," I said dryly. I felt Alex pulling me closer to her in a protective manner.

"Sweetheart, I've been so worried about you," Josie went on, ignoring the low growl Alex released. "It was all I could talk about in therapy this week. I must say, I'm surprised you didn't call me."

"It was one date."

"We have a connection, Stephanie," Josie went on. "If it wasn't for that idiot doctor in the emergency room." She huffed as I tensed. "I have real issues with her."

"You're not talking about my baby sister, are you?" Alex asked in a controlled yet frightening tone.

"Oh, no." Chris gasped in fear. "I've seen that look before. Things are about to get ugly."

"Would you like to dance, Chris?" Rita asked hurriedly, and with that, they disappeared, leaving me wedged between an angry Alex and the clueless issue girl.

"Who are you?" Josie had the nerve to snap at Alex.

"I'm Stephanie's partner," Alex said dryly. I felt no need to correct her. I liked the way it sounded when Alex referred to me as her partner.

"I don't think so," Josie challenged her.

"And I think you should leave." Alex growled.

"You look like you have some anger management problems," Josie retorted as if that was going to save her.

"And you look like a bleeder," Alex said coldly. I could see the bartender stiffen from behind the bar preparing for trouble.

"Okay, that's it," I said finally as I stepped away from Alex positioning myself between the two. I placed a calming hand on Alex's chest. "Josie, goodbye." I waved my hand at her to shoo her away, then turned to Alex. "Alex, go drink your water and give the bartender a little something extra for worrying him." Alex muttered something under her breath and slinked over to the bar and followed my instructions. Josie just stared at me.

"Look, Josie, I'm with Alex." Again, I liked the way it sounded. "Now please leave because frankly you are working my nerves." Josie looked horrified as she stomped off. I just rolled my eyes and turned my attention back to a certain beauty who was pouting as she sipped her water. I walked over to her.

"She seemed nice," Alex jested. "How did you ever let her get away?"

I slapped her playfully on the stomach and held a cautioning finger. "It's a good thing it's your birthday," I warned her. "You know, she did," I added thoughtfully.

"Did what?"

"Seem nice," I tried to explain. "When I first met her here, she seemed perfectly normal. It wasn't until I got her out in the light of day that she turned out to be a complete wacko."

"Welcome to the world of lesbian dating."

"So are you enjoying your birthday?" I threw out in an effort to change the subject.

"Hmm, I liked my presents."

"The flowers or the balloons?" I asked.

"The balloons, but that wasn't the best one."

"No?"

"Nope," she teased. "The best one was the one received in my bedroom earlier tonight."

"What was that?" I feigned innocence. "Oh, you mean this?" I reached up and curled my fingers through her hair and pulled her down to me. I pressed my lips against her and kissed her. The kiss deepened quickly as I ran my tongue across her lips. She parted her own lips and granted me access into the warmth of her mouth. I pressed my body against hers, my senses reeling from the feel of her hands roaming down my back. We broke the kiss as the need to breathe became overwhelming.

"Yeah, that was the one." Alex moaned as I teased her forearm by tracing a pattern on her bare skin with my fingers. Not for the first time that night, I was happy that she had me check her blazer.

"I don't think so," I offered playfully. "As I recall, I had just started to grant your birthday wish when we were interrupted."

"Seems to be a pattern with us." She laughed. "Dance with me?"

"Are you trading your earlier wish for a dance?" I toyed with her.

"No," Alex answered seductively. "I still want to finish that, but if we try to do that here, I think we might get arrested. For now, I'll accept a dance."

"Okay," I agreed as I took her hand. "Just one thing, is Chris staying with you tonight?"

"Not a chance."

"Good." I squeezed her hand and led her onto the dance floor.

As we stepped out onto the dance floor, our bodies instinctively pulled together. We swayed in perfect rhythm to a remix of *Downtown*. As she pulled me even closer to her, I felt my breath escaping my body. I was certain that my heart would stop beating at any moment. As the next song started, I ran my hands up her arms. I was completely unaware of the music or the other people dancing around us. At that moment, my only lucid thoughts were of her. I felt her hand gently grip my waist. We moved closer together. Our bodies pressed together, only our breath separating us. All of this done under the veil of dancing. We swayed in time as our hips melded together. Her breath was hot against my neck. My hands found the way down and were caressing her well-toned backside.

Suddenly, the music vanished, and I heard the DJ thanking everyone for coming as the room was flooded with bright white lights. The spell would have been broken if only we weren't still standing there holding each other. We both sighed as we spotted Chris and Rita approaching us hand in hand.

"The ugly lights are on, time to go." Chris grunted, seemingly upset.

"Ugly lights?" I questioned.

"That's what they call it when the house lights come on at the end of the night," Rita merrily explained. "Often between the drinking and the dimly lit dance floor, you never get a good look at who you're with. The end of the night can prove to be quite disappointing if not shocking at times."

"I'm hungry," Chris said suddenly. "Who wants to get something to eat?" she asked as we just stared at her dumbfounded. "What?" She snarled.

"How can you be hungry again?" Alex scoffed.

"I'm a growing girl." Chris patted her well-toned stomach.

"Unbelievable." Alex grumbled.

While we waited in the seemingly endless line for the coat check, Chris managed to convince us to go to an all-night diner in the South End. Chris also managed to get Rita's email address with relative ease. The girl was smooth; I had to give her that. I was secretly pleased to see Chris and Rita hitting it off. Of course, my pleasure was born from a selfish desire to keep Chris as far away from Alex as possible. Alex stood beside me the entire time, her arm never leaving my waist.

"Chris, when is your flight?" Alex asked suddenly. Her fingers caressed my waist. "Are you sure you have time to catch a bite to eat?"

"Not a problem," Chris reassured her with a coy smile. "I can catch a shuttle out in the morning."

"It is morning," Alex pointed out.

"Trying to ditch me?" Chris made an attempt to sound playful but fell short as a hint of bitterness crept through. Chris's question was followed by an awkward silence. It was Chris who finally broke the silence. "The truth is that I'm not expected back at the office for a few days. I can fly back anytime."

"Uh-huh" was Alex's only response.

"I thought I could spend some time in Boston," Chris added, once again trying to sound nonchalant and failing miserably. "We could get some work done on the case."

"Unbelievable," Alex muttered.

It didn't take a rocket scientist to put the pieces together. Chris, thinking that Alex would be alone on her birthday, flew up to Boston in hopes of catching her in a vulnerable state. I had to give credit where credit was due, it was a good plan. It would appear that I had thrown a monkey wrench into Chris's plans, and she was none too happy about it.

"Fine," Chris spat out when we finally retrieved our coats. "We'll just grab a bite to eat then drive back to Prowers Landing so I can pick up my rental and be on my way." Chris seemed to be conceding but not entirely, I couldn't help but notice. I quickly did the math in my head. By the time we would leave the club, drive across town, eat, and drive back to Prowers Landing, it would be about time for Alex and I to go to work.

She certainly was a clever girl. Since she wouldn't be sleeping with Alex, she was making damn sure that I wouldn't be, either.

There was no way I was going to give up so easily this time. There had been too many missed opportunities and far too many misunderstandings. I felt that Alex was ready to invite me to spend the night. I pulled her closer and leaned up so I could whisper in her ear. "Feel like playing hooky tomorrow?" I suggested in a husky tone.

"Why, Dr. Grant?" she answered me with a slight blush and a lustful gaze.

She never answered me, though. Perhaps I had read the signals wrong. *No way,* I thought to myself.

***

I was questioning myself once again while I sat in a small diner at four a.m. Chris had ordered an enormous amount of food and was taking her time eating. I ordered coffee, while Alex had settled on the clam platter. Another hour passed as Chris rambled on endlessly about anything and everything. I was on my seventh cup of coffee when I noticed that Alex had grown strangely quiet. I looked over at her with concern as I noticed that her normally dark complexion had paled.

"Hey, I just noticed something," Chris said suddenly, breaking me from my thoughts. "I haven't seen you light a cigarette all night."

"I quit." Alex groaned in a somewhat confused state.

"I've heard that one before," Chris replied in disbelief.

"It's true," I defended Alex. "She hasn't had a cigarette since Halloween."

"No kidding?"

I looked over at Alex when there was a slight pause in the conversation. She looked terrible. "Are you all right?"

"I'm fine," she offered with a wave of her hand. "Just a little tired." Although I didn't believe her, I decided to let it go for the moment. Chris went back to talking about her favorite subject, which was, of course, herself.

"I find it hard to believe that no one asked you out in high school," I said to Chris about twenty minutes later. Somehow, she had managed to engage me in conversation.

"It's the truth, no one asked me out," Chris explained a half hour later. "All the boys thought I was too tall. By the time I was sixteen, I was already six feet tall. When boys finally decided that I was interesting, I discovered that I wasn't interested in them. Of course, my not dating caused some concern with my parents. I remember the day I graduated from law school they were so proud. I decided it was time to tell them the truth about myself. My Mom burst into tears, and my Dad threw me out of the house. I haven't spoken to them since."

"Their loss," Alex said bluntly as she absently rubbed her temple.

"Not all of us can have parents like yours, Alex," Chris replied earnestly.

Alex smiled slightly. "Oh, yeah, my coming out was easy," she said in a shaky voice. "I was seventeen, and they walked in on me and my girlfriend making out in my bedroom. They were relieved when I started dating boys again. Then after I went away to school, I decided it was time to sit them down and have 'the talk.' I was terrified, and I will never forget what they said."

"Well, what did they say?" I asked.

"Do we look stupid?" Alex said with a chuckle. "That was it. From then on, they just accepted me for who I was."

"What about your parents, Stephanie?" Chris asked.

"They're both dead."

"I'm sorry," Chris said with genuine kindness.

I was about to thank Chris for her kindness when I noticed that Alex was shaking slightly. "Alex?"

"What?" she answered absently.

"I think we need to get you home," I said quickly.

"Probably just the tequila," Alex tried to explain as she slumped over slightly.

"Chris?" I called to her in alarm. Without a word, Chris jumped out of her seat and was helping Alex up.

"I'll get the car," Chris offered.

"I'll get the check," I volunteered.

Alex stumbled as she stood. Her face turned an unnatural shade of green.

"I think maybe I'll take her to the ladies room first," Chris said quickly as she rushed Alex toward the restrooms at the back of the diner.

I motioned for the waitress and paid the check. I raced toward the restroom to help them. Just as I approached the bathroom, the door swung open. Chris struggled to keep a hold on Alex. I moved quickly and helped Chris drag her outside to the car. As we placed Alex in the backseat, I felt her forehead, shocked to find that she was burning up. She mumbled incoherently.

"I don't think it's the tequila, sweetie," I said to Alex. Chris and I switched places. She looked after Alex in the back while I drove.

"Based on the way that ladies room looked, I have a bad feeling about the clams," Chris nervously offered as I sped off, trying to remember the route to the hospital.

When we pulled up to the front of the hospital, I put the car in park and rushed over to assist Chris with Alex. Chris reached into Alex's pocket, only to have her hands swatted away. "Hey, I'm not trying to feel you up." Chris snapped. "I need to get your wallet." She reached down again and was once again pushed away. "Stephanie?" Chris pleaded. "We need her insurance card." I nodded, understanding the urgency. I slipped my hands inside Alex's jacket and reached in the pocket of her jeans and pulled out her wallet. Not only did Alex not refuse my advances, she pulled me closer to her. "Jesus, Alex." Chris laughed as I pulled myself away from Alex's embrace. I pulled her insurance card from her wallet and handed it to Chris and shoved Alex's wallet into my pocket.

Just then, a security guard began barking at me to move the car. "Do you know if her mother is still listed as her contact person?" Chris asked me quickly.

"Probably." I hopped into the car. "Oh, Chris!" I called out to her as she was entering the ER. "I think Nicole is on duty tonight. You might want to have someone page her," I suggested as I pulled away. I was taken aback by the stunned look on Chris's face.

Chapter Twenty Eight

I parked the car in one of the parking garages and ran off to the emergency room. The place was full of people. I found Chris and asked what was happening.

"They're seeing her now," Chris said. "By the looks of it, the clams at the diner were a big hit tonight. You were right, Nicole is on duty, and they paged her. That should make this fun." She sighed.

"What do you mean?"

"Let's just say there's no love lost between Nicole and me." Chris grunted. "I can't believe that someone allowed her to practice medicine."

"Really!" I shot back.

"Look, I'm sorry. Let me try to explain. Nicole was booted out of med school because of her drinking. I watched her drag her family through hell and back. She lied to them, stole from them. The entire time I was with Alex, I never once saw that girl sober."

"Well, that's not the person I know," I countered. "I don't think you're being fair to her."

"Fair to her?" Chris laughed. "What's fair about being a spoiled brat who has no problem with sucking free legal services from me, then running to her sister telling her to dump me?"

"Hold on," I tried to calm her down. "Now let's be honest here. Granted, using you was wrong, which I'm willing to bet she has already apologized for." Chris nodded in agreement. "But if you were Alex's sister, how would you feel about her relationship? You told me yourself that you're a womanizer."

"Honestly?" Chris asked slowly. "I would never let my sister be involved with anyone like me. But then again, my sister is a nun, so I don't need to worry about it."

We sat in the busy waiting room and awaited news on Alex's

condition. The wait was becoming unbearable. After hearing Chris's take on Nicole, I didn't feel like talking to her.

"Tell me something, Stephanie?" Chris asked suddenly.

"Sure," I said nonchalantly.

"Did you know what I was up to tonight?"

"You mean keeping us out so late that we couldn't have time to do anything when we got home?" I said with a shrug. "Oh, yeah, I figured it out fairly quickly. That's why I suggested to Alex that we both call in sick today."

"I knew I liked you." Chris smiled in response. Then she grew quiet for a moment before speaking again. "There's something you should know. I really do like you, but I love Alex. I fell for her the first moment I saw her. We started at the firm at the same time, and she just took my breath away. But Jessica Gunnarsson was there first. I stood back and watched the two of them together for six very long months."

"Eight months," I said absently.

"No, it was six," Chris corrected me. "It's not something that I'm likely to forget. The two of us ended up becoming friends, and I had given up on ever being with her. Then one night, it happened. I couldn't believe it. Then I screwed it up. You see, I want Alex back, yet I don't want her back. I know she doesn't love me. The one thing I want is for her to be happy. If you can make her happy, then…look, what I'm trying to say is, don't ever hurt her."

"I won't," I said frankly. "Now can I ask you something?" I asked her. "If you love Alex this much, why did you cheat on her?"

"Good question." Chris sighed. "The first time was pure lust, nothing else. The second time was because I got away with it the first time. Then I guess I kept doing it because deep down I suspected that she knew, and she wasn't going to leave me. I thought I could have my cake and eat it, too. Or maybe I suspected that she didn't love me. I think that was the real reason I was sleeping around. I think I wanted to get caught. Perhaps that's why I brought that woman home to our apartment. Just my luck, it proved to be one betrayal too many."

I tried to process everything that Chris was telling me. There was something nagging at me that I couldn't quite put my finger on.

It wasn't what Chris had just confessed to me, it was something Alex had said to me before.

I was closing in on the answer when Chris interrupted my thoughts. "So tell me, just what is going on with you and Alex?"

"It's complicated."

"I've already heard that line from Alex, so give," she pushed.

I couldn't believe I was doing this, but I answered her honestly. "For starters, when we met, I was already involved."

"Oh." Chris seemed to understand.

"With a man."

"Excuse me?"

"I didn't know I was gay," I explained further.

"That explains it then."

"That explains what?"

"Well, you know about Jessica," Chris began slowly. "But do you know about Brenda?"

"Brenda?" I asked, recalling that I had heard Nicole mention her once. "Who the hell is Brenda?"

"Brenda was Alex's first girlfriend," Chris said as her face twisted in an odd expression. "The one from high school. She dumped Alex for a guy, giving Alex the old 'it's been fun, but it's not like I'm a queer or anything' crap. Then she ends up marrying this guy and had the nerve to ask Alex to be the maid of honor at the wedding."

"What a bitch!" I exclaimed a little too loudly as the entire waiting room turned around and stared at me.

"Basically," Chris agreed. "Nicole didn't take it too well, either. She beat the crap out Brenda. She ended up getting arrested for drunk and disorderly and assault and battery. The charges were dropped since Brenda wasn't in a hurry to explain the situation to anyone. Everyone agreed that it would be best if Alex wasn't a member of the wedding."

"The two of them certainly look out for each other," I said.

"Yeah, well, Nicole didn't need an excuse for getting loaded and starting a brawl."

"Again, not the person I know."

"What are you doing here, snake?" A familiar voice snapped me out of my thoughts.

"Leech," Chris retorted to Nicole.

They glared at each other for a moment; it appeared there would be no cease-fire coming any time soon. "How is she?" I asked, not caring about the tension that was clearly flowing between the two of them. They could kill each other later, the only thing I cared about was Alex's health.

"She's going to be fine," Nicole reassured me. I felt a weight being lifted until Nicole added, "But…" Nicole began, and my chest tightened. "There's a problem." Nicole sat next to me and placed a hand on my arm. "It was food poisoning. As you can see, we've had a run of cases on that tonight. So far, it looks as if Alex is going to be just fine. She's hooked up to an IV getting some fluids. The doctor would like to keep her here overnight just for observation. The attending physician agrees. Here's the problem, Alex wants to go home."

"So what's the problem?" Chris interrupted. "If she needs to be in the hospital, just explain it to her."

"I wasn't talking to you, jackass," Nicole hissed.

"I think—" Chris began to argue.

"Enough!" I growled, stunning both of them. "Now behave, the both of you. Nicole, what aren't you telling me?"

"It's just that…" Nicole stammered. "Well, Alex is…"

"Spit it out," I pushed.

"She's afraid," she finally admitted.

"What?" Chris said with disbelief. "Please, she isn't—"

I held up a cautioning hand to Chris. "She's terrified of having to stay overnight in a hospital," Nicole said quietly.

I didn't need to know why. I could see the pain on Nicole's face of having to reveal Alex's secret. "Is it medically necessary for her to be admitted?"

"It would be a wise choice, but no, it isn't necessary," Nicole said. "It's just a precaution. Dr. Chang isn't going to release her, though, unless she knows that someone will be with her constantly for the next twenty-four hours."

"That isn't a problem," I assured her. "I'm not planning on leaving her side even if you do admit her. Does this mean I can take her home?"

"Thank you." Nicole sighed with relief.

"Hold on," Chris butted in. "If the doctor thinks she should stay…"

"No! End of discussion," I said firmly, surprised when Chris shrank back.

"She's been asking for you," Nicole said. "Funny, she didn't mention you, pond scum," Nicole shot out at Chris, who just glared in response.

Nicole led me into the treatment area. On the way, she explained that they had pumped Alex's stomach, and they had started her on antibiotics and something to help her stop vomiting, which I needed to continue after she got home. She also explained that Alex was pretty much out of it, and she might be confused on and off for the next few days.

Alex looked terrible when I was led into the curtained area. I brushed her hair off her face and took her hand. She smiled gently up at me. "I'm taking you home," I whispered to her. She just nodded in response and squeezed my hand. Nicole spoke to Alex's doctors and convinced them to release her into my care. Once she was stable enough, Chris and I drove Alex home and put her to bed. I made up the couch for Chris and rushed downstairs and changed into a T-shirt and sweats and raced back upstairs. I peeked into the bedroom to find Alex resting comfortably.

"Long day, huh?" Chris said from behind me.

"No kidding." I sighed as I turned to her. She had taken a shower and was wearing Alex's robe. I was too tired to get angry. "Chris, I need to talk to you."

"I'm sorry if I was out of line at the hospital."

I smiled at her sincere offering. "You were fine. There's something bothering me, and maybe you could help me out with it."

"Shoot." She plopped down on the sofa.

"Don't lawyers need to account for their time for financial reasons?"

"Always," she said with a smile. "Billable hours make the world go round."

"Alex isn't the type who would screw something like that up, is she?"

"Not a chance," she answered with curiosity.

"So for her not to able to account for her whereabouts is very unusual?" I pushed a little harder.

"Tell me about it." Chris groaned in frustration. "That woman could probably tell you what she ate for breakfast every day for the past decade."

"She doesn't eat breakfast," I added absently as I tried to piece together my thoughts.

"I know that," Chris snapped.

"Sorry. I'm just trying to put something together here. If you could just hear me out." She nodded in agreement. "You and Alex were friends before you were together. She told me that many times."

"Yes."

"Keep in mind that I'm a little socially awkward. When you're that close to someone, you tell them everything, like who you're dating, right?" Chris nodded again. "Would there be any reason why you wouldn't tell someone about a person you're dating?"

"Lots of reasons," Chris said. "You're embarrassed for some reason, like you know your friend wouldn't approve. Then, of course, if you're seeing someone who is involved or if you're involved and you're having an affair."

"I can honestly say that none of those would have occurred to me."

"What can I say?" Chris teased. "So where is all this leading?"

"A couple of things I've heard tonight don't fit," I tried to explain. "Alex told me that when she first met you, she was involved. The two of you didn't start dating until later. When I asked her about that, she lied to me and said she must have made a mistake. The other thing is that you told me she was with Jessica for six months."

"That's right," Chris said in a bewildered tone.

"But some time ago, Alex said it was eight months." I hoped that she would get the connection without my having to tell her.

"You must have been mistaken."

"Chris, I have a PhD in history." I sighed. "I live for details. I hate to say this, but I think Alex knows exactly where she was on those dates in question."

"What are you saying?"

"I'm saying that she was involved with someone she didn't want anyone to know about," I spoke carefully. "Not then and certainly not now."

I watched her as the information sank in. "Jessica." She finally realized.

"I think so," I said. "I'm just guessing, but I also think that the husband knows, and that's why he's going after Alex."

"Well, this is just peachy." Chris groaned. "I'll have to look into this. Damn it! If what you're saying is true, then I spent three years of my life with someone who was on the rebound. This night has just sucked."

"I'm sorry."

"It's not your fault," she grumbled. "I'm going to get some sleep so I can fly home later."

Without a word, I left her with her thoughts and went into the bedroom and crawled into bed with Alex. I felt her shift slightly and wrap her arms around me. I set the alarm so I could call the office in a few hours. Then I turned out the light and curled into Alex's embrace and began to drift off. "Stephanie?" a very sleepy Alex called out.

"Yes, Alex?"

"Next year, can we do something different for my birthday?" She yawned as she pulled me closer.

"Absolutely," I promised as we both fell asleep.

Chapter Twenty Nine

I muttered a nasty word when the alarm went off. I called the office and explained to Louisa that we would both be out sick. I could hear her chuckling when I told her this. I could only assume that like most everyone else on campus, she assumed that Alex and I were dating. Through her snickering, I convinced Louisa to contact Alex's TA and that I would be emailing her lecture to her.

I managed to climb out of bed and make it to the living room. Passing through, I noticed that Chris had left already.

"Sure, spread botulism and run, you coward!" I groused. It was safe to say that I had been in better moods, but a lack of sleep after spending the night in the emergency room will do that to a girl.

My body was dragging, yet somehow I managed to find Alex's laptop. Her password took me a few tries until I tried Wonder Woman. Admittedly, it was a lucky guess. I found the files and emailed them out. Having accomplished my tasks, I headed back toward the bedroom and some much-needed sleep.

Someone knocking on the front door halted my retreat; again, I found myself cussing. I felt bad for using colorful language when I found Mrs. Giovanni standing on the other side holding two large plastic containers. Without a word, I accepted the food she thrust at me.

"Stephanie, you no look so good," she said, her accent showing as she bustled into the apartment. "Nicole called and told me everything." She shooed me toward the kitchen. "Now this one is plain broth. Nicole said you should try to get Alex to eat some of this." She took one of the containers from me and placed it in the refrigerator. "Clean!" she said with joy. "I never see it clean before. I knew you would be a good influence on her. Now this one is for you. Chicken soup, I made it this morning." She shook her head in horror. "Clean but empty." She pointed to inside the refrigerator. "You girls don't eat right. Always going out late to eat, see what happens," she chastised me.

I chuckled slightly, offering no defense for my actions. I knew that Mrs. Giovanni never understood why anyone would go out to eat in the first place.

"Mrs. G, would you keep an eye on Alex?" I asked wearily. "I need to get some stuff from my apartment since I'll be staying up here for a few days."

"Go." She shooed me away.

"Thank you." I sighed heavily. "What about you? Is there anything you need done?"

"No, I'm good," Mrs. Giovanni said with a dismissive wave. "The food order you did for me last weekend was good. I'm going to my son's for the holiday. I wanted the family to come up here, but his wife insisted. They think I'm too old to cook for everyone." She snorted angrily. "Now someone has to drive up here in the snow."

"When is the snow coming?" I asked, knowing the woman never missed the weather report.

"The smiley man on channel four said it is coming soon. I don't know why he's happy that it's going to snow, but he was smiling. Now go get what you need so you can get some rest." Once again, she was shooing me. I had to admit, Mrs. G might be four-foot-nothing, but she could motivate anyone to get moving.

Upon returning to Alex's apartment, I found Mrs. Giovanni dusting. "You don't need to do that," I tried to stop her.

"Alex is sleeping," she told me while she continued to dust.

I thanked her and sent her on her way as quickly as I could. The woman loved to talk. Normally, I found her a little difficult to understand, but she was a wonderful storyteller just the same. That day, all I wanted was a hot shower and to climb back into bed.

I was exhausted by the time I re-entered the bedroom. The sight of Alex trying to stand unnerved me. "Stop!"

"I'm going to be…" She gulped. I understood immediately and dropped my belongings and rushed to her side.

"Okay," I reassured her. "But you can't do it alone." With my assistance, Alex made it to the bathroom. I held her hair back while she became ill.

"I don't understand why I can't." She moaned weakly from her spot in front of the toilet.

"Because there's nothing in your stomach," I tried to explain. "I'm going to run a bath for you." This little trip into the bathroom provided the perfect opportunity to change Alex and the bedding, as well. I started to run the water as Alex muttered something about a shower. "I don't think so," I said softly. "You don't have your sea legs yet. Stay here, I'm going to get you something clean to put on." Alex groaned weakly in response, pressing closer to the toilet.

Upon returning to the bathroom, I found her still lying there with her face against the porcelain. I quickly tested the water, turned off the faucet, and returned my attention to Alex.

"Okay, Wonder Woman, let's get you into the tub." I assisted her to a somewhat standing position.

"What are you doing?" Alex mumbled as I began to undress her.

"You might enjoy your bath more without your pajamas."

"Oh," she said absently as she tried to help with the removal of her clothing.

"Not to worry," I reassured her. "I saw everything you had to offer last night."

"Really?" She stepped out of her flannel lounge pants. "And?" she asked as I helped her into the bathtub.

"Well, with the exception of the unnatural shade of green your skin had turned, I enjoyed the view." I handed her a clean washcloth and soap.

She shook her head in confusion. "My head hurts so much. Why isn't anything making sense?"

"You're very sick." I patted her gently on the shoulder.

"Is that why I feel like I've been run over by a semi?"

"Probably. Now if you promise not to drown yourself, I need to change the sheets on the bed." She gave a mock salute, but her glassy-eyed expression concerned me. Reluctantly, I left her and tore the sheets and blankets off the bed. I then fluffed up the feather bed, put on clean sheets and blankets, and raced back to the bathroom.

Much to my relief, I found that Alex had managed to clean herself without drowning. My relief proved to be short-lived when she struggled to stand up. "Hold on, tiger, I need to wash your hair."

"How did you know about that?"

"Know about what?" I lowered the shower massage and retrieved her shampoo.

"Tigger, David used to call me that."

I wanted to ask why; instead, I focused on washing her hair. I massaged her scalp, smiling at the soft murmurs she released. I thought I would like to do this again, preferably when I wasn't exhausted and she wasn't delirious. After Alex was cleaned and dried, I helped her change and put her back into bed. Immediately, she began to toss and turn. I went to the kitchen, heated the broth, and grabbed her medicine, water, and a sports drink I brought up from downstairs.

Alex held down most of the broth, took her medicine, and drank everything I gave her. I tucked her back into bed and took her dirty linens and clothing to the laundry room. I threw everything, including the clothing I was wearing, into the washing machine before heading back to the bedroom. I hadn't given a thought to my own nakedness until I walked into the bedroom and quickly realized that Alex was awake. I blushed furiously and buried my face in my hands. "Beautiful," I heard her mutter. I looked up to find that she had rolled over and went to sleep.

"Yup, that's us in a nutshell. I'm naked, and you're so sick, you fall asleep." I threw up my hands in defeat and crawled into bed.

***

I never knew food poisoning could be so nasty. Most of Alex's symptoms passed over the next few days, mostly because she slept a lot. The worst was the lingering confusion, although she seemed more and more coherent but not consistently. I kept Maureen informed about Alex's state of health, and it was agreed that Alex's teaching assistant would give her midterms.

I thanked the heavens for Mrs. Giovanni, who came by frequently to check on her and bring food. Alex was keeping more down, but her diet was still restricted to broth. By Sunday evening, I was exhausted. I was looking forward to the day when Alex would wake and not need to have everything explained to her as to why she was sick.

I also spent my time fielding calls and texts from Chris and

Nicole. Chris updated me on the case against Alex. Nicole managed to convince her parents not to come up and to just let Alex rest. She was taking the train up so she could sit with Alex in the morning while I was at work.

I set the alarm and crawled into bed with Alex. Even though she was fast asleep, she pulled me into her arms. This had been our routine for the past few days whenever I crawled into bed with her. It didn't take long for me to drift off to sleep.

***

The dream was so vivid. I was touching Alex, and she was caressing me in return. I moaned as I felt her suckling my nipple, my legs opened for her, and she pressed her thigh between them. Out of instinct, I lifted my knee and slid my thigh between her legs. "My God, she's wet!" My eyes flew open; this was no dream! I found myself lying beneath Alex, our legs entwined just as I had been dreaming. Much to my surprise, my hands were underneath Alex's nightshirt cupping her breasts. I quickly pulled my hands from her.

"Stephanie," she called out dreamily.

Her hips swayed in a slow gentle movement, causing my hips to follow her lead. Our legs and hips rocked together in a slow rhythm. She pressed her body tightly against mine and allowed her lips and tongue to feast on my neck.

"Oh, god." I moaned as I felt our desire touch even through our clothing. I needed to stop what was happening. Alex wasn't awake or aware of what she was doing. While my mind screamed at me to stop her, my body fought its own battle. I continued to rock against her, and my hands slid down her strong back to her buttocks. I grabbed her cheeks and pushed her against me.

"Oh, yes." She moaned as our pace became more urgent.

My thighs trembled as my breathing became ragged. All too familiar demons chose that moment to arise. I was so close to something I had never experienced before. I felt her body reacting in a similar fashion. We were both so close, and it was so wrong. It was a struggle, but I managed to gently push her away. Alex rolled off of me without protest and drifted back into her slumber.

"It's the right thing to do," I told myself as I tried to regain control of my breathing. "If we're going to make love, I want us both to remember it." I collected myself and climbed out of bed. I grabbed a clean T-shirt and a fresh pair of boxer shorts and headed into the bathroom.

Two things occurred to me as I took a long cold shower. The first was that what I said to myself was true. With the gentleness of the moment and the way our bodies connected, I was making love to her. For the first time in my life, it wasn't just sex, I had been making love to someone. The second thing I realized was that if Alex was that good when she was sound asleep, I really wanted to know what she was like when she was wide awake! Damn, it would probably kill me, but what a way to go!

After climbing back into bed, I tossed and turned for hours before finally returning to sleep. Fortunately or unfortunately, I wasn't awakened by any more erotic dreams. The next morning, I awoke and reached out for my companion. I was surprised to find Alex's side of the bed empty. I heard the shower running in the bathroom.

"Idiot." I growled as I looked at the alarm clock noting that I had a good two hours before I had to get up. I threw the bed covers aside and followed the sounds of running water.

I rapped on the glass shower door and was greeted by a startled gasp from inside. "Are you all right?" I called out in a tense tone. The water stopped, and the door opened slightly. Alex's dazzling blue eyes peered out shyly. For the first time in days, she looked like her old self.

"I'm fine," she said shyly.

"Can you stand up okay?" I pushed, wiping the sleep from my eyes.

"Yeah," Alex said in a confused voice.

The telephone rang, and it took me a moment to realize that it was my cell. "I need to get that. You be careful."

"Oh, okay," Alex said, still confused by my actions. I waved a dismissive hand at her and stomped off into the bedroom.

"Hello?" I snarled into the telephone.

"Whoa." Chris chuckled on the other end. "Someone is grumpy."

"I need sleep, Chris." I took a calming breath before continuing. "I'm sorry, it's been a long couple of days."

"How's our girl doing?"

"Much better. She's in the shower."

"That's a good sign." Chris sighed with relief. "Maybe when she has her strength back, the weather will change and send the two of you a nice rainstorm."

"What is it with you and the rain anyway?" I asked, not really wanting an answer.

"It's not me," Chris said seductively. "It's her. It makes her...how do I put this delicately...it makes her horny as hell."

"If that was delicate, I would hate to hear you tell a children's story." I shook my head until the meaning hit me. "Wait, really?"

"Oh, yeah, and it's not just the rain," Chris continued. "Rain, sleet, snow, any change in the weather sets her off. I swear that woman is a sexual barometer."

"Uh-huh," I squeaked out as my mind reeled at the implications of what Chris had just told me.

"Well, I just wanted to check in." Chris sounded far too pleased with herself. "Glad to hear she's doing better. I'll be emailing some information to you later. Talk to you soon, bye."

"Bye, Chris," I replied sheepishly, thinking about what I had just learned. "I need to start following the weather reports."

Alex entered the bedroom in a clean pair of navy sweatpants and a well-worn Harvard T-shirt.

"How are you feeling?"

"Like I've been kicked in the head by a mule," Alex grumbled as she ran her fingers through her hair. "I've got one hell of a hangover. I swear my thirties are turning into some kind of cruel joke. In my twenties, I could party all night and hit the gym in the morning before working a twelve-plus-hour day."

I groaned, realizing that Alex was still unclear about what happened after the clams attacked. "Alex..." I began slowly.

"I should feel better later," Alex interrupted me. "I mean, if you still want to play hooky, that is? I must admit, I was more than a little surprised to find you in my bed this morning. I feel a need to ask, did I forget something important?"

"Almost, Alex, sit down." I patted the bed next to me. She complied, although her startled expression remained in place. I took another calming breath as I tried to figure out the best way to explain everything to her. Somehow, it had been easier when she was delirious. "Alex, you don't have a hangover."

"That's not what my head is screaming."

"I'm sorry I was so forward in the bathroom, but I was afraid that you might fall."

"Okay?" She looked at me oddly.

"Alex, what day is it?"

"Friday," she said as she continued to stare at me.

"No."

"No?"

"Today is Monday."

"What?" She gasped. I watched as she tried to process what I had just told her. "Monday? How can that be?"

"You remember going to the diner after dancing?" I asked. She nodded. "Well, you and half of Boston ended up with food poisoning. The board of health shut the place down. It was in yesterday's *Globe*."

"Food poisoning?" Alex was trying to put the pieces together.

"You were very sick, so Chris and I took you to the ER at MGH. The doctors wanted to keep you overnight, but you weren't thrilled with the idea. Nicole and I arranged it so they would release you. For that to happen, someone had to stay with you. I volunteered." I took a breath and allowed her to catch up on what had happened.

"I remember something…" Alex said absently. "You coming to me and saying that you were taking me home."

"That's right," I confirmed. "Now climb back into bed. You still need your rest, and frankly, so do I."

"But if it's Monday, I have midterms to give."

"No, you don't," I argued. "Your TA is giving them. I emailed your exams over to Louisa on Friday. Maureen has already signed you out for the rest of the week and your cousin Anthony closed up your house in P-town. Your sister is on her way over to stay with you while I go to work. There's nothing you need to do except get some rest." Having said that, I crawled back under the covers and waited for her to join me. Finally, she crawled into bed with me. I released a sigh, realizing that she wasn't going to fight me on this.

"You did all that for me?" She curled up next to me.

"Yes," I said with a yawn.

"Thank you," she said sweetly.

"You're welcome." I yawned again. "Now go to sleep. I have a couple hours left before I need to get up."

"I can't believe you did all that for me," she repeated. "Thank you."

"Anytime." I yawned. "Now shh. I need sleep." I snuggled against her.

"Stephanie?"

"Ugh!" I groaned.

"Sorry, but I seem to recall a few other things that have me confused."

"Such as?" I growled and lifted my head to face her and found her blushing.

"Well, for some reason, I recall you standing in my bedroom naked."

"I can explain that," I stammered. "I was doing laundry and decided to wash what I was wearing. We were alone in the apartment, and I thought you were asleep."

"Well, that makes sense." She nodded. "I do that all the time. One of the advantages of living alone."

"Okay, if that's settled, can I get some sleep?" I pleaded, hoping that was all she remembered.

"Did you give me a bath?" she went on.

"Yes," I nervously answered. "Whenever you needed to change your clothes and get cleaned up, I helped you."

"That was sweet of you," Alex said honestly. "But there's something else...I can't seem to sort out what was real and what was a dream."

"Alex," I cut her off. There was no way we were talking about that when I was sleep-deprived. "You slept most of the time. I'm sure everything will come back to you. Please, I need to get some sleep."

"Sorry." She snuggled against me again and placed my head on her chest.

I listened to her heart beating steadily, and once again, we were both fast asleep. I was awakened by the sound of the alarm clock.

Alex stirred slightly as I cursed and shut the annoying clock off. I showered and changed into a pair of jeans and a white turtleneck. I glanced outside, noticing the frost building up. Winter was definitely on its way.

I went to Alex's walk-in closet and grabbed a black wool sweater. I hoped that she wouldn't mind. I also prayed that when she woke up, she would remember what day it was. I brewed a pot of coffee for me and Nicole. I quickly learned that Nicole shared her sister's addiction for caffeine. I toasted a bagel and ate it while flipping through my paperwork.

I was placing my work into my briefcase when I heard footsteps approaching the apartment door. I was snapping my briefcase shut when I heard noises still shuffling around outside. I peeked through the peephole and chuckled at the sight I was spying. I swung the door open quickly, startling Nicole and Roger the cop caught up in a major lip lock. Roger blushed as Nicole laughed.

"Stephanie," she greeted me. "Thanks again for the ride, Roger." She kissed him gently on the cheek.

"Nice to see you again," Roger said shyly to me.

"Officer," I replied with a smirk as Nicole brushed past me.

I closed the door and gave a knowing look at the younger Kendell woman. "You know you can get cooties by doing that."

"It's true," she agreed. "We learned that in med school. Unlike when you stick your tongue down my sister's throat, which is perfectly hygienic."

"Nicole," Alex barked from the bedroom doorway. "You have the manners of a goat."

"At least I'm not a nag."

"Okay, play nice, you two," I warned them as they rolled their eyes in unison.

"I see that you have returned to the world of the living, Alex," Nicole noted, effectively changing the subject. "How is she today?" She directed this comment to me.

"She still has a headache, but she's been keeping down more food. Nothing solid yet, and she's not delirious any longer, I think." Alex growled at me. "She also showered by herself this morning," I continued, ignoring Alex's obvious discomfort.

"I also went potty by myself." Alex grunted. "What am I—a

two-year-old?"

"Alex, you were very sick," Nicole tried to calm her down. "If it wasn't for Stephanie, the doctors were going to admit you."

Alex pouted in response. "I have to go," I explained. "I'm taking the car if that's all right." I asked Alex, who nodded.

"Why not?" Nicole said. "She's grounded." She pointed to Alex. "And I'm not allowed to drive yet."

Alex looked at Nicole with surprise. "I was going to tell you later," Nicole said. "I went to see that judge, and I have my learner's permit." She reached into her pocket and produced a long white sheet of paper with her picture on it. "I had a very long talk with the judge, and he could see that I've changed. But if I screw up again, he made it very clear that I'll be looking at some serious jail time."

"What?" Alex snapped. "Nikki, you should have let me handle this for you." Nicole held up her hand in protest.

"I have to do these things myself," Nicole said. "And he's right. I should have been locked up for what I did. I'm an ER doctor. I know better than to get behind the wheel of a car after drinking. I could have killed someone."

The two remained silent for a moment. Alex headed for the kitchen. "Where are you going?" I asked her briskly, effectively stopping her in her tracks.

"I smell coffee," Alex said shyly.

"No."

"Why?" She whined like a child.

"Alex, no," Nicole confirmed. "You were dehydrated, no caffeine."

"But," Alex whimpered.

"Maybe by Wednesday," Nicole suggested.

"Wednesday!" Alex gasped in horror. "But...but today is Monday. It is still Monday, isn't it?"

I rushed to Alex's side as she whimpered. "Yes, sweetie, it is still Monday," I reassured her. "Two more days and you can have some coffee. I'll get the hazelnut blend you like so much, okay?" I patted her on the shoulder.

"It's not fair." She pouted as she tugged on the sleeve of the sweater I was wearing.

"I know." I comforted her, wrapping my arm around her waist. "It's not fair."

"You get to have coffee, and Nikki can have coffee." Alex continued to whimper, then a surprised look crossed her face. "Is that my sweater?"

"Gotta go," I said hurriedly as I dashed into the kitchen and filled my travel mug. I returned to the living room and gathered my belongings and threw on my coat. There was no way I was giving up that sweater. It was comfortable, warm, and most importantly, it smelled like Alex.

"Oh, sure, rub it in." Alex snorted as she pointed to my travel mug. I just shrugged my shoulders and headed toward the doorway with Alex following me. "Have a good day at work," she said softly, then as if it was the most natural thing in the world to do, she lowered her head and placed a gentle kiss on my lips.

We broke apart, both startled by the kiss. "That was..." Her voice trailed off.

"I know," I said, thinking about how perfectly normal it seemed for her to send me off to work with a goodbye kiss.

"Could we do that again, but could you take a sip of coffee first?"

"Oh, sure, use my body to satisfy your caffeine jones. I feel so cheap." Taking pity on her, I took a healthy sip of coffee.

Alex lowered her head once again as I pursed my lips to greet hers. I gasped slightly as she ran her tongue across my lips. Instinctively, I parted my lips and allowed her entrance. I moaned, not caring that she was simply trying to taste the coffee I had just consumed. The kiss deepened as she wrapped her arms around me, pulling me closer as our tongues battled for control. Our bodies melded together, thoughts of feeding Alex's caffeine addiction no longer a concern.

"Are you saying goodbye to the girl, or are you giving her a dental exam, Alex?" Nicole teased.

Alex growled and sneered at her. "I have to go." I patted Alex gently on the arm. "Have fun with your sister."

"Stephanie." Alex's sultry voice stopped me. "It looks nice on you. The sweater, it looks good on you." She smiled sweetly at me.

"I could definitely get used to starting my mornings like this," I sighed as I finally left the apartment. Behind the now closed door, I could hear some choice words in French being tossed around.

Chapter Thirty

I was walking on air as I stepped out onto the front porch. Then I was greeted by a most unwelcome sight. The image of Courtney climbing out of her car made me feel sick.

"This is going to be fun," I cursed silently.

"Hi." She greeted me with a forced smile. I didn't respond, I couldn't, far too afraid that I would say something inappropriate like her mother having an unnatural relation with a barnyard animal. "I heard Alex was sick, and I wanted to give her this." I noticed that her hand was shaking as she handed me what appeared to be a greeting card sealed in a lavender envelope.

I accepted the card gingerly, taking note that she had dotted the "I" with a little heart. *God how young is this kid?* I cast an icy glare down at her.

"Fine," I grumbled as I tried to push my way past her. The events of the past few days had only convinced me further that Rita had been correct. Courtney set me up, and I fell for it.

"Wait," she called out as I was heading toward Alex's car.

"Oh, goodie." I rolled my neck, fighting against the urge to smack her. "Courtney, what could you possibly want?"

"I owe you an apology."

"For?" I retorted coldly. There was no way I was going to make it easy on her.

"I think you know," she mumbled, unable to look me in the eye. I stood there waiting. I needed to hear her say it. "For the morning after Halloween. I lied to you, and you were right—I was being a bitch." I released a breath I hadn't realized I had been holding. "You don't need to worry about the card," she went on to explain. "It's just a thank you. She's been so nice to me helping me study for the bar exam and all. The firm I work for is so small, and I have to put in a lot of hours. None of the lawyers there has any time to spare and—"

"I'll see that Alex gets this," I cut off her ramblings, deciding it was time to let the girl off the hook.

"Thanks," Courtney said quickly. "Again, I'm sorry for lying to you. I don't know why I did it."

"Don't worry," I said warmly. "You'll grow out of it."

"Hey. Enjoy your holiday!"

"You too," I offered as I deactivated the car alarm.

"Thanks," she responded but remained standing in place. "Stephanie, I'm still a little confused about something."

"What?" I sighed as I glanced at my watch.

I watched as she shifted nervously from one foot to the other. "I ran into Peter back home in Providence last week," she began cautiously. "And well, the thing is, he kind of gave me the impression that the two of you were still together. I couldn't figure it out since all Alex talks about is you. That and I heard the two of you were pretty hot and heavy at The Galaxy last Thursday."

"What did you just say?" I blurted out in horror.

"Which part?"

"About Peter," I impatiently prompted.

"Well, I...um..." she stammered. "I ran into him, and we exchanged the usual 'funny running into you' thing. I asked about his holiday plans, and he said something about the two of you spending the holiday with his family. I thought it was strange since Alex told me that the two of you split, and I've seen you at Alex's early in the morning."

"No, I broke up with Peter on Halloween," I spat out. "I haven't even seen him since then. I swear if you're lying again," I threatened her.

"I'm not, I swear," she frantically defended herself. "I just thought I should say something to you, sorry."

"No, I'm glad you did." I steadied myself. "Thank you."

***

My encounter with Courtney was strange, to say the least, then again, I never experienced a normal gathering with little Miss Perky Bits. I shrugged it off for the moment, gathering my messages from Louisa before heading off to give my first exam of the day. While my students were busy with the midterm, I studied my messages. Most of them were from Peter, wanting to know my plans for Thanksgiving. Granted, I wasn't looking forward to spending the holiday alone, but there was no way I was going to spend it with Peter and his family. I needed to have a chat with him and find out what was going on. I didn't trust Courtney and for good reason.

After I administered my last exam for the day, I headed directly to my office and pulled up my emails. Once again, many were from Peter. Frustrated, I searched for my cellphone. It quickly became obvious that I had left it at Alex's. I thought it was just as well since I really didn't want Peter to know my cell number. His constant emails and calls to the office were bad enough.

"Peter, it's Stephanie," I spat out harshly.

"Stephanie, where have you been?" he spat back in an accusing tone.

"What?"

"I'm sorry," he offered weakly. "It's just that I've been calling you for days. I didn't get an answer at your apartment. I can't help if I'm jealous."

I tried to calm myself before I lost all control. "I'm sorry I flew off the handle," I apologized. "Alex has been very ill, and I've been staying with her."

"Thank God."

"Did you run into Courtney last week?" I asked him carefully. "You know that girl we met on Halloween."

"Yes," he said after a brief silence. "I...um..."

"Peter?"

"I'm sorry," he sputtered. "Look, I'm having a hard time telling people about this. I still don't understand it, and well, I really don't believe it."

"Oh, Peter," I tersely began. "I know this has been hard, especially after all the years we've been together."

"About Thursday?" he began hopefully.

"No." I was gentle but firm.

"But—"

"I'm sorry, but it's over." I felt my head throbbing as I tried to choose the right words that would leave no room for misunderstandings. "I know the timing sucks. Take care of yourself." I hung up before he could say anything. After the holiday, Peter and I were going to have a very long talk. It was time he knew the entire truth.

When I returned home, I found Alex and Nicole in a fierce battle over some video game. "Did you two have a nice play date?" I asked them, noticing Mrs. Giovanni puttering around. "Ah, saving the world from zombies."

"Some of us are," Nicole gloated.

"Harvard law and Stanford medical, money well spent," I snickered.

"Zia Maria, I can clean my own apartment," Alex groused. She threw her hands up in defeat while Nicole cackled. Mrs. Giovanni, for her part, ignored Alex and continued to dust.

"I'll put this away," Nicole offered, breaking down the XBox.

For my part, I put my briefcase down and slipped off my shoes and went over to the sofa and joined Alex. "Help," she whispered to me.

"Mrs. Giovanni?" I called out. "Why don't you take a break?"

She shrugged and complied with my request. "How was school, Stephanie?" Mrs. Giovanni asked.

"Good, thank you, and how was our patient today, ladies?"

"She ate some soup and toast," Mrs. Giovanni said.

"How did she do with the soup?" I ignored Alex grumbling next to me.

"Good," Nicole answered. "She's much better. Keep her on the antibiotics and no coffee until Wednesday, then only a little. Keep up with the fluids. You might want to keep an eye on how much she urinates," Nicole suggested. "If she gets plenty of rest and things keep going this way, she can enjoy a nice meal on Thursday."

"Hello!" Alex shouted. "I'm sitting right here, you know."

"Don't listen to her," Mrs. Giovanni scolded. "She's been a pain in the ass all day." I choked at Mrs. Giovanni's choice of language. "She kept trying to sneak upstairs and work on her computer or do laundry."

"I did not," Alex lied.

"She did," Nicole confirmed.

"Rat." Alex snarled.

"Zia Maria finally got her to sit down," Nicole explained, ignoring Alex.

"How did she manage that?"

"She threatened me," Alex grumbled.

"I did not!" Mrs. Giovanni protested.

"She did," Alex teased.

"That fresh mouth of yours is gonna get you in serious trouble someday, young lady," Mrs. Giovanni scolded.

Alex ignored her. "Come on, Zia Maria," Nicole said. "You promised me dinner before I had to leave."

"Okay, but first, I heat up the plate I brought over for Stephanie," Mrs. Giovanni said in broken English. "Eggplant parmesan."

"I'll eat it later," I said. "Thank you for doing that. You two go eat." They said their goodbyes and left us alone.

I reached to the back of the sofa and grabbed the blanket that rested there and covered Alex. "I don't know how to thank you for everything you've done for me over the past few days," Alex said with sincerity as she moved part of the blanket over my legs.

I couldn't help thinking that she could spend the rest of her life with me. Thinking that might be a little pushy, I just told her to forget it as I snuggled closer.

"Stephanie, I've been meaning to ask you something," she shyly began. "What are you doing for Thanksgiving?"

"Nothing."

"Well, it's just that...well, I've been wondering..." Alex stammered.

"Yes?"

"Well, I...um...I meant to ask you this before...would you like to spend it with me and my family?" she finally said, then blew out a breath as if she had just run a four-minute mile.

"I'd love to," I answered her quickly before she could change her mind. "So where is the family gathering—the compound in Hyannis?" I joked.

"No, the estate at Chestnut Hill," Alex said plainly. "The family lost the property on the Cape years ago."

Oh, my, God she's not kidding. How am I going to fit in with these people? I silently panicked. Suddenly, I was terrified, even after meeting Nicole.

"Don't worry," Alex reassured me as if reading my thoughts. "It won't be all that. It'll just be my sister, who you already know. If you can survive Nicole's antics, the rest of the family will be a piece of cake."

"Who's going to be there?"

"There's just Mom and Dad and Nukumi, of course."

"Nukumi?"

"She's my great-grandmother, you'll love her. She's Haley Ballister's daughter-in-law, so the two of you can talk about that."

"Thanks."

"Stephanie, now that we're alone, I need to ask you something."

"Okay?" I shivered nervously, uncertain as to where this was going. The look in her eyes drew me in, filling me with an overwhelming urge to get closer to her. She licked her lips, her gaze drifting down. My heart was racing, then she pulled away.

I shivered at the abrupt movement but decided to let it go for now. I pulled myself up and ran my fingers through my hair. "So what did you want to ask me?" I tried to hide it, but I knew my voice was shaking.

Alex leaned over to the coffee table and handed my cellphone to me. "Now before you say anything, I need to make something perfectly clear, this is all Nicole's fault."

"Oh, this is going to be good."

"Your phone chimed, and Nikki picked it up and saw that there was a text from Chris. Thinking that it was for me, she read it."

I opened the phone and quickly read the message that began, *I got these names from a friend of mine. Guess what two things these women have in common. Talk to you soon, Chris.* The message was followed by a long list of names.

"Again, I want to make it clear that I had no intention of invading your privacy. However, I'm more than a little curious as to why my ex-girlfriend sent you a list of women's names. Care to enlighten me?"

Chapter Thirty One

I wasn't ready to go into this with Alex. In fact, Chris and I had agreed that she would be the one to tell Alex if my suspicions were correct. Now there was no way to avoid it. I couldn't lie to her.

"Stephanie?" Alex pushed in a strained voice. "Come, on what is it? I know some of those women," she added absently.

"Alex..." I started carefully, hating what I was about to do. "You and these women have something in common."

Alex stared at me blankly. "What is it? Please, tell me what is going on,"

"Jessica Gunnarsson," I said quickly, then just as quickly braced myself for her reaction.

"Well, Jessica has certainly been a very busy girl," Alex wryly responded. "But that still doesn't explain..."

"Wait, you're not upset."

"No, should I be?"

"Frankly, yes."

"Why?"

"Because there are so many."

"And?" Alex laughed. "I'm sorry, I don't mean to laugh, but I learned the painful truth about Jessica quite some time ago."

"But so many?"

"I get it!" Alex snapped before wincing. "Sorry," she apologized. "I'll admit to see it in writing is a bit much. But Jessica is my past. Any feelings I had for her are just that, the past. I got over her years ago." Her voice was firm and honest.

"I'm sorry." I caressed her arm.

"That still doesn't explain why Chris sent you these names," Alex continued. "And what did she mean by these woman have two things in common?"

"The first thing is Jessica and the other thing is…" I said very carefully.

"Now wait a minute!" Alex jumped in. "I don't know what Chris is trying to pull here. I've been tested for everything, and I do mean everything. Several times, in fact, mostly because of Chris and Jessica."

"That's good to know," I said without thinking. I pulled my arm away from her as I realized not only what I had said, but what it implied.

"And you?" she asked me with a mischievous smile.

"I had a full physical when I joined the faculty at Prower. It included all the blood work under the sun," I said proudly, then feeling a little adventurous, I added a little something. "You could eat off of me."

Alex was suddenly plagued with a coughing fit. I patted her back as she gasped for air.

"You okay there, sparky?" I teased her as she regained control. She held up a hand to indicate that she was fine. "Do you need some water?" I only felt slightly guilty for her present condition.

"No thank you," she croaked out. I gave her a few moments to regain her composure. "So are you going to tell me what this is all about, or are you just going to torture me all evening?" she finally managed to ask me.

"Tough call," I said dryly as I debated the possibilities. "Define torture." I wiggled my eyebrows at her in a suggestive manner. Okay, I was stalling, but no one said I couldn't have a little fun while I did it.

"Stephanie?" Alex pleaded in exasperation.

"Fine," I finally caved. "First, let me explain that I had no intention of telling you this. Chris was the one who lost the coin toss." Alex just stared at me blankly. "I think Chris got these names from a bartender in the city. I mean, who else but a bartender knows all the dirt on who is knocking boots with whom?"

"Knocking boots?" Alex scoffed. "Tell me, did you learn that expression at Yale?"

"Anywho," I continued, ignoring the jab at my alma mater. "Chris was working on an idea I came up with. Well, it was more of a theory, really." I stopped my ramblings when Alex cleared her throat and rolled her hand in a *get on with it* motion. "Well, to make a long story short..." I stammered.

"Too late."

"Okay," I conceded. "All of the women on that list and you were not only involved with Jessica Gunnarsson, but also are now being or have been investigated by the New York District Attorney's Office." Alex's eyes widened at the revelation. "To be more specific, they are being investigated by Simon Brenner." I blew out a long cleansing breath and waited for the other shoe to drop.

It came quietly. "He knows" was all Alex said, then for a very long time, she said nothing at all. "Jessica, you idiot." Alex suddenly snarled in disgust. "She must have written it down somewhere, probably in the damn organizer she never let out of her sight. Or that damn organizer she's chained to. All of it must be in one of them, names, dates, how else could he have known when I was..." She stopped suddenly as her face grew ashen.

"When you were with her," I finished for her. "And how long you were with her."

Alex hung her head in shame and rubbed her eyes. "Chris knows all of this?" she asked numbly.

"Yes."

"God, she must be pissed." Her voice drifted off as she spoke. She lifted her head and looked at me. "You know the funny part of this fiasco is that if it had been any other attorney handling this case, I would have just come clean from the get-go. The firm assumed that because of my prior relationship with Chris that if I had anything to hide, I'd tell her."

"Ironic."

"Tell me about it," Alex agreed. "Chris was the one person I couldn't tell about this. I didn't want her to know what an idiot I had been falling for Jessica's lies again. More importantly that I had turned to her because of it. How did all of this come out in the first place?"

"That was my fault."

"How did you come up with this?" Alex appeared to be impressed. "I mean, I know how intelligent you, are but this is incredible."

"First off, you are a terrible liar, Alex Kendell," I eagerly explained. "You are also as anal as the day is long."

"Thank you, I think."

"You told me you were with Jessica for eight months. Chris said it was six. Not a detail either of you would've screwed up. Then you said something about being involved when you first met me. But you weren't with Chris at the time. When you tried to cover up the slip-up, I knew you were lying. That's when I started to put the pieces together and came up with Jessica."

"You're a very clever girl, Stephanie Grant," Alex said with genuine sincerity. "You have a little Laura Holt in you."

"Now who is she?"

"Did you never watch television?"

"Apparently, not as much as some people." I scoffed.

"Timing is everything." She sighed thoughtfully. "Take us, for example. If things had been different, then so much we've put each other through would have never happened. Then there's Jessica. The first time I met her, I was clueless, hell, I was a kid back then. When I found out about her husband, I broke up with her immediately. A short time later, our paths crossed, and she told me that she and her husband were separated. Little did I know that Jessica's version of being separated meant she hadn't seen him since breakfast. Of course, when I figured it out, I walked away. I don't blame her, really. She grew up in a different era, and coming out was never an option for her."

"She may have to, she's your alibi."

"She won't."

"But she —"

"She won't," Alex repeated. "I've already asked her."

"She's just going to let her husband railroad you?"

"Yes," Alex confirmed without any hint of emotion.

"This certainly explains a great deal to me," I said bluntly. "Now I understand why you ran away from me. The way I kept putting off breaking up with Peter. After what Jessica had pulled, then there's Brenda, of course."

"How do you know about Brenda?"

"Chris."

"What else has she been telling you?"

"Nothing," I lied.

"Stephanie?"

"I swear that was it. Scouts' honor. Look, it's raining." I couldn't resist teasing her.

"No!" Alex blushed furiously. "Oh, god, she didn't?"

"What?" I answered with feigned innocence.

"Oh, my God!" Alex buried her hands in her face.

Then suddenly, her words were echoed through the wall. "Oh, my God!" Which was quickly followed by, "Yes! Yes, baby, yes!"

"They're at it again." Alex groaned. "Shavonne has a new girlfriend. It sounds like they're almost finished." The sounds continued until someone loudly thanked Jesus.

I stared at the wall thinking the last of my questions had just been answered. Courtney must have heard the couple, as well, and decided it would be a good way to screw with me.

"So that's who I heard on Halloween night."

"Who did you think it was?" Alex asked in bewilderment.

I didn't answer her as I struggled to find a way to explain the bizarre events. I knew it was time to put my cards on the table and tell her everything. Yet there I sat struck mute.

"I think I need to go to bed." Alex yawned. "You'd think that after all the sleep I've had in the past few days I'd be wide awake."

"Alex, wait, there's something else you need to know."

"There's more?" Alex asked in a frightened tone.

"Yes," I said with a slight smile, trying to reassure her. "It isn't anything horrible. I now know why you shut me out before I broke up with Peter. Do you know why I avoided you after I did?"

"Frankly, no." Alex's voice was as smooth as velvet. "I'm more than a little curious. I thought of a million reasons why. Maybe you needed more time or weren't interested in me. I was going insane. Finally, I just backed off and stayed away. I was trying to give you some space."

"I understand that now, but at the time, I didn't." I had to laugh at the situation. "I thought you were dating Courtney."

"What? She's a bit young for me, don't you think? Well, she's not that young."

"Yeah, right." I got up off the sofa and went over to my

briefcase and retrieved the card Courtney had given me earlier. I walked over to Alex and handed it to her. "From Courtney." Alex looked at it briefly before tossing it onto the coffee table.

"She dots her I's with little hearts? Maybe she is that young," Alex conceded. "That still doesn't explain why you thought I was dating her. I only had the one date with her, and you were there for most of it. In fact, I kissed you that night."

My only response was to jerk my thumb in the direction of the wall that had previously been filled with the sounds of passion. "How could you think that?" Alex countered in a horrified tone. "You were the one I was making out with the night before and that night, as well. Did you really think I could kiss you, then bed her?"

"Not entirely."

"What does that mean?" Alex asked me directly. "I only went out with her in the first place because of you."

"Excuse me?"

"You still hadn't said anything to Peter," Alex explained. "Yet you were flirting with me, but he was still in your life. I knew that until you ended things with him, I could never be in your life. I told you that more times than I can count. Finally, one night out of desperation, I went to the club. Courtney asked me out, and against my better judgment, I said yes. It was a stupid attempt to get over you."

"Alex," I pleaded with her. "I understand that now, but at the time, I didn't know if I was coming or going."

"After the way we touched each other, how could you think that I would sleep with that girl?" Alex protested. "Damn it, Stephanie, even as sick as I was over the past few days, last night, I dreamed about touching you."

I let it slide, thinking there wasn't a need to tell her that she wasn't dreaming. There was far too much happening. I had started out trying to be honest with her. Pissing her off hadn't been my intention.

"I think that we need to slow things down here," she said heavily. "Take a break from whatever this is."

"How much slower would you like to go?" I spat out, realizing that I was being dumped. "I mean, without my moving back to

Connecticut?"

"Stephanie," she protested. "Maybe we should just be friends for right now."

"Fine," I shouted in anger as I tore her sweater off my body and tossed it at her.

"Keep it," she offered. "It really does look good on you."

"You can't have it both ways. You can't just dump me, then try to flirt with me." My anger was building. "I know how I feel, and there are things you don't know. But if you want to play at being buddies, then fine. Frankly, I'm tired of the games." Having said that, I stormed out of her apartment and raced downstairs.

My heart sank when I realized that I did not have my house keys. "Crap." I scowled as I stomped back upstairs and stormed back inside Alex's apartment. Having to go back inside really took the glory out of my storming off. "I forgot my keys," I bellowed, gathering up my belongings. "Your aunt is staying with you tomorrow. The instructions for your meds are on the bottle."

"Stephanie?"

"Don't."

"I'm not dumping you," she choked out. "But we can't start something now."

"Whatever you are running from this time, get over it and soon!" I shouted and stormed back downstairs. Of course, once I entered my apartment, I realized that I had left most of my clothing upstairs. "Forget it!" I snarled as I tore off my clothing and climbed naked into my futon. I spent a sleepless night trying to figure out just how things spun out of control so quickly.

Chapter Thirty Two

Wednesday morning, I gave my last midterm for the semester and told my students, "Happy Thanksgiving." I turned in my paperwork and wished everyone at the office a happy holiday and picked up Alex's midterms from her teaching assistant. I started to walk home in the cold when I was greeted by the sound of a car honking its horn. For a brief moment, I hoped it was Alex. I turned and spotted a familiar black Honda.

"It's much too cold to be walking," Hal called out to me. "Care for a lift home?"

Hal and I chatted about the weather and the upcoming holiday. He was grateful for the time off, and he planned on spending it with his girlfriend and her family. I didn't elaborate on my plans, not really knowing just what they entailed. More than likely, I'd be spending the day with a microwave dinner and a good book.

I looked at Hal's well-pressed suit and noted that he was a classy dresser in men's and women's clothing. We arrived at our house in no time. I thanked him as I let myself into my apartment. I looked around thinking about turning on the television while wallowing in a pint of Ben and Jerry's.

"What happened?" I asked for the hundredth time. I still couldn't understand how in the blink of an eye Alex had decided that we were meant to be really good friends. I heard a thud on the stairs and knew who it was. "She's so clumsy."

I jumped when she knocked on my door. I assumed it was her since Alex was the only one who consistently tripped on the stairs.

"Hello?" I greeted her coldly.

"Truce?" Alex offered shyly.

"Hmm," I grunted.

"Still want to spend the holiday with my family?" she asked

hesitantly. "I'd really like it if you came."

"I don't know," I said honestly.

"I meant what I said about keeping your friendship."

I stood there staring at her, my mind telling me one thing and my heart another. I hated that the two were in constant conflict lately.

"Please," Alex pleaded. "I don't think I could bare it if I lost your friendship."

"Fine," I agreed reluctantly. "Do you need me to drive since I'm not entirely sure you should be out of bed?" I don't know why I agreed but there I was ready to drive to Newton.

After she reassured me that she was fine, I packed an overnight bag and met her at the car. The cold winter air sliced through my body, making me thankful that Alex's car had heated seats. As we drove down the highway, it began to snow. I found myself wondering if what Chris had told me about Alex's reactions to the changing weather were true.

The snowfall grew heavy along with the number of cars on the road. Alex's sex drive was no longer my primary focus. I offered another silent thank you for all-wheel drive. The constant whirring of the windshield wipers began to wear on me. With each swipe, it reminded me that neither of us had spoken a word since we headed out.

The silence was unbearable. For some unexplainable reason, I wanted to scream. I was wondering if this was what finding love was really like. I found it difficult to understand that I would find that one person I wanted to be with for the rest of my life, only to end up miserable. I thought that I should have stayed home, not looking forward to sitting down to dinner with her family.

"Stop the car!" I shouted, unable to withstand the silence any longer. My chest felt tight, alerting me that I was on the brink of a full-fledged panic attack.

Alex was visibly shaken. My guess was that having her passenger screaming somehow unnerved her. She managed to pull the car over safely into the breakdown lane. Not without several other cars honking their horns in anger. Once the car came to a stop, I jumped out, slamming the door behind me. Alex followed me as I began to pace on the snow-covered pavement, all the while fighting against the need to start hyperventilating. Her face was painted with fear as she tried to calm me down.

"You're such a jerk!" I finally shouted, startling her even further. "I met you in August, and from the first moment I saw you, I knew. I knew! You're the one, and because of this, my life has been turned upside down." I blew out a heavy breath as I finished, not certain my words made any sense but somehow not caring. The only thing I cared about was that I could finally breathe.

"I never asked you to turn your life upside down," Alex argued.

"Didn't you?" I countered loudly. "You encouraged me every step of the way. Just tell me why, now that everything is starting to make sense, you're running away again."

She just stood there looking guilty with her hands stuffed into the pockets of her camel hair coat, closing her eyes and lowering her head.

"Don't!" I screamed. The anger in my voice began to frighten me. I felt as if I was fighting to stay alive. "Is this why I came out? So you could leave me? Tell me why. Just tell me why you're running away from me, from us."

"Because I have no secrets." Alex's voice trembled. "In a matter of a few weeks, you know everything there is to know about me. We never even dated, yet you know my entire past. I'm completely exposed. You even stepped in and solved my legal problems. I've nothing to offer you."

"What about your heart?"

"I tried that. Every time I asked you out, I got shot down."

"I thought that you were dating Courtney!"

"That's another reason we should stop this. How could you not trust me like that?"

"Because when you did bother to come home, she was there."

"I was helping her study for the bar exam," Alex helplessly tried to explain. "Damn it, you know me. How could you think that I would be so shallow as to sleep with her, then ask you out?"

"Because she told me that she had slept with you," I fired back. There it was, finally out, and it felt good.

"What?" Alex gasped.

I took a few breaths and collected myself before speaking. I couldn't screw this up, I had to make her see what I had seen and why I thought what I thought. "The morning after Halloween," I explained calmly. "Courtney told me that the two of you slept together."

I watched as Alex's expression changed rapidly from stunned to outrage. "That little…" Alex sputtered. "I swear to you, Stephanie, I never touched her. The only reason she spent the night was because she was in no condition to drive. When she tried something, I let her down gently. I explained that I wasn't interested. I was also very honest about my feelings for you and how it looked as if we might finally have a chance to explore a relationship. She said she understood."

"Of course she did." I had to laugh. "Being the bright girl that she is, the first thing she did was run to me and tell me about having sex with you. She knew I'd back off." I shook my head at the irony of the situation. "I didn't discover the truth until very recently."

"Yes, she's a very clever girl," Alex said coldly. "She made certain she got to you before I did. You must have thought I was a first-class jerk asking you out after sleeping with her." Alex shivered as she spoke.

"Jerk was one of the nicer things I was thinking about you," I confessed. "There's something else. I didn't realize that you were asking me out, for a date I mean. You were, weren't you?"

"Yes," she asserted before her face dropped. "I keep forgetting this is all new to you."

"So now that this is all out in the open, where does this leave us?" I looked at her hopefully, surprised by the tears now running down her face. I rushed to her side.

"We need to get out of the snow." She sniffed, taking me by the hand.

Once we were safely inside the car, I watched as the normally stoic woman dried her tears and collected her thoughts. "Alex, what is it?" I took her hand in mine.

"I'm not running away. I took the position at Stanford. With my leaving, I didn't think it would be a good idea to start something."

"That's it? I'm not thrilled, but it's only for six weeks. I'll miss you, but—" She held up a shaking hand and stopped me.

"Stephanie, I'll be gone for four months."

"Four months? Four freaking months?" I shrieked before I took a moment and calmed myself. "This is not the end of the world. After all the crap we've been through, four months is a mere drop in the bucket. When did this happen?"

"Right before my birthday. Had I been thinking clearly on that day, we wouldn't be sitting here now."

"Oh, of course, we would. Apparently, we're jinxed."

"You could be right."

"Why did you agree to it?"

"I thought that the time apart would be good for us." She sighed. "Somehow, my going to California would give us the distance that we needed and maybe our friendship would survive. Then the other night, everything was coming out, and suddenly, I realized what I had done, and I panicked. How could we start seeing each other now? I'll be leaving in a few weeks, and it's not fair to you. You just came out. You should be out meeting women and dating."

"You are insane," I said in dismay. "I've already gone out and met other women. One of whom landed me in the emergency room, thank you very much. Do you want me to go out with other women?"

"No."

"Then what's the problem?" I asked her directly. "I know how my heart feels…I love you now, and I will still love you four months from now."

"You can't know that," she warned me. "But if it is true and when I come home and we both still feel the same way, then let's start things off right this time. What we've had up until now has been…I honestly don't know what it has been."

"Bedlam."

"Pretty much." She laughed in agreement. "For now, let's just be friends and put all this tension behind us."

I thought I'd rather put her behind me, but I could go along with it even if I thought the whole idea was ludicrous.

"So can you wait?" she asked me sweetly.

"I've spent my whole life looking for you," I confessed and gently touched her cheek. "I can wait until…"

"April," she concluded with a heavy sigh. "I'm not being

foolish. You could meet someone while I'm away."

"So could you," I argued. "But we'll do it your way and leave it up to the fates. Deep down, I know that we're meant to be together. I also know that even though I don't agree, I can try. Though I doubt we'll wait."

"What do you mean?"

"We've had better reasons than this to keep our hands off each other, and we've failed miserably."

"Stephanie…"

"I'm serious," I offered in my own defense. "I'll go along with this plan of yours, but I'm telling you right now, you'll never make it."

"I'll never make it?" Alex snorted as she started the car and pulled back into traffic.

"You won't."

"And what makes you so certain that I'll be the one to cave in?" Alex protested in a cocky tone. "I'm an adult, and I think I've behaved fairly well under the circumstances."

"Sure, whatever you say," I answered blithely.

"I'm serious about us waiting."

"I know, and I promise to behave myself."

"But you don't think I will?"

"Nope."

"And just why not?" Alex was on the defensive. "As I recall, most of our close calls weren't initiated by me."

"True. You're right, I'm sure you can control yourself for the next month and a half." Silently, I was begging for her to take the bait. I was peeved that overnight she had come up with the colossally ridiculous idea that after everything we should just be friends while she's on the other side of the country.

"That's right," she sternly countered.

"Uh-huh."

I allowed her to drive in silence while she stewed over what I had said. I knew that I had challenged her, and it was just a matter of time before she would bring the subject up again. "I can show as much restraint as the next guy," Alex snapped finally.

"Of course you can." I patted her to reassure her.

"You really think I'm going to cave in?" Alex whined at the

thought that I could doubt her.

"Yup," I said with a smack of my lips. "I'll even bet you on it."

"Challenge my morals, will you? Fine, you're on. So what's the bet?"

"Loser installs a shower massage in my apartment for while you're in California."

"What? How did you learn about shower massages?"

"It's a recent revelation. I'll need a new one while you're away."

"Why are you so certain that I'll lose?"

"Just am."

"Fine, when I win, you can..." Her voice trailed off.

"Picturing the possibilities?"

"No," Alex lied. "I just can't come up with anything right now. I'll let you know when I do."

"Uh-huh."

"I'm serious."

"Alex..." I was enjoying this little game perhaps a little too much. "One of the reasons I think I'll win is because of that dream you had the other night."

"It was just a dream," Alex defended herself.

"No, it wasn't."

"Of course, it was. Not to burst your bubble or anything, but you are certainly not the first woman I've had an erotic dream about."

"Yeah, about that, it wasn't a dream," I said simply as if I was telling her the time of day.

The car swerved briefly out of control. After a few frightful moments, Alex regained control of the vehicle. "What are you saying?"

"It really happened."

"No, it didn't."

"Yes, it did," I smugly confirmed. "You woke me up, and even though you were asleep, you were fondling me." I watched in amusement as her jaw hung open. "I know I should've stopped it sooner than I did, but it felt—"

"Right," she concluded in embarrassment. "How far did things go?"

"Let's just say, not as far as they could have," I said with a blush, recalling the feel of her body moving against my own. "I ended up taking a very long and very cold shower."

"No more sharing a bed," she declared, clutching the steering wheel. "Let's just change the subject."

"Fine by me, nice weather we're having." She growled irritably at my observation. "Gotcha!" I thought triumphantly. I meant what I had said. I spent a lifetime looking for her, and if I had to wait until April to be with her, I would. April! The gods certainly must be bored.

Chapter Thirty Three

As we entered the Chestnut Hill section of Newton, I couldn't help but gasp at the sight of the grand houses that lined Commonwealth Avenue.

"Do your parents know I'm coming?" I asked shyly as I watched one mansion after another pass by.

"I told them I was bringing a friend," Alex said as she pulled into a long driveway. The exterior property was surrounded by a large brick wall. The best way to describe the house was grand.

"Oh, my God!" I gasped in horror seeing the large white columns that adorned the front. "This is where you grew up?"

"Yes. Why?"

"It's...just so..." I fumbled, regretting my rash decision to come. "I grew up in a two-bedroom apartment that is smaller than the apartment you live in now."

"Oh?" she said in an embarrassed tone. "Would it make you feel any better to know that up until just a few years ago the bank owned most of it?"

"No."

"The roof leaks, the heating is shot, and if it wasn't for the fireplaces, you'd freeze at night."

"Well, in that case, how could you bring me to such a dump?" I teased, trying to ease the sudden tension between us. "Come on, it's cold out here. Will Nicole be here?"

"Sure, she lives here," Alex said as we retrieved our bags.

"Good, maybe she can teach me some new words in French. Let me take the bags, you're still recovering." I tried to ease my nervousness about meeting her parents.

"Trust me, Nicole is not the person you should learn any new words from. Not if you ever want to be able to have a conversation in public, that is."

"Right, and you have such a pure mouth, Harvard."

I looked at the massive oak door adorned with brass; I felt downright shabby. I glanced at my worn-out wool coat and faded blue jeans. Suddenly, I was thinking that I should have changed before leaving Prowers Landing. Alex placed her hand on the small of my back and swung the door open.

"Come on, it's cold out here." She flashed me a reassuring smile as she whisked me in the house.

We entered the grand foyer, and I dropped the bags, my mouth hanging open. "Oh, wow."

"Are you all right?"

"Sure," I sputtered slightly. "Yeah, I'm good. You should have a little something to eat."

"Still taking care of me?" she asked in a lilting tone.

"No," I tried to brush off the compliment. "I brought your exams, as well."

"Chicken soup and homework, you're the best." She gave me a playful nudge.

"Never let it be said that I don't know how to show a gal a good time," I jested, still looking around thoroughly amazed. "Actually, I don't know." I dropped the bags to the floor.

"You're doing just fine."

"Alexandra, I heard you were coming home!" a happy voice exclaimed.

"Matilda!" Alex squealed, hugging the older dark woman. "Dropping off some pies, I hope," Alex added when she finally released Matilda from her grasp.

"Yes." She smiled. "And who is this?"

"Dr. Stephanie Grant, this is Matilda Rupert, my mother's law partner and best friend since before I was born."

Ms. Rupert and I exchanged our greetings before she and Alex fell into a comfortable conversation about Matilda's grandchildren.

"Great day in the morning!" a deep voice boomed from a room somewhere off to our left. I was a little startled by the outburst.

"Dad's home!" Alex gleefully exclaimed.

"Yes, he's been watching football all day." Matilda snickered. "Not to worry, your mother made certain he lit a fire in your room for the two of you."

"The two of us?" Alex grimaced as I chuckled. Matilda just stared at us blankly. "Hold on, it's the middle of the afternoon. How can he be watching football? There aren't any games until tomorrow."

"Who knows?" Matilda shrugged. "If there's a game on, that man can find it. I need to get going. Nice meeting you, Stephanie. And, Alex, don't be a stranger. You know where I work."

"Yes, ma'am."

Matilda left us standing there just as a booming voice accused the referee of being blind.

Alex moved our bags to the winding staircase and took me by the hand. "Come on, time to meet Dad." Alex gave me a gentle tug on my sleeve and led me to the room the shouting had been coming from. She opened the door, revealing a large den with mahogany wood covering the walls. In the center of the room sat the largest television I had ever seen in my life. A silver-haired gentleman was reclined in an oversized leather armchair.

Wrapped up in the game and with his back to us, he failed to notice our entrance. "Great day…" he began to shout once again.

"…in the morning! You call that a pass!" Alex bellowed.

"Alex!" he screamed with delight as he jumped out of his chair and rushed over to her. He swept her up in his arms. His brown eyes twinkled as he set his daughter down, taking a step back from her. "Let's have a look at you, child. How are you feeling?"

"Much better, Pops."

"And this is?" He smiled at me.

"Dr. Stephanie Grant, this is my Dad, Jefferson Adams Kendell the third." He took my hand gently as Alex made the introduction.

"Jefferson is fine," he scolded Alex. "You're a doctor?" he asked eagerly.

"Relax, she's not that kind of doctor, Pops. I told you about Stephanie. She's the colleague I'm working on the book with."

"So you're a bookworm like my little girl then?" Jefferson teased Alex as he reached up and ruffled her raven hair.

"Pops!" Alex protested indignantly.

"What? Not getting too big for your britches, are you?" he taunted. "I can still take you over my knee."

"You've never spanked any of us." Alex laughed. "Who plays football on the day before Thanksgiving?"

"Classic sports," he said with pride.

"So this is an old game?"

"What's your point?" He groaned.

"No point." Alex chuckled. "Basically, you're not really watching the game. You're just hiding in here so Mom won't catch you smoking your cigars?"

"I am not smoking," he lied.

My God, it's genetic! I thought wryly.

"Nice try," she chastised him. "Next time, try cracking a window."

"Speaking of football," he cut in before Alex could lecture him. "When your Mother told me you were bringing home a friend, I got an extra ticket for the game tomorrow."

"The game?" Alex gasped as her face paled. "Oh, no."

"Something wrong?" he asked with concern.

"No," she blurted out. "Not a thing. We should go find Mom."

"Okay then." He turned his attention back toward the television. "Oh, by the way, I lit a fire in your room so the two of you will be warm tonight."

"About that, Dad. Stephanie and I are not..."

"Of course not." Jefferson laughed. He had the same laugh as his daughter. I was amazed by the way their personalities matched.

"Where's Mom?" Alex groaned in defeat.

"In the kitchen with Nukumi," he said absently.

"Amazon!" Nicole called out from the doorway. "And you brought the blonde." Nicole raced over and hugged both of us. "Now how are you feeling?"

"Much better," Alex said.

"And you, how is the knee?" She directed the question toward me.

"No problems," I reassured her.

"Good." Nicole smiled. "I have something to show you, Alex." Nicole was practically beaming.

"She doesn't know yet?" Jefferson asked.

"No, I was saving it as a surprise, Pops." Nicole reached in the pocket of her jeans and pulled out a plastic chip.

"Nikki, your five-year chip!" Alex swept her up in a hug. "I'm so proud of you, little sister."

"It's still one day at a time," Nicole said as Alex released her. "I never thought I would see the day when I would earn this," she said proudly as she clasped the chip in her hand.

"Great day in the morning!" Jefferson shouted once again. I couldn't help but notice he was facing the window and not the television.

"What is it, Pops? Another bad play?"

"No," he said grimly. "The whitest woman in America just pulled up in a taxi."

"Grandma's here!" Alex and Nicole shouted in unison.

"Someone had better go and warn your Mother," Jefferson advised gravely.

"I will," Alex and Nicole jointly volunteered.

"Cowards." Jefferson scoffed. "Go ahead then." He waved to his daughters.

"Wait, the pool!" Nicole stopped us. "Drinking, homosexuality, Democrats, or those people? I'll go with homosexuality."

"Drinking." Alex shook her head. "She'll be thirsty."

"I'll have to go with Nicole on this one," Jefferson said. "Sorry, Alex, but the new girlfriend."

"She's not my…ugh!" Alex groaned. "Never mind. I'm sticking with drinking, and I say ten minutes for those people."

"Five," Jefferson casually threw out.

"No way," Nicole argued. "Matilda already left. I'm going with fifteen."

"Standard wager?" Jefferson asked. "I'll need to pay the cab driver. Lord knows she never has any money in that gawdy purse of hers."

"Of course," Nicole said.

"What the hell was that all about?" I asked in confusion as we made our way from the den down a long corridor.

"Just wait," Alex said simply as we entered the kitchen.

The kitchen was a mix of modern fixtures and colonial architecture. At the stove stood a woman with jet-black hair that appeared to be graying slightly. By her stature and chiseled features, I could see just where Alex and Nicole had gotten their striking good looks from. She flashed a familiar brilliant smile at us as we entered the kitchen. Seated in a wheelchair at the kitchen table was a tiny woman with gray hair. Her tanned features reminded me of something out of a southwestern painting.

"Alex," her mother greeted her, pulling her into a warm embrace. "Nukumi, Alex *est ici*."

The elderly woman smiled up at Alex, who made her way over and bent down and kissed the frail woman on the cheek. *So, this is what families are supposed to be like,* I thought to myself as I watched them interact.

"Mom, this is my friend Stephanie Grant," Alex introduced us.

"Welcome, Stephanie." Her Mother greeted me with a warm hug that surprised me.

"It was very kind of you to invite me, Mrs. Kendell," I shyly offered.

"Paulette, please," she said. "Nukumi, *ceci est* Stephanie, *la nouvelle petite amie d'Alex*."

"No, Mother," Alex protested. "Did you put them up to this?" Alex asked Nicole in an accusing manner.

"Now would I do that?" Nicole chuckled as she climbed up to sit on one of the kitchen counters.

"Yes, you would, you little rat."

"Hush, girls," Paulette scolded her bickering daughters.

"What did I miss?" I had to ask since it appeared that the Kendell siblings were not going to volunteer any information.

"My mother just introduced you as Alex's girlfriend."

"Mom," Alex began wearily. "Stephanie and I are just friends."

"It's true, Mrs. Kendell," I added, finally deciding it was time to help Alex out.

"Paulette," she corrected me once again. "Mrs. Kendell is my mother-in-law."

"Speaking of the wicked witch of the east," Nicole cut in with an ominous tone. "She's here."

"*Merde*," Paulette grumbled as Alex's eyes widened at her expression. Heck, even I knew that one. I could detect a slight tsk from Nukumi, who obviously disapproved of her grandchild's use of language. "Put me down for drinking and seven minutes," Paulette announced.

I was about to ask what was going on when an extremely thin and overly pale woman burst into the kitchen. Although she was very well dressed, there was something about her attire that was the definition of ostentatious. Perhaps it was the fur coat and jewels in the middle of the afternoon. That or the way her makeup appeared to have been applied with a spatula. She was definitely trying to appear much younger than she was. I didn't want to be the one to tell her that her attempt failed miserably.

"Why is it that I'm forced to meet with my family in the cook's area?" she demanded in a shrill tone.

"Because I'm cooking," Paulette tersely explained, turning her attention back the stove. "I find it easier to do that in the kitchen."

"Children." The woman snarled at Alex and Nicole.

"Good afternoon, Mrs. Kendell, ma'am," the siblings responded absently in unison.

"*Sorciere*," Alex muttered under her breath.

"What was that, child?" Mrs. Kendell demanded.

"Do you really want to know?" Alex challenged.

The elderly woman wisely chose to ignore Alex's challenge. "Child, get off of that counter and fetch me a martini," Mrs. Kendell ordered, thumping her cane on the floor for emphasis.

"Mother," Jefferson spoke firmly. "I've explained to you before that we no longer keep alcohol in the house."

"Nonsense." She sniffed.

"You know it's the truth," Jefferson asserted.

"Ridiculous." She sniffed once again, something I was quickly becoming annoyed with. "Why on earth would you do that?"

"Because I'm an alcoholic," Nicole said dryly. "Everyone, including me, is more comfortable with my living in a house where there isn't any liquor."

"There are no drunks in the Kendell family," she protested in horror. As she did, money began to exchange hands around her. I watched as Nicole and Jefferson handed over twenty-dollar bills to Alex and Paulette. "For the last time, get down off of the counter and fetch me a martini."

I noticed something familiar in the manner in which Mrs. Kendell spoke. It was the same way the matrons back in New Haven spoke with their lips barely moving. They could be saying, "Nice weather we're having," yet it always sounded like a putdown.

"Our children have been allowed to sit on the counters since they could lift their bottoms up there," Jefferson countered.

"It's uncivilized," Mrs. Kendell chastised him. "And I repeat, there are no drunks in the Kendell family."

"That would explain Father's twelve-martini lunches."

"Don't be fresh, Jefferson," she responded coldly. "I don't know why I even bother coming over here. I just came to wish everyone a happy Thanksgiving, and once again, I find myself being treated in a most unpleasant manner."

"Mrs. Kendell, we don't celebrate Thanksgiving out of respect for Nukumi," Alex spat out in a terse manner.

"Please," Mrs. Kendell scoffed. "The poor thing doesn't even speak English."

I looked over to where Nukumi was sitting happily shelling peas. She seemed unaware of what was happening around her. For the briefest of moments, I wish I could be as oblivious as she was. It was quite clear that Jefferson's mother was a first-class snob who didn't care about her family. It was also painfully clear by the reaction of her family that the household rules had been pointed out to her on more than one occasion. I did not like this woman, perhaps it was the way the temperature dropped the moment she entered the room.

"I don't understand what it is with these people," the obnoxious woman continued. "They come to this country and can't be bothered to learn English. Yet we're expected to accommodate them. If it wasn't for us, they would have been exterminated years ago."

At that moment, everyone checked their watches, then handed over their money to Paulette. I was beginning to catch on as to what was happening.

"For starters, Nukumi's people lived here long before the pilgrims showed up," Alex scolded her. "And the only reason they faced extinction at all was because of people like us."

"Don't get fresh with me, young lady." Mrs. Kendell shot an angry glare at Alex. I made a protective step next to Alex. The woman took a quick glance at me, then looked away in disgust. "Such an insolent child. You never should have given her a boy's name."

"We named her after my sister," Jefferson groaned.

"Your sister's name is Alexandra, not Alex." She pointed her cane at him. To his credit, Jefferson didn't even blink.

"Do you want to play?" Alex whispered in my ear.

"Yes, please," I whispered in response, eager to do whatever I could to upset this woman. Alex pulled me in front of her and wrapped her arms around me tightly. I played along and reached up and caressed Alex's cheek. Alex in turn lowered her head and began to nibble delightfully on my neck. I honestly didn't know which felt better—our touching or knowing that we were pushing the old witch's buttons. I could see Alex's father smiling from behind his now very uncomfortable mother. The woman's complexion actually grew even paler than before at the sight of us cuddling like lovesick teenagers. She must have been extremely upset to have her disgust show through all that make up she was wearing. More money was passed around.

"Why is it every time I come into this house you people are throwing money around?" she choked as Alex continued her exploration of my neck.

"The family collection, of course," Paulette said as she tucked the money into a cookie jar. "This money is for helping orphans in Ethiopia, care to contribute?"

"Always throwing your money away on these silly causes of yours." Mrs. Kendell sneered, clearly disgusted. "You should pay more attention to what's going on under your own roof." She shot a look of disgust at Alex and me.

This proved to be all the prompting that Alex needed. She placed her fingers under my chin and raised my head to look at her. I swallowed hard as she lowered her lips to mine and captured them in a passionate kiss. I didn't care if everyone was watching. Personally, I would have made love to Alex then and there if I thought it would kill this nasty old woman. Then again, even if it didn't kill her…

"Where is David?" the old woman demanded, breaking the spell.

Alex's body tensed as she pulled her lips from mine. Everyone, including me, just glared at her in amazement. I wasn't even a part of the family, and I knew enough to know that David's absence was a sensitive issue. The look of pain on Paulette's face was unmistakable.

"Mother!" Jefferson snapped in anger. "I think it's time for you to go." Nicole and Alex were instantly by their mother's side. As the two tried to comfort their mother, I heard an angry voice coming from the front of the house.

"Mother, are you here, you crazy old woman?"

"In here," Jefferson called out.

An older redheaded woman with sparkling blue eyes stormed into the room.

"Thank goodness, she got away from me again," she exclaimed. "Two days ago, she slipped out and went on a spree at Tiffany's. Jefferson, I'm so sorry. Good God, you made Paulette cry! How long has she been here?"

"Long enough." Alex groaned.

"My darling nieces, anyone have a cigarette for Auntie?"

"Ladies do not smoke, Alexandra!" Mrs. Kendell scolded as Nicole handed her aunt a pack of cigarettes.

"I quit," Alex mumbled.

"Good." She nodded, extracting a cigarette from the pack before handing it back to Nicole. "And who is this?" She turned her attention toward me.

"Dr. Stephanie Grant, my Aunt Alexandra Wigginsworth."

"A pleasure." She greeted me with a warm and firm handshake.

"Wigginsworth? Any relation to Arnold Wigginsworth of the Smithsonian?"

"My father-in-law."

"I worked with him on a dig at a ghost town in Montana about three years ago."

"You did?" Alex gaped.

"Ah, beauty and brains. Hold on to this one, Alex." She smiled at me. "Come along, Mother, you've wreaked enough mayhem for one day." She hustled the griping older woman out the door.

Jefferson returned and brushed his children aside as he took his wife lovingly into his arms. "I'm sorry, baby," he comforted Paulette. "I think maybe you should lie down for a while. Alex can finish up here. After all, she is the best cook in the family."

"Excuse me?" I exclaimed.

"Alex, you didn't do that again, did you?" her mother asked her in an accusing tone.

"What? No, I wouldn't…I mean," Alex tried to defend herself.

"Stephanie, you must forgive my thick-headed daughter." Paulette sighed. "She's always telling her girlfriends that she doesn't know how to cook."

"Hey, tell a woman that you can cook, and you will never see another restaurant," Alex argued. "Besides, I have to be in the mood to cook. For me. It's an all-day project. And for the last time, Stephanie isn't my girlfriend."

"Yeah, right." The group collectively scoffed.

"Apologize to Stephanie," Paulette scolded her. "Now."

"I'm sorry," Alex muttered as Nicole laughed while Jefferson and Paulette excused themselves.

"This simply confirms what I've suspected for some time."

"Can't put nothing past you, can I?" Alex said with a slight hint of flirtation.

"Honestly, Stephanie," Nicole chimed in. "You really should get this one to cook for you. Her chocolate chip pancakes are the best."

"Really?" My mouth was watering already.

"No," a tiny voice protested from behind us. "Her lasagna and that cheesy garlic bread is the best."

I turned in shock to find Nukumi smiling back at me. "I thought you didn't speak English," I stammered.

"Of course I speak English," Nukumi confirmed. "It was one of the things that saved me from the reservation when the Catholics arrived to save all of us heathens." I stood there dumbfounded as I tried soaking in this revelation. "Mi'Kmaq are my people. We are from New Brunswick. Also Maine, which is where I was living when I met my husband."

"And like most East Coast Canadians, you speak English and French."

"I prefer French when Jefferson's mother is around," she confessed. "I find it easier to deal with her if she thinks I don't understand her."

"I told you that Nukumi was Haley's daughter-in-law," Alex reminded me as she began to chop celery like a master.

"You are so busted, Professor Kendell," I teased her as I

watched her culinary expertise. She wiggled her eyebrows playfully.

"Are you the one who is writing the book with Alex?"

"Yes," I answered her respectfully.

"Nicole, child, I am finished here," Nukumi said gently as Nicole slid off the counter she had climbed back up on. She went to take the bowl of peas from her. "You help your sister, child. I'm going to visit with Stephanie. Come with me, and I will show you some of my mother-in-law's papers. You must help me, though. My spirit may move freely, but my body is imprisoned."

Alex stopped what she was doing and undid the brakes on the wheelchair. She showed me what to do and how to move the chair properly.

"Go ahead," Alex insisted as she placed a hand on my shoulder. "I have to warn you of something. Nukumi knows things." I just stared at her blankly. "Trust me, she just knows things."

"Uh-huh." I didn't have the slightest idea what she was talking about.

***

I managed to wheel Nukumi into her room without any problems. She instructed me to open a large hope chest that was filled with books and papers. She directed me as to what I should remove. I handled each item with respect as I placed them on the bed.

"Come give me your hand." She spoke so softly, I had to lean in to hear her. I sat on the bed and offered her my hand, which she clasped gently. "You have come home," she said as her eyes smiled up at me.

"Excuse me?"

"You have been searching for two things since your birth," she said tenderly. "Love and a family. This is your family now."

"Nukumi, Alex and I are not lovers."

"There is more to love than just the physical," Nukumi chided me. "That will come sooner than you expect. Although you have already suspected that it would. You have captured each other's hearts. When your heart found Alex's, you found your way home. I know you are troubled that she has not told you what is in her heart. You spoke first and are bothered that she did not say the same."

"How did...?" I stammered, thinking that this was getting

creepy. Everything she had said was the truth. It did bother me that I had told Alex that I loved her, and she failed to say the same. She said she cared for me and so many other things, but she hadn't said she loved me.

"I will tell you," she said warmly as she patted my hand. "You sit and listen like you did with your grandmother."

"How did you know that I told her I loved her?"

"I just know," she said. "Not to worry, child, she loves you, and when you hear her tell you, you will no longer have any doubts about the path that you have chosen, or I should say the path that has chosen you. Trust me. Paulette and Jefferson adore each other. Theirs is a perfect union. Their children grew up knowing this, seeing it every day through the good times and the bad. Each of them assumed that they too would find what their parents had. Not understanding that finding the one person is not as easy as it would appear. Each of them gave their hearts to the first person who asked for it. When their own relationships failed to live up to their parents', it hurt them deeply.

"Alex was proud and felt that she needed to make her parents proud of her. Since her heart had failed her, she threw herself into her work, thinking that money would make her happy. It didn't. The day she walked away from everything, she assumed that she had failed. Even though she started to walk a path true to herself, her heart was still cold. Until now, you have melted her heart. Never doubt this. She needs you to let her love again. She is afraid, but don't let her fear stop her from loving you.

"David, being the middle child, tried to do everything his big sister did. He loved a woman for a long time, and she was a good woman. But she was not the one. When she left him, he was lost and met people who misled him. He will find his way home soon. After the snow kisses the dawn a few more times. Nicole, the wild child, was the baby. She never wanted for anything. Alex and David were always there for her. No matter what, they would protect her. What she needed was to fly, and you cannot truly fly if you know there's someone there to catch you. Nicole hid instead of flying, thinking she could hide inside a bottle. She knows all of this now, and she is finally free."

"I don't need to know all of this," I tried to explain to her.

"You do," Nukumi said with a slight nod. "You look at Alex and wonder why she won't let you in. They grew up watching the perfect couple, and when their own relationships failed to meet this level of perfection, Alex and her siblings learned something very new to them, they learned fear."

"Why are you telling me this?"

"Because this is now your home," Nukumi said with a quiet smile. "You have brothers and sisters because your father called many places home. Do not hate him for his weakness. This hatred has already controlled you for far too long. Your father never meant any harm. He was young, and no one ever taught him the importance of responsibility. Your mother was also young and unable to resist his charms. Stephanie, do not seek out your other family, you will not be welcomed. Embrace your new family."

"How can you know all of this?" I hoped that perhaps she was wrong, yet prayed that she was right.

"I just do," she said. "You are in Alex's blood. Not to worry, she will see that soon."

I sat there staring at her, mystified by her words, my rational side telling me that it was simply the ramblings of an old woman. My voice of reason did nothing to still my rapidly beating heart.

Nukumi decided to let me off the hook and changed the subject. She told me about Haley. I listened to her stories carefully. I found myself envious of what Haley and Eleanor shared so easily. I know that at times I still had my own doubts of how quickly I came out. Was it really the right choice, or did I jump into this without thinking? Why after everything I had felt and admitted was I still having these doubts?

"Because you are afraid," Nukumi said, breaking me out of my musings. "You followed your heart, and now your head is trying to rein you in like a wild steed. Since you decided to travel this road, how do you feel about yourself?"

"I'm uncertain," I admitted as she stared at me in disbelief. "Damn, how do you do that? I feel like for the first time in my life, I truly know who I am. But everything happened so soon!"

"Trust your heart. Allow yourself to be happy." She was still clasping my hands, still smiling that knowing smile. "Now let me tell you how I met my husband. There was a man, I know that isn't your cup of tea, but he was the most handsome man. The first time I saw him, I almost fainted."

***

I nodded in agreement as Nukumi started telling me about her childhood. I was thankful for the change in subject. Nukumi was in Maine trying to avoid being put on a reservation. She met a naval officer who, as she had already said, was the most handsome man in the world. Despite her being much younger than he, they fell in love and married quickly, each knowing they found the one. Once he left the military, they settled in Salem to be closer to Robert's mother. She never had the opportunity to know Eleanor since she had passed on years before Nukumi had been born. But Nukumi explained that Eleanor's presence could always be felt.

After Haley's death, it was Robert who had placed the stone between their grave markers. Nukumi and Robert decided to spend their twilight years traveling. Just at the time she thought she was about to become a crone, she was surprised. It was not the change of life she was experiencing, she was pregnant. Her son Graham was Paulette's father. I badgered her constantly for more details finding the story was fascinating.

Chapter Thirty Four

Night had fallen while we had been talking. Our conversation ended when there was a knock on the door. Alex peeked her head into the room to let us know that dinner was ready. I assisted Nukumi out to the family dining room as Alex trailed behind us. Once Nukumi was settled, Alex pulled me aside.

"I put our bags in my old room," she nervously explained. "I can't seem to convince anyone that we're not a couple."

"Don't worry about it, it'll be fine."

"There's just one more thing," Alex whispered. "It's about the game tomorrow…"

"Girls, please, sit down," Jefferson called out.

As we took our seats, I couldn't help noticing how tense Alex seemed to be. I wondered if I should stay up late and wait until she was asleep before going up to her bedroom. Dinner was wonderful. Alex didn't eat much since she was still feeling the effects of the clams from her birthday. I listened to the conversations during dinner. I could not believe how everyone exchanged stories. The banter never ceased during the meal. I was surprised to be included in the chatter. This was a real family! The way they laughed and talked over each other, these people truly cared for one another. Growing up, I wasn't allowed to talk during a meal. The only time the conversation became stilted was when David was mentioned. His absence had created an immeasurable void.

In an effort to deflect the conversation away from David, Nicole turned the conversation toward politics. I was amazed by the people they knew and spoke of so casually. People I had only read about in the papers. I started to feel out of my element when Jefferson noticed my discomfort.

"Stephanie, is everything all right?" he asked sincerely.

"Everything is wonderful, thank you, Mr. Kendell."

"Please call me Jefferson," he implored me. "Now about the game tomorrow…"

"Oh, God." Alex groaned as her body tensed.

"Are you okay, sis?" Nicole asked from across the table. "It's not your stomach, is it?"

"No. I'm fine, really."

All eyes were on Alex, who was squirming in her chair. "Alex, what is it?" her father asked with concern.

"Nothing, really," she lied.

"Are you sure?" Paulette chimed in. "It's college football, so there won't be any shenanigans."

"He didn't cheat," Jefferson blurted out. "There was no concrete evidence that he cheated."

"I never said Tom Brady cheated," Paulette countered with a sly smirk. "I only said he could have cheated."

"Why would he?" Jefferson argued.

"Mother is a Giants fan," Nicole gleefully explained.

"For which I forgive her," Jefferson teased. "Enough about that, I managed to get us great seats for tomorrow."

"Crap," Alex muttered, pushing her plate aside.

"Alex, there's something going on. Every time I mention the game, you get all tense," Jefferson pushed.

"What game?" I asked, hoping to distract everyone's attention from Alex. Not knowing what was going on, I was concerned.

"*The* game, Stephanie," Jefferson boasted. "The only football game that matters. I've been taking the family to the game since before Alex could walk. In fact, it's where I proposed to Paulette."

"We're going to freeze our asses off," Nicole offered, eyeing her sister.

"As long as we win, who cares?" Paulette tossed out.

Alex whimpered. I turned to her, truly concerned by the fearful look on her face.

"One of the proudest moments of my life was when my baby told me she was going to law school at my alma mater," Jefferson continued, unfazed by Alex's discomfort.

"Oh, so you're a Harvard man?" I said absently, still not fully understanding the problem. Then it hit me like a ton of bricks.

"Harvard?" I muttered to Alex. "So *the* game would be…"

"The annual Harvard versus Yale game, of course," Jefferson proudly exclaimed.

"Oh, no," I whispered to Alex. "How bad is this?"

"I don't know. It's never happened before," Alex said through clenched teeth.

"Will someone please tell me what is going on?" Jefferson asked in concern.

I looked around to find everyone staring at us. I gave Alex's hand a gentle squeeze and decided to offer myself up as a sacrifice. Knowing that full well it was no big deal for Alex to bring home a woman, but a Yalie was quite a different story. Alex and I may end up sleeping in separate bedrooms yet.

"I think I know what's going on." I gulped, twisting my napkin nervously.

"Well, enlighten this old man," Jefferson urged me on.

"My undergraduate degree is from UConn."

"Fine school," he commended me.

"Thank you," I said quickly, then I took a deep breath before lowering the proverbial boom. "However, my advance degrees are from Yale."

Everyone was staring at me as the room fell into an eerie silence. I held on to Alex's hand for dear life while wondering how much a taxi back to Prowers Landing would cost.

"Now, Pops, I know how much the game means to you and Mom," Alex offered in my defense.

"Stephanie?" Jefferson addressed me in a stern voice.

"Yes, sir?" I squeaked.

"Have you ever been to the annual game?" he cross-examined me.

"No, sir. I don't really understand football."

"Then I will have the pleasure of teaching you the game tomorrow while you're wrapped up in a Harvard fleece," he gently offered. "But if Yale wins...which they won't...you're walking home."

"Agreed, sir."

"Stop calling me sir," he grumbled. "I can't believe this is what was worrying you, Alex. Despite the fact that she's a Yalie, I find your girl perfectly charming."

"She's not my..." Alex started to protest. "Never mind."

Everyone relaxed over dessert while Jefferson tried to teach me about the finer points of football and just why Harvard was going to crush Yale. After everyone had finished eating, we cleared the table. Everyone, including me, helped with the cleanup process. I felt like part of the family as we all joked around in the kitchen. Then I helped Alex put Nukumi to bed and retrieved Haley's papers that she had offered me to read. Nicole left for work, and the elder Kendells excused themselves for the night.

It was late, and there we were. Everyone else had left or was in bed. I stood there staring, curious as to what was going on behind the smile she was sporting. She didn't say a word as she took my hand in hers and led me upstairs to her bedroom.

Chapter Thirty Five

Alex opened the door to her bedroom and allowed me to enter before her. The room was lit only by the fire blazing in the fireplace. In the middle of the room was a four-poster bed. I jumped slightly as I heard the door closing behind me. I placed the papers I was gripping tightly on a bureau near the door. My palms were sweating as I just stood there feeling like a virgin on her wedding night.

"I'll get the light," Alex said softly from behind me.

"Oh, okay."

I spotted my overnight bag on the floor and picked it up, wondering what I should do next. Alex's body brushed against mine as she passed me on her way to the nightstand. I swallowed hard as I watched her bathed in firelight. She reached for the lamp on the table, then stopped her movements. Alex turned and gazed at me with an intensity I had never seen before. I dropped my bag and crossed over to her quickly. She met me halfway, and without a word, we found ourselves wrapped up in each other's arms. Our lips pressed together as our bodies met. The heat was unbelievable as our mouths parted and our tongues met, dancing together with passion.

We gasped as we broke apart as the need to breathe overcame us. "I'm terrified." I gasped. In response, she placed her fingers gently on my lips and silenced my fears.

"I love you," she sweetly whispered. "And I want to make love to you." She kissed my neck while her hands trailed down my sides. I felt her tugging my turtleneck out of my jeans and strong hands sliding up under the material. I arched my back as she cupped my breasts gently. Then suddenly, her touch vanished, and she stepped slightly away from me. I panicked for a brief moment before my fears were quieted with a tender kiss.

"Why now?" I gasped.

"I can't fight it any longer." She confessed with a shy smile.

Alex lifted my shirt from my body and tossed it onto the floor. Her hands found their way to my bare shoulders, and I trembled from her touch. Alex pulled me toward her and wrapped me in her arms. I captured her lips and kissed her passionately. I felt my bra depart my body and fall to the floor.

"How do you do that?" I moaned against her lips.

She laughed lightly as she pulled her lips from mine. "You inspire me," she whispered hotly in my ear.

She looked at me as her hands ran down my face, then lowered to caress my neck. My skin trembled from her touch. "You are so beautiful," she said softly as one hand descended farther and cupped my breast. Nimble fingers teased my nipple, her gaze never leaving mine. I shuddered as I felt my nipple becoming erect. Her eyes closed slightly as she lowered her head and captured my nipple in her mouth, teasing it slowly with her tongue and teeth. I moaned deeply as my head spun out of control. I ran my fingers through her dark hair and found myself pushing myself farther into her mouth.

I thought I would collapse as she moved her mouth to my other breast and lavished it with the same attention. I could feel my passion growing between my legs as she feasted on my breast. Her tongue moved from my breast and kissed and tasted its way down my cleavage. Her hands covered my now aching breast and teased my nipples until I thought I would explode. I groaned deeply as Alex's mouth sampled my exposed skin moving across my chest and down my ribs and lavishing attention to my abdomen. Her hands never left my breasts until she had sunk to her knees.

My body went cold as her kisses ceased and her hands left me. I felt a surge of warmth as she unbuttoned my jeans. My heart raced faster and faster. I felt the denim being pulled down my body. She paused briefly to remove my shoes and socks. Then she lowered my jeans to my ankles, and I eagerly stepped out of them. I stood there before her clad in nothing but my panties while she kissed her way up my thighs.

I opened my legs to her as she ran her strong determined hands over the sheer fabric of my panties. She looked up at me with a lustful gaze. The intensity was captivating and made me gasp in anticipation. I knew what she was asking. "Yes." I trembled not in fear but with desire. Slowly, she slid my underwear down my thighs, her mouth following their path. I stepped out of my panties, and Alex's mouth retraced its path back up my body. I was on fire from her touch and shaking from the power of what was happening between us. I felt her hands hold me tightly as I opened myself up to her even farther.

A cry escaped my lips as her warm breath blew gently across my blond curls. Her tongue slowly teased me. "Please," I begged, slightly embarrassed by my eagerness and wetness as I pulled her closer. I felt her tongue exploring my passion, and I moaned as I felt it enter me. Her tongue parted me slowly and teased me as she plunged it in and out of my opening. I whimpered when it departed, only to moan again as she tasted me. "Oh, Alex...yes." I growled as she thrust two fingers inside of me and captured my throbbing clit in her mouth.

Wrapping my fingers in her hair, I pulled her farther into me as my hips thrust against her. Her movements became more rapid and directed. My knees became weak as I gasped for air. Somehow, she held me upright as my hips thrust wildly. I could feel my body trembling and was suddenly frightened. I leaned back to find a desk behind me. With one hand, I held on to the desk tightly, while the other hand was firmly attached to the back of Alex's head.

I could feel one of Alex's arms wrapped tightly behind my back. I closed my eyes to keep the room from spinning while Alex's fingers and tongue quickened their pace. Shades of crimson filled my head as a strange buzzing began in my ears. My body shuddered uncontrollably. My screams were trapped in my throat struggling to be free. With each thrust of my hips, I was eager to feel more of what Alex had to offer. I felt her responding to my neediness, taking me deeper. I opened my eyes briefly and swooned at the sight of her crystal blue eyes staring up at me from between my thighs.

"Oh, God, yes!" I screamed, my voice finally freed. Alex responded by sucking my throbbing clit harder. "Yes...oh...yes...Alex..." I screamed louder and louder as my body exploded in ecstasy. I was gasping for air as I began to collapse against the desk behind me. Alex lay her head gently against my stomach while her fingers remained inside of me. My body continued to tremble with the waves of aftershocks from our passion.

Alex kissed my stomach gently; her fingers teased me once again. I tried to catch my breath as her ministrations began once more. I reached the crest much faster this time. I screamed over and over again as she kept pleasing me. I was losing my grip on the desk, and my body started to slide. Before I realized what was happening, Alex had captured me in her arms. I was panting, trying to ground myself as she embraced me tighter. Alex kissed me gently, and I tasted myself on her lips.

"Was it…did I please you?" she asked me tenderly.

"Are you joking?" I croaked out since my voice was spent. Alex held me tighter. "I don't think I can stand much longer," I said weakly.

"Shall I take you to bed?" She moaned hotly in my ear. My legs trembled from her offer.

"Can't walk that far," I said in a daze. Without a word, she lowered my trembling body onto the plush carpeted floor and lay beside me. She caressed my breast as I tried to control my breathing.

After a few moments of lying in her arms, I regained my composure. "What are you thinking?" She kissed my brow.

I snuggled in closer to her. "You'll think it's foolish," I said shyly.

"Never," she cooed softly into my ear.

"It's just that I…thought I was frigid," I admitted in embarrassment. She laughed at my admission. "Don't laugh." I swatted her playfully.

"I'm sorry," she said in a serious tone. "Why would you think that?"

"I never experienced an orgasm before tonight." I swallowed hard as I tried to explain this.

"I think we dispelled that myth," she said proudly.

"Twice," I confirmed, feeling positively giddy.

"Never?" she asked thoughtfully.

"I came close a couple of times," I said. "When I was a teenager with a friend, then the other night with you."

"When I was asleep?" She laughed, and I poked her in the ribs.

"Sorry." She turned toward me, looking thoughtfully into my eyes. "Stephanie," she began in a seductive tone. "I am just beginning. I'm going to make love to you until you scream out my name and beg me to stop."

I trembled at the thought of her proposition. "Is it always like this?" I asked nervously. "Is this what it's like between women?"

"Sometimes," she said soothingly. "It really depends on the women. There have been women I've been with who probably think I was the worst lover they've had."

"I find that hard to believe."

"Sometimes it comes down to emotion," Alex said. "If your heart isn't there or you just don't click physically, then it's just sex. I think we connect, and as I said, I want to make love to you."

"We do, it feels like you're a part of me. I can't believe I used to think sex was tedious."

"I know," she agreed as she brushed my lips tenderly.

"And will I make love to you?" I asked hopefully yet uncertain as to what the rules were.

"Yes," she purred, her hands roaming my body. "Some women like only to please. Others prefer only to be pleased. Personally, I like to give and to receive. I find both very pleasing. For the moment, I only wish to become lost in you. There's so much more I want to do with you...to you."

"More?" I swallowed hard with anticipation.

Her body was on top of mine, and she teased my nipple with her tongue. I pulled her closer as she continued to tease me with her teeth and tongue. I felt her hand glide down the naked curves of my body. Once again, I was driven by desire and opened myself for her. I moaned helplessly as she teased my wetness. Slowly and gently, she ran her thumb against my clit. She raised her head and looked deeply into my eyes. I felt as if she could see inside of me and somehow she could see my soul. I felt her fingers pressed against my opening. I arched my hips, begging her to enter me. Gently, her digits entered me, her gaze never breaking contact with mine.

My center pushed against her hand, demanding more as I pushed harder against her. She responded by increasing her movements with her fingers and thumb, teasing me into a frenzy, all the while looking at me. It was as if I belonged to her and her to me. I did scream her name over and over again as she entered me over and over again. Each time, I was certain that my body could not reach the same level of ecstasy. Each time, Alex had proved me wrong.

I was amazed how my body continued begging for more, and Alex never failed to answer my urging. My level of frenzy became overwhelming as I clawed at her back, tearing her shirt in the process. She responded by removing the torn garment with one hand and offering one of her breasts up to my eager mouth. My lips captured her nipple eagerly. I groaned in disappointment when she removed her breast from my mouth.

"Give that back," I panted. She smirked slyly as fingers pumped in and out of me in a steady rhythm.

Alex kissed me and lowered herself down my body, leaving kisses and goose bumps in her wake. She nestled between my thighs. Her fingers continued their steady movements, and her tongue replaced her thumb flicking across my throbbing clit. I lost control—and at one point consciousness—as she feasted on my desire. I regained my awareness, and Alex held my body tightly as I rose steadily against her mouth.

"No more," I pleaded as she purred gently and kissed the inside of my thigh. She pulled herself up my sensitive body and lay beside me, wrapping me in her loving arms. "I need to catch my breath."

I lost track of time as we lay comfortably in each other's arms. I felt her heart beating and the warmth of her body as she held me. She pressed against my back, and I could feel her nipples becoming erect. It was all the encouragement I needed. My body was once again in a full state of arousal. I turned to her and pressed my lips to hers and kissed her deeply. I loved the taste of her, and my body craved to taste more of what she had to offer.

Boldly, I guided her onto the floor. Alex offered no resistance as my body pressed against her. I grew more eager as her hips arched in response to my touch. My hands trembled as I felt my way down every curve of her gorgeous body. I felt the waistband of her jeans, and I ran my hand across the well-worn material. I stopped, suddenly feeling uncertain.

"I don't know what to do," I admitted fearfully.

She gazed deeply into my eyes and smiled. "Do whatever you

want to do. I trust you," she whispered. "I'll tell you if you do something I don't like." I licked my lips and gazed at her half-naked body. I lowered my head and circled her nipple with my tongue. Her moans encouraged me on. I captured her breast in my mouth and sucked it slowly. "Harder," she begged, and I fulfilled her request and feasted on her. I turned my attention to her other breast and lavished it with the same attention.

I was spurred on by her sounds and movements, allowing my instincts to take over. I unzipped her pants and pulled them from her body as she raised her hips to assist me. Her underwear quickly followed. My focus turned to the dark patch nestled between her luscious long legs. I knew what I wanted—what I needed. I lowered my hand to her as she gasped in anticipation. I hesitated slightly, and her hand reached for mine, sensing my hesitation. "Yes." She moaned as she guided my hand to her wetness. Her body welcomed my touch in so many ways.

My hand cupped her wetness, and my heart raced from the feel of her pressing against my touch. "Please…" she begged me. "…need you now…" She moaned again as my fingers entered her. My fingers began a slow and steady rhythm as they pumped in and out of her. With my thumb, I circled her button as she had done to me. Incredibly, I discovered that as I pleased her, I found myself increasing in my own desires. I now understood what Alex had meant by giving and receiving. My own desire was all-consuming as I lowered myself to her. When I tasted her passion for the first time, I almost came again. I fumbled at first, but soon, I found my way with her gentle encouragement. I held her body as she responded to my touch. She moaned and begged for more. I felt like I was a part of her as she cried out in ecstasy. I couldn't stop myself, I wanted her to explode again. Spurred on by my desire, my fingers began their insistent pace once again. I lifted my head so I could watch her face as she went over the edge.

Despite the winter chill, our bodies were covered in sweat. Alex reached for me, and I climbed up her body. She pulled me to her, and we became lost in a frantic kiss. Our hands explored each other's body freely and urgently. Our legs entwined as our hips moved together in perfect rhythm. With urgency, our bodies pushed harder and harder against each other's wetness. Within moments, our screams of release blended together. Exhausted, we collapsed into each other's arms.

"I can hear your heart beating."

"I can't believe this is happening." She sighed with relief. "All of those months of being so close to you and being afraid to touch you. Not being able to look into your eyes fearing that you would see how much I wanted you...how much I loved you. Every time we touched, it frightened me. I was afraid that I wouldn't be able to let you go. Fearing that it would be the last time I would be able to hold you."

"And you were the one who wanted to wait until April," I gently teased her. "By the way, you owe me a shower massage." She laughed at my teasing. A sudden terrifying thought came to me. "Oh, my God, your parents!" I said, suddenly recalling our passionate screaming.

"No worries," Alex reassured me. "Their room is in another wing of the house. Trust me, they didn't hear a thing."

"Thank God." I relaxed slightly. "Another wing of the house? This is going to take some getting used to." I stood slowly on unsteady legs, my head spinning slightly. I reached out to her, which she accepted eagerly and stood up equally unsteady. "Take me to bed."

"I like the way you say that," she murmured, leading me to the bed. She pulled back the covers before lowering herself onto the bed and drawing me to her. I curled up next to her as she covered us with the blankets. Our exposed bodies touching proved to be far too much of a temptation, and we began all over again. With each touch, we wanted more, and there seemed to be no stopping our desires. It wasn't until Alex noticed that the sun had already risen that we stopped.

"We need to take a shower," Alex said playfully. "No funny business," she warned me.

Fortunately, there was a private bathroom off of Alex's bedroom. The privacy proved to be too much of a temptation for both of us as we made love in the shower. Finally after the water turned cold, we somehow managed to get clean. As we were drying ourselves, it only took one look from Alex to find us making love on the bathroom floor. After a second more subdued and cold shower, we managed to dress ourselves. It was no easy task, and I was forced not to look at Alex, knowing the slightest look from her would start my heart racing once again. The way I felt amazed me. Never before had I experienced such passion. To want someone so desperately. I knew in my heart it wasn't simply Alex's body that I craved; I yearned for her mind, body, and soul.

Chapter Thirty Six

We arrived in the kitchen and were greeted by an all-too-knowing smirk from Nicole. Alex blushed as she poured coffee for the both of us. Our gazes met as she handed me the steaming mug, which I almost dropped from the intensity of her look. Somehow, I managed to hold on to the mug and thanked her.

"It's amazing that after a full night's sleep, the two of you seem to be exhausted," she said sarcastically.

"Shut up." Alex yawned.

A short while later, their parents joined us. They too seemed to be glowing. Alex and Nicole just rolled their eyes at the sight of them. After everyone had been properly caffeinated and dressed, we were prepared to leave. Jessup, a neighbor, came over to stay with Nukumi while we were out. He didn't seem to mind the time away from his wife's dinner preparations, and in fact, he seemed to look forward to it. Nukumi obviously liked him, even though she didn't seem to care for the idea of needing a sitter. After all, the woman was well over a hundred years old, and even though her mind was as sharp as a tack, her body was not. We piled into the family Land Rover and made our way into Cambridge for the game.

Jefferson, true to his word, guided me through the entire game. I think the other family members were relieved that he had someone to take under his wing. This kept him occupied so they could sneak off and find refuge from the cold. It appeared that the only true fan of football was Jefferson. Thankfully, Yale lost. Although it was a close game, Harvard pulled it out with a field goal. By the end of the game, I knew more about football than I ever needed to. A small price to pay for spending time with Jefferson, and truth be told, I enjoyed it. But it now appeared that I had become Jefferson's new football buddy.

After returning to Chestnut Hill, dinner preparations were in full swing. "Thanks for sitting with Pops all morning," Alex said as she gave me a tender kiss on the lips.

"I enjoyed it."

"Good because he asked if it was okay if he invited you to more games."

"I'd like that."

"Really?" Alex seemed surprised.

"Yes, really." I swatted her playfully. "I like sports, and I like your dad."

Alex gave me another tender peck on the lips.

"Ahem!" Nicole cleared her throat loudly. "No smooching in the kitchen, you two! It's bad enough when I walk in on Mom and Dad." Alex muttered something in French and brushed past Nicole.

"You know we need to teach you French since you'll be spending more time around here," Nicole pointed out.

"Don't you teach her anything!" Alex growled from behind us.

***

Dinner was a wonderful affair with the food and conversation. The warmth that surrounded the table made me a little teary-eyed. How truly wonderful it must have been to grow up with such love and sense of family. No wonder Alex and her siblings expected to find the same in their own relationships.

After dinner, Alex and Nicole assumed the cleanup duties. Their parents volunteered to help out at a shelter in Boston. I was pleased to learn that this was an activity they participated in year-round and not just for the holidays. Nukumi was tired, so Alex took her to her room. I was shooed from the kitchen by the Kendell sisters. I suspected that they wanted to talk in private. I went to the family room and sifted through the papers that Nukumi had given me the day before. There was a letter that interested me greatly. It was from a woman named Annabel Freewoman.

Annabel Freewoman
17 Charles Street
Boston, Massachusetts
July 17, 1880

My Dearest Eleanor,

I understand that you now travel by the name Sarah Moorehouse for reasons that I think I can understand. My heart was full to see you alive and well. I had heard that you had passed on when the Union army burned Greenwood to the ground. Imagine my delight at learning that the rumors were false. Not to worry, my dear friend, I will not reveal your secret. I owe you so very much, including my life. I remember those days working in the fields, you were my only ray of sunshine. You kept your brother from taking my virtue and opened the door of knowledge. If you had not taught me to read and write, the good Lord knows that even this simple correspondence would not be possible.

At the time I never fully understood the risk you were taking by teaching us the skill of reading. Now I know that your generosity could have cost you your life. Possessing this skill made life easier for me once I found my way North.

You also taught me to love. We were so very young when we discovered our passion. Do not worry, my sweet, I know your heart was never truly mine. I knew that each time you left for Baltimore, there were others who warmed your bed. It was true for me, as well.

I wanted to thank you for my freedom. I can never forget how you saved my sister and me, stealing us away under the cover of darkness. I will cherish your final words to me as we parted for the last time. "Live well." And I have. Each day, I greet the morning a little more slowly as the years pass, but I greet the morning and thank the good Lord for sending you into my life. And having found you again, I can finally express my emotions. I thank you for your courage and kind heart.

Not to worry, my sweet, I know your heart belongs to another. As does mine. Her name is Claudine, and we have shared our lives for over ten years now. I can see that you and your woman share the same love as I carry for my sweet Claudine.

I cannot help but think that it was God's hand that orchestrated our chance encounter last evening. I thank him or whatever forces brought you back into my life. I would enjoy keeping our friendship. I know that you are not well and traveling is difficult. Your words can always reach me. Claudine and I own a small bakery on Charles

Street.

How is this possible, you ask? I can hear your curious mind at work already. Claudine is fair-skinned and can easily pass for white. She lied when she came North and claimed to be a war widow. We both worked hard at the bakery, which is how we met. When the owner passed on, I used our savings and the money you gave me when you sent me North to buy the shop from the owner's widow. Of course, everyone assumes I work for Claudine. If they only knew how demanding I can be on the poor woman.

As I said, your words can reach me here since we live above our shop. Your letters would be most welcome by both of us.

My best to you and your lady.

Lovingly,
Annabel

***

"Hey, Stephanie," Nicole called to me, breaking me out of my musings. "What are you doing?"

"Just going through some stuff Nukumi gave me." I looked up at her. "This one is a letter from a woman named Annabel Freewoman."

"She was quite a lady herself from what I understand," Nicole said thoughtfully. "Her name before she ran away from the Ballister plantation was Annie Ballister. After she escaped, she made her way up to Boston and ran her own business with her lover. From the letters I've read, she gave all the credit to Eleanor. Of course, all Eleanor really did was help her start on her journey. In the end, it was Annabel who was the one to survive leaving the South during a very troubling time."

"These women faced what must have seemed like insurmountable forces, yet somehow survived," I said absently. "When you think about it, we freak out if our Internet connection goes out. If we're not connected to our computers, civilization as we know it will come to an end. These women couldn't even vote, and still they stood up and fought for their freedoms. The problems that I face in my life seem so insignificant in comparison."

"I can't imagine what they had to endure," Nicole agreed. "There are references to Stephan and the other white men on the plantation taking what they wanted from the female slaves."

"Annabel and Eleanor were lovers at one time?"

"From what I gather." Nicole shrugged.

"That must have been what she meant when she caught her brother with Haley." My mind reeled with information. "Haley wrote that Eleanor said something about him still sniffing after her women. I get the impression that her brother must have been fully aware of her orientation."

"Hard to say. I got the impression that Eleanor had many lovers before settling down with Haley. Most of her own writings and whatnot, including the family Bible, were lost when the plantation burnt down."

"That would explain the lack of information on her headstone," I noted. "Back then, the only records of births would have been in the family Bible." I pondered over this as I sifted through more papers. "Sorry. I just get caught up in these things."

"Don't worry about it." Nicole waved off my apology. "I'm used to it, what with the folks and Alex. Growing up in a household full of lawyers, things can get pretty intense. That's why I became a doctor. I just had to be different."

"You're different, all right," I teased her. "I'm confused by something. You're a doctor, but Chris said you were thrown out of med school."

"That snake." Nicole growled. "I finished med school, surprisingly enough. I even survived my residency in California and passed the boards. But I screwed up, and no decent hospital wanted me. When I sobered up, I was forced to start over in many ways. This is my second chance, and I'm no fool. I know if my last name wasn't Kendell, I'd be selling hemorrhoid cream at CVS."

"I watched you in the emergency room. You're good at what you do."

"I love it," Nicole admitted. "I always assumed that I would go into private practice. But there's something about the ER. I think that's where I belong."

"But what about the pressure? Aren't you worried that you might—?"

"Drink," Nicole finished for me. "It was never the pressure that got to me. It was more the lack of it. Everyone seems to think that there was some kind of catalyst for me being a drunk. Truth is, there was no trauma, no event that sent me off the deep end. I started drinking the way everyone does. At some point, I couldn't tell you when, I was hooked. There's a chance that it's genetic from the Kendell side or just luck of the draw. Who knows? Like most alcoholics, I just like to drink." She shrugged at the thought. It was clear Nicole stopped looking for the why and only dealt with the reality of the situation. I had to admire her for that. "The Amazon told me to tell you that she's upstairs in the bedroom grading papers."

Alex is in the bedroom, so why am I down here? I wondered as I stood quickly.

"Feel like taking a walk?" Nicole offered.

"Umm…" I stammered.

Nicole laughed as I blushed. "I know she's upstairs, and the folks are out. Humor me," Nicole said gently. "Besides, making her wait will be good for her, and I thought I told you to let her rest while she was recovering."

"Not my fault," I argued.

"That's not what I heard."

"Oh, and did you and your sister have a nice chat in the kitchen?"

"Yes, as a matter of fact, we did." Nicole flashed that famous Kendell hundred-watt smile at me. "Now get your coat, and we'll take a walk around the grounds."

"A walk around the grounds?" I shook my head at her statement. "I don't know if I'll ever get used to the way you people talk."

"What?" Nicole asked in confusion.

"Couldn't you just say let's go for a walk in the yard?"

"The yard? Huh." Nicole just shook her head and led me to gather our coats.

We went outside through the back. As I looked around, I realized that the property extended past the pine trees I had seen through the kitchen windows. It looked more like a state park than someone's home.

"Still want to call it a yard?"

"Wow!" I gasped. "I can't begin to imagine what it was like to grow up with all of this."

"Doesn't guarantee you happiness, sweet pea," Nicole pointed out thoughtfully.

We walked in silence for a short while, taking in the refreshing cool night air as the light layer of snow crackled beneath our feet. I looked up into the clear winter sky and marveled at the stars.

"Beautiful, isn't it?" Nicole said. "David would love this, he knew every constellation." I said nothing, knowing the gap David's absence had created. "When he first fell in with those people, we all thought nothing of it," Nicole continued absently, lost in her memories. "After all, a little religion wasn't a bad thing. I was certainly in no position to throw stones. Then he started to change and become more withdrawn. Then he was gone, and it was too late to save him."

I kept quiet, letting Nicole set the pace of our walk and conversation. I couldn't imagine the hell this family was enduring. It was one thing to lose a member of your family, it was another to have a son refuse to see you. Not knowing how he was or where he was. Nicole walked steadily, lost in her thoughts.

"You should have seen us when we were kids," Nicole said proudly, breaking the silence. "Alex always had to be the best and the brightest. And she was. David had to do everything she did. Whenever you saw Alex, there was David tagging along behind her. Of course, I had both of them wrapped around my finger." Nicole laughed at the thought. "When we were little, David and I would sneak out of our bedrooms and climb into bed with Alex and beg her to read to us. She would argue, but we always wore her down. She read to us almost every night of our childhoods, and it had to be Winnie the Pooh. We never wanted to hear anything else." Nicole chuckled again.

"Is that why David called her Tigger?" I asked, thinking of how sweet it must have been for those three children.

"Yeah," Nicole said with a smile. "David said she did Tigger's voice the best."

"She did the voices?" I smiled at the idea of stoic Alex Kendell doing voices for the characters of Winnie the Pooh.

"Yep," Nicole confirmed. "She did them all—Pooh, Owl, Piglet, the entire hundred-acre wood. Looking back on it now, it's hard to believe that she really isn't that much older than us. She'll make a great Mom someday."

"She will," I agreed wholeheartedly. "I can see her rolling around with the kids…what am I saying?" I stopped myself from thinking so far into the future.

"Why did you stop?" Nicole asked, seeming to understand.

"I think it's a bit premature to start…you know, making plans," I muttered in my defense. "The truth is, Alex and I haven't even been on a date yet."

"Oh, please." Nicole laughed again. "I've been on thousands of dates, that doesn't mean anything."

"That's a lot of men."

"Mostly," Nicole said with a shrug. "Anywho…" Nicole changed the subject as I wondered if she had just implied what I thought she did. "…several years ago, I came home for Thanksgiving, and I was drunk, of course. Alex started to rip into me. I gave it right back to her, only I was cruel. For some reason, I seemed to enjoy hurting people when I was drinking. I said something about my being a drunk, David was dysfunctional, and Alex was a dyke. The three D's, I liked to call it, and somehow, I thought it was funny. I started up about David again, and that was it. Alex and I got into it big-time. I could say whatever I wanted about her, but David was off-limits."

"It must have been horrible."

"It was," Nicole said. "Alex ended up tossing me out of the house before dinner. I started to rant about how she was a hotshot lawyer with a beautiful girlfriend yadayadayada. Only I was truly cruel about it. Imagine my surprise when Alex pointed out that not only wasn't she a lawyer, but she and Chris had split up. She was going to school and living with Mom and Dad. Who knew, right?" I just nodded in agreement. "Apparently, I did and simply forgot that all this happened over a year ago. I lost an entire year of my life."

"Is that when you stopped drinking?"

"No, that would have made sense." Nicole sighed heavily. "It was an almost a year later. I broke into the house thinking no one was home. I needed money. I was pretty much living on the streets at that point. I was going through Alex's things looking for money when I found a tattered copy of Winnie the Pooh. That was it. Alex found me curled up clutching that book to my chest and crying like a baby. I will never forget how truly frightened she looked at that moment. The only thing I could say was, 'Alex, I need help.' She took me to my first meeting that night. So why is she telling me all this, you ask."

"No, I think I know why."

"My sister means the world to me, and I almost lost her once."

"And if I break her heart, you will break my legs."

"No." Nicole laughed slightly. "I'll send Zia Maria over with her cast iron frying pan." I could tell by the tone of her voice and the look on her face that Nicole was serious. I also had little doubt that Mrs. Giovanni would not hesitate to chase me around with her well-worn skillet if I hurt her favorite niece.

"Lucky for me that I am madly in love with your sister and would never do anything to hurt her," I said firmly, hoping to calm her fears and save my hide.

"I'm not worried about you, just letting you know how I feel," Nicole said with a reassuring smile. "Stephanie, I can see in your eyes every time you look at her how deeply you love my sister. Don't let her screw this up. I know she seems like a strong woman, but truth be told, at times, she can be an emotional coward."

I allowed her words to sink in as I thought back to events at the hospital and how truly frightened Alex was. We walked in silence enjoying the night until the need for warmth became overwhelming. We made our way back to the house, and Nicole left to get ready for her shift at the hospital. It would appear that late nights and holidays were a part of Nicole's retribution.

Jefferson and Paulette arrived home exhausted from their duties at the shelter. Nicole's ride arrived, and she said her good nights to all of us, explaining that she would be home by Saturday morning. I was now eager to rejoin Alex upstairs in the bedroom.

"Stephanie," Paulette called out to me. "Jefferson and I were just going to enjoy some hot chocolate by the fire. Come join us." It was not a request. Suddenly, I was feeling very popular.

I put my overactive libido on hold and agreed, knowing that I was about to receive more grilling regarding my intentions. I couldn't blame them. I wished that I had someone in my life who cared that much for me. I wondered that perhaps I did and she was waiting upstairs.

I couldn't help pondering the possibility that she was naked before chiding myself for being a pig while I was sitting with her parents. I watched as Jefferson stoked the fire and Paulette entered with a carafe filled with hot chocolate and three very large mugs.

"Should I get Alex?" I volunteered hopefully, not looking forward to being double-teamed by her parents.

"Let her relax. I'm certain she could use it after being so sick," Paulette said in a soothing voice as she poured the hot chocolate and handed a steaming mug to me. I accepted the beverage with shaky hands. "Relax, Stephanie." Paulette smiled as her blue eyes twinkled. "We're not going to interrogate you."

"We aren't? I was looking forward to that," Jefferson teased me with a false scowl.

"Jefferson," Paulette cautioned him. "You'll have to excuse him. You know that when the girls started dating, he decided it would funny to be cleaning his rifle when their young men arrived to pick them up."

"Rifle?" I gasped.

"Paulette, you're scaring the poor girl," Jefferson chastised her. "Stephanie, drink your hot chocolate, and I promise not to bring out any firearms."

"Yeah, I'm scaring her." Paulette scowled. "Now as I was saying…" Paulette lowered herself onto the large comfortable sofa, and I found myself sitting between the two of them. I suddenly felt very helpless, realizing that I was trapped between the two attorneys. "We're not going to threaten you in any way. I'm quite certain that our little Nicole has already done that. The girls are very overprotective of each other. Plus, I had a chat with Nukumi. She told me that you're joining the family. I've learned to trust what my grandmother tells me."

"Okay?"

"We wanted to thank you for taking such good care of Alex while she was ill." Paulette patted my arm gently. "Nicole told us that if it wasn't for you, the doctors would have admitted her."

"I wouldn't have let that happen," I said in a determined tone.

"We know, and we thank you for that," Paulette said tenderly. "Did either of the girls explain to you why Alex is afraid of staying in the hospital overnight?"

"No, and I didn't want to pry. I just wanted what was best for Alex."

"I'm very pleased to hear that," Paulette said and sipped her hot chocolate slowly.

"We were on vacation," Jefferson began slowly, his eyes tearing up slightly at the memory. "It was a little town in upstate New York. The kids were little, and it was wintertime. We thought a nice walk by the lake in the snow would be fun."

"We only turned away for a moment," Paulette said absently, then shook her head, bringing herself back to the present. "Those words parents fear the most. Someday, you'll understand what I mean. When we looked back, the kids were gone."

"When we found them, all hell had broken loose," Jefferson finished for Paulette. "Nikki and David had wandered out onto the lake. Alex went after them. Somehow, she understood it was dangerous to walk on the ice that time of year."

"She got them to safety," Paulette picked up for Jefferson. "But the ice cracked, and she fell through and was trapped underneath."

"You must have been terrified." I gasped at the thought of poor Alex being trapped in the icy water.

"To say the least," Paulette said. "We managed to get her out and rush her to the hospital. It was a small hospital, and they adhered very strictly to their policies. David and Nicole were not allowed to visit, and Jefferson and I were not allowed to stay once visiting hours were over. We wanted to fight them, but since it was only for few nights, we gave in. We had no idea how truly frightened Alex was since, true to her nature, she put up a brave front. All she wanted to know was that David and Nikki were all right. She didn't believe us when we told her that they were fine since she wasn't allowed to see them. She was only nine years old and left alone while she was sick and terrified. She put on a brave face when we saw her, but we didn't know how painful it had been for her until after she had been released."

"Those bastards!" I blurted out before I could stop myself.

"Sorry," I apologized for my outburst.

"Why?" Jefferson comforted me. "They were bastards. All they had to do was let one of us stay with her or allow her to see her brother and sister. Instead, they let a frightened little girl cry all night without any comfort. Ever since then, Alex has been afraid of staying overnight in a hospital."

"Stephanie, I'm curious about something," Paulette began carefully. "You haven't mentioned your family. Why is that?"

"I'm an only child and lost both my parents at a young age. I was raised by my grandmother. She passed on a few years ago."

"I'm so sorry. I shouldn't have pried," Paulette said. "Nasty habit with me."

"No, it's fine," I said honestly. "Alex is the same way, direct yet very giving. Now I know where she gets it from."

"We can be brutally honest, to say the least." Paulette laughed lightly.

"That's my fault," Jefferson confessed. "I grew up in a household that never talked about anything. Secrets were kept, and no one was happy. Then I met Paulette and saw what a real family could be. We don't keep secrets, and sometimes, it can be overwhelming, but my children can always tell us everything."

"Except that one of your dinner guests went to Yale," I couldn't resist teasing him.

Chapter Thirty Seven

I left Jefferson and Paulette snuggling by the fire and made my way upstairs. I found Alex deep in thought and covered with papers.

"I was beginning to worry about you," she said softly without looking up.

"I was with your family." I gazed at her body illuminated by the light of the fire.

"They really like you," she said brightly.

"I like them, too." I thought about how much I wanted to kiss her and how nice it was not to have to second-guess my emotions.

"I'm amazed that some of these kids got into college in the first place," she said as she shuffled her paperwork.

"How's it going?" I stole a glance at her cleavage that was slightly exposed.

"Almost finished."

"Good," I responded with a sly grin.

She looked up at me and smiled; her eyes were clouded with passion. A wave of heat rushed over me as she pushed the paperwork aside and held out her hand to me. I felt a spark as our fingers touched and watched in amusement as she blushed slightly. Alex pulled me onto her lap, and I straddled her hips. My hands rested on her broad shoulders. I ran my finger across her soft inviting lips as she sighed deeply. I licked my lips unconsciously, thinking only about how her lips would taste. Our kisses were magic. Everything about us seemed to fit like a puzzle finally finding its missing pieces.

"We really should get some sleep," she suggested in between tasting my lips and neck.

"Of course," I said in a sultry tone, pulling away from her slightly. I lifted my sweater from my body as she watched me intently. Slowly, I undid each of the buttons of my oxford shirt, her gaze never leaving the motions of my fingers. Finally, I removed my bra and exposed myself to her. I gently cupped one of my breasts and offered it to her. She accepted my offer while her fingers

374

explored the curve of my breast. I moaned with excitement when her tongue finally greeted my skin. When she took my breast into her mouth, all thoughts of sleeping were pushed aside.

***

After exploring each other with our hands and mouths, we found ourselves naked still on top of the bed covers with our clothing surrounding us. Alex's long body stretched across mine as my hands caressed her back, slipping down the length of her body. She shifted slightly to accommodate the differences in our sizes. I found myself opening to her as she settled between my firm thighs. We both moaned as the wetness of our passion met.

My gaze captured hers, and I smiled as our bodies moved together. I clasped her firm cheeks and pressed her deeper into me. Our movements were gentle; for the first time, I knew our dance would not be interrupted. For that moment in time, there was only the two of us. I had found my way home, and my home was here in this woman's arms.

"I love you," I whispered, my heart soaring from saying the words without fearing what would happen next.

"Say it again," she whispered in return as our sweet gentle movements continued.

"I love you, Alex." I released a needy moan, my body melding against hers.

"I love you, Stephanie, and I never want to let you go."

There was no hurriedness to our movements; our bodies moved together in a slow sensual dance. My heart raced, and our passion grew, inspiring me to pull her even closer. Slowly, we rocked against each other until we fell together, holding each other tightly as our bodies merged into one. Making love to Alex that night had been sweet and gentle. We simply touched the intensity born purely from emotion. Nestled together, we shared kisses filled with promise. The kissing continued as we climbed under the covers and wrapped arms around each other, drifting off to sleep comforted by the beating of the other's heart.

***

When I awoke the next morning, I was still wrapped in Alex's arms with my head lying on her chest. I lay there listening to her steady breathing. I felt her stir slightly, then her fingertips ran down my back. I looked up to find myself captured once again in a sea of blue.

"Good morning," Alex whispered, placing a tender kiss on my lips. I lifted my hand to her face and gently traced the outline of her jaw.

"Good morning. Sleep well?" I snuggled in closer to her.

"Hmm." She sighed contently, closing her eyes as a blissful smile crossed her lips.

Her lips proved to be far too tempting to resist. I had only intended a simple good morning kiss. Nothing was ever simple between us, as I found myself quickly deepening the kiss. I felt her body respond, and soon, I was on top of her. Our bodies melded together in a demanding urgency. I couldn't wait. The previous night had been about a gentle sharing of our souls. That morning, however, was all about the driving passion and lust her touch inspired within me. I ran my hand down the length of her gorgeous body and brushed her dark triangle. The wetness pooled between her thighs sent me over the top. With two fingers, I teased her silky folds as she opened herself to my touch. I eagerly accepted her offer as my hand cupped her mound. We were both ready, and I knew what we both wanted. I was inside of her before I realized it. Her hips greeted my touch as I quickly increased my motions.

I grew more excited as her body rose against my hand. I moaned as I felt her hand greeting my wetness. Our bodies rocked in harmony. Despite the coolness of the morning air, our bodies were covered in a blanket of sweat. "Stephanie!" she cried out as her body arched off the bed. I followed her quickly over the edge and collapsed against her.

We lay together riding out the pleasant aftershocks of our passionate union. She held me tenderly as our breathing slowly returned to normal and our ability to speak returned.

"We should go downstairs and have breakfast," Alex suggested as she held me tightly.

"I prefer breakfast in bed." I growled as I kissed the length of her body. She eagerly allowed me to taste her. I feasted upon her until she screamed out my name. I pulled myself up and climbed the length of her body and kissed her quickly on the lips. "Now we can go downstairs." I said playfully. She just smiled sweetly. I never saw it coming as she flipped me over and turned her body. Lying side by side, her mouth buried in my wetness and mine in hers. Our tongues tasted each other as fingers probed. I could hear her moaning from between my thighs as I screamed her name into her wetness.

***

Sometime later, after a very short yet entertaining shower, we got dressed and finally entered the family kitchen for breakfast. "You missed breakfast," Paulette said dryly, We simply blushed in response. "If you want something, you'll have to cook."

Alex nodded to her mother and began to fix us breakfast while I put on a fresh pot of coffee. Nukumi watched us carefully and smiled at our playful exchange.

"Who's in the gym?" Alex asked curiously.

"The gym?" I muttered under my breath.

"Nicole," Paulette said in a concerned tone.

"I thought she was working today," Alex pressed.

"She has to go back in, but she has some downtime for a while."

"What's wrong?" Alex pushed.

"She won't say, but she's punching the stuffing out of the bag."

"How long has she been at it?" Alex sighed deeply.

"Over an hour."

I watched as Alex went over to the built-in refrigerator and removed a bottle of Gatorade. "I'm going to check on her."

Her movements were cut off by the sound of Nukumi's voice. "No, send Stephanie."

"*Pourquoi?*" Alex questioned her curiously. Nukumi refused to answer, and Alex sighed heavily, handed me the bottle she was holding, and pointed me toward the hallway. "You're up. Second door on the right and down the stairs."

"And just what should I do when I get there?" I asked in a panic. Alex shrugged in confusion. "Is Nukumi ever wrong?" I pleaded, uncomfortable with the whole idea of invading Nicole's space.

"Never."

"Well, if she's right about this one, I think instead of going to a football game, your Dad and I should take Nukumi to the track," I joked as I nervously clutched the bottle I was holding.

"We've tried that," Alex quipped. "She doesn't like gambling."

I made my way down the staircase to find a full gym complete with free weights, Nautilus equipment, punching bag, and a sauna. I padded my way carefully across the matted floor and watched in amazement as Nicole worked out her frustrations on the heavy bag suspended from the ceiling. My fear dissipated when something caught my eye as Nicole's leg swung around and connected with the bag.

"You're not distributing your weight properly," I said with certainty.

"What?" Nicole snapped angrily as she turned to me with a feral gleam in her eyes.

"Your balance is all over the place," I said, not feeling the slightest bit fearful of the anger in her eyes.

"Whatever." She shrugged, and I handed her the bottle of Gatorade. "Thanks." She accepted my offer and drank down the blue liquid quickly. She set the bottle down and unwrapped her sparring gloves. "So how'd you end up drawing the short straw?"

"Maybe I just missed you."

"Should Alex be worried?"

"Nice staffs," I said as I noted the collection on the wall. "So who's the expert with them?" I made idle conversation, hoping that she would take the bait. If she possessed half of the competitive streak her sister did, it wouldn't take long.

"All three of us," Nicole said, trying not to reveal anything. "Mostly it was Alex and me. David lost interest after he got his driver's license."

"Tae Kwan Do?"

"Bojutsu," she corrected me.

"Who's better—you or your sister?"

"I am."

"Really?" I baited her.

"Yes," Nicole said angrily. "I have better control over lowering my center of gravity. I don't know if you've noticed it or not, but my sister is a bit of a klutz."

"Interesting."

"What, you're doubting me?"

"It's just from what I just saw—" I toyed with her.

"I was upset," Nicole flared before she realized that I was playing her. She blew out an exhausted breath and hung her head. "Very good," she said finally. "I guess there's no way I'm getting out of here without telling you, am I?"

"I don't think I'm going to get breakfast until everyone upstairs knows that you're okay."

"I lost a patient last night...suicide. Twenty-seven-year-old guy who couldn't understand that things can get better. It hit me hard, and I needed to blow off some steam."

"I'm sorry."

"Thanks," she blew out after a taking a moment. "Oh, and for the record, I am better than Alex."

"Since you're a big ole straight girl, I'm going to assume that we're still talking about staffs," I teased her as she flashed me a cocky grin. "You little fence-hopper you." I gasped, knowing I had hit the nail on the head.

"You lesbians always have to put a label on things," she chided me playfully. "So you ever spar...with staffs, I mean?"

"Me? No. Looks like fun, though."

"I used to really be into it. It was one of the things I lost when the drinking got out of control." She picked up a towel and wiped the sweat from her brow. "I've been thinking about getting back into it."

"So have you and Alex ever gone after the same girl?" I changed the subject.

"Nope, most of the time, I'm attracted to men."

"Good to know. It's a little upsetting to come out at my age to find that my girlfriend's sister has slept with more women than I have."

"These things happen," Nicole jested. "It's nice to finally see the two of you together."

"Everything okay down there?" Alex called down to us.

"Yeah, we're good," Nicole called. "Stephanie called me a fence-hopper."

"Well, you are," Alex retorted.

"Ugh." Nicole groaned. "Thanks for everything, Stephanie. I need to get cleaned up and get back to the hospital."

We went back upstairs, and Nicole brushed past her family with a wave. I felt Alex's arms wrap around my waist; instinctively, I pulled her closer to me. "She lost a patient last night," I explained. "It hit her hard, and she needed to blow off some steam."

"Wow." Alex sighed deeply. "I don't know how she does it."

"She loves what she does," I said, letting her know in my own way to just let Nicole do what she needs to do.

"Come on, breakfast is ready." Alex nudged me.

***

The rest of the weekend proceeded in much the same fashion. We spent time with the family. I was beginning to feel more and more at ease with the Kendell clan, although their brutal honesty could be shocking at times. Growing up, the person closest to me was my grandmother, and she and I never really talked about anything. I did make one observation: As a group, the Kendells shared almost everything, but individually, without the security of the family, they could be very guarded with their emotions. I began to understand that their openness with me stemmed from the fact that I was viewed as a member of the family. It pleased me and frightened me.

I scored some extra points with Jefferson during a friendly game of touch football. Jefferson insisted that I be on his team, so he could teach me more about the sport. When I proved that I could actually throw the ball, he was thrilled beyond belief. Our team, which consisted of Jefferson, Paulette, and me, crushed Nicole, Alex, and Jon-Michael, Paulette's brother who had dropped by one afternoon. We also played board games at night. I learned quickly not to play Trivial Pursuit with Alex. The woman was a wealth of useless knowledge.

At bedtime each night, Alex and I would rip each other's clothing off and drive each other to the brink of insanity. I felt like I was living in a dream world.

We spent the early hours of Sunday morning rolling around in bed. Then it was time to pack. For the first time during our visit, we managed to make it downstairs in time for breakfast. We said our goodbyes, and after being hugged and kissed by everyone at least twice, we drove off. Alex promised to call, so they would know we arrived home safely. The drive home was pleasant, despite the overwhelming traffic. We talked, laughed, and sang along to the music on the radio.

It was joyous until we got closer to home, and I began to worry about being away from the safe cocoon of family. Prowers Landing meant coming down after an incredible high.

"Getting quiet on me?" Alex asked just after we crossed the town line.

"What happens when we get back?"

"Well, that depends," Alex responded dryly.

"On?" I asked with trepidation.

"Have you finished grading your midterms?"

"Yes."

"Then I say we unpack the car," Alex offered in a sultry tone. "I call my parents and let them know we got home in one piece. We don't unpack—"

"No?"

"No, and we don't grade papers. Instead, we take advantage of arriving home early."

"How so?" I teased her as I ran my hand across her thigh.

"If you keep doing that, we might not make it back to Prowers Landing in one piece," Alex warned me. Despite her warning, I kept caressing her thigh. "What are you worried about?"

"That when we get back to reality, things will change."

"They will," Alex said flatly.

"Oh?" I sighed fearfully.

"In a good way, I promise."

I smiled at her response and wished that the roads would suddenly open up. I was more than a little anxious to get home so I could take Alex to bed and make love to her all night long. I never thought I could feel this way about someone. I seemed to need to be with her constantly. I never believed that I could want sex this much. Finally, we approached our street. I felt my excitement growing as we neared the house. Perhaps that was why I didn't notice the car parked out front. We pulled into the driveway and climbed out of the car. Then I saw him approaching.

"What is he doing here?" I looked over at Alex in horror.

She seemed to be unfettered by the sight of him. I, on the other hand, was dumbfounded and suddenly felt exposed. This was proving to be far too surreal for me. I closed my eyes, hoping that his image would vanish. When I reopened them, he was still there, coming closer and closer.

Chapter Thirty Eight

"Peter, what are you doing here?" I asked in a frightened tone.

His face dropped at my question and his eyes teared up. "Well I…" He stopped when he looked over at Alex. I was irked by his expression. He looked at her as if she was the one who was intruding.

"I'll take our bags in," Alex said calmly. "I need to call my parents and let them know we got home." She grabbed our bags and started to walk away. She approached me, and for a brief moment, I was terrified that she might kiss me or show some other sign of affection. Confused by my reaction, I just stood there wondering why I felt so unnerved. For a brief moment, I felt uncertain about everything. I shook off the feeling, realizing that it wasn't shame I felt, I just did not want Peter to find out this way. I had hurt him enough.

"It's all right," Alex whispered to me tenderly. "I'll be waiting for you upstairs." She gave Peter a shy wave and retreated into the house.

"Peter, why are you here?"

"This is going to sound silly," he said softly. "I drove up on Thursday."

"Thursday? What have you been doing all this time?"

"I got a room in town," he sheepishly explained. "At first, I came here because I thought you might be lying about having plans for the holiday. When I arrived and found you weren't home, I was embarrassed. I already told my parents that we couldn't make it for Thanksgiving. I had nowhere to go. I drove over here every day hoping to find you."

"Peter…" I started to say as my heart was breaking for him.

"Don't say anything, I feel like an idiot."

We went inside to the warmth of my apartment. I felt sorry for him as I watched him slump down onto my futon. I went into the kitchen to brew a couple of cups of coffee. I wondered if he had now figured things out when he saw Alex and me together. I watch the coffee drip into the glass pot, and I could hear Alex's footsteps above me. By the sounds, I could tell exactly which room she was in and what she was doing. I knew when she put our bags onto her sofa.

Funny how I didn't question that she took my belongings to her apartment. It just seemed like the natural thing to do. I knew when Alex was talking on the telephone. I watched the coffee sputter out its last hiss. I listened as Alex began to pace around her living room. Coffee in hand, I joined Peter, telling him to take off his coat, which he did reluctantly. I sipped my coffee as he stared into his cup.

I silently prayed that he would just say something so we could get this over with, and I could go upstairs to be with my lover. A part of me felt guilty while another part of me was angry with him for intruding. I had no idea which would win out.

"I must look like a total jackass."

"No," I said, hoping in a small way I was comforting him. I was torn between helping my best friend and listening to the sounds of my lover pacing frantically above us.

"You know, I told myself that I was coming here so you wouldn't be alone," Peter said absently. "Truth is, it was because I wanted to see you. I also didn't want to face my family. I wasn't comfortable knowing that when I arrived without you, I would have to tell everyone all at once that you left me. When I came here and you were gone, I felt like everything had just slipped away. Of course, I assumed that you were with him."

"Him?" I asked in puzzlement, realizing how quickly that option was no longer one that I considered.

"The guy you met when you first came to Prower," he said. "Boy, I was relieved when I saw you with Alex," he added with a hint of a smile.

I cringed, knowing that he had assumed I had left him for another man. It was one of the moments I seemed to be facing more and more. Everyone faces them. It's a small life-changing choice. I was offered the perfect opportunity to tell him everything. He had most certainly opened the door for me. No matter how much more this was going to hurt him, it was time to just be honest.

"Peter, there is no him," I carefully began, bolstering my courage.

"I knew it." He sobbed as he slumped back, looking like he had just gone ten rounds with a prizefighter and lost.

I took a deep breath. Taking in his disheveled appearance, I braced myself for one of the hardest things I would ever do. Then Peter did something I was completely unprepared for, he started to cry. Honestly, it made me angry at first. Telling him that our time together was a lie because I didn't know who I was, was hard enough. Add him sobbing like a small child, and it was impossible.

I couldn't do it. Instead, I held him as he sobbed for over an hour as I whispered, "I'm sorry." Finally, he collected himself and left with a promise that we wouldn't lose touch with each other. I felt a pang of guilt as I watched him drive off. I hoped that I had made the right decision by not being completely honest with him.

By the sounds I could hear from Alex's apartment, she too had watched Peter drive off. I stopped and listened to her footsteps as I locked up my apartment. She went from the living room directly into her bedroom. I climbed the staircase fearful that Alex would run away from me once again. I went to knock as I approached her door, but I stopped and tried the doorknob first. I breathed a sigh of relief as it opened. I walked in and closed and locked the door behind me. With each step I took as I approached her bedroom, I prayed that my presence would be welcomed.

Upon entering the bedroom, I found it dimly lit by candlelight and Alex in bed. "I'm sorry," I apologized to her. "He's having a hard time letting go."

"Don't be sorry," she said in a comforting tone. "I can't blame him. You're quite a woman. I understand that at one time Peter was your best friend. How are you doing? It couldn't have been easy for you."

"I'll be fine."

"What can I do?"

"Tell me that you are completely naked under those blankets," I pleaded, hopeful that the scene that surrounded me was an invitation. Without a word, Alex pulled back the bed covers and revealed her naked form to me. Greeted by the tantalizing vision before me, I licked my lips. My heart raced as I crossed over to the bed, stopping only to remove my shoes. In the few short months I had known this woman, I went from being thoroughly convinced that I was incapable of sexual desire to being dominated by it. I joined Alex on the bed, too eager to stop and undress myself. I kissed her warm mouth and explored her naked body. Nothing mattered at that moment. The only thing I wanted, the only thing I could think of, was how much I wanted to please her.

My mouth trailed an eager path across her neck as I pressed my body against hers. I blazed a trail across her skin, needing to taste all of her. I slowed my motions as I reached her breasts; I wanted to take my time. I teased her nipples between my fingers, realizing that I was becoming obsessed with her breasts. The mere thought of them filled me with desire. I circled her already erect nipple with my tongue, teasing it until I felt Alex's hand on the back of my head lowering me to her. I pressed harder as I took her breast into my mouth and feasted on it. I lavished its twin with the same attention as I lowered my hand down her body and was happily greeted by her wetness.

"How can you be ready so fast?" I moaned against her skin.

"I've been like this since we got in the car." She groaned as I entered her. "More," she pleaded, and I granted her request eagerly.

I watched her body arch against my hand and was awestruck by her beauty as she climaxed. She collapsed against the bed in a heap as she pulled me with her. I kissed her brow as her body continued to tremble with the aftershocks of my touch. When her body finally stilled, I removed myself from her. Lifting my fingers to my face, I inhaled the musky scent that was Alex. I brought my fingers to my lips and tasted her essence. I heard a soft growl emanating from her. I gazed into her smoky blue eyes as she pulled me to her. As we kissed, our lips parted slightly, and I felt her entering my mouth. Her hands raced down my body and unbuttoned my pants. Without hesitation, she lowered them down my hips.

"Take me..." I pleaded on the verge of begging. "Now! I want you now!" I moaned my need for her, and she responded to my needs. My words surprised me. There had been a time when I wouldn't have thought such things, and now I found myself screaming them as I begged her to take me. "Harder," I commanded as I rode her hand.

"That's it!" I groaned heavily as I grasped her wrist and plunged her deeper inside of me. With one final scream, I collapsed on top of her. She pulled me into her arms and held me close to her naked body. I snuggled up to her still half-dressed and not caring.

Once we caught our breath, she placed two gentle fingers under my chin and lifted my face to hers. "Let's go slower this time." She kissed my lips tenderly. Alex rolled me on to my back and undressed me very slowly, stopping to kiss my body as my skin was revealed to her. I would halt her exploration so I could touch her with tender inviting caresses.

"I love you," I murmured as my fingers touched her with a light feathery touch. I shivered from the mix of the cool air and her touch once my body was completely exposed. Alex pulled the bed covers around us.

Tucked in for the night, even though it was still the middle of the afternoon, we freely touched each other. With each touch and kiss, our desire grew stronger. Our pace remained slow and gentle, and this proved far more intoxicating. I touched and kissed every inch of her body, and she did the same to me. At one point, we just held each other, kissing tenderly as our bodies nestled against each other. It was as if we had become an extension of the other. Our passionate exploration continued throughout the evening. It must have been sometime around dawn when we found ourselves locked in an embrace gasping for air, our hips rising in urgency, one inside the other. Our tired voices lett one last scream out. Exhausted, we curled up into each other's arms and drifted off to sleep.

***

Far too soon, I was awakened by the sounds of Alex's alarm clock. I rolled over her sleeping form and slapped the snooze button harshly. I rolled back over and caught a glimpse of her breast peeking out from under the comforter. I licked my lips hungrily; the temptation proved to be too much for me. Slowly, I ran my fingertips across her exposed nipple. It excited me as it became hard from my touch. Alex moaned deeply from her slumber. Surprised, I pulled my hand away.

"Don't stop," she whispered.

I pulled the comforter down slightly to reveal the object of my desire. I cast a shimmering glance at her before lowering my head to feast on her. As I circled her nipple with my tongue, the alarm clock screamed out once again. We both reached for the offending object. Alex managed to slam the snooze button. Giggling like children, we retreated under the covers and began what I hoped would become our morning ritual.

When the alarm clock announced its presence again, we were far too busy to cease our activities. I dragged myself up from underneath the covers. While I fumbled for the clock, we did not stop making love. Meaning only to silence the clock, I managed to send it crashing to floor. We were far too wrapped up in each other to notice. We only cared that the clock had finally stopped interrupting us.

It wasn't until much later when we were dressed and ready to leave for work that we noticed the shattered remains of the alarm clock.

***

The first day back at work seemed to be dragging on forever. I reluctantly separated from Alex so we could go teach our classes. My students were pleased with their grades from the midterms. Not as pleased as I was, knowing that I had reached them. Alex was busy playing catch-up from the days she had missed, and as a result, I saw very little of her. I found myself staring at the clock willing it to move faster so Alex and I could go home. Then something occurred to me. It was time for lunch anyway. I grabbed my wallet and made my way across campus to the campus store. I giggled slightly as the clerk put my purchase in a bag.

"Hey, Stephanie," Maureen called to me. I waved to her as she approached the cashier. "How was your holiday?" she asked as the cashier rang up her purchase.

"The best," I said with a tad too much gusto, making me blush.

"Uh-huh," she said slowly, studying me carefully. "Why don't we grab lunch at the cafeteria and eat in my office?"

"Sounds great."

***

I put my feet up on the coffee table in Maureen's office and dug into my salad. I was happily munching away when I noticed that she was staring at me.

"So what did you get at the store?" Maureen tried to make small talk.

"I needed a new alarm clock, and what did you buy?"

"A book for Ben." She showed me the book on ancient Egypt.

"Is your oldest taking after Mom?" I said with a smile as I handed the book back to her.

"I think so." She sounded proud. "Mort and I have talked about when the kids are older, I'm going to start going on digs again. Ben should be old enough to go with me. If he's still interested, that is."

"He will be," I said with the same goofy grin that had been plastered on my face all morning.

"You never know, kids change their interest from day to day."

"It would be nice to share it with him, though," I said, then took a sip of my coffee. Over the brim of my mug, I noticed that she was still studying me. "Do I have something on my face?" I finally asked.

"You had sex," she exclaimed. "Don't deny it."

"I don't know what you're talking about."

"You're glowing, so don't try to tell me you haven't been at it all weekend." Maureen's bluntness caused me to choke on my coffee.

"You know, it's your shyness I admire the most." I coughed as I checked my blouse to make sure I hadn't spilled on it. Maureen stared at me and awaited an answer to her question.

"Getting laid has made you witty."

"Okay, I had sex this weekend." I tried to sound nonchalant about it. "Happy now?"

"I knew it! You know what's funny, I had a meeting with a certain tall, dark, and gorgeous coworker of yours, and she had the same glow about her."

"Fancy that."

"Come on, share," Maureen pleaded with a pout.

"Share what?" I feigned innocence.

"Ugh." Maureen growled. "So did you?"

"Did I what?" I continued to torment her.

"Stephanie?" she whined. "Come on, give an old married woman a break here. Did you and Alex?" I blushed and wiggled my eyebrows at her inquiry. "Well, it's about time. I thought the two of you were never going to come to your senses." Maureen blew out a frustrated breath. "How are you going to handle her being in California?"

"I don't know. Four months is a long time, and this is all still so new for us."

"Mort and I went through the same thing." Maureen patted my hand gently. "We had just started dating, and I was committed to go on a dig in Greece for the summer. It was hard, but look how well it worked out for us."

"Thanks."

"So how was it?" she asked happily.

"Maureen!" I gasped as I swatted her arm.

"How was what?" an all-too-familiar voice asked from behind us. Maureen's jaw dropped at the sight of Alex entering the office.

"Paybacks are a bitch, Maureen." I felt positively evil. "Maureen was just asking—" I began as Maureen blushed furiously.

"Stephanie, don't forget that I'm your boss!" Maureen tried to stop me.

"About our sex life," I finished, much to the surprise of both of my companions. Maureen groaned and buried her face in her hands.

"What did you tell her?" Alex finally managed to squeak out.

"Well, I was about to tell her it was good," I said flatly.

"Good?" Alex asked. "Is that all?"

"Hey, I don't want her to get jealous." I smirked, looking up into those captivating blue eyes. "The poor girl might have a heart attack if she knew how truly amazing you are in bed."

Alex stood beside me and caressed my cheek with her thumb. I leaned into her touch and gazed deeply into her eyes.

"Yuck." Maureen scoffed. "I think I'm getting a cavity."

"See, I told you she would be jealous," I pointed out. "No offense, Maureen, but you did ask."

"I have to go," Alex said. "I just wanted to see you."

"Have you eaten?" She held up a cup of yogurt in response.

"You need more than that," I said as she opened her mouth in an attempt to argue. "Alex, go get a sandwich or something." For a moment, she looked like she was going to put up a fight. Instead, she agreed to stop off at the cafeteria.

Maureen chuckled at the sight of the normally stoic Alex being ordered around by little old me. "Okay, now that she's gone, tell me everything," Maureen instructed me eagerly.

"Everything?"

"Well, not everything." Maureen laughed. "But you know, how did it finally happen?"

"We decided to spend the holiday with her family."

"Wait, you did it in her parents' house?"

"Yeah." I sighed happily at the memory. "Fortunately, it's a very big house. The whole drive down there, Alex kept explaining how we shouldn't get involved until after she got back from California. I don't know what deity to thank, but we ended up sharing a bedroom."

"Let me guess, all of Alex's plans flew right out the window." Maureen sighed happily. "I'm glad. I mean, I understand that the timing sucks, but the two of you belong together. Now that you're home, how is it going?"

"So far, so good."

"Speaking of good," Maureen prodded.

"Amazing, earth-shattering, I think we broke the sound barrier more than once," I confessed, blushing furiously. "I can't explain it. Before, sex for me usually ended with me saying, 'Yeah, we're done, get off me.' With Alex, I swear if we didn't have classes to teach today, we'd still be in bed. It's crazy, I don't know what happened to me over the past couple of months. Whatever it was, I'm so glad it did. For the first time in my life, I feel like I'm living *my* life."

***

After lunch with Maureen, the rest of the day dragged along slowly. Around five thirty, Alex finally returned to our office. She just gave me a knowing smile, and without a word, I gathered up my belongings and walked with her down to the car. We drove home in blissful silence. As we entered the foyer of the house, I grabbed her fiercely and kissed her deeply. Unable to wait any longer, I struggled to find my keys and dragged her into my apartment. I closed the door behind us and pushed her up against it. I kissed her hard, not hiding my desire as I pulled her overcoat off her body. I continued to kiss her as I struggled to rid myself of my coat, as well. I slid my thigh between her legs and ground our hips together.

I was on fire as I pulled her shirt out of her pants. I slid my hands up her taut abdomen and across her ribs, feeling my way up under her bra. She moaned my name as my eager fingers brushed against her nipples. It was all the encouragement I needed. I sank to my knees and unzipped her pants. I found myself yanking her slacks and underwear down her body, allowing them to rest around her ankles. Alex opened herself to me. Eagerly, I took her into my mouth. I held her steadily as her body rocked. I felt her hand pressing against the back of my head, guiding me to take her deeper. Feeling her need urged me on. I tasted her harder, deeper, faster, bringing her closer to the edge. Her body trembled as her hips arched, and I knew she was close to her release. I held her tightly as my tongue plunged deeper inside of her. Alex clutched the doorknob for support. I felt the wave crash over her as she exploded against me. I held her trembling body as I kissed her thighs. Once I felt her body steady itself, I stood and wrapped my arms around her waist and held her.

Within moments, we had undressed each other and climbed under the covers of the futon. Time passed slowly as we made love. Each moment seemed frozen in time. With every touch, my body craved more of what I had denied it for so very long. It was if I had locked my heart away and only Alex possessed the key.

Chapter Thirty Nine

One Friday afternoon, I was sitting on Alex's lap in our office. We were making out like a couple of teenagers. "Someone could walk in," Alex warned me between kisses.

"The door is shut," I protested as my hands freely explored her body.

"Stephanie—" I placed my fingers on her lips and silenced her. I lifted myself up off her lap, took her hands in mine, and pulled her into a standing position.

"I love the way you say my name," I murmured.

Alex looked at me curiously as I placed her hands on the desk and stood behind her. My hands roamed across her back, enjoying the feel of the wool sweater she was wearing. "Stephanie?" Alex squeaked as my hands cupped her jean-clad behind.

"Shh." My hands roamed to her hips and snaked around to the button of her pants. I pressed my center into her backside as I undid the button of her jeans, then slowly lowered the zipper.

"We can't." She moaned as I lowered her jeans and underwear down her body.

"We can," I whispered huskily as my hands now caressed her exposed bottom.

"Someone could walk in." Alex moaned again as I urged her legs open with my thigh. "We shouldn't, not here." Her words of protest were cut off by the sound of the zipper on my jeans being lowered.

I watched in amusement as she clutched her desk hard. "This is your fault," I teased while lowering my pants and underwear. "You've turned me into a wanton woman." I lifted the hem of the black turtleneck I was wearing. I pressed my wetness into her naked cheeks as she bucked her hips in response with a deep growl. "Do you want me to stop?" I increased the rhythm of our movements.

"No," she answered heavily as her hips matched my movements. I grabbed her hips and bucked against her furiously. We were both close, our bodies trembling. "Ah, yes, baby." She moaned as she held on to her desk for dear life.

"Well, I see the two of you have worked out your differences," a voice said with a slightly bitter tone from across the room.

"*Merde*!" Alex shouted as she pushed herself away from the desk and pulled up her pants. "Chris, what are you doing here?" She growled as I hid behind her, putting my own clothes back on.

"Enjoying the show," Chris chuckled lustfully.

"Don't you know how to knock?" Alex demanded as I continued to cower behind her.

"I did knock," Chris said defensively. "I guess you were too occupied to notice."

"Kill me now," I grumbled from behind Alex.

"Hi, Stephanie," Chris chirped brightly, seeming to enjoy my discomfort.

"Chris." I growled, finally emerging from behind Alex. I took my place on the corner of Alex's desk and folded my arms across my chest and glared at Chris.

"Chris, are you here simply to fulfill your voyeuristic fantasies, or is there a reason for this intrusion?" Alex asked her heatedly.

"Why so hostile? I'm just here to update you on the case. Not that there was ever anything to it in the first place. Half of Simon's bogus attempts to get even with the women in his wife's life couldn't get an indictment from the grand jury. Normally, good old Simon could get a Tic Tac indicted."

"Chris," Alex pushed.

"Anywho, I went to see Jessica, and she refused to help me out. In fact, she denied everything."

"I could have told you that would happen." Alex snarled.

"I had to try. Now Simon was another story. He completely freaked when I went to see him. He also denied everything, then asked me just how well I knew his wife."

"You're surprised?"

"No," Chris said frankly. "But I need to do this by the book.

This has the potential of becoming a huge scandal. I had to offer Simon an out. My next stop is a meeting with his boss."

"With the evidence you've collected, that should just about wrap everything up," Alex agreed. "So tell me, why the trip up here? You could've told me all of this in a text."

"I was coming to Boston anyway. I thought it would be fun to tell you in person, and I was right. That was fun."

"I get it. You have a hot date in town, and now you can charge the firm for your trip," Alex grumbled.

"I have a lecture to give on the Knights of the Golden Circle," I said as I looked at my watch in disgust.

"Who?" Chris blinked.

"Secret society that may or may not still exist."

"Don't forget the part about how cranky they are about that act of Northern aggression," Alex teased me before giving me a kiss. "I'll see you later."

"Yes, you will," I whispered before saying goodbye to Chris, who despite what she had said, did not look happy.

***

On Saturday morning, I was awakened by Alex urging me to get dressed. Not her usual morning request, so I was intrigued as to just what she had in mind.

"It's Saturday," I tried to argue, wiping the sleep from my eyes.

"Yes, it is, and it's cold out, so dress warmly."

"Alex, honey, what fiendish plot are you brewing?"

"I simply want to spend this beautiful day with my new girlfriend."

"Girlfriend?" I couldn't help smiling. "Wow, you have no idea how glorious that sounds."

"I think I do," she seemed to be boasting. "From the first moment you walked into our office, I have been positively smitten."

"Me too," I confessed. "I'm going to miss you when you're in California."

"I know." She shook her head. "When the opportunity first presented itself, I thought, 'Great, with a tenure slot opening up, this will be good for me.' Now I don't care if I get the spot."

"It's important," I argued, finally dragging my tired body out of bed. "I won't lie. I wish you didn't have to go, but your career is important. What is that—Vivaldi?" I added when a sudden blast of music invaded the room.

"Must be Hal." She rolled her neck. "I swear when they divided this house into apartments, they used the cheapest material possible."

"Someday, you'll fix that." I yawned and stretched my arms over my head. "I need a shower and coffee."

"I'll brew the coffee," she promised.

"What's the hurry?"

"I want to get there early."

"Get where?" I asked, shuffling toward the bathroom.

"The tree farm," she shyly confessed. "Not to get ahead of things, but this will be our first Christmas together."

"First?" I smiled before giving her a quick kiss. "You're making my morning, you know that, don't you?"

"I'm trying."

***

Once dressed in warm clothing, we drove north to a tree farm and went shopping for a Christmas tree. Cutting down my own Christmas tree was something I'd never experienced before. My grandmother just picked up the smallest tree she could find on Christmas Eve. I knew it was because it was all we could afford. After she passed away, I didn't bother. There I was running through the woods, stuffing snow down Alex's back and cutting down our own Christmas tree.

Alex strapped the tree to the roof of the car while I shook the snow out of my boots. When we stopped for lunch, I couldn't stop thinking how much I loved my life. I knew that I should be worried, but the way everything felt right was impossible to ignore.

"You're staring," Alex disrupted my thoughts.

"Can't help it," I admitted. "I know it's silly. We've only been together for little more than a week."

"Ten days. The best ten days of my life."

***

Once the tree was lit and decorated, we sat on the sofa sipping champagne and watching the tiny white lights twinkle. "Beautiful." I held Alex's hand and looked at the tastefully decorated tree.

"Truly," Alex said as I turned to find that her comment was directed toward me and not the Scotch pine that had overtaken her living room.

"I love you." Since saying it the first time, it seemed that I couldn't say it enough. Alex reached out and took me by the hand and led me into her bedroom.

Once again, sleep was not in our future. We were awakened by the joyful sounds of Tigger bouncing, thanks to the new clock I had purchased. It thrilled me that she woke up laughing each time it went off.

"I love this thing," she'd say, playfully slapping the top of Tigger's head to hit the snooze button.

***

Our days began to fill up between teaching, work on the book, shopping, and my new favorite pastime of making love. The only time we were apart was when we were teaching and one time when Maureen dragged me to the athletic center. I in turn dragged her out shopping.

"I can't believe how good you are," Maureen rambled on, referring to the outing. "Seriously, you're a natural."

"Really?" I crinkled my nose thinking how nervous I was when I realized that Maureen had dragged me to the athletic center to see how I would handle myself in the batting cages.

"You can hit, throw, and run." Maureen was beside herself. "I'm thinking of starting you on first or pitching."

"I always wanted to play." I couldn't help smiling. "Okay, focus. I need to find the perfect Christmas present, but I don't want it to be too much. Everything I look at screams materialistic."

"You're in a tough position," she agreed. "When Mort and I went through this, there weren't any major holidays to deal with. The two of you haven't been together all that long, yet you've been through a lot."

"It is hard, we haven't been dating that long."

"You haven't started dating." Maureen scoffed.

"We go out."

"No, you get food when you come up for air in between bouts of hot monkey sex," she blurted out, causing an elderly woman next to us to glare at me.

"Do you stress over what to get Mort?" I threw out in an effort to change the subject.

"No, we know each other so well, it's easy." She waved it off. "The only thing is, we have to rein in the romantic gifts so we don't gross out our kids. What about a scarf?" She held one up.

"I don't know."

"What are you two doing for the holiday?"

"We're spending it at her parents' house." I sighed happily. "We'll be there until after the first. Her mom texted me the other day, she's excited that I'm coming. It's strange going there. I love her family, but they're from a different world."

"How so?"

"They don't have a yard, they walk around the grounds," I tried to explain. "The house is a mansion with wings. The Kendell fortune may not be what it used to be, but their definition of a lack money is far different from mine. Oh, my God, that's it!" I exclaimed.

"A Wonder Woman statue?"

"It's a Wonder Woman M&M dispenser." I held up the three-foot sculpture. "Does this not say Alex?"

"Actually, it does."

Chapter Forty

"Everything okay with Mrs. G?" I asked one afternoon. I was sitting on Alex's sofa working on my laptop while enjoying a clear view of the tree.

"I took her shopping, which is always an adventure." Alex chuckled, dropping her keys on the coffee table. "The tree looks nice, doesn't it?"

"It does," I couldn't help smiling.

"I told you it wasn't too big," she teased, slumping down beside me. "Zia brought up your apartment again."

"She's a funny lady." I shook my head. Mrs. Giovanni had been dropping hints about me moving upstairs since I spent most of my time at Alex's place. "The studio has come in handy." I blushed, thinking of the numerous times our passion overwhelmed us to the point we were unable to wait until we could get to Alex's bedroom.

"She has a point," Alex tossed out, shrugging off her coat.

"Huh?" I sputtered.

"At the very least, we need to put you on my insurance so you can use the car while I'm gone."

"I—" I began to protest.

"I can't let the car sit," she said, relieving the sudden sense of panic. "The snow is only going to get worse, and you'll need to get around. I'd be grateful if you helped out Zia Maria while I'm gone."

"Absolutely. We have a review day on Wednesday," I readily agreed. "I'll go into town so I can go to the DMV and change my license from Connecticut to Massachusetts."

"RMV," she corrected me. "I'll drive you into town. I have some last-minute shopping to do. What's in the box?" She pointed to the carefully wrapped Wonder Woman I had placed under the tree.

"Nice try." I smirked. "Need I remind you that Santa is

watching? Are you doing all of this to avoid installing a shower massage in my studio?"

***

The first stop on Wednesday was the Registry of Motor Vehicles. After waiting in an endless line and filling out stacks of paperwork, I was finally approved and had my new picture taken. Then we rushed over to Alex's insurance agent, so she could have me listed as a driver on her car. I still felt somewhat uncomfortable with this. But Alex was right. I would be using her car mostly to run errands for Mrs. Giovanni and to drive to school until the warmer weather returned. Since the car was less than a year old, she needed to list me as a driver for extra protection.

After we finished this and some more tedious errands, we walked around Boston. Something in a window of a small shop on Charles Street caught my eye. I managed to send Alex off to the CVS down the street by lying about needing more wrapping paper. The moment I saw her entering the store, I ducked into the small shop.

It was simple, yet beautiful, just like Alex. It was a small onyx pendant set in silver, which was perfect since Alex never wore gold. I did some haggling with the shop owner. He tried to sell me the pendant at an outrageous sum of money, claiming that the piece was from the colonial period. I shot him an angry glare and explained my credentials and just why the colonial period wasn't a possibility. He quickly dropped the price. I was more than a little pleased with myself as I tucked the box into my pocket. I glanced back at the store and smiled when I noted the address. Seventeen Charles Street. It seemed that the past was once again guiding me. The pendant and candy dispenser were the perfect gifts.

I was startled when Alex touched my arm. "I'm sorry." I quickly gasped. "I was just looking at Annabel's shop. We should head home before the traffic turns insane."

***

That night, we ended up nestled on the sofa sipping wine. I rested my head on her shoulder, and we just sat there staring at the tree and each other. It was a simple heartwarming moment. I knew then that I was turning into a complete mush ball. I smiled, enjoying the moment, until I remembered that the time for her to leave was just around the corner.

"Penny for your thoughts," she whispered before kissing the top of my head.

"I'm going to miss you."

"I'm going to miss you, too. Maybe we could schedule some trips to see each other. I know you worry about money a lot." She added alerting me that she was well aware of my nasty habit of over worrying about money. "What if you didn't have to pay rent?"

"Alex?" I wasn't prepared for what she had just offered. "Your aunt needs the money," I protested.

"Hear me out." Alex held up her hand. "First off, for some reason, my aunt is under-charging you by at least a grand. I own my place, which you'll be looking after during my absence. My replacement will need a place to live. Zia can charge them the real rent, and you can stay here rent-free."

I was stunned, to say the least, torn between joy and sheer terror. "What happens when you come home?" I asked hesitantly.

"Stephanie, if for some reason our relationship does not survive our separation, do you plan on staying downstairs from me?"

"Not a chance in hell," I said firmly. "It was hard enough before we started seeing each other. I couldn't go through that again. I just don't know about moving into your apartment."

"Look, if when I come home, it's too soon for us to be living together, then we go back to the way it was. I have to admit, I kind of enjoy being able to use your apartment when we can't wait to get upstairs."

"I don't know," I began slowly. I wanted to say yes, feeling confident that our relationship was solid. I reminded myself that Alex and I had known each other less than a year, and there was a little matter of my pride. "I'm not really comfortable with you paying my way," I finally confessed.

"I wouldn't be paying your way," Alex argued. "I'd simply be paying the utilities, which I'm responsible for regardless. If it makes you feel better, you can take over the cable bill. I'll set it up with my accountant."

"You have an accountant?"

"Of course, with the house and my investments."

"Oh, of course." I chuckled, then I caught myself and sighed heavily. "I just don't want to feel like you're supporting me." I had to be honest, it was the only thing keeping me from accepting her offer. I had worked my entire life to become independent.

"I wouldn't be," Alex protested. "You'd be paying everything that isn't covered by the rent."

"But I wouldn't be paying rent," I tried to reason with her.

"Because there is no rent to pay on this apartment," Alex countered. "Zia Maria would be receiving more money than she would have if I was staying in town."

"But you'll be paying rent in California."

"I'm staying in faculty housing for free," Alex deflated my point quickly. "I'm house-sitting for another professor who will be on sabbatical. So it won't cost me a dime to live there." I listened to her argument, and it made sense. "I have a newsflash for you, Stephanie. You make more money than I do. The only reason I have more money is because I invested well. The interest I make off of my portfolio covers this house, my car, and helps out my family. If I lost my job, I would be in trouble just like everyone else."

"It's not like I ever use my apartment anymore. Most of my clothes are up here." I laughed. "I was just thinking about this joke Rita told me. What does a lesbian bring on a second date?"

"A U-Haul." She snickered. "It's an old joke, honey. Look, we won't really be living together if that's what's bothering you. I'm going to be on the other side of the country, and when I get home, we can talk about our living arrangement."

"It would be nice to save some money. Not to mention how much I love your apartment."

"So you're saying yes?" Alex asked carefully.

"Yes." I leaned into her body. "Now kiss me."

The sweet gentle kiss quickly deepened, leading into further exploration and inspiring me to remove her clothing. "Don't you ever get enough?" She gasped, her hands roaming my body.

"Never."

"Good."

***

The next morning, we moved most of my belongings upstairs,

most of which took up residence in my office on the second floor. It was the twenty-third, and classes were over. I wondered where the month had gone. My only plans for the rest of the day were simple—make love to Alex and to find food at some point before making love to Alex once again. I wanted to make it last all night and commit her body to my memory. At times, our lovemaking was rushed, driven solely by a lust that neither of us could control. Other times, we took everything very slowly, wanting each moment to last forever. That night was a night to take things slowly. With each touch and every lingering kiss, we were lost in each other. I remember thinking that I could spend an eternity caressing her breasts.

The next morning, I awoke blissfully as Alex lay sleeping beside me. I played with her tousled hair while she slept peacefully. I nuzzled my nose into her neck and inhaled her scent. I knew that Alex would not be awaking any time soon, so I reluctantly climbed out of bed and threw on a pair of sweats and a T-shirt that belonged to Alex. I loved wearing her clothes. It was like carrying a part of her with me. I made my way into the kitchen and brewed a pot of coffee. While the coffee was brewing, I dug out some of the papers that Nukumi had given me and settled down onto the sofa with them and began to read. Once the coffee was ready, I retrieved a cup and returned to the bedroom. Alex was still fast asleep. I decided to read from Eleanor's diary. From her words, I sensed that life did not always run as smoothly as Haley had viewed it.

***

July 1863

I find it hard to rally the men after the loss we have endured over the past few days. My thoughts turn to my beloved Haley. I thank the good Lord that my injury was not serious. I will return to her. I also thank the Lord that my secret has remained just that—a secret. The men are restless. Perhaps a trip to Mrs. Moorehouse's will lift their spirits. It will be a long trek from Pennsylvania, but the men deserve some entertainment. We have faced the Yankees and have been driven back each morn. Russell, my second in command and my dearest friend, and I fought bitterly today. His spirits brightened when I told him of my plans for our trip.

His joy was short-lived when I revealed to him the true reason I wished to visit with Mrs. Moorehouse. I planned to take Haley as my wife. "But, lad, you cannot," he scolded me. "She's a whore." His words had angered me so that I drew my sword without hesitation.

"I will thank you not to call her that!" I told him. "I am fond of the lady." I will never know if it was the sincerity of my words or the tip of my blade pressed against his neck that made him apologize.

It hurt me to argue with him. I admire Russell in many ways. He is very much my elder. If it were not for my station in life, it would be him leading this unit. I rely heavily on his advice. We both fight for the South because this is our home. Neither of us supports slavery, although our reasons differ greatly. I, like our great leader General Lee, feel that slavery is abhorrent. Unlike General Lee, I do not believe that slaves should be watched over like these men and women were children.

Russell, like many others, does not share my opinion. Russell's reasons are more practical. For a man of his station, finding honest work is difficult. Why pay a man to work when you can simply buy a slave who is forced to work for you? Russell came to this glorious land in hopes of finding a better life. The life he found was cold and unwelcoming. America, although built entirely by foreigners, does not easily welcome outsiders. Will this country ever grow to be what our forefathers fought for it to be?

Russell's harsh words had cut through me. I cannot help but believe that this conflict has made whores of all of us. I fight for a cause that I do not embrace in my heart. As the road to the end nears, I am all too aware that the South will fall. As proud Southerners, will we ever survive the defeat?

My feelings for Haley trouble me. I love her dearly as I have loved no other before her. The fact is there have been so many before her. Haley was angered when I told her of the number of women from my youth. The Boston marriages are a simple tradition for my station. Most of my companions went on to marry appropriate suitors. I knew in my heart that this was not a road I would travel willingly. I followed my heart, and it led me to Haley.

I accept our lives together, but she often becomes jealous and angry over the fact that I have kept company with so many. I find that odd since she has made her wages by entertaining men. If I see her again, I will offer her my hand. Perhaps it will quiet her fears. I know it will quiet my own. For I know in my heart that there shall never be another for me.

It is her smile that keeps me going during these bloody days. At night, I try to rest, but faded echoes of the cannons haunt my dreams. I pray that I will find peace in my beloved Haley's arms. For now, I try to sleep. At dawn, we bury the dead.

***

Eleanor's words seemed so troubled. I personally could see why Haley was troubled by Eleanor's past. In so many ways, her suspicions mirrored my own. Alex had known so many women. Would she find someone new when she traveled to California? Could I measure up to the passion she must have known in her life? Face it, Chris alone must have been quite an education. Alex stirred slightly as I wondered if this beauty who lay beside me would eventually break my heart.

"Good morning," she whispered as she looked up at me. "What are you doing?"

"I was just...working." I smiled at her loving expression, suddenly filled with a sense that she would never hurt me.

Overwhelmed with emotion, I placed my coffee cup on the nightstand and Eleanor's diary on the floor. I rolled on top of Alex and kissed her gently.

"Did I say good morning?" I murmured, kissing my way down her neck.

"No." Her voice trembled.

"Good morning." I growled as I assaulted her neck.

Encouraged by the guttural moan she released, I continued my journey tasting her skin. I teased her nipple with my tongue. The more I teased her, the tighter she held me. My fingers traced their way down her body. I could feel her opening herself. It was an invitation I could not refuse as I slid my fingers inside of her. Her wetness greeted my touch. Nothing excited me more than her passion. Just knowing that she wanted me could send me over the edge. I could feel her excitement growing, and my fingers thrust harder. She screamed my name as her fingers dug into my back as she tried to hold on.

"I like the way you say good morning," she croaked breathlessly. "I still find it hard to believe that you're new at this."

"You inspire me," I said brightly, snuggling against her and listening to the beating of her heart. "Would you like some breakfast?" I asked once she caught her breath. She didn't say a word as she smiled knowingly in response and lifted my face to hers and kissed me deeply. Within moments, I was screaming her name as she feasted on my wetness.

***

Later, we finally managed to drag ourselves out of bed and into the shower. Meaning only to bathe ourselves, we soon found it impossible not to caress each other. We finally finished our shower when the water turned icy cold. We dressed and packed the car with our bags and presents for the family. Then we took a casual stroll into town and had a real breakfast at the Java House. Upon returning home, we went upstairs to rest before facing the holiday traffic.

I watched her profile as Alex absently ran her fingers through my hair. "Do you have any idea just how truly beautiful you are?" She looked intently into my eyes. It was all I needed. I reached up and kissed her. I lowered her onto the sofa and began to unzip her jeans when a sound from downstairs startled me. There was someone knocking on my apartment door. I lifted my head and listened.

"Stephanie?" I heard Peter calling out before he knocked once more.

"Damn it." I scowled as I pulled myself up. "Man up, will you?" I growled at the intrusion.

"What is he doing here?"

I gazed down at her, knowing that I wanted nothing more than to finish what we had just started. Sadly, there was Peter to deal with.

"I'm sorry, I'll get rid of him."

"Don't be silly." Alex sighed as she stood and zipped her pants. "He probably just wants to wish you a merry Christmas. I didn't mean to snap, he must be having a hard time with this. I certainly would be. Why don't you invite him up?"

"What?" I stared at her in amazement.

"It might help him adjust to things," she explained thoughtfully. "You know, seeing us together."

Just when I thought things were going well and my life was nothing short of amazing. Unable to respond to her suggestion, I felt a full-fledged panic attack starting to grip my chest. I knew Alex was not going to take this well.

"Stephanie, is there a problem?"

"No," I said a little too quickly. "Just let me talk to him."

As I was saying the words, I heard his footsteps ascending the staircase.

"Stephanie?" Alex began slowly. "He doesn't know about us, does he?" Her voice was very calm and controlled, perhaps too controlled.

"No."

"It's all right," Alex said in the same overly calm tone that was beginning to worry me. "I understand."

"You do?" I asked with suspicion.

"Of course," Alex said and caressed my arm reassuringly. "Finding out that you're gay must have been hard enough on him."

I said nothing, incapable of moving or thinking. Despite the fact that I had every intention of telling Peter everything, Alex was not going to respond very well when she learned that I hadn't.

"Oh, my God!" she said sharply, and there it was. Before I even told her, she knew. "You didn't tell him!" Alex hissed in disgust.

There it was—all of her fear and doubts confirmed in a single moment. Not only that, it was literally knocking on her door. She stood there staring at me with disbelief. With each rap on the door, she seemed to be one step away from completely freaking out.

"Alex," I carefully began. "When I ended things, I told him that I wasn't in love with him."

"But..." Alex said in a strained voice. I sensed that she was struggling with her emotions. "You've talked to him since then. I seem to recall that he assumed there was someone else. I'm guessing that he thinks this someone else is a man, which I am mostly definitely not. Seeing us together last month could make him think that you haven't moved on. The poor sorry bastard probably thinks the two of you are going to get back together."

"No," I tried to argue, reaching out for her. "I've told him repeatedly that it's over. I'm going to tell him everything. Just not right now."

"Don't," Alex snapped as she pulled away from me. "Are you ashamed of me?"

"No," I said firmly and without hesitation.

"Are you ashamed of being gay?"

"No," I said again with the same firmness. "He's in pain. How can I add to that?"

"Tell him," Alex ordered me sternly.

"On Christmas Eve?" I gasped in horror. I wasn't certain what stunned me more—that she had told me to do it now or that she had out and out ordered me to do it.

"Tell him," Alex repeated. "Trust me. In the long run, you'll be doing him a favor."

"Let me handle this," I fought back. "I'm going to tell him in my own way. But it won't be today."

Alex looked as if I had slapped her. I couldn't bear to see the pain in her eyes. I had to turn away.

I opened the door to find Peter standing on the other side.

"Hey," he said with a goofy grin. "I was about ready to give up. I had a feeling you'd be up here. I think it's really nice that you have a neighbor you can be buddies with." I grabbed him by the arm harshly and led him back down the staircase.

Things were already going badly; I understood why Alex had snapped. The entire situation must have seemed like a bad flashback. I tried to calm myself and focus. The woman I loved was in a panic, and her next course of action would be to run. I had to deal with Peter quickly, then go back upstairs and reassure Alex that I was not like the others.

"Ouch," he exclaimed when we reached the bottom of the staircase and I spun him around.

"Peter, what are you doing here?" I demanded harshly. Silently, I was pleading that he would just wish me a merry Christmas and be on his way.

"Stephanie," he began. "I want us to stop playing games," he happily exclaimed as I felt the bile rising in my throat. "When we first split up, you led me to believe that there was someone else. But it's pretty obvious that isn't the truth. I understand that you needed time apart before we took the next step."

Oh, my God, Alex was right! As the words screamed through my mind, I watched in horror as he got down on one knee.

"I was planning on doing this in private." He laughed nervously and looked up. "But here goes," he merrily continued.

I followed his line of vision and was horrified to see Alex standing there. Her face was ashen as she leaned against the wall for support. Her eyes seemed to be begging me to stop him and tell him the truth.

"Stephanie?" Peter called for my attention. I turned, and much to my horror, he was still kneeling on the floor with a jewelry box opened to reveal a diamond ring. "Marry me?" he triumphantly concluded, looking extremely pleased with himself.

I felt my lips moving, yet no sound came out. Instead, I burst into tears. "Darling, say yes," he pleaded as I wept. "Alex, help me out here?" he implored her.

Fearfully, I looked to her. My heart sank when she turned away, walking back upstairs before slamming her apartment door behind her.

"Stephanie?" Peter called to me once again. He was still smiling, still so hopeful. For the life of me, I failed to see how he thought this was a good idea.

"Peter, get up." I wiped the tears from my eyes and took him by the hand and yanked him to his feet. "Peter..." I gulped, trying to gather my wits. "I'm sorry, but the answer is no."

His smile quickly vanished as he shoved the ring back inside his coat pocket. "I'm sorry," I repeated. "I care for you, but I'm not in love with you."

"You keep saying that, but—"

"But nothing," I cut him off, my world still spinning out of control. "There's something I need to tell you." I tried to calm myself as he turned, staring out the window in the front door. Not having him facing me made it easier. "I didn't fully understand my feelings for you until I came to understand myself. I'm a lesbian."

"What?" he shouted as he turned to me in anger. "How can you say that?" The vein in his head was throbbing.

"Because it's the truth," I said calmly, mistakenly thinking that if I was calm, it would calm him down.

"You can't be gay!" he shouted even louder, his face turning bright red.

With his last outburst, Hal appeared on the stairwell wearing a formal evening gown. "Is everything all right out here?" Hal asked me with concern.

"What is it with this place?" Peter shouted. "Is everyone who lives here a homo or what?"

I recoiled at the hateful words. I had never expected him to react this way. Hal, on the other hand, was not offended. He was accustomed to this misconception.

"My good man, I am not a homosexual," Hal responded confidently.

"Listen, pal!" Peter spat out in a hostile manner. "First of all, this is none of your business, and second of all, you might be a little more convincing if you weren't wearing a dress."

Hal just sighed and rolled his eyes before he explained dryly, "I'm a transvestite, not a drag queen."

"Who gives a—" Peter snarled.

"Peter!" I cut in quickly. "Just calm down. Hal, I can handle this."

"I am calm," Peter snapped, curling his hands into fists.

"I'm not convinced," a calm and familiar voice said from behind us.

We turned to find Shavonne standing there in uniform. "I'd be more convinced if you stepped back about two feet." Shavonne spoke with a calm yet authoritative voice. Peter just stared at her blankly. "Hal, why don't you go back inside?" Hal obeyed and returned to his apartment. "Now," she returned her attention toward Peter. "Why don't you step back, sir?" Peter failed to comply with her request. He just stood there glaring at me. "Stephanie, what is your friend's name?" she asked me in a mild tone without taking her gaze off of him.

"Peter," I said nervously.

"Peter?" Shavonne said. "Do me a favor and look at your hands."

He cast a glance down, seemingly shocked to see his hands

clenched into fists. He dropped his hands suddenly and backed up against the wall.

"Good," Shavonne said in a soothing tone. Peter just stood there shaking.

"I wouldn't hurt her." His voice trembled.

"I know," Shavonne continued to soothe him. "But you know someone who would." It wasn't a question. Somehow, she just seemed to know. "You're not him, Peter."

"No, I'm not," Peter choked.

Shavonne stood with him as he calmed himself and caught his breath. I knew that the sight of his hands clenched in anger had frightened him, and I knew why. His father beat him and his mother on a daily basis. They finally ran off one night while he was at work. Peter and his mother lived in a shelter for over a month. He swore that he would never be like him. He would be like the man who raised him, his stepfather who was a kind and decent man. The guilt I felt over this situation made me sick.

Shavonne talked with him for a while, and when she was finally convinced that he would be all right, she agreed to leave us. "Oh, and just for the record, Hal may enjoy wearing women's clothing, but the guy would have kicked your ass, son." She then touched me gently on the shoulder. "Will you be all right?" she asked me with concern. I simply nodded in response. "God, I hate the holidays," she muttered as she made her departure.

We stood there in silence for a few moments. "Is it true?" Peter finally asked in a defeated tone.

"Yes," I said quietly.

"Why didn't you tell me?" he asked. "All these weeks, I had convinced myself that maybe there was still a chance for us. You should have told me. I would've been hurt, but at least I would've known the truth. All this time, I just thought you had lied about there being another guy. I guess in a way you did lie."

"No, letting you believe it was the lie," I choked. "I just didn't want to hurt you any more than I already had."

"Now that is a lie," Peter said. "You did it because you didn't want me mad at you."

"What do you mean?"

"I mean that you're afraid of losing the people in your life."

Peter sighed dejectedly. "You'll do anything to keep people from getting mad at you. You weren't protecting me, you were protecting yourself." I felt a stab of truth in his words. "When did you know?"

"I've had these feeling since I was a teenager," I confessed. "I fought them and pretended they weren't real. Until I met Alex."

"Alex?" he said absently.

"Alex and I are lovers."

"When?" he asked suspiciously.

"Thanksgiving."

"Stephanie…" His voice was strained. "How can you be so cruel? Letting her watch as I was proposing? Well, that explains why she drove off."

"What?" I raced out onto the porch, and my heart lurched when I discovered that her car was gone. I couldn't believe that I was too wrapped up in Peter's craziness that I never heard her leaving. "What have I done?" Peter joined me out on the porch. I turned to him. He put his hand up and stopped me.

"I don't want to talk to you," he said firmly and walked off without looking back.

Chapter Forty One

I raced to Alex's apartment and confirmed what I already knew—she was gone. I paced back and forth, wringing my hands while wondering what I should do. I had nowhere to go. My apartment was empty since Alex's replacement agreed to sublet it. I could only assume that she went to her parents' house. I hoped that was what she did. I was fearful of the thought of her just driving around with the idiots out there celebrating the holiday and possibly drinking and driving. I could call her parents, but if she wasn't there, I didn't want to worry them.

I tried her cellphone, which went straight to voice mail. I was frustrated. I knew she needed space, but I needed to talk to her and make things right between us. I was sick to my stomach knowing that the most important person in my life just walked away, and I was the cause.

Exhausted, I went into the bedroom and collapsed on the bed in tears. I lost track of time as I wept. Somewhere in the back of my mind, I knew the sun had set. I tried calling and texting with no success. Each time I tried, the feeling of dread that was quickly consuming me grew.

I jumped when I heard the living room door close. I sprung off the bed and raced into the living room. "Alex?" I called out. I was startled as the lights went on, and I saw Nicole standing in the living room.

"Hate to disappoint you," Nicole quipped. "It's the younger, cuter version," she added with a wink and looked for a place to extinguish the cigarette she had been smoking.

Without a word, she went into the kitchen to retrieve an ashtray. Unceremoniously, she plopped down onto the sofa and lit another cigarette. "Did you know I got my driver's license back?" she said nonchalantly as she blew smoke rings. "In my sister's infinite wisdom, she let me take her precious car out for a spin. Actually, she sent me out to score her some cigarettes. Which I gladly agreed to do since I'm out, as well."

I looked at her suspiciously as she extinguished her smoke. "You drove all the way here from Chestnut Hill in holiday traffic?" I asked in bewilderment. "Where does she think you went for cigarettes—Bangladesh?"

"I haven't a clue." She shrugged. "But I shut my cellphone off, so she couldn't track me down."

"I thought you were out of cigarettes." I pointed to the pack she had placed on the coffee table.

"I must have forgotten about them," Nicole said with a smirk, which quickly vanished, and her face grew serious. "She's pretty upset."

"So you came here to break my legs." I sniffed, feeling sick over hurting Alex.

"No," Nicole said softly. "I told you before that I would let Zia Maria handle that. But since she's out of town at the moment, I guess I'll have to grant you a reprieve."

She gave me a moment to collect my thoughts as I fought back the tears. "Stephanie," she said finally. "Did you know that I've been married five times?" I just stared at her curious as to why she was telling me this. "It's true," she confirmed. "Not once did I make it to my first anniversary. One of the things I learned from those experiences is that it only takes one time of not thinking before you speak to end a relationship. You and Alex have not done that yet."

"It's my fault." I began to sob, the tears getting hold of me once again.

"She blames herself." Nicole jumped up and wrapped her arms around me. I just stared at her as she released me. "For running and for not staying to talk things out," Nicole said. "By the look on your face, I can see that you feel the same." I just nodded in response as she wiped the tears from my face. "Get your coat." She gave me a gentle push. "Go on, get your coat. I think Alex needs to talk to you more than she needs to smoke."

***

I followed Nicole's instructions, and we were on our way to Chestnut Hill. We talked on the long drive down to Newton. I was terrified not knowing what I should say to Alex. Nicole told me to calm down and speak from my heart. By the time we pulled into the Kendells' driveway, my heart was racing. As we stepped onto the front porch, Alex stormed out.

"Nikki, where the hell have you been?" she shouted, and her face dropped when she saw me. Before I knew what was happening, we were in each other's arms. Both sobbing and apologizing.

"I should have stayed," Alex choked out. "I should have trusted you. I don't know why I didn't stay."

"No, you were right." I sobbed. "I should have told him."

"No." Alex comforted me as she pulled me closer. "You know him better than I do. I let my fears get the better of me. I shouldn't have freaked out like that."

"I told him everything about me and about us."

"That must have been awful," Alex said, softly brushing away my tears.

"Well, he hates me." I sniffed, leaning into her hand. "But it's finally over. No more hiding the truth. I was afraid I had lost you. I never want to feel like that again."

"Never," she vowed, placing a kiss on my lips. "Now let's go inside, it's freezing out here." She draped her arm around my shoulder and led me into the house. "Wait." Alex stopped suddenly. "I brought in the presents, but I left our bags in the car. I wasn't sure that I was going to stay."

"I'll get them," I volunteered. "I don't think Nicole locked the car. Speaking of Nicole, where is she?" We looked around to find ourselves quite alone. We heard laughter coming from inside of the house and realized that Nicole had thoughtfully gone inside. "Go inside, darling, I'll get the bags. Go on in, it'll give me a moment to fix my face," I prodded. Alex bent down and kissed me once again, then retreated happily back into the house.

I made my way carefully through the snow back to the car. As I opened the back hatch, my breathing hitched as I spotted a dark figure hiding in the bushes. I was frozen with fear as the man shifted to conceal his presence. I swallowed hard as I stood there frozen in place. My body was shaking as I tried to work up the courage to run.

My heart hammered against my chest as he moved. There was something hauntingly familiar about him.

"Stephanie?" Alex called to me from the porch.

The man's blue eyes widened in fear at the sound of Alex's voice. He turned and bolted across the icy front lawn. "Oh, my God!" Alex jumped the railing and slid along the ice as she ran after him. Somehow, she managed to catch up with him by a large oak tree. "Wait," I heard her pleading with him.

My feet finally started moving when Nicole emerged on the porch.

"What is going on?" she asked in confusion. "She's not looking for the cigarettes, is she? I honestly didn't buy any."

"There was a man hiding in the bushes."

"What?"

"Alex ran after him."

Nicole looked frantic as she spied the two of them by the tree. Her face dropped as she too hopped over the railing and raced to the scene unfolding under the oak tree. Admittedly, she was far more graceful than her sister.

I followed after Nicole as quickly as I could. She reached Alex and pulled her away from the stranger. Nicole reached out to him, only to have him push her away and step back, yet making no effort to run. He just stood there, and they backed away, giving him his space. I stopped suddenly as I approached them. Seeing the three of them together, I knew instantly who he was.

"Please, don't run. They want to see you," Alex pleaded.

He sobbed as his sisters cautiously approached him. Slowly, they wrapped their arms around him and just held him. I walked back to the car to allow the three of them some privacy. I retrieved our bags from the car and headed into the house. Walking into the Kendell home unannounced somehow seemed perfectly natural to me.

"Well, there you are," Jefferson greeted me with a big hug as I set the bags down.

Paulette followed, hugging me tightly and wishing me a merry Christmas. "Nukumi said I needed to set a place for you at the table. But she also told me to add one more," Paulette explained.

"Goodness only knows what that's about unless she finally got one wrong."

"Perhaps not," I said quietly as I cast a glance at Nukumi, who just sat by the fireplace smoking her pipe. "You should come with me."

"Are those girls having a snowball fight?" Jefferson seemed hurt. "Well, not without me, they don't."

"You need to come outside."

They looked at me with confusion as I led them into the cold winter air. They stared out into the night, looking for some explanation. I watched their faces change as the image of their three children approached the house.

"David?" Paulette sobbed quietly, bringing her hands to her face as Jefferson pulled her close.

"Look what I found," Alex tried to lighten the mood as they stood together at the bottom of the steps.

Alex and Nicole stepped back slightly as David hesitantly stepped onto the porch and approached his parents. Jefferson and Paulette wept as they wrapped their arms around their son's body. I smiled at the sight of Nicole and Alex holding on to each other. David was led into the house by his parents. Nicole and Alex followed putting their arms around me, as well, as we entered the house.

David's parents had yet to release him. Nicole watched the scene with tears in her eyes. I removed my coat and hung it in the hallway. I took my place by Alex's side and wrapped my arm around her waist as we stepped into the family room followed by the rest of the family. I walked over to the fire with Alex to warm myself. I looked down at Nukumi, who was still puffing away on her pipe and rocking in her rocking chair.

"You're beginning to scare me," I confessed. She just smiled back and continued with her rocking. "How did you know?"

"Listen to the earth, and it will speak to you," she said flatly. "Follow the wind, and it will guide you." Then she went on rocking without further explanation.

"What the hell does that mean?" I whispered to Alex.

"I have no idea," Alex blew out. "She has been saying that for as long as I can remember. Then again, there are times I swear she just makes crap up."

"Finally, the entire family is together." Paulette wiped the tears from her face as she held David closely to her.

"Not yet." Nukumi smiled knowingly. "Not everyone has arrived. There will be many more to join the family. After I have gone on my way, the first two will come. Window shopping can prove to be very inspiring." She winked at Alex and me, then went on with her rocking.

"Something you want to tell us?" Nicole teased Alex with a playful nudge.

"No," Alex shot back firmly. "I don't think I really need to explain the improbability of that to you, Doctor."

"Oh, that's not what you claimed in the ER last month." Nicole snickered.

"What's this?" Jefferson asked.

"When Alex was being treated for food poisoning, she boldly announced to me and everyone else in the room that she could too get Stephanie pregnant, then she threw up on my boss's shoes," Nicole explained much to everyone's delight. Embarrassed, Alex buried her face in my shoulder. I patted her gently as I laughed along with the rest of the family.

"I did not." Alex protested.

"Fine, you just threw up on my boss's shoes."

***

Nukumi's predictions aside, the family settled in. David seemed timid at first, so much so that everyone approached him carefully. He still seemed overwhelmed. Despite my desire to get to know him, I kept away. The family gathered around the Christmas tree and sang carols. Alex was right—they were not a gifted group vocally, and recalling the lyrics was a challenge. No one cared, we just sang and enjoyed the fire and the tree.

Alex and I were seated on the floor next to the fireplace. I was nestled in front of her, happy to be wrapped in her arms. The tree was gorgeous, trimmed with antique ornaments and white lights. In the middle of *Deck the Halls,* at least I think it was supposed to be *Deck the Halls*, David began to sob. The singing ceased immediately.

"Don't stop," he pleaded, wiping his eyes. "I'm just happy to be home at last. You have no idea what it's like seeing all of you again. I was watching from the window afraid to come in. The people at the church had me believing that I was no longer welcomed here. Being here with all of you, I can finally see clearly how they deceived me."

"It's good to have you home, little brother," Alex said gently.

"It's good to be home." He sighed heavily. "Everything is the same. Well, almost. Nikki, you're sober. No drink in your hand, and you seem so happy and full of life."

"Clean and sober for over five years."

"I'm proud of you," David said with a smile, then turned his attention toward Alex and me. "And you, Tigger, no cigarettes." I could feel Alex hold me tighter when David used his nickname for her. "I can see that you may have found something better to hold on to." He smiled at me as I blushed.

"Time for the formal introduction." Alex pulled me closer. "Stephanie Grant, I would like you to meet my brother, David Ballister Jefferson Kendell."

"It's nice to finally meet you." I smiled up at David.

"The pleasure is mine." David blushed. "How long have the two of you been together?" he asked with genuine interest.

"Not long, Thanksgiving weekend was when we first..." Alex stopped hesitantly as the family erupted in laughter at her revelation. Alex buried her head in my neck and whispered, "Kill me now."

"*Moi, cheri.*" Paulette laughed. "It's not like this is news to us."

"Yeah, the two of you aren't exactly quiet," Nicole added. There was a collective groan from the rest of the family as I buried my face in my hands. "What?" Nicole tried to defend herself.

"Too much information, dear," Paulette chastised her.

"So how did the two of you meet?" David asked, changing the subject quickly.

"We work together," Alex said, thankful for the diversion.

"Oh, so you're a lawyer, as well?"

I felt Alex stiffen, and I became acutely aware of how long David had been absent. "David..." Alex began slowly. "I'm not a lawyer any longer. I gave it up a long time ago," Alex nervously explained. "I'm a history professor at Prower University. It makes me happy."

David's shoulders slumped sadly. "I feel as if my life has been going on without me." The sorrow was evident in his voice.

"You're home now, son," Jefferson said tenderly. "You are home, aren't you?" The nervousness was plainly written across Jefferson's normally stoic features.

"Yes, Dad, I'm home." He straightened his body and looked around the room with a misty gaze. "I'm home," he repeated confidently. "I'm not going to lie and tell you that this is going to be easy. But I want my life back. I want my family back!" David's comments were followed by a tearful round of hugs. "Speaking of being home, where am I going to sleep?"

"I'll get a fire going in your room right now, son," Jefferson immediately volunteered.

"Wait." David held his hand up, and everyone held a nervous breath. "There's something else I need to feel like I've truly come home."

He looked toward Alex and smiled, then cast a glance toward his father. Jefferson nodded his understanding and left the room without a word as the rest of the family settled in comfortably around the fire. Jefferson returned with a withered book and handed it to Alex, then took a seat next to Paulette. With the family gathered around Alex, she opened the book, and without looking at the words, she began to read. "Twas the night before Christmas..."

I was impressed by Alex's narration of the familiar holiday classic. She never missed a word throughout the entire telling of the story. I also quickly figured out by the tear-stained faces that surrounded me that this holiday tradition had not been observed since David's departure. I finally felt like a part of a real family, and I knew then just how much I belonged with them. It was if they needed me as much as I needed them. After Alex finished reading, Jefferson and David went upstairs to prepare a fire in his room. The rest of the family made their way into the kitchen to finish dinner preparations.

I stood to join them when I felt Alex's firm grasp pulling me back down. "We'll join them in a second. I need to hold you for a moment," Alex said softly.

I snuggled against her body, enjoying the warmth she offered me. "He's home, he's really home." She sighed deeply as I pulled her closer to me. "A few hours ago, things seemed so bleak. I was afraid that I had lost you and..."

"Shh." I held her tightly.

"Thank you." She kissed the top of my head. "You have no idea how much you being here for this means to me. The family is all together finally, and I can't begin to tell you how happy I am that you're now a part of the family." My breathing quickened at the implication. "You are, Stephanie," she reassured me. "I know you never had a real family, but you do now. I want to thank you for not giving up on us. I've never loved anyone as deeply as I love you. It's like I spent my entire life looking for you. Does that make any sense?"

"Yes," I said firmly. "I feel like I've come home. All of this is a bit overwhelming at times, but I know I belong with you."

"You do, and don't you ever think about leaving me." Alex held me tightly. "Besides, if we ever broke up, I think my family would go ballistic."

I reached up and pulled her closer to me and kissed her gently. I certainly hadn't intended to start anything in the middle of her family's house, but I lost all sense of reason when I felt her tongue teasing my bottom lip. I parted my lips as Alex quickly accepted my invitation. My breathing grew ragged as she explored my mouth. My hand began to caress her breast.

"Ahem!" I heard from the entryway. I looked up, startled to find Jefferson waving a cautioning finger in our direction.

"Hey, Pops," Alex greeted him with a gulp.

Jefferson flashed us a knowing smirk and left the room. I wanted to crawl into a hole, I understood that Jefferson was a very understanding man, still I doubted he was happy to see me feeling up his daughter.

Alex and I quickly retreated to join the rest of the family in the kitchen. After dinner, everyone shared in the cleanup, then everyone with the exception of Nukumi, who had been put to bed, was enjoying a snowball fight on the front lawn. In between activities, Alex and I stole kisses under the mistletoe. In many ways, I felt as if I had entered a dream world. When the clock struck midnight,

Jefferson and Paulette sent everyone off to bed. Although David and Nicole protested, Alex and I did not. As Alex and I climbed the staircase, I caught a glimpse of Jefferson and Paulette necking under the mistletoe. It warmed my heart to be surrounded by so much love.

***

We entered our bedroom, and my gaze never left Alex as she stoked the fire and pulled down the bedding. The sight of her warmed me to the depths of my soul. I knew what I wanted for Christmas, and she was standing right in front of me. I approached her slowly as a playful smile crept across my lips. She took me into her arms, and we exchanged a tender kiss. I watched the firelight dance in passion-filled eyes. Slowly, Alex undressed me. She caressed my body as she removed each article of clothing.

"Opening our presents a little early?"

"All I want for Christmas is to wake up next to you," Alex whispered hotly in my ear.

"You do know how to say just the right thing."

Chapter Forty Two

I was awakened by the sound of gentle tapping on the bedroom door. I looked over with bleary eyes at the clock on the nightstand. It was just after seven in the morning. Alex rubbed her eyes sleepily. She looked at the clock and groaned. Then suddenly, she smiled brightly and climbed out of bed. I felt a chill as she left the comfort of our bed. Alex quickly gathered some clothing. She put on a pair of sweatpants and a T-shirt, then tossed similar items to me. I just looked at her like she had lost her mind. Granted, it wasn't the first time she had seen this expression on my face. She just continued to grin like an idiot as I grudgingly put on the clothing she had offered me.

The tapping on the door continued as Alex climbed back into bed and snuggled up to me. "Come in," her voice creaked. The door flew open as Nicole and David scampered in like children and jumped on the bed.

"Santa came," they chanted repeatedly as Alex laughed at their antics.

"Come on, sleepyheads, time to get up," Nicole demanded as she tickled Alex.

"Stop it." Alex laughed as she tried to swat away Nicole's hands.

"Hey, I'm the baby." Nicole pouted.

"Suck it up," I teased Nicole as she rolled off Alex.

"I'm sorry, Alex, it was my idea," David admitted sheepishly. "I just had to. I wanted this small part of the past."

"It's okay," Alex said with a smile. "At least you knocked, not like when we were kids."

"When we were kids, you didn't have a girl in your room."

"Unlike some people." Alex laughed as Nicole wiggled her eyes suggestively.

"There are no secrets in this family," I noted.

"Nah." Nicole scowled. "Where's the fun in that? Now come on, we have muffins to bake."

Alex sent her siblings off, so we could wash up. I took a quick shower and threw on a pair of flannel lounge pants and one of Alex's T-shirts.

"So you caught Nicole with a girl?" I brushed my hair and stopped suddenly, noticing a telltale bruise on my neck. I swatted Alex and pointed to it. She just smiled proudly.

"When she was a teenager, there was much I didn't catch Nicole with in her room," Alex said. "Boys, booze, girls, she was a handful. She drove my parents crazy. She never really seemed happy then. Now all she does is work, and she's the happiest I've seen her in years."

"Hmm." I sighed thoughtfully. "I never did anything wrong. I didn't want to upset my grandmother. Except for this one time." I blushed at the memory.

"What?"

"She walked in while I was…you know."

"Tell me," Alex purred hotly into my ear.

"I was touching myself," I admitted with a blush.

"What happened after that?"

"She just walked out of the room, and we never talked about it."

"Why not?" Alex asked in puzzlement. "I mean, it's only natural. Of course, when Mom sat me down to talk about it, I thought I would die of embarrassment."

"My grandmother didn't discuss such things. After that, I was just too embarrassed to do it alone. I was always afraid that she would walk in again."

"What do you mean alone?" Alex licked her lips suggestively.

"I had a friend," I admitted with a furious blush.

"Do I get a show?" Alex whispered hotly in my ear as my knees buckled.

I pushed her away gently as her hands roamed under my shirt. "Cool off, pal," I warned her. "Your family is waiting on us." I held up my hairbrush in a threatening manner. "I'm telling you, with such randy behavior, I wouldn't be surprised if your stocking is filled with coal."

"Spoilsport," she grumbled as we exited the bathroom.

Feeling playful, I pulled her aside before we could depart from the bedroom. "But if you're a good girl today, I could arrange a private performance tonight," I suggested seductively in her ear, then I licked her neck. I felt her shiver from my touch as she squeaked in response.

Alex and I arrived in the kitchen and began preparing the muffins. Nicole made a pot of coffee while Alex and David each prepared a bowl of batter.

"What can I do?" I watched the three of them working in unison.

"Grease the muffin tins," Nicole suggested. "Everything is on the table. I'll get Nukumi." Nicole bounced off while I began greasing the muffin pans. Nukumi and Nicole entered the kitchen.

We spooned the batter into the tins I had prepared as Nukumi lit the oven. David prepared chocolate chip muffins, while Alex prepared a batch of blueberry. The blueberries, I was told, were handpicked from the bushes on the property. Once the tins had all been filled, we handed them off to Nukumi, who placed all six trays into the oven.

I was amazed at the quantity until I was told how many people would be stopping by to extend holiday greetings. It occurred to me that this tradition of baking the muffins together probably started when the Kendell children were very little. Nukumi would have been there to handle the actual baking. When the cleanup of the kitchen had been completed, the sweet aroma of coffee and fresh-baked muffins filled the air.

All of us settled around the kitchen table and peacefully drank our coffee. I learned that this part of the tradition led all three of the Kendell offspring to an early addiction to caffeine. I was surprised that the Christmas morning baking tradition had for some reason ceased as the siblings grew older and their lives led them in different directions. This was the first time in many years that they had shared this part of their past, and I felt honored that I had been included.

As the morning passed, their parents awoke and joined us. We gathered around the tree and exchanged gifts. There were even gifts for David that had been set aside over the years in hopes that he would return. No one in the family failed to remember me in the celebration. It was clear that I was accepted as a part of the family.

Throughout the day, many people did drop in to wish the Kendell clan happy holidays. I was amazed by the diversity of the Kendells' friends. They differed not only in ethnic diversity, but in their social standings, as well. I grew up in New Haven, where almost everyone was white. I stood out because I came from the working class. I still remembered how it broke my grandmother's heart when she was forced to accept food stamps.

Another thing that impressed me with the Kendells was that many of the gifts lacked materialistic value. Many were handmade or simply a donation to someone's favorite charity. As people came and went, David often shied away. When old lady Kendell made her appearance, he disappeared completely. I watched in amusement as the family made their wagers at what insensitive comment the old woman would utter next.

***

The next few days continued to be magical. The days were filled with family activities, and the nights were filled with Alex. One night, we went for a walk around the grounds. As we walked, I played with the necklace Alex had given me on Christmas morning. It was a single black pearl on a silver chain. Just above the pearl was a single one-carat diamond. I loved it more than any other gift I had ever received. We walked in silence hand in hand and breathed in the cold night air. I was silently dreading the holidays coming to an end. The new year would mean Alex would soon be off to California.

On New Year's Eve, the Kendells hosted a party. There were so many people, and I stayed close to Nicole and David while Alex was getting ready. It was slightly formal, and I was pleased with my black velvet dress. The only jewelry I wore was the necklace Alex had given me. I felt a shiver and turned suddenly to see Alex descending the staircase. My breathing stopped as I cast a fiery gaze over her body dressed in a red silk gown that was cut perfectly to fit her gorgeous body. Her hair was braided in the back, which served to highlight her chiseled features, and I thought I would drool when I noticed that her broad shoulders and magnificent back were exposed.

"Breathe, stupid," Nicole whispered to me as she gave me a playful nudge.

I choked as I finally allowed the air to enter my lungs. Alex approached me and bent down and gave me a kiss on the cheek. "You look incredibly beautiful," she purred into my ear. "Happy New Year," she added and began to pull away. I clasped her head and drew her back down to face me, then with all the strength I could muster, I growled.

"I want you now." Overhearing my bravado, Nicole choked on her beverage. I scanned the room quickly and was relieved that only Alex and Nicole seemed to have heard my comment.

Alex was blushing at my comment and squeezed my hand tightly as she whispered, "Later." I spent the rest of the evening trying to capture her under the mistletoe.

Some of the guests were disappointed that no alcohol would be served during the evening, but the majority didn't seem to care. For the first time in my life, I watched midnight approach without witnessing a single drunken occurrence. Alex and I shared a kiss at midnight, which soon proved to be overpowering. Quickly, we disappeared without saying our good nights to anyone. Once safely locked in our room, we began our own celebration.

***

The following day, we stayed in bed longer than we should have. After finally dragging ourselves out of each other's embrace and out of bed, we showered and packed the car. We returned to the house and said goodbye to the family. Nukumi stopped us on our way out. I adored the woman, but her little predictions were beginning to make me nervous. Thankfully, all she did was hand Alex a present.

"It's for both of you, and it's for neither of you."

"Nukumi, someday you're just going to say what you mean." Alex laughed as she opened the package.

"What is it?"

"A pair of drums," Alex said, mystified, holding up one of the small handmade drums. The family seemed stunned as they asked to see them. Then they just stared at Alex and me with a wide-eyed expression. Their reaction was odd, to say the least.

"Nukumi, you made these?" Alex asked. Nukumi just nodded. "How do you think this is going to happen?"

"Window shopping" was all Nukumi offered as an explanation.

"Uh-huh." Alex just stared at her, then shook her head in amusement. "Thank you, they're beautiful."

***

When we returned home, I unpacked as Alex put on a pot of coffee, then went across the street to check on Mrs. Giovanni. I started the laundry once everything, with the exception of Nukumi's gift, had been put away. I left that on the coffee table wondering what the significance a tiny pair of drums had. Alex returned, and I asked after Mrs. Giovanni. Alex told me that she was well and sent her regards.

"What should we do with this?" I motioned toward Nukumi's gift. "They're very beautiful. The detail is amazing."

"I don't how she managed. Her eyes aren't what they used to be." Alex just stared at the package. "Not to mention, her fingers are riddled with arthritis."

"Do I want to know why they freaked you out?"

"The beating of a drum is an important tradition," she thoughtfully began. "For Nukumi's people, everything has a spirit—people, plants, animals, and the Creator. The beating of the drum represents the heartbeat of the Creator. We hear that drumbeat for the first time in the womb from our mother's beating heart." I stared at her blankly as she ran her fingers over the delicate carvings. "Nukumi made drums for every child, grandchild, and great-grandchild. It's a tradition...Nukumi's way of announcing a new arrival to the family. Sometimes before the parents even know that a little one is on the way. My mother still has my drum on the desk in her office. From what I understand, when Nukumi gave my parents my drum, it was a little upsetting. They had only recently become engaged. I was early."

"Okay, now I'm even more confused," I mumbled at the implication of Nukumi's gift as I left the room to retrieve some coffee for us.

I returned to the living room to find Alex studying the gift carefully. I handed her a cup of coffee and settled in next to her. She took a long sip of the brew and set her cup down, then set down my mug, as well. "Okay, let me see if I can explain this." She clasped my hands. "Keep in mind I'm still convinced that sometimes Nukumi makes crap up just to screw with us. The drums are a gift for *our* children."

"Excuse me?" My eyes widened as she finally said what I had suspected since this conversation began. "I think it's a little early in our relationship to be talking about this. And it's not like it's going to happen by accident despite your boasting in the emergency room."

"You're right," Alex agreed and put Nukumi's gift in the bedroom closet.

"Why don't we play with your M&M dispenser instead?"

"Cool!" She leapt off the sofa and raced into the bedroom.

"You put it in the bedroom? Really?"

***

We let the conversation go for now, then we focused on what little time we had left together. For the next few days, we rarely left the bedroom. We made love continuously until it was time for me to drive Alex to Logan Airport. She waited until the last possible moment before leaving my side. She kissed me with such passion I thought my already unsteady legs would give out entirely. As she made her way to the gate, I noticed the shocked expressions on some people's faces, and I didn't care. I wanted the world to know that I loved this woman.

"Get over it," I snapped at one woman who seemed overly horrified.

Chapter Forty Three

Alex's absence proved to be painful and interesting. She called me the moment she landed, and we each expressed how we were already missing the other. As much as I missed her, there wasn't a doubt in my mind that not only would we survive this, but we would also become closer because of it. We spoke to each other two or three times a day, and thanks to modern technology, we also exchanged some rather intimate emails and texts.

The day before the start of the new semester, I was greeted with another surprise. One that I was quite unprepared for. I had been working on the finishing touches to the first draft of our manuscript when suddenly a loud crash from downstairs alarmed me. I raced out the door and down the staircase to my old apartment. Just inside the doorway, I found a petite redhead picking up the shattered remains of something as she cursed loudly. The new tenant had arrived with a bang.

"Need a hand?"

She looked up as her piercing green eyes stared back, and I gasped in recognition. It seemed that my life wasn't going to settle for dull.

"Caroline?"

"Stephanie?" she responded, equally surprised.

Caroline Jennings had been a classmate of mine at Yale, and apparently, she was the woman who would be subletting my apartment. At Yale, we were on somewhat friendly terms, until one night when I decided to pull one of my nights of drunken experimentation. The memory came flooding back to me. That night in her dorm room with our bodies wrapped together in passion as we kissed. Seeing her again was more than a little bit of a surprise. It had the potential of becoming a full-fledged disaster. If there was a God, Caroline would develop total amnesia and forget that night and how I ran away and never spoke to her again.

"This is a surprise," she echoed my thoughts. "You don't by any chance know where a gal could score a broom, do you?" Caroline asked, easing the tension between us.

"There's one in the closet over there." I released a sigh of relief. I rushed over to the tiny closet off of the kitchen and retrieved the broom and dustpan. "I'll get this while you unload your stuff. When I'm finished, I can give you a hand."

"Thanks," Caroline agreed and left me alone. I swept up the broken glass and deposited the remains into the trash. I replaced the broom and dustpan, then joined Caroline outside as she unloaded the U-Haul. We didn't really speak much as we unloaded her belongings. Although there wasn't any furniture, there was more than I had expected. I began to wonder how long Caroline planned on staying.

"Thank heavens this place is furnished," she said. "Although I'm always leery about sleeping in a strange bed."

"The futon is almost new," I sheepishly told her as I helped her unpack.

"You seem to know this place pretty well. I'm assuming that you live in the building. Either that or you just like to wander the streets looking for damsels in distress."

"I'm upstairs for now. This is, or was, my apartment. I bought the futon in September. You should be safe."

"Oh?" she said in a curious tone. "Wow, I'm finally sleeping in your bed?" She planted her hands on her hips. "And where is it that you're sleeping?"

"I'm taking care of Alex's, I mean Professor Kendell's, place while she's away." A faint blush crept across my cheeks.

"I see," she said slyly. "Tell me, is there any chance Professor Kendell will choose to stay in California?"

"No!" My answer was swift and harsh.

"Too bad." She sighed. "I was hoping to be picked up by Prower full time. Positions are becoming harder to find these days."

"I know," I said, slightly more relaxed. "I just joined the staff last semester."

"Ah, so you were the one who beat me out of the position."

"Sorry."

We engaged in more chitchat while we unpacked her boxes. I offered to follow her, so I could drive her back after she returned the van. After this was done, I drove her back to the house.

"I need to thank you for everything you've done," she said politely. "Let me take you to dinner, and we can catch up on everything. It has been a long time."

Her offer seemed innocent enough, and she seemed to lack any animosity toward me, so I agreed. It felt nice to be able to mend some fences from my past. We agreed on getting takeout from the Chinese restaurant. As we were sitting on the futon in what was now her apartment eating kung pao chicken, Caroline filled me in on what she had been up to since Yale. It seemed to me that Caroline moved around a great deal.

"How is Peter? That's his name, isn't it? I remember how he used to follow you around. I always wondered if you ended up with him simply because you couldn't shake him." Her odd statement caught me off-guard.

"At the moment, he hates me. We broke up a few months ago, and it didn't end very well."

"Really?" she cooed, her hand landing on my thigh. "After all this time? Then again, I didn't get why the two of you were together. So tell me what happened."

I wasn't really listening. I was far too busy staring at her hand. "Um, okay," I sputtered, brushing her hand aside.

"My mistake." She held up her hands. "You know how touchy-feely I can be."

And that in a nutshell was the problem with Caroline. The time we did hang around together at Yale, she was on me like white on rice. Doing the math in the here and now, I found it disturbing given the considerable age gap between the two of us.

"You were saying? About the breakup," she prompted when I turned mute.

"I came out."

"It's about time!" She applauded as she inched slightly closer to me. "You know I was very hurt by you."

"I'm sorry about that. I didn't understand myself back then."

"No kidding." She had the bad manners to laugh. "Does this mean that you're out and about?" she asked seductively as she leaned in closer and dipped her head slightly. Knowing what she was planning, I pulled away.

I was flabbergasted that she had tried to kiss me. Nothing that had transpired that afternoon was the least bit romantic in nature. Yet there she was scooting closer for another try.

"Uh, no thanks, I'm very involved," I quickly rebuffed her second attempt.

"I won't tell if you won't," Caroline teased as my eyes widened in disbelief. "Hey, I'm just kidding." She laughed slightly. "So tell me about her."

"Actually, my lover is Alex Kendell," I proudly told her, not missing the way she pursed her lips.

"But she's in California."

"Don't remind me." I groaned. "But even though she's out of town, we're fully committed to each other. I'm going to go out on a limb and guess that there isn't someone special in your life?"

"Good Lord, no." She laughed heartily.

"Okay then." I faked yawning. "It's getting late, and I have a Skype date tonight."

***

"What is that behind you? Is that sunshine?" I asked during the Skype session with Alex a couple of weeks later. "I couldn't help noticing the golden light streaming in from the window behind you."

"Is it still snowing there?"

"Yes." I groaned. "They canceled classes again. The weather has been so bad, we're way behind schedule. Not my online classes, but the others are going to run into June at this rate."

"That sucks." She pouted for me. "Are you in the bedroom?"

"Yes, what do you have in mind, my little pervert?"

"Sorry, we don't have time for that." She pouted again. "I was just curious as to why I don't see Wonder Woman."

"Oh, well, she decided she'd be happier upstairs in your office," I quipped with a shrug. "If you want, I'll bring her back down here. It is your bedroom, after all."

"No, she can stay upstairs, and as for whose bedroom it is, that's debatable," she said. "Hey, tell Maureen thank you for the pics she sent. Looks like you're going to be a real asset for the Relics."

I was thrilled that she was smiling. "I'm looking forward to when we can practice outside, not that the center isn't nice."

"I can't wait to see you play. Maureen is over the moon about how good you are." She grimaced when she looked at her watch.

"That time already?"

"Yeah," she whimpered, playing with the pendant I had given her for Christmas. "I miss you."

"I miss you, too." It was my turn to pout. "I love you."

"Love you more. Sorry, I have to go."

"Not all of us get snow days. Talk to you later."

"Count on it."

***

The moment we disconnected the call, I felt miserable. I never knew that I could miss someone as much as I missed her at that moment. Time seemed to pass slowly without Alex. Even though we spoke every day, there was still an inexplicable void. Watching Caroline settle into Alex's side of the office at the university made me uncomfortable.

But there was very little about Caroline that didn't make me uneasy. She hadn't changed much since our days at Yale. She was charming, I couldn't deny that. But just like in grad school, there was something shady brewing just below the surface.

It didn't take a rocket scientist to figure out that from day one, she had set her sights on Alex's job. I couldn't shake the feeling that the job wasn't the only thing of Alex's that she had set her sights on. The woman would not stop flirting with me, no matter how many times I pointed out that I was not interested. She'd just laugh it off, pretending that she was joking. Call me crazy, but I don't find rubbing up against a coworker every chance you get a joke.

Sadly, this was the same woman I knew in grad school. Sleeping with Caroline was something I would be eternally grateful I missed out on. Her flirtatious nature and underhanded approach to gaining long-term employment weren't the only things bothering me. On more than one occasion, I noticed her flirting with some of her female students.

It may be archaic, but Prower had strict rules against the faculty having personal relationships with the students. The rules had been in existence before the enactment of sexual harassment laws. The penalty for violating the rule ran both ways. In theory, this would protect a member of the faculty from false accusations. The only exceptions to the rule were if there had been a prior relationship. This clause existed so that spouses of faculty members could take classes if they wanted to. They were still unable to enroll in courses taught by their significant other.

For Caroline's sake, I hoped she wasn't pursuing things past the flirting stage. I wanted to give her the benefit of the doubt since as far as I knew, she had yet to cross the line. In the meantime, I buried myself in work and learning about softball.

I answered my cell, furrowing my brow when I saw who was calling. "I'm not practicing today."

"Oh, come on," Maureen whined. "My kids have another snow day. I thought if we took them to the batting cages, they'd burn off some of their excess energy."

"Your kids?" I couldn't stop laughing before I agreed.

***

Late on one Saturday afternoon, I had Alex on speaker phone, so we could work on some of the revisions our editor requested. We had been at it for hours, and I was thrilled that we had finally reached the end.

"That should do it," I said in exhaustion. "I'll email these out tonight."

"I miss you."

"I miss you, too," I said, finding myself pouting once again.

"What are you wearing?" she asked in a mischievous tone.

"Wouldn't you like to know?" I teased.

"Yes, yes, I would" came her frantic response. "I knew we should've Skyped."

"We get less work done when we can see each other," I pointed out. "Why don't you tell me how great the weather is out there again?"

"Yeah, yeah, it's seventy-two. Now what are you wearing?"

Just as I was about to spin a yarn about a fictional sexy outfit, there was a knock on the door. "Damn, there's someone at the door." I sighed.

"I'll let you go," Alex offered in a dejected tone.

"No," I whined in protest. "I want to finish this conversation. I'll get rid of whoever it is, then I'm going to go into great detail and describe to you what I'm wearing." I heard a very pleased murmur coming from the other end of the line. I opened the door and found Chris standing in the doorway with an annoyed look on her face.

"Well, nuts." I groaned deciding that Alex's ex-girlfriend was a definite mood killer.

"Hello to you, too." Chris snorted and entered the apartment without invitation.

"Who is it?" Alex asked, clearly annoyed.

"Avon lady," I teased as Chris laughed.

"So what are you doing with the Avon lady, or don't I want to know?"

"She was just about to show me her samples," I continued as Chris ignored me and made her way into the kitchen.

"Uh-huh?" Alex responded.

"Bring me a cup, too." I called out into the kitchen. "Alex?" I returned my attention back to her.

"I'm here, baby." Her sultry voice sent shivers down my spine. "Are you going to tell me who was at the door?"

"It's just Chris," I explained as Chris offered me a cup of coffee.

"Thanks a lot." Chris scoffed as she plopped down onto the sofa.

"What does she want?" Alex asked in a miffed tone of voice. "Never mind. Tell me about you. What are you wearing?" I could hear her breathing becoming ragged.

"I can't." I laughed uneasily.

"Sure you can... Alex encouraged me. "Go into the bedroom...and...."

"Alex." I told her there was no way I was going to do what I knew she was suggesting. "You're on speaker phone." I was blushing from head to toe.

"Which is why I suggested you step into the bedroom," she reasoned.

"Okay, that's enough." Chris blanched, motioning for the phone.

"Chris wants to talk to you."

"Rats," Alex grumbled as I muted the speaker.

I handed the telephone to Chris and sat on the sofa and sipped my coffee. It wasn't unusual for Chris to stop in. Lately, she had been driving up on the weekends to visit Rita. Sometimes, she'd stop in to check up on me. It was nice that the two of us were getting along. I knew there would always be a slight awkwardness in our relationship, but that was to be expected since I was with her ex-lover.

"Hey, Alex..." Chris chimed cheerfully into the receiver. "Did you get my email?...I know...no, I'll tell her...I don't know...me? I'm just checking out your girlfriend. She looks very hot today...such language! Did you learn that at Harvard? Seriously, how could you leave her behind? You know if I was any other kind of woman...oh, wait, I am that kind of woman...Whoa! You eat with that mouth?...Calm down, I'm in town to see Rita."

I listened as they chatted for a while longer, then Chris said her goodbyes and handed the phone back to me. "Hey," I said softly.

"Hey yourself. I'm afraid that I have to go." She apologized. "I love you."

"I love you, too." My heart skipped a beat as we exchanged our goodbyes.

"I had forgotten what a great phone voice she has." Chris sighed thoughtfully.

"You had to tease her." I poked her.

"I couldn't resist." Chris scoffed. "Don't worry, she trusts you, and she knows that I wouldn't try anything. Strange after all these years, she finally trusts me. If I was her, I'd be more concerned about that hot little number who moved in downstairs. This is going to sound strange, especially coming from me, but I don't trust her."

"Get in line. I think she's after Alex's job."

"Yeah, her job, that's what she's after," Chris offered knowingly. "I sent Alex an email this morning. A certain assistant district attorney in New York resigned his position unexpectedly yesterday."

"Simon Brenner?"

"He didn't have much of a choice," Chris confirmed. "It was either resign or be brought up on charges for prosecutorial misconduct. The really big news is that he also left his wife. Jessica called my office late last night screaming that I had ruined her marriage."

"You ruined her marriage?"

"I must have." Chris laughed slightly. "Lord knows it couldn't possibly have been all those women she slept with."

"Amazing. I thought I had some delusional self-rationalizations. Does this mean that Alex's legal troubles are over?"

"It does."

"Thank goodness."

"Rita and I were wondering if you had plans for next weekend," Chris asked suddenly.

"Not that I can think of," I said without thinking. My only immediate thought was how much I enjoyed Chris referring to Rita as if they were a couple. "Probably just the same old thing, why?"

"Would you like to join us for dinner Friday?"

"Sure." I shrugged, then it hit me. "Wait! Valentine's Day, no thank you. I have no desire to be a third wheel."

"No, you wouldn't be. We just thought that with Alex away and all..."

"No."

***

Chris tried in vain to get me to agree, but I stood firm. The following morning, Rita called me. Rita proved to be far more stubborn than Chris. After an hourlong debate, I finally caved in and agreed to join the pair for dinner on Friday. Not feeling good about caving, I decided I needed some fresh air and went to check on Mrs. Giovanni.

I started down the staircase, halting when I spotted Cheryl Cooper leaving Caroline's apartment. When Cheryl caught my eye, she blushed furiously and ran off. I looked at my watch, thinking that this was not a good sign. Cheryl was a history major, and she was leaving Caroline's apartment at nine o'clock on a Sunday morning. I needed to have a little chat with Caroline very soon. When I stepped out onto the porch, I found Hal standing there holding the Sunday paper and looking grim. It was more than a little obvious that he too had seen Cheryl.

"This is not good, Stephanie."

"It doesn't look that way," I said shyly. "I'll have a talk with Caroline."

"You need to report her to your department head." Hal was adamant.

"I don't know anything for certain," I lied, knowing there could be no other explanation for the morning's events.

"It's not the first time I've seen one of her students sneaking out first thing in the morning," Hal explained. "It's against university policy. I haven't said anything yet, but this does put both of us in a very awkward position."

"Let me talk to Caroline. Maybe there's a reasonable explanation."

"Fine," he conceded. "But if there isn't and you don't turn her in, I'll have to. These are kids we're talking about. The powers that be at Prower want them to focus on their education. For no other reason than that, I agree with the policy. I just never thought I would have to turn someone in. I've never thought of myself as some kind of stoolie."

"I know," I agreed with a heavy sigh.

I checked on Mrs. Giovanni and found her trying to shovel her driveway. I immediately took the shovel from her. I couldn't understand why she needed to clear the driveway since she didn't drive. I shoveled her driveway and walkways, then I ran a few errands for her. After that, I joined her for a cup of tea and filled her in on how Alex was doing. After two cups of tea, I returned home. I stopped and knocked on Caroline's door and braced myself.

"I was just thinking about you," she cooed. "Come in."

"I need to talk to you."

"Really?" She smiled slightly. "I'm intrigued."

"I saw Cheryl Cooper leaving your apartment this morning."

"And?" she responded coyly.

"You do know about the university's policy, don't you?"

"Cheryl is an adult," Caroline said in a dismissive manner.

"The university doesn't allow any leeway in these matters."

"Relax," Caroline said with a wave of her hand. "Nothing happened. The poor kid just needed someone to talk to. You remember what it was like, being that young and confused."

"All right," I said, not completely believing her. "But if this happens again, I'll have to go to Maureen. I'm sorry. In the university's eyes, if there is something going on and I don't report it, I could lose my job."

"Don't sweat it." Caroline shrugged. "Nothing happened, and Maureen let me know in painstaking detail of all the dos and don'ts at Prower. Now sit down and relax. I was just going to watch some television and have a glass of wine. Why don't you join me? A hell of a dull way to spend the weekend, I know, but other than you, I don't really know anyone here."

"No thanks, I have things to do."

She pretended not to hear me and opened a bottle of wine and turned on the television. I stood there for moment with my mouth hanging open. "Um, it is still morning." I couldn't help sputtering. Granted I had an early start to the day but it was just past ten.

"And?"

"Okay, then enjoy your breakfast."

"Stephanie?" Caroline's pleading voice halted my retreat. "Do you ever think about that night?"

"Yes," I said honestly. "I feel terrible about the way I treated you. The worst part is that it wasn't the first time I did something like that.

"I think about that night." She sighed regrettably before taking a sip of wine. "I was crazy about you. I think that when I invited you over that night, somewhere in the back of my mind, I knew I was going to try to seduce you."

My mind once again drifted back to that night. The talk and the wine and the kiss that had driven me insane. Before I knew what was happening, I was kissing her back, and she was pushing me down onto her bed. As we lay on her bed, our bodies became entangled. Her hand had slid up my sweater, and she caressed my breast. It was the sudden jolt of pleasure that had snapped me into reality. I jumped off her bed, made some feeble excuse, and ran out of her dorm room. I had wanted her so much then, and I was too frightened to act on my impulses.

"You must have hated me," I said, shaking the old memory off.

"I was hurt more than anything." She moved closer to me. "I blamed myself."

"No, it was me. I wanted you, but I was a coward."

"And now?" she asked in a sultry voice, closing the gap between us. She reached out and caressed my arm.

"Now I'm in love with someone else," I spat out, jerking away from her.

"She's not here," Caroline pointed out in a husky tone as she grabbed me and pressed her lips forcibly to my own. Without hesitation, I pushed her away from me, knowing that whatever passions I had once felt for her were long since dead.

"What is wrong with you?" I yelled, pushing her away from me. "Just so we're clear, I'm in love with my girlfriend!" I spun on my heels to leave.

"So you're just going to walk out on me for a second time?" she sneered bitterly.

Her words stopped me cold as I spun around seething with anger. "Do you honestly think that you're going to guilt me into bed?" I spat out. "Even if I was single, I wouldn't touch you with a ten-foot pole." Having said this, I stormed out of her apartment.

Chapter Forty Four

The following week passed slowly as Caroline and I kept a chilly distance from each other, which was fine by me. I did speak to Hal and relayed the conversation I had with Caroline concerning Cheryl Cooper. We both agreed to let it go for the moment. I could tell by his demeanor that he didn't believe her story any more than I did. We hoped that Caroline's common sense would kick in.

On Friday, I returned home very tired and completely agitated. I wasn't looking forward to dinner. If it had been any other night, I would have been thrilled.

The thing that really frosted my cookies was that I had sent Alex a dozen roses and had yet to receive a phone call from her. I didn't even get an email, text, or voice mail. Nada, nothing, zippo! It was very strange, indeed, especially since I tried getting in touch with her, and she was nowhere to be found.

As I entered the apartment and set down my briefcase, an uneasy feeling crept over me. Something was wrong. I knew in an instant that I was not alone in the apartment. I reached for the softball bat I had left by the door after Maureen and I had gone to the batting cages to practice the day before. I gripped the bat tightly as I scanned the apartment. My breathing hitched when I heard a sound coming from the bedroom. I entered the bedroom, and my heart sped up when I heard the water running in the shower.

I stood there thinking I should call the police while wondering what kind of thief stops to take a shower. I stepped carefully into the bathroom and yanked open the shower door. I was greeted by a loud screech. I dropped the bat the moment I saw her in all her glory.

"Stephanie!" Alex gasped. "You scared the life out of me."

"I scared you?" I laughed as my gaze wandered freely over her naked form. I removed my coat quickly and dropped it onto the floor and slipped out of my shoes. Fully dressed, I stepped into the shower and wrapped my arms around her.

"I missed you," she murmured into my ear.

"Kiss me," I demanded breathlessly.

Alex obeyed without hesitation as her lips soon found my own. Her hands struggled to unbutton my blouse. I halted her movements and reached down and tore open my blouse, the buttons scattering across the shower floor. We both engaged in a struggle to remove my clothing as the warm water drenched our bodies. The water soaked my clothing, making it difficult to remove, as it clung tightly against my form. Yet somehow we managed to release me from my clothing. Throughout the struggle, our lips continually sought out each other. Finally free of my clothing, I stood naked before Alex. My eyes glazed over as I watched her tall lean body sink to its knees as her hands caressed me.

I allowed the water to embrace me as Alex kissed my thighs. I opened my legs to her, eager for her touch. "If this is a dream, please don't let me wake up!" With the first flick of her tongue, I knew this was no dream. I braced my hands against the wall of the shower and further opened myself to her. With passion-filled eyes, she looked up at me as she parted my lips. I trembled as she teased me.

"Damn!" she sputtered as she suddenly ceased her movements.

"What is it?" I gasped.

"Water up my nose," she stuttered in dismay.

"Get up here before you drown." I laughed as I pulled her up to me, shutting off the water before wrapping my arms around her.

"Making love in the shower always seems like a good idea." She coughed as we stepped out of the shower.

"I don't know, sometimes it works," I said as we grabbed some towels and dried off. "If you recall, we put a dent in your parents' water bill."

"Oh, yeah." She moaned softly.

"I can't believe you're here."

"I was going to surprise you at the office, but after seven hours on a plane, I felt all grungy."

"Finding you naked in the shower was a lot more fun."

"I hope I'm not interrupting any plans that you might have made," Alex added with a sudden shyness. "I just couldn't hold out for another nine weeks."

"Let me make a quick phone call, then I'm all yours."

"Oh?" Alex said with a slight frown.

"I did have a date with two women tonight," I teased her as I wrapped myself in a towel and made my way into the bedroom as Alex followed closely behind me.

"You've been a busy girl. Here I thought you might be lonely without me."

"Oh, you have no idea." I sighed before I explained how Chris and Rita took pity on me, then bullied me into joining them for dinner. I grabbed my phone and dialed Rita's shop.

"Rita, it's Stephanie."

"Hey, what's up? You're not going to back out, are you?"

"Afraid so," I answered brightly.

"Now, Stephanie…" she began to protest.

"Sorry. No offense, but I just got a better offer," I said as Alex nibbled my shoulder.

"I see," Rita said suspiciously as I moaned in response to Alex's attention.

"Oh, yeah." I groaned. "You wouldn't believe what I found in the shower when I got home."

"Do tell," Rita encouraged me.

"I'll give you a hint. She's tall, has amazing eyes, and you once saw her streaking down a hallway." I lost my train of thought as Alex's lips moved to my neck. "And, um, I have to go." I moaned. I could her Rita laughing at me as I hung up. "Don't stop."

"Let's drive down to Provincetown," Alex purred into my ear.

"Now?" I gasped as the heat of her touch sent a jolt through my body.

"I'll make you dinner," Alex encouraged. "We can sit by the fire or sip champagne in the hot tub."

"Hmm." I moaned as the image of Alex in a hot tub floated through my thoughts.

"Is that a 'yes'?" she taunted me as my body went cold from her departing touch.

"What do I need to pack?" I asked as I finally cleared my head.

"Personally, I like what you're wearing at the moment." She purred as she tugged on the towel I had wrapped myself in. "But then again, it is very cold outside."

We dressed quickly and tossed some clothing in an overnight bag. We hurried down the staircase, and as luck would have it, we ran into Caroline. Actually, I ran into Caroline, almost knocking her to the ground.

"Sorry," I said quickly.

"My pleasure," Caroline purred as she steadied herself, touching my backside in the process. I pulled away in disgust. "Where are you running off to in such a hurry?" she asked in a husky tone. "I was hoping that perhaps we could..." She stopped suddenly, finally noticing Alex behind me. Of course, she would have noticed sooner if her gaze hadn't been firmly staring at my cleavage. "Oh...I see you have other plans." She sneered as Alex took her place by my side.

"Alex Kendell," Alex introduced herself as she placed her arm around my waist in a possessive manner.

"Caroline Jennings, I'm your replacement."

Only in your dreams, I thought coldly. Much to my relief, Alex chuckled at Caroline's statement.

"Sweetheart, we should get going if we want to beat the traffic," I said quickly, knowing that Caroline was about to dig her heels in. Caroline was no match for Alex, and I didn't want to waste any time watching her try to start some kind of pissing contest. I had more important matters to attend to. Alex placed her Ray-Bans on her face and led me out to the car. Caroline was fuming as we made our departure.

"She seems interesting," Alex teased as she pulled the car out of the driveway.

"She's a pill," I responded in distaste. "I think she's after your job."

"That's not all she's after, is it, sweetheart?"

"Yeah, about that."

"It's okay."

"Thank you," I said, happy that she wasn't going to freak out. "So you're not bothered by her."

"Of course I am. I'm jealous as all hell. But if you and I don't trust each other, then we're right back where we started. I don't know about you, but I wouldn't want to live through that again."

"Amen to that." I squeezed her hand gently.

We drove in silence for a few moments. "I love you, Alex," I said as I squeezed her hand once again. "There's something I need to tell you."

I looked over at her and watched her body tense slightly. I needed to tell her about my past with Caroline. Based on the fiasco that happened with Peter, I had more than learned my lesson. I told her everything about what had happened in college to Caroline's present-day advances. When I had finished, she thanked me for being honest and kissed my hand.

"Are you all right?" I asked, slightly fearful of her response.

"Yes," she said sweetly. "The world is filled with people like her. You're a beautiful woman. There are going to be a lot of women and men alike who are going to try to seduce you. I love you, and I know you love me. That's all that matters. That's not to say I won't get upset at times."

"I spent my entire life looking for you," I said honestly. "Until there was you, I don't think that I was really alive."

"You're going to make me cry," Alex said softly.

***

We drove on, enjoying each other's company. It was getting late, so we decided on a quick dinner from McDonald's instead of Alex cooking. She apologized repeatedly as we drove toward Provincetown. I didn't care about the food; we were together, and that was the only thing that really mattered to me. It was late when we finally arrived in P-town. I was thankful for the Subaru's all-wheel drive as we maneuvered our way through the narrow snow-covered streets. Alex's summer place was small but quaint. She unlocked the gate to the driveway, and I pulled the car in.

The windows were covered with dark shutters. Alex explained that they were heavy storm shutters that would protect the glass from any unforeseen weather conditions, and we could open them with a switch from the inside. I couldn't help thinking just how much I wanted to see the house in the summer.

We rushed into the house from the cold and began turning on the lights. Alex opened a few of the shutters so we could enjoy the view. The view of the ocean was breathtaking. Alex built a fire, and as I warmed myself by the fire, she went outside to the deck and started up the hot tub. She needed to uncover it, heat the water, then test it to ensure that it was safe to use. I looked around the house with curiosity. It was one floor with a bedroom at the back and a smaller one in the front of the structure. The living room and kitchen meshed together with a deck leading off of the kitchen. It was perfect. The only thing that troubled me was that I knew I was not the first woman Alex had brought here.

Alex shivered as she re-entered the house. She absently rubbed her hands together and scanned the contents of her wine rack.

"Crap, Chris has been here," Alex grumbled as she pulled a bottle of champagne out and set up an ice bucket and placed the bottle in so it could chill. "I wish if she was going to sneak down here, she would at least replace the wine she uses," Alex complained. "Stephanie? What's wrong, honey?"

"It's silly," I mumbled. "Chris has been here." I gave an embarrassed shrug. "I guess I never stopped to think about it before. That you made love to her in the bed that we share."

"No, I didn't," Alex reassured me. "The bed I have now is something I bought when I moved to Prowers Landing. It was all part of my new life. You're the only woman I've shared it with. As for this place, that's a different story. If it bothers you, we can get a hotel room," she offered sympathetically.

"No." I sighed with relief as I relaxed slightly. "It bothers me a little, but knowing that you would rather try to find a hotel room in the middle of the night than make me uncomfortable gives me all the reassurance I need."

"I'll tell you what, how about in the spring we redecorate this place from top to bottom?"

"Deal," I agreed eagerly. "Could you get the key back from Chris?"

"How about we just change the locks and the alarm code?" she suggested as she crossed over to me.

"Even better. Now where is that hot tub you promised me?"

"I'm afraid it won't be warm for a while yet."

"What are we going to do in the meantime?" I teased her as I began to remove my clothing, dropping each article on the floor. Alex smiled back at me as she started to remove her clothing, as well. We stood there naked bathed in firelight, and for a brief moment, we simply stared into each other's eyes. She wet her lips in anticipation, beckoning me to come closer.

I ran my fingers delicately over her skin, leaving a trail of goose bumps behind. I reached down and took her by the hand and led her into the bedroom. We made love slowly as our cries of passion matched the howling of the night wind. Later, we found ourselves lounging in the hot tub as we sipped champagne.

***

"I can't believe that you flew all the way across the country just to see me." I sighed with contentment as I pressed my body against her naked form.

"I had to see you." She wrapped her arms tightly around my waist.

I leaned in and kissed her neck with desire. My hands roamed freely, and she guided me to float in the water. The thrill of the bubbling water and the freedom of floating added to my excitement. I pressed my center against her firm abdomen and continued my explorations. I could feel her hands cup my backside, pressing me harder into her.

Making love this way was a new experience for me. The night air was cold against my skin, mixing with the warmth of the water and the heat from Alex's body. I could feel Alex's hand pressing between our bodies as she cupped my mound and stroked me gently. My body arched in response as she entered me. My head tossed back, I looked up into the night sky filled with stars as Alex's touch grew more insistent. I became lost in a dream world as she entered me. The night sky seemed to explode as I released myself for Alex.

Several explosions later, we decided it was time to go inside. I raced into the house as Alex shut down the hot tub and covered it for the night. The night air was far too cold for me to endure as I ran directly into the bedroom and climbed under the covers.

Even though I was still shivering from the cold, I had never felt so relaxed in my life. The combination of champagne and the soothing water from the hot tub blended with the passion of our lovemaking had relaxed every muscle in my body. I shivered violently as Alex drew back the covers and joined me in bed. Wrapping me in her arms, she warmed me quickly. My breathing slowed as I drifted off to sleep in her warm embrace.

***

I awoke the next morning still wrapped in Alex's arms as she slept peacefully. I unwrapped myself and let her continue to sleep as I went into the kitchen. The cupboards were most definitely bare. I stepped back into in the bedroom to find Alex still fast asleep. I relit the fire, then proceeded to shower and dress warmly. Then I walked outside and made my way in the direction that I hoped would lead me into town. As I explored the seaside village, I was captivated. Most everything had been boarded up for the winter, but there were still many shops open for the townies. I found a bakery and bought coffee and several Danish pastries.

Upon my return, I found Alex still fast asleep. I wanted to wait for her to awaken, but my hunger won out since I was completely famished from the previous evening's activities. After I ate several Danish pastries and drank my coffee, I gathered up the clothing that we had left lying around the living room. Then I curled up onto the sofa by the fire with some work from school.

A few hours later, Alex finally emerged from the bedroom. She could not look more adorable if she tried. Her hair was a complete mess, and she had thrown on a tattered pair of sweats and a baby doll T-shirt that said *Fight like a Girl*.

"Sorry I slept so late." She yawned as she stretched. "My body is still on West Coast time."

"S'okay." I smiled brightly as she ran her fingers through her long dark hair. "I'm sorry I fell asleep on you," I apologized. "I couldn't help it after…" My voice trailed off as I blushed, unable to complete my words.

"I know." She winked back at me.

We spent the rest of the weekend blissfully walking around town. The cold New England weather often proved to be overwhelming for us. We decided to only go out when we needed to eat. When we weren't hopping into bed or the hot tub, we spent the rest of our time together cuddling by the fire, where we shared our thoughts, dreams, and our bodies. I realized that the time we had been apart had actually brought us closer together.

I loved seeing her, but the endless hours chatting on the phone, video chatting, and texting had enabled us to get to know each other. I was still dreading her leaving again. On Sunday morning, we packed up, locked up the house, and drove back to Prowers Landing.

Sadly, Alex had a flight back that evening.

***

We rushed out of car and raced toward the house, eager to spend what little time we had left in bed. As we approached the front porch, I was startled to see Cheryl Cooper exiting the house. I just shook my head in disbelief and waved off Alex's inquiring look. As we entered the foyer, we were greeted by Hal.

"Hello, Alex." Hal greeted her with surprise. "When did you get back?"

"I'm just in for the weekend."

"That's nice," Hal muttered as he shifted uncomfortably. "Look, I know the two of you probably would like to be alone right about now, but I really need to talk to Stephanie."

I nodded in agreement and understanding. The three of us went upstairs with a slight reluctance. Alex excused herself and went into the kitchen to make a pot of coffee. Hal sat silently for a moment, then he let out a heavy sigh and began to recount the details of the weekend. It would appear there had been a steady stream of female students coming and going from Caroline's apartment, most of whom were clueless to the other's existence. When some of them discovered that they were not as special as Caroline had led them to believe, it resulted in more than one altercation. It was apparent that Caroline had gone way beyond simply breaking the rules. This woman was some kind of predator. Hal explained that he could no longer remain silent. I told him not to worry I would go to Maureen first thing in the morning. Hal seemed relieved that he would not have to be the one to blow the whistle.

After Hal's departure, Alex turned to me. "She's sleeping with her students?" she asked in astonishment. "That will get you a ticket out of town very quickly."

"I warned her."

"Nobody wants to be a squealer," Alex tried to tease me as I turned sullen. "Look, I honestly don't know if I agree with the policy or not, but it's there, and everyone knows about it. It doesn't matter if you've been here a month or a decade, you touch a student, and you're out."

"You don't agree with the policy?" I was curious.

"We're talking about consenting adults," Alex tried to explain.

"Have you ever been interested in one of your students?"

"No."

"Why not?"

"Because they're...kids," Alex admitted, seeming to understand the policy a little better. "Point taken."

"Professor Kendell," I said firmly as I stood and took her by the hand. "Do you really want to debate this issue now?"

"No, Dr. Grant, I do not," she responded in a deep tone as she led me into the bedroom.

Chapter Forty Five

The following morning, I paced outside of Maureen's office. Finally, I summoned up the courage and knocked on the door. "Come in!" Maureen bellowed from inside.

"Great, she's already in a bad mood, and I'm about to make it worse," I mumbled as I entered her office. She was on the phone. She waved to me, and I closed the door behind me.

"So there's no way you can return?" she pleaded in a frazzled tone. "I understand…talk to you soon." She hung up and slumped in her chair as she groaned in disgust. "I was in such a good mood this morning." Maureen grimaced. "My kids actually made it out the door on time. That should have been my first clue that this day would wind up being a complete disaster."

"I'm afraid I'm about to make it worse," I said carefully.

"You're not running off to California, as well?" she joked.

"No." I swallowed hard, not certain how to tell her about Caroline. "It's about Caroline Jennings."

"I already know," Maureen said in a serious tone. "This morning, three of her students came forward and admitted to having an affair with her."

"Oh?"

"What an idiot." Maureen groaned as she looked up at me. "I was just on the telephone with your girlfriend. I begged her to come back. Seeing you here, I now know why she wasn't surprised to hear from me."

"What happens now?" I asked.

"The students are on probation," Maureen explained grimly. "It could have been worse for them. They could have been dismissed."

"And Caroline?" I asked with trepidation.

"I have to fire her," Maureen stated adamantly. "I can't believe

452

she did this. We almost hired her for the position we gave to you. One of the things that prevented that was that I had heard rumors that she had a history of seducing her students. When she came in to fill in for Alex, I explained to her that there was no gray area in this matter." Maureen's telephone rang, and she answered it promptly. "Thank you, Louisa…send her to my office." Maureen concluded the brief conversation with a hint of remorse. "I hate doing this," she said after she hung up and began to massage her temple.

I left without saying a word, eager to make my exit before Caroline arrived. Sadly, I wasn't fast enough.

"Good morning, Stephanie," Caroline beamed.

"Hi," I muttered, unable to look her in the eye as I brushed past her, making a hasty retreat to my office. I gathered my belongings, having no desire to be present when Caroline returned. Louisa entered and handed me a new assignment sheet. Maureen had already divided up Caroline's classes amongst the faculty. I knew all too well that was not going to sit well with the rest of the faculty.

I thanked Louisa and tried to get moving before all hell broke loose. If only I had moved just a little quicker. Caroline stormed out of Maureen's office and made a beeline straight toward me.

"You couldn't resist, could you?" Caroline snarled bitterly. I looked at her and felt nothing but pity for her. "You just could not keep your mouth shut!" This time, Caroline was actually shouting at me.

"I didn't turn you in," I said calmly. "Granted, I was going to, but someone else beat me to it. Three students, Caroline. I'm willing to wager that they only came forward because they failed to make the short list this weekend. A woman scorned times three. What in the hell were you thinking?"

"Kids!" She snarled.

"That's right, they're kids, and you used them."

"Bitch!" she screamed in response. "It's so easy for you, isn't it? I guess when your girlfriend's last name is Kendell…"

"Don't," I warned her furiously.

"Whatever." She grunted and pushed past me. I took the opportunity to get the hell out there.

***

When I returned home late that evening after a very heated staff meeting, I was exhausted. Many of Caroline's classes were dumped on me. It made sense. I was most definitely low man on the totem pole when it came to seniority. I spent the remainder of the day teaching my classes and trying to sort out Caroline's. After reviewing her lesson plans, grades, and syllabus, I came to the conclusion that I would need to start from scratch. Her lesson plans made no sense, and the grades contained far too many discrepancies. The students would freak, but it was the only fair way to do this.

My body was aching, and all I wanted was to soak in a very warm bath. My phone vibrated, alerting me that I had a message. I smiled when I saw that it was from Alex. I dropped my briefcase, not caring that the door was still open. I just stood there reading the message.

It was typical Alex explaining that she had talked to Maureen and hoped that I was okay. She also told me to drop everything and take a long hot soak. She loved me, and she would call in the morning. I smiled and sent her a voice text, thanking her and telling her that I loved her.

"How sweet," a voice slurred from behind me, and my body tensed. I turned to discover Caroline standing, or at least trying to stand, in the doorway. The woman was more than a little drunk.

"Great, this day just keeps getting better and better!"

"Tell me something, Steffi pooh," she slurred. "What is it about this Alex bitch that is so damn fascinating?"

"Get out!" I demanded.

"No." She snarled. "Not until you tell me about your girlie." She weaved as she stepped into the apartment.

"Get out."

"What is it, hmm?" She made her way over to me and attempted to stare me down. "She's not that good-looking. Is it the money?"

"I said get out," I repeated loudly as I stood up to her.

"Tell me, Steffi pooh," Caroline continued, ignoring my request. "What's the great Alex have that I don't?" Then she reached up and tore open her blouse and began to cup her own breast.

"It's probably because she's so amazing in bed," a firm voice said from the still open doorway. I looked past Caroline to find Chris standing there very confidently.

"What the…" Caroline sputtered as she turned toward Chris. "Who da hell are you…say, you're kind of cute." She stumbled toward Chris and reached over to touch her. Chris just pushed her hands away as she rolled her eyes in disgust. The entire display was pathetic.

"I think you should leave," Chris said firmly.

"Why?" Caroline slurred in a cocky manner.

"Because the lady asked you to," Chris asserted as she straightened out her body to its full intimidating height and stared down at Caroline. Chris's imposing stature eclipsed Caroline. She looked up at Chris and muttered something incoherent and stumbled out of the apartment.

"Charming." Chris sneered as she carefully watched Caroline make her departure.

"Thank you." I sighed with relief as I rushed over and slammed the door closed and locked it. "She was beginning to make me nervous."

"What's her problem anyway?" Chris asked. "I mean, other than the gin or whatever that was she took a bath in."

"She got fired today."

"I know," Chris said. "That's why I'm here. Alex rang me up and asked me to let her know that there would no problem in releasing her from her lease."

"You flew up here just for that?"

"No," Chris said with a slight uneasiness. "As of this weekend, I'm living in Boston."

"Oh?"

"Well, it's not official yet," Chris hedged. "I gave my notice at the firm. I was going to tell you Friday, but since you had a better offer…"

"That I did. So what inspired your desire to relocate?"

"After all these years at Wainwright and Griggs and all the hard work I put in, not to mention saving their butts from Simon Brenner, I was certain that I was well on my way to becoming a partner. It was made painfully clear to me that I was not. So I walked."

"I'm sorry."

"I'm not," she said with conviction. "Unlike my ex-girlfriend, I like the law and I love being a lawyer. It's time for me to become the type of lawyer I always wanted to be. I still need to pass the bar here, but I like Boston, and I think I might try my hand at private practice. For now, I'm staying with Rita. Is any of this going to be a problem for you? I like you, Stephanie, and I wouldn't want you to feel uncomfortable."

"I'm fine with it," I said warmly. "I like you, too. Granted, at times, things can be a little awkward. But so long as you don't poison my girlfriend again, I think things will be fine."

"I'll try not to." Chris smiled in return. "Tell me about little Miss Muffet from downstairs. Why is she mad at you?"

"She blames me for her losing her job. She also hates me because I won't sleep with her."

"I don't get it." Chris shook her head in confusion. "There's a long list of women who have shot me down, but not once did I ever show up at their apartment drunk off my ass."

"I find it hard to believe that someone has turned you down."

"It happens. I'm not Madonna." Chris chuckled. "Why was she fired?"

"Sleeping with her students."

"They can't fire her for that," Chris said as I watched her legal mind going to work.

"It was in her contract, and she had been warned when they hired her that it was against university policy."

"The contract is one thing." Chris shrugged. "If they went out of their way to give her a special warning, I'm going to assume she has a history with this sort of thing," Chris went on, lost in thought.

"I think so," I said. "You don't think she could fight this, do you?"

"She could," she said. "If she has done this before, then she probably knows just how to handle it. If she's smart, she knows that the university would do anything to avoid a public scandal. They'll settle and she'll walk away with a big check and no stains on her record. The only thing she needs to worry about are a few rumors and innuendo."

It was too incredible to believe, but it made sense. Caroline had been bouncing from one college to the next. No doubt adding notches to her bedpost along the way and cashing in on it, as well.

Chris was probably right. Caroline had pulled this before. I managed to convince Chris to crash on the sofa for the night instead of driving all the way back to town, only to drive back in the morning.

***

The following morning, I made coffee while Chris took a shower. Alex called to see how I was doing, and I retold her the events of the previous evening, including Chris's suspicions. Alex agreed with Chris that Caroline was probably using her lesbian affairs with students as a way to cash in. Chris walked out into the living room just as the conversation was beginning to get interesting. She rolled her eyes and trotted off into the kitchen to fetch some coffee while I ducked into the bedroom and finished my conversation with Alex.

After Chris left, I took a much-needed cold shower. When I was leaving the apartment, I could hear screaming coming from down below.

"Who in the hell do you think you are?" Caroline screamed as she stood in the foyer dressed only in a bathrobe.

"As I have already explained, I represent your landlord," Chris said dryly.

"Alex Kendell is not my landlord," Caroline screeched indignantly.

"Technically, she is," Chris pointed out in a rather bored tone.

"Well, you can tell her that I'm not going anywhere," Caroline snapped back in a cocky manner.

"That's fine," Chris said in the same monotone voice she had maintained throughout the conversation. "No one is telling you to leave. You can stay as long as you pay your rent. I'm only here to inform you that you're free to go. Given the circumstances, you won't need to worry about your lease."

"I'm staying," Caroline spat back. "I'll need to stay here since my lawyer is filing a lawsuit against the university."

"Really?" Chris smirked in a cocky manner.

"That's right, lawyer girl." Caroline snarled as she planted her hands firmly on her hips. "I don't know what kind of law they practice in whatever podunk town you're from, but here in the big city, things are different."

I cringed and waited for Chris to rip Caroline a new orifice.

Surprisingly enough, it never happened. "Do tell?" Chris baited her.

"I'm suing for wrongful termination and sexual harassment," Caroline said proudly.

"Are you insane?" I finally said, having grown weary from watching this display.

"I have a strong case," Caroline quipped in my direction. "I'm also planning to sue Alex Kendell, as well, since she's the catalyst behind all of this."

"I see." Chris nodded thoughtfully. "Except you don't have a leg to stand on."

"Yeah, right." Caroline sneered in distaste.

"Well, for starters, Alex Kendell is on the other side of the country," Chris pointed out. "You were dismissed from your position because you violated your contract."

"Prove it." Caroline snarled, all full of herself.

"The students came forward," I pointed out.

"Students?" Chris cooed pleasantly. "As in more than one?"

"Three," I said.

"They'll never testify," Caroline gloated. "Those girls would be far too embarrassed if their families found out."

"I don't know. Out of three of them, one might be just angry enough with you to do that," Chris noted. "As for sexual harassment, what is your basis for that claim?"

"Dr. Grant was constantly making sexual overtures at me, and when I refused her advances, she used her influence with Alex Kendell to have me fired," Caroline said in a hurt tone.

My jaw dropped as I realized this woman was using me to get to Alex's mythical fortune. Chris laughed in her face. "Miss Jennings, you're not filing any lawsuit," Chris said very calmly.

"And why not?" Caroline snarled, refusing to back down.

"First off, that podunk town I'm from is New York City. Perhaps you've heard of it?" Chris stressed. "I'm with one of the top firms in the country, and I'm very good at what I do. For starters, all I need are the statements those three students already made. Then I'll look into your past. I'm sure out there somewhere is an old colleague who would love to expose you for the lying bitch that you are. After that, it shouldn't be too difficult to prove the only mistake the university made was to hire you in the first place. Now as for Dr. Grant, I would personally love to testify about how I found you in her apartment tearing your clothes off in a drunken stupor while she was yelling at you to leave."

"You won't do that," Caroline cooed in a confident manner. "If you do, then I'll be forced to call Professor Kendell and tell her that you spent the night."

"And?" Chris asked in confusion. "She knows that, and she also knows that I slept on the couch."

"What?" Caroline sputtered in a shaky voice, knowing that her bluff had been finally called.

"I know it's hard to believe that not everyone is a big skank like you. Women like you give the rest of us a bad name," Chris said bitterly. "Now as I was saying, you are not being asked to leave this residence, but you are free to go."

Caroline stomped off in a huff and slammed her apartment door. Chris turned to me, shaking her head. "That woman makes me look like a virgin."

***

Chris had made her point, and Caroline Jennings was gone for good. By the time I returned home from work that evening, she had packed and disappeared. None of us heard from her again. I had to ask myself how it was that at one time I had found that woman attractive. Granted, it was a long time ago, but that kind of warped personality just doesn't pop up overnight. I also had to ask myself if her recent advances were so she could gain some kind of leverage for herself. Was I a ticket into Prowers Landing or to Alex? Perhaps I was just another conquest.

As the weeks passed, I forgot about Caroline. It was spring, and that meant that Alex would be home soon. It also marked the start of the softball season. I was pitching and doing fairly well, so Maureen was thrilled. I didn't understand why she was so happy since we were ranked number nine out of fifteen teams. Stan explained to me that we had never finished above last place.

On an unusually hot day in April, I was standing on the mound. We had won our last three games, and now it was the top of the ninth, and we were tied at five-all. If we could pull this win off, the team would move up in the rankings. Maureen had been ready to explode throughout the entire game. I struck out the first batter, and I had one ball and two strikes against the second batter. I took my stance and was just about to release the ball when I spotted a familiar face peeking out from behind the backstop. I released the ball, which sailed off nowhere near the plate.

I tried to calm myself as I watched her make her way over to the bleachers. I took a deep breath and tried to focus. My next pitch fared better but not good enough.

"Ball three," the umpire called out.

"Okay, this is not the end of the world," I tried to calm myself. "So it's a full count with the score tied in the last inning, no problem! Just don't look at her, and you'll be fine."

I heard Maureen call for time as she ran over to me from first base. "Stephanie?" Her voice squeaked. "Are you all right?" I shook my head. "Damn, I knew I shouldn't have let you pitch all nine innings," she chastised herself.

"It's not that." I whimpered as I stared at my feet. "Look over at the bleachers."

"Why?"

"Look who just showed up." I smiled as I pointed over to Alex. "My God, she looks good."

"Oh, she came home early." Maureen sighed, then snapped back into her coach mode. "No time for that. Just don't look over there."

"I can't help it." I pouted. "It has been a long time."

"Let me put it to you this way," Maureen spoke carefully. "Two more outs, and you are that much closer to taking her home."

"Get your ass back on first base."

Maureen ran back to first, and I threw out my next pitch. A swing and a miss. The next batter went down in flames. Three pitches and three strikes. What can I say? I was suddenly motivated. Maureen ran over and hugged me. I shook her off and started to head toward the bleachers when Maureen grabbed me.

"Not so fast, hot stuff." She tugged my shirt. "You're up. Remember?" Reluctantly, I tossed my glove in our dugout and grabbed my bat. Once the warmup was completed, I turned to Maureen.

"We're not going into extra innings," I spat out as she laughed. I stomped over to home plate like a woman on a mission.

The first pitch was perfect. I knew the moment the bat made contact with the ball that my prediction had been accurate. I flung my bat to the ground and rounded the bases with ease. Once I crossed over home plate, my teammates surrounded me. I knew they were happy, but I had other things on my mind as I tried to pull myself away from the celebration.

I looked for Alex in the crowd until I found her carefully putting my gear together in the dugout. She stepped out onto the field with my equipment bags tossed over her shoulder. I pushed my way over to her and without saying a word and not caring who was watching, I reached up and pulled her to me. Without a word, we became wrapped up in a heated kiss.

Once the need to breathe overwhelmed us, we parted. I reached down and tugged on her belt and pulled her to me.

"Let's go home."

Epilogue

Well, that was it. Oh, the book did well and it still causing a stir with some conservative historians. However the splash was just enough to garner Alex the vacant tenure position. So, that was how my journey began and ended. Well, not quite how it ended. It is now one year later. September, in fact, and classes are starting in a few days. I find myself standing on the pitcher's mound once again. This time at the end of the season in the championship game. I feel good, we're one strike away from walking away with the title for the first time. But it's not the game that's making me smile. It's one face looking out from the crowd. I smile in her direction, then turn my attention back to the task at hand. I know the instant the ball leaves my hand how good it is. The batter swings and misses. We win. My teammates already know I won't be joining them for the celebration. I need to get my girl home.

You see, yesterday we found out that she was carrying twins. Of course, we already suspected that. Nukumi told us last year. Even though she left us months ago, before Alex got pregnant, we can still feel her with us. Oh, and if you are wondering, it was window shopping. Alex and I had been walking around Boston. For some reason, we found ourselves standing in front of a maternity shop holding hands and watching the people inside. Without speaking, we knew what we wanted. What we wanted was to complete our family.

Soon we will. I just wished that Nukumi had warned me what life was going to be like with a very pregnant Alex. It doesn't matter. I would have found my way to her and our children anyway. It's where I belong. It's my home.

The End

ABOUT THE AUTHOR

Boston native Mavis Applewater started writing at the request of a very wise woman; she claims that is why she married her. She is the author of five full length novels, *The Brass Ring, My Sisters Keeper, Tempus Fugit,* Goldie Winner *Whispering Pines and Checkmate the second Caitlin Calloway Mystery.* She has also penned four collections of shorts stories including *Home For The Holidays* Goldie Finalist for best Erotica. She is looking forward to the release of *Remember When, Blair's Bounty* and the first *Harper Winston* thriller.

CPSIA information can be obtained at www.ICGtesting.com
Printed in the USA
LVOW01s0900150815

450252LV00033B/1626/P